NEIL LANCASTER is the No. 1 digital bestselling author of both the Tom Novak and Max Craigie series. His first Craigie novel, *Dead Man's Grave*, was longlisted for the 2021 McIlvanney Prize for Best Scottish Crime Book of the Year. The second Craigie novel is *The Blood Tide* which has topped several ebook and audio charts. He served as a military policeman and worked for the Metropolitan Police as a detective, investigating serious crimes in the capital and beyond. As a covert policing and surveillance specialist he utilised all manner of techniques to investigate and disrupt major crime and criminals.

He now lives in the Scottish Highlands, writes crime and thriller novels and works as a broadcaster and commentator on true crime documentaries. He is a key expert on two Sky Crime TV series, *Meet, Marry, Murder* and *Made for Murder*.

@neillancaster66
@NeilLancasterCrime
www.neillancastercrime.co.uk

Also by Neil Lancaster

The Max Craigie Novels
Dead Man's Grave
The Blood Tide

The Tom Novak Novels
Going Dark
Going Rogue
Going Back

NEIL LANCASTER

THE NIGHT WATCH

ONE PLACE. MANY STORIES

HQ
An imprint of HarperCollins*Publishers* Ltd
1 London Bridge Street
London SE1 9GF

www.harpercollins.co.uk

HarperCollins*Publishers*
1st Floor, Watermarque Building, Ringsend Road
Dublin 4, Ireland

This edition 2022

1
First published in Great Britain by
HQ, an imprint of HarperCollins*Publishers* Ltd 2022

Copyright © Neil Lancaster 2022

Neil Lancaster asserts the moral right to be identified as the author of this work. A catalogue record for this book is available from the British Library.

ISBN: 9780008518479 (HB)
ISBN: 9780008551247 (TPB)

MIX
Paper from
responsible sources
FSC™ C007454

This book is produced from independently certified FSC™ paper to ensure responsible forest management.

For more information visit: www.harpercollins.co.uk/green

This book is set in 10.7/15.5 pt. Sabon by Type-it AS, Norway

Printed and Bound in the UK using 100% Renewable Electricity at CPI Group (UK) Ltd, Croydon, CR0 4YY

This book is dedicated to my wonderful
sisters, Judith and Helen
We did OK, right?

1

SCOTT PATERSON YAWNED as he left the dark streets of Edinburgh and drove towards the leafier suburb of Ravelston. It was pitch black, dry and cloudy, and the city was deserted this early in the morning.

His head felt heavy after spending the evening with some pals in a nice pub in the centre of town. He'd drunk some champagne, smoked a joint, and snorted a line of Charlie, so whilst he probably shouldn't have been driving, he was hardly drunk. He was, however, knackered after a whirlwind of emotions and celebrations. A few days ago, he'd been given a 'not proven' verdict at the High Court. He'd gone from facing a life sentence in Saughton Jail to freedom, and it was all a little hard to take in. He settled with pleasure into the soft leather seat of the BMW X5, and yawned again. Time to go home and continue getting reacquainted with the wife.

His phone buzzed on the seat next to him. He picked it up and looked at the screen, his eyes widening as he saw the name of the caller. Jackie McLennan. *The* Jackie McLennan. A man to be feared and revered in equal measure.

'Jackie, my man,' he said.

'Scotty, I just heard. You're out of Saughton and dinnae tell me, eh?' a rough Edinburgh accent barked in his ear.

Jackie was a serious face from the Edinburgh underworld with fingers in all sorts of pies. Scott hadn't seen him for a while, but then he hadn't seen anyone after almost a year on remand in Saughton Jail, awaiting trial for a rather nasty murder.

'Ach, you know. Been busy, catching up with my lady and my boys.'

'Aye, I guess. So, a not proven then. You jammy bastard, how'd you pull that off, eh?'

'Innocent as a wee lamb. The cop in charge got fucked by my lawyer, and the rest is history. What a shame, eh?' he guffawed.

'Fucking Teflon-boy, you are. Rumours were, you were bang-to-rights for a life stretch.'

Paterson opened his mouth to retort, but paused, distracted by movement in his rear-view mirror. A big, dark car suddenly pulled out of a side street. It was accelerating hard to catch up with him. Within seconds, it closed the distance until it was only a few feet from his bumper. Its bright halogen headlamps pierced the darkness, flooding his car with blinding, white light. Scott was a man of the world, and a car that close, with its lights on full beam, meant only one thing.

Trouble.

Either a cop car, or worse, a rival gang. The cops didn't bother him too much. He had a gram of coke in his pocket, and a small knife in the door of the car, but he could either ditch those before the cops pulled him, or just brazen it out. Worst case, if it was a lone cop, he would intimidate the life out of the bastard. Scott was used to doing that. At well over

2

six feet tall and close to eighteen stone of solid muscle, it wasn't hard. A tooled-up rival gang was a different matter altogether. He'd made plenty of enemies in his years as a gang enforcer for hire, and he was always ready for trouble. His hand gripped the phone, his eyes dropped to the door pocket where he was reassured to see the glint of the lock-knife.

His jaw set tight, and he growled softly, under his breath. No one fucked with Scott Paterson. Not the cops, and certainly not some wee gadgies wanting to make a name for themselves.

'I'm gonna have to go, Jackie. I've got company.'

'You okay?'

'Aye, someone on my tail. I'll call you later.' He hung up without waiting for a reply, hoping Jackie wouldn't be offended.

Then it happened. He watched in the rear-view mirror as an arm came out of the pursuing car's window. It clamped an oscillating blue light on the roof.

Fuck. Cops. Even worse, not regular cops, but a specialist unit by the look of the car, a decent-sized SUV with a covert light. They probably had him under surveillance, but he was sure he hadn't seen anyone. Only been out a few days and the bastards were already trying to fuck him over. Anger flared in his chest like sudden indigestion.

Paterson floored the powerful BMW and roared off, gathering speed along the long, straight road. The cop car accelerated, too, but Scott was making good ground. Seeing the junction ahead he swiftly turned right onto Strachan Road, heading towards Ravelston. He mashed his foot to the floor again. The BMW screamed as it sped along, tyres protesting. Soon the streetlights ended, and he found himself on

Ravelston Dyke Road. It was a dark and lonely stretch, lined with woodland on either side. The cop car briefly disappeared, so he quickly lowered the passenger window. Reaching into the door pocket, he tossed the lock-knife out over the low wall and into the woodland, closely followed by the small wrap of cocaine. He checked his rear-view mirror, to see the pursuing cop car screech back into view in hot pursuit, blue lights strobing and flickering through the surrounding trees.

He smiled to himself, his confidence rising now the contraband was gone, and he was certain they couldn't have seen him ditch it. If they were CID officers, they'd never have a breath machine with them and they'd certainly never have a field drug test kit. If he made enough of a fuss, they'd probably leave him alone. Police manpower in this bit of Edinburgh was shite, and they'd have no desire to wait for ages with an angry Scott Paterson. They were almost universally fucking cowards.

As quickly as he'd accelerated to get away from the pursuing police car, he stamped on the brakes and pulled to the side of the road, just past the entrance of the empty car park of Ravelston Golf Course. He sighed, totally relaxed now. They had nothing on him at all, he chuckled to himself, his eyes glued to the rear-view mirror.

The cop car stopped close behind him, almost touching his rear bumper, headlights on full beam, the pulsing blue light blinding him.

'Jesus suffering fuck,' he said to himself, flipping the mirror up to avert the beams of light. Turning to the wing mirror, he saw the cop car door open, and a shadowy form step out. Through the glare he could just see the cop's hi-viz ballistic vest as it began to move towards him. Cheeky bastard, he thought. He was going to make his life a misery.

He'd only seen one person get out of the car. Whoever it was had made a big mistake.

Paterson decided that he was going to stay put. The fucker could come to him. He turned the music up and began to scroll through Facebook on his phone. The photos from his celebration a few days ago were there, and he grinned at the pissed carnage that had ensued.

A full minute had passed before he looked up again. The lights were still burning into the back of his car, but there was no sight of the cop. He killed the music and squinted, trying to see what the hell the pig was playing at. Was he trying to freak him out?

He looked down at his phone again, but he couldn't concentrate. Something tickled at his subconscious. He'd been stopped by cops a million times, and they always approached the car. They were usually all over him like a cheap suit. Suddenly, the cop car's headlamps and blue flashing light died, and the BMW was plunged into darkness.

'What the fuck?' he murmured, wishing that he hadn't tossed his blade.

He looked at the car behind him. It was quiet and inert in the gloom, as shadowy and ominous as the night itself. He leaned out of his open window and strained to hear, but his engine was too loud. He pressed the ignition button, and the BMW fell silent. Everything was suddenly shrouded in darkness. The only sound was the engine ticking as it cooled, and the soft breeze whispering through the trees. The silence was almost physical in its intensity. He flinched at a rustling noise from the edge of the woods beside his car. He swivelled his head towards it, his eyes wide, but could see nothing through the deep, impenetrable blackness.

'Fuck this for a game of soldiers,' he said, opening the door and stepping out, pulling himself up to his full height, muscles tensed, massive shoulders squared. 'What the fuck is going on?' he bellowed towards the car.

Nothing. He felt a prickle along his spine as he waited. There were no other cars, no one else on the street. At that moment, the full moon broke through fast-moving clouds and a shaft of light hit the car, momentarily bathing him in a pale glow. Long shadows crept across the road and then vanished into the trees as the moon disappeared.

'I'll have my fucking lawyer on you bastards,' he shouted, his voice loud, but without the furious anger of before. He walked up to the silent cop car that was black enough to melt into the night. There was no sign of a blue light on the roof, and nothing on the dash. What was the stupid bastard up to? Despite the cool autumnal air, a bead of sweat ran down his spine. His heart thudded. He swallowed and turned towards his car.

As he strode back, he glanced around once more. Again, nothing. He tried to stay calm as he peered through the still-open door of his vehicle. The interior light was on, illuminating everything in a soft glow. It would be fine. He would just drive home and forget this ever happened. But he couldn't escape the feeling that he was missing something.

Then he saw it.

His car key had gone. It was no longer in the slot next to the steering wheel.

Paterson groped around in the footwell, hoping it had fallen onto the floor, but after a moment, he stopped. He stood up, blinked, balled his hands into tight fists. His nails dug into his palms as he took a ragged breath and his insides turned to ice.

'Where the fuck are you?' he yelled, but he sounded scared. His words were quickly swallowed up by the surrounding trees and the deep, velvety night.

There was a faint cackle of laughter behind him. The snap of a twig under a boot. Paterson froze. He turned slowly, looking into the undergrowth for the source of the noise. Something moved, came out of the dense trees, a slow-moving shadow, only just visible. He gasped, sucked in a lungful of air.

The shape approached, one arm outstretched, clutching something.

Scott Paterson cried out in terror and turned to sprint into the darkness.

He ran for his life.

2

FERGUS GRIGOR KISSED his wife gently on the cheek. He stared down at her as she lay asleep in their narrow double bed. She stirred and turned to look at him.

'You're awake early,' she murmured, stroking his cheek.

'Morning. I'm going for a run, I can't sleep.'

'You're mad,' she said, with an exaggerated yawn and a stretch.

'You love me for it. It's why you married me.'

'No, I married you for your huge wallet and athletic physique. Make sure you bring me coffee when you get back. Where're you going?'

'Just around the headland. It's looking like a beautiful day. Honeymoon weather,' he said, stroking her long auburn hair.

'Aye well, it's honeymoon weather every day in the Maldives, but your daft bloody job put paid to that, eh?' she said without resentment, referring to the holiday that they'd cancelled because of his overrunning trial. So instead of two weeks in the Indian Ocean, they'd had a long weekend in a lighthouse keeper's cottage at Dunnet Head.

'We'll do it soon, *Mrs* Grigor. I promise.' Fergus leaned forward and kissed his new wife once more.

'Yeah, whatever, counsel,' she said, burying herself in the duvet again and closing her eyes, a trace of a smile on her face.

Fergus chuckled, stood up and left the room, pulling his running vest over his head. He quickly put his well-worn trainers on and let himself out of the small, whitewashed cottage right next to the lighthouse at Dunnet Head. The most northerly part of the United Kingdom.

The wind whipped in from the Pentland Firth as he broke into a jog along the path and out into the empty car park. It was normally busy with tourists, but the season was drawing to a close, and it was still early. Very early.

Fergus marvelled at the starkly beautiful sweeping expanse of open landscape that stretched inland for what seemed like a hundred miles; stark, bleak, and almost devoid of trees. There wasn't much that could withstand the battering of the almost constant wind. To his right, lay a vast sheet of cobalt-blue sea that glittered all the way to the horizon. It was, as always, uncompromisingly beautiful, particularly on a morning like today.

The sun rose in the east, beginning to chase away the early chill. He was thankful for the brisk wind blowing in from the Firth, keeping the bloody midges away. Had it been still they'd have chased him along the path, thirsty for a morning drink.

He breathed deeply, tasting the ozone tang of the sea, and a wave of satisfaction swept over him. He picked up his pace as he hit the coastal track, leaning into the roaring wind. He continued along the path beside a stone wall that separated him from the hundred-metre drop to the rocks below. As he rounded the bend, he got a view of the grey, jagged cliff plummeting down to the crashing waves.

A faint noise carried in the wind as he jogged, and he slowed his pace a touch. There it was again, a faint cry that fought to be audible against the rush of the wind. His brow furrowed. Surely there was nobody about at this early hour? He'd seen no campers, and the other cottage was empty. Was it an animal?

There it was again. Definitely a cry, or a wail, coming from the direction of the bird species information board that was set against the wall. He stopped and listened, his breath even and controlled.

Suddenly, he jumped, startled, as a throaty wail erupted. It seemed to be just the other side of the wall. He climbed up the rough stonework and looked over at the few metres of scrubby grass that led to the cliff edge.

His heart began to pound.

A pair of bright white sneakers, an empty bottle and a rucksack sat on the grass in between the wall and the edge of the cliff.

He swallowed and reached into his pocket to locate his phone. He looked at the screen, but saw the familiar icon indicating no signal.

He jumped over the wall, landing two-footed on the tussocky grass. The wind buffeted his vest against his body and tousled his curly hair, as he cautiously approached the sneakers and bag. His heart seemed to be trying to beat its way up and out of his throat. He squatted and picked up the empty bottle to look at the label. Grant's whisky. He glanced towards the edge, considering his next move. Dare he risk a peep over? If anyone had jumped, there'd be no saving them. He'd have to go back to the cottage to get a wi-fi signal to alert the authorities. He took a step closer to the sheer drop. Before he could understand what was happening, he was hit by a massive impact that smashed into his back and tore his breath from him in a whoosh. It felt as though he'd been struck hard with a baseball bat, or even a fucking lorry. His body exploded with pain and he dropped, face first, hitting the rough grass like a felled tree. The morning sun began to fade, until there was only an inky wall of impenetrable blackness.

3

A LOW MIST ENGULFED the car park of Ravelston Golf Course, in the affluent suburb of Edinburgh. The first rays of the morning sun had begun to emerge to warm the chilly autumn air.

A uniformed officer moved aside the blue-and-white scene tape, and Detective Chief Inspector Donald 'Donnie' Watson drove into the car park in his Major Investigation Team pool Ford Mondeo. He pulled into one of the bays next to a white liveried CSI van. Getting out, he shivered and for the first time in a while, wishing he had worn a coat. His thoughts turned, as they often did, to his small place in Alicante, and the prospect of his imminent retirement. Another day, another murder, and another step closer to his pension.

'Cold, this morning. Winter's coming,' he said moodily as he looked across at his deputy Detective Inspector Marnie Gray. She pulled her long, lean frame out of the passenger seat, an Airwave radio handset in her hand. He buttoned up his thin suit jacket, which was futile against the penetratingly cold mist. The Scottish haar. Even on a warm day, it could cut through clothing like a knife.

'Stop moaning, man, you should have listened to your

ma and brought a jacket,' said Marnie. She was young for a DI, close to six feet tall, smartly dressed and with an almost permanent wide smile and piercing jade-green eyes. Nothing seemed to faze Marnie, which was probably why she was destined for greater things. He was fast realising that he was something of a dinosaur in the modern, more informal police service. He scowled at his use of the word. *Service*. They were a force, not a bloody service.

'Who found the body?' said Donnie.

'Dog walker. A couple of hours ago, just after sun-up. But the duty officer thinks he's been there for a wee while.'

'Shite, the press will go mental for this.'

'I've already alerted press office. They're on standby,' said Marnie.

'I think you'll find that's my responsibility, Marnie. I'll decide media strategy when it's appropriate. Bloody gutter press will be all over us if press office tip the wink, you know how leaky they are,' said Donnie, his voice hard-edged. Marnie was competent, but she had ideas above her bloody station, he mused.

'Just trying to get ahead of the game, sorry,' she said with no trace of contrition.

'Who was the duty officer?'

'Gordon Campbell,' said Marnie, raising her eyebrows.

'Oh jeez, not "Cordon Gordon",' muttered Donnie.

'Aye, the very same.'

'Go and check for CCTV in the clubhouse, Marnie,' said Donnie, turning away from her.

'It'd be a pleasure, *sir*,' said Marnie, with far too much emphasis on the word, as she turned towards the clubhouse.

A grin stretched across Donnie's face at this little exercise in establishing just who was in charge.

He recognised Jimmy Duggan the crime scene manager, dressed in a forensic overall and overshoes, dragging his heavy metal case from the back of the white van. Jimmy was a small, compact figure, with piercing grey eyes that were only partially shielded by thick-framed spectacles. His hair was jet black, and thick, and as always, he had a hint of a five o'clock shadow. However often Jimmy shaved he always had a fuzz of stubble emerging on his jaw.

'Morning, Donnie. Did I witness a slightly aggrieved Marnie?'

'Possibly, she's trying to throw her oar in too much, as normal. You had a look, yet?'

'No, I'm not long here myself. Seems I also managed to upset Cordon Gordon by telling him that his scene control was a bag of shite. Stomped off in a proper hump. Cold morning, eh?' said Jimmy, yawning, and rubbing his hands together. His accent was pure unadulterated Dublin, unchanged by many years with Scottish police.

Jimmy was a good man with a lot of experience who had been working in forensics almost as long as there had been forensics. He placed his kit box on the ground and opened it, briefly checking the contents against his kit register, in typical Jimmy fashion.

'All present and correct, Jim?'

'Rule of seven Ps. Prior Prevention and Planning Prevents Piss-Poor Performance.'

'Now how many times have I heard that?' said Donnie.

They walked up the sloped pathway together, coming out

at the front of the green wooden-framed clubhouse that sat in front of an expanse of trees and fairways.

'Morning, boss,' said a middle-aged, dark-haired man. DS Mark Fagerson was striding over the grass from the course towards them, clutching a clipboard. He too wore a forensic oversuit, the hood down and a surgical mask pulled under his chin. His hair was immaculately cut and styled with too much product, and his grin revealed a row of too-white teeth. He pulled back the sleeve on his suit and looked at a sparkling and expensive-looking watch.

'Morning. I didn't expect you for a while, only just checked the cordons myself.'

Donnie sighed to himself, wondering when detective sergeants began to wear watches that cost two months' wages. 'Morning, Mark. What do we have?'

'This is gonna be a bad one, boss. Definite Cat A, I'd say. Call came in not long ago from a dogwalker. Body is in that first small group of trees over there.' He pointed towards a cluster of birch trees a hundred metres into the course.

'I think I'll make the call on what cat it's going to be, if that's okay with you,' said Donnie, referring to the gradation system for murders. Cat C was the lower grade, normally applied where the offender was known, and there was little risk to the public. Cat A meant the opposite. Offender not known, high profile, a danger to the public and a reputational risk to the force. Donnie's stomach lurched – he really didn't need it, not at this time of his service. This was likely to be his last murder inquiry, and he'd hoped for a nice simple domestic, or some drunken nonsense, with a remorseful suspect handing himself in. It was somehow unfortunate timing that he was now

16

available, having just finished a long and difficult court case. If only this had happened last week, he thought to himself.

'Fair enough,' was all that Fagerson said.

'Scene secured?' said Donnie with a sigh.

'Aye. Duty officer had made the scene far too bloody small, as Cordon Gordon always does. The inner cordon is secured as the whole group of trees. I have to say it's a horrible place.'

'How so?' asked Donnie. He wanted the details, not stupid opinions.

'It's in a bog, a nasty hole with a load of muddy Baltic-cold water that stinks of shite. Although I've only been to the outer reaches of it.'

Donnie shook his head. 'Outer cordon?'

'The whole course, boss. Easy enough to secure, but Gordon wasn't happy and he's stomped off in a huff.'

'Aye, Jimmy had words with him as well. I'll have a chat to Cordon Gordon about this. Common path of approach?'

'Aye, sorted and marked out.' Mark pointed to the long line of evenly spaced small plastic shapes, which looked like miniature traffic cones leading through the mist to a lonely copse of trees.

'You been in and looked?' said Donnie, his face firm.

'No chance, I know how you feel about that. All I've done is secured the cordons and sorted approach for follow-ups. Just the two uniforms who got the initial call went in, and once they found no signs of life, they backed off and called it in. They did well, boss. No one else has been in apart from the paramedic crew, as one of them is authorised to pronounce life extinct.' It always struck Donnie as daft that a cop could never officially assume that someone was dead. Even if the head had been removed from a body, they had to have a healthcare professional to certify life extinct.

'Do we have a PLE from them?'

'Aye, here it is.' Fagerson handed over a signed form.

Donnie glanced at the page before handing it back to his DS.

'The uniforms didn't hang about. Said the place was bloody spooky.'

'Spooky? What the fuck has happened to cops, eh? If I'd told a DS a scene was spooky when I was in uniform, I'd have been called a bloody Jessie.'

'It's a bit grim, boss.'

'Jesus, I need to bloody retire,' said Donnie, shaking his head again.

Despite his moans, Donnie was impressed. On so many occasions he would attend murder scenes and every bugger had been in for a gawp. So much could be lost with a few misplaced size ten boots by curious cops. Now they were here, the scene secure, they could process it properly. The golden hour. That period where you had to secure and preserve the evidence that would disappear if you didn't act fast.

'Nice work,' Donnie said as he turned to face Jimmy. 'Okay, Jim, let's get step plates, and go for a look.

'Mark, anything I need to know before then, like why you think it's a Cat A that's about to ruin my day, and possibly the remainder of the time I have left in the job?'

'Perhaps it's best you see for yourself, boss.'

'You ready?' said Donnie to Jimmy, both clad in full forensic clothing, gloves, masks and overshoes.

'I'm ready. You know not every SIO does this anymore?'

'Madness. How can you know the context of the photos, plans and videos without having seen it yourself with your own eyes? Bloody amateurs.'

Donnie pulled his mask down, his chin set firm. It was time. That first appraisal of the scene that all SIOs should make. That first opportunity to see what they were dealing with. To take in the tableau of murder that would never be the same again once the CSIs started their work.

They followed the cones that marked the common path of approach towards the blue-and-white scene tape. It surrounded a copse of trees in a small depression that seemed to be overgrown with gorse. A solitary uniformed cop, clutching a formatted scene log, stood in front of the tape, his flat cap pulled low on his head. He was already noting the arrivals. As they approached, he nodded at Donnie. 'Careful in there, sir. It's slippery as hell. Could do with wellies,' he said.

'When I want advice, son, I'll ask for it,' growled Donnie. The cop coloured a little.

They walked up to the edge of the slight depression and carefully descended the slope. They waded through knee-length wet grass, immediately saturating their flimsy overall trousers. The bottom of the slope was just as the cops had described it. Mud, putrid puddles, and a dank, boggy odour. To the right it was reasonably dry, and the going was more solid. Donnie wrinkled his nose. It was definitely colder down here, where the mist had settled above the water.

'What a shite-hole,' said Jimmy as he transferred the step plates to his other hand.

'Not gonna disagree with you, there,' said Donnie.

'Aye, just looking for best approach point. Whoever brought

him here avoided all the mud, so we best go through it, so we don't spoil any footprints. Any marks in the drier area will be indistinct, as the surface looks hard, so if we stick to the mud we'll be grand.'

'Aye, grand. I hate working with you, sometimes,' said Donnie.

'Let me get the plates in, then he's all yours, for your first look.'

Donnie allowed Jimmy to advance to the body. They could see it slumped against the slim trunk of a silver birch.

Jimmy placed aluminium step plates in the untouched muddy ground at intervals between the bottom of the slope and the corpse, noting in his book as he did. He carefully checked each piece of ground. After a few minutes, he was satisfied, and he nodded at Donnie. It was time.

Donnie advanced slowly and deliberately, using the step plates, each one squelching as he moved until he was standing behind the corpse. Fortunately, the earth around the tree was dry and firm. The first thing that occurred to Donnie was the size of the man. He was wide and beefy, and even sitting against the tree you could tell that he was tall. His shovel-like hands were positioned behind him on either side of the trunk, almost as if they had been secured together, back-to-back. Donnie squatted, and looked closely at the wrists. The left one sported a glittering Omega, and he wasn't surprised to see deep indentations and some bruising. This man had been bound, or possibly handcuffed; by the look of those bruises, he was guessing the latter. He breathed in deeply, the mask sucking in against his face, trying to detect any smell of alcohol or chemicals. Nothing, beyond the boggy stench of the woodland.

He moved around the body, noting the expensive-looking leather jacket, Armani polo, and mud-stained Boss jeans, all saturated with either blood or possibly the loss of control of the victim's bladder. He turned his gaze to the man's head, noting the neatly styled hair, the way his head slumped forward. Across the front of his Polo and jacket was a bib of almost-black blood. Donnie squatted again to look at the wound and the man's face. A deep, clean gash ran from his left ear to his throat, exposing glistening tendons and a flash of severed windpipe.

As his eyes moved up to the man's face, Donnie's heart skipped a beat.

He'd seen those cruel, angry features, the beefy physique, for every day of the past eight weeks at the High Court. Despite the rigor mortis that had seemingly frozen his face into a terrified grimace, there was no doubt.

This was Scott 'The Axe' Paterson.

The same Scott Paterson who had only last week been acquitted of murder. Well, by acquitted, he really meant, 'not proven', in that strange peculiarity of Scottish law. Neither guilty, nor truly innocent. The Crown had just not satisfied the jury to the required standard. A failure. Donnie wasn't one for history, or hyperbole, but Sir Walter Scott's description of a 'not proven' as a 'bastard verdict' always seemed appropriate.

Scott Paterson's eyes were open, but clouded and empty.

Donnie stood and looked at the whole scene, taking it in, imprinting every detail on his memory. He circled around the body anti-clockwise, opposite to his previous pass. He took in the grooves in the ground where his heels had dug into the compacted soil, and noted that Paterson's fingernails were well cut, and there appeared to be no debris or blood traces. No struggle, no defence wounds. Nothing.

Somehow, someone had managed to overpower the eighteen-stone man-mountain that was Scott Paterson, handcuff him to a tree and slice his neck with absolutely no signs of a struggle. A cold-blooded and sadistic execution.

Donnie shuddered, and it wasn't because of the cold, dank and unpleasant copse that was the murder scene.

This was most certainly a Cat A murder.

4

DONNIE STOOD ON the fairway by the copse of trees, scribbling in his decision log. He was thankful that the haar had cleared and a pleasantly warm autumn day had emerged, only tempered by the stiff breeze. There was nothing worse than hanging around for bloody hours, freezing your goolies off and waiting for the CSIs to process a scene. He normally left once he'd visited, but he really wanted to speak to the pathologist to get her early findings.

A small knot of journalists had already begun to gather in the car park, fortunately well away from the scene, thanks to Mark's decent management. This was going to attract plenty of attention once the details got out, particularly as Paterson had only got his 'not proven' a few days ago. They always put two and two together, and often arrived with a sum of about 300.

The forensic pathologist had arrived quicker than he had expected, after only a few hours. She was currently performing her initial scene exam behind the tarp which had been erected around Paterson and the birch tree.

Donnie was actively considering lighting a cigarette, and

his desperation for a strong coffee was becoming overwhelming, when the slight, almost petite figure of Dr Elsa Morina emerged from the scene, and ducked under the tape, pulling off her surgical mask and slipping down the hood. Her deep auburn hair cascaded out like a wave. She blinked heavily at the assault of the sunlight.

'Morning. You look a bit tired,' said Donnie.

'Late night, you know how it is,' she smiled, her face pale but brightening. She always looked too young and feminine for a forensic pathologist from Edinburgh University, thought Donnie. As if she belonged behind the perfume counter at John Lewis, rather than out here in a bog, examining a corpse. As always, her smile was framed by bright scarlet lipstick.

'Strange one, this,' she continued, her brow furrowed.

'How?'

'Well, there are no signs of a struggle. I can't be sure, but the angle of the cut suggests to me that it had been inflicted by someone standing in front of him as it's shorter than I would expect from a rear-inflicted cut. It seems to me that the cut started just below the left ear and was dragged across the carotid until it severed the trachea where it stops. He had clearly been handcuffed, or restrained, but I just can't see why there was no evidence of a struggle. There's nothing – it's almost like he put the cuffs on himself. The bruising is definitely ante-mortem, possibly because his wrists are so bloody huge that bruising was inevitable.' She had a trace of Eastern Europe in her accent, but her delivery was flawless.

'Drugged?' said Donnie, digesting this information. The concept of Scott 'The Axe' Paterson not putting up a fight with anyone was almost beyond comprehension. His whole life had been getting into – and generally winning – fights. The cops who had arrested him in the past knew him as a ten-man job, because he was so big and powerful, and he never came quietly.

'Nothing I can tell here, it'll have to wait for tox; I'll know more later. Are you coming to the PM?'

'Aye. Early thoughts?' said Donnie.

'I'll know more after the PM.'

'A strange one.'

'Yep, Cat A, I'd say. It seems to me that someone wanted to make a point here. Why not just shoot him? Why subdue, restrain, and then slice? I'm no behaviouralist, but to me that seems almost ritualistic.'

'Jeez, don't say that, Elsa. Any idea how long ago?'

'I hate guessing but rigor is fully in place; he's stiff as a board. Best estimate is six to eight hours, possibly more, but you know my feelings on time of death. How urgent for the PM?'

'Top priority. The bloody press is going to be all over this one.'

'I saw when I came in. Half a dozen of them set up with cameras. Are you going to give a statement?'

'Aye, I don't think I have much of a choice. When and where for the PM?'

'Either later today, or sometime tomorrow, at RIE, I'd hope. Funnily, we aren't so busy, but I'll call you to confirm. All depends if I can get a lab tech. Right, he's all yours and feel free to get him shifted to the mortuary. Have you spoken to the fiscal?'

'Aye. CFIU are aware and they've authorised for a special PM already. I'm sure an email will be waiting for you when you get back.'

Jimmy Duggan emerged from the forensic screen. 'All finished, Elsa?' he said, slightly hesitant.

'Yes, carry on,' said Elsa, not looking back at the crime scene manager. 'I've not hit the office yet, as I came straight from home. I'll call you later, Donnie.' Elsa nodded and marched away towards the car park.

Donnie nodded at Fagerson, who had just joined them. 'Over to you, Mark. Get the body across to the Royal Infirmary.'

The DS nodded, checking his watch, which glittered too much for a cop, as far as Donnie was concerned. 'I had them on standby, they'll be here soon. PolSa search team are expected soon, too, for the fingertip search, so I don't expect that this will be a long one. It's a simple scene, boss,' he said, recording something in his notebook.

'Too simple. Far too simple. How the bloody hell did someone do it without a struggle?'

'Drugs?'

'Aye, maybe, but that begs the question, how did they carry all eighteen stones of him here and secure him against that tree?'

'Have to wait for PM, but the press isn't going to like the fact that he was acquitted of murder last week.'

'Not proven, Mark. The bastard was guilty as sin. It was only the absence of corroboration – and let's be honest here, other than his nearest and dearest, no bugger is going to miss him, eh?'

'Press are wanting a statement,' said Fagerson, changing the subject.

'Well, I'll give them something very brief. I want this scene processed and closed and an urgent team meeting at Leith. We are going to need every bugger on this; in fact, we may need to ask for reinforcements.'

'Incident room is open already, and HOLMES is up and running. We even have an operation name.'

'What is it?'

'Operation Saturn.'

'What? That's shite, who picks these bloody names?'

'Computer generated.'

'Aye, right, anyway, where's Marnie?'

'Speaking with the course manager up at the clubhouse.'

'Right. See you later. No shortcuts here. Every bloody blade of grass needs to be gone over. We have missing handcuffs and a missing murder weapon.' Donnie nodded and walked off towards the clubhouse.

Marnie Gray was coming out as he approached, talking into her radio, the picture of efficiency.

'How we getting on?' he asked her.

'Clubhouse shut at ten thirty last night. Last member of staff gone by eleven. No one saw anything,' Marnie said, looking at her clipboard.

'CCTV?'

'Not working.'

'Bloody typical,' muttered Donnie.

'Broke a few days ago, and they're still waiting for an engineer.'

'Bugger. I need to give the bloody leeches over there something before we move Axe Man. Come on, stand by me and look confident.'

They both moved off towards the small cluster of perhaps half a dozen men and women, all clutching cameras, chatting and smoking. They began snapping as Donnie and Marnie approached.

'DCI Watson, have you identified the body yet?' a small man at the front asked, still clicking away.

'Ladies and gentlemen, as you are probably aware, I'm DCI Watson from the Major Investigation Team at Leith. I'll give a very brief statement now, and once facts emerge, I'll be sure to keep you all updated via the Police Scotland Press Team. At around seven this morning, a dog walker found the body of a man in a small copse of trees on Ravelston Golf Course. We're undertaking a full investigation in relation to this incident now, and a major investigation team is currently engaged in enquiries to formally identify the victim – a man in his late thirties – and ascertain how he died. We're appealing to witnesses who may have been in the vicinity of Ravelston Golf Course any time from 10 p.m. last night to come forward as they may have vital information,' Donnie paused to draw breath.

A sudden babble of competing voices exploded. Donnie simply raised a hand until the pack quietened.

'No questions, right now, sorry. I don't know enough, yet.'

A voice from the left – a small, youngish, compact figure, with sharp eyes and a shaved head – spoke in a soft, enquiring voice. Donnie recognised him as Shuggie Gibson, a freelance investigative journalist turned blogger who he had clashed with on one occasion. Shuggie had no camera, only a small voice recorder in his hand. The look on his face was unfathomable.

'Detective Chief Inspector, I'm hearing that the deceased is Scott Paterson, who was acquitted of murder at the High Court last week, a murder your team investigated. Can you confirm this?' His voice was low, tinged with the tones of Glasgow.

All the other reporters turned to look at the newcomer, who was clearly not part of their little club.

'It would be inappropriate of me to elaborate further, I'm afraid,' said Donnie, his insides churning, and feeling his face begin to flush.

'Are you connecting this murder to the death of Chick Wilson in Perth five years ago? I'm hearing that there are similarities between the two cases,' the small man said, his face impassive.

'Sorry, Shuggie. Nothing right now, we'll brief more fully later,' said Donnie through gritted teeth.

'Have you connected this murder to the death of his advocate a few hours ago?' the journalist said, his eyes shining.

'No idea what you're talking about,' said Donnie, feeling ice grip his insides, trying desperately not to show the shock that was coursing through his body.

'DCI Watson, have you not heard that Fergus Grigor, who was the advocate for Mr Paterson's recent trial, died this morning at Dunnet Head? Fell or was pushed off the cliffs. Officers are on scene and investigating as we speak.'

All the journalists turned, opened-mouthed, to look at Shuggie. One thing any journalist hates is to be beaten to a story, and Shuggie had stolen a march on all of them, including the police.

'Sorry, I've no information on that. Now you'll have to excuse me.'

'Are you not worried that they have been killed within hours of each other? Is this another one of the coincidences that seem to follow you and your team around?'

29

'No comment. This is a fast-moving inquiry, and there'll be a press release once we have more information.'

'DCI Watson, do we have a serial killer at large?'

'No further questions, any other enquiries please contact the press office at Police Scotland. Thank you.' He turned to Marnie and whispered, 'What the hell was that?' then moved to walk back towards his car, the fading voice of Shuggie Gibson ringing in his ears.

5

MAX CRAIGIE SCOOPED the burger from the grill on the big barbecue on the deck outside his cottage overlooking the Firth of Forth in Culross. He slapped it between a bun, put it on a plate and handed it to a compact and tough-looking man with short greying hair and twinkling eyes who was sitting on a patio chair.

'I could say something about the presentation,' said Niall Hastings in a soft Scottish accent with a smile, as he opened the bun and squirted a dollop of ketchup on the charred patty. Despite being a native Scot, Niall had lived down south in the Home Counties for many years and had married a local woman in Hertford. They lived in a nice house just outside the city with their three kids.

'Stop moaning, man. There's also tattie salad over there.' He pointed to a bowl on the table.

'You spoil us,' Niall said taking a huge bite.

'Jeri?' said Max, handing a similar and inelegantly prepared burger to a petite redheaded woman sitting next to Niall, her hand resting on his leg.

'Ooh, looks lush, Max,' she said as she accepted the paper plate.

'I can't believe that your best pals from London come up to see you and the best you can serve is a bogging-looking burger. If I wasn't a vegetarian, I'd be offended for them, but you know, meat is murder, and all,' said DC Janie Calder, Max's partner at their small, covert unit at Police Scotland.

'Since when were you a vegetarian?' asked Max.

'Last week,' said Janie.

'Latest fad?' asked Max.

'Someone's influence,' said Janie, jabbing her thumb at Melissa, who smiled. Melissa was Janie's girlfriend, and they had quickly moved from being casual to what seemed to be a serious relationship. Melissa was ditzy, fun and energetic, the opposite of the more serious and considered Janie. Janie had a complicated relationship history, but in the last few months she seemed to have settled particularly well with Melissa who was a surveyor in Edinburgh.

The tall, slim form of Katie, Max's wife, appeared out of the patio doors of the cottage, with a tall jug of Pimm's, smiling widely. 'More Pimm's, anyone?' she said, looking at the group, squinting in the watery autumn sun. 'Max, those burgers look bloody awful. Tell me you bought something better than that?' she said pouring Pimm's into some glasses on the table.

'What is this? Have-a-Go-at-the-Chef Day?' said Max, sipping from a glass of cranberry juice.

Niall and Jeri had flown up to spend a few days with Max and Katie. They'd had a great time walking in the hills, with Nutmeg, Max's little cockapoo, and generally chilling. They'd all been friends when Max and Niall had served together on the Flying Squad a few years ago, but they hadn't been together for some time. The barbecue was the final meal before they caught their flight back down south later that afternoon. Janie and Melissa had turned up out of the blue, and it had been a pleasant way to spend the afternoon.

'You back at work tomorrow?' said Max to Niall through a big bite of charred burger meat.

'Aye. Midway through a pain-in-the-arse blagging job at a newsagent in Tottenham. We're going through the lad's door early with an armed team, so I'm in at four, hence why I'm drinking bloody Coke,' he said.

'Ouch,' said Janie.

'Aye. I've kind of had enough of it, you know. The hours are just bloody horrible – I did a hundred hours overtime last month,' said Niall.

'Good for the bank balance,' said Max.

'Not that he's ever around to spend it,' said Jeri. 'The kids never see Niall, so it's lucky they love going to their granny's place or we'd never get to spend any time together,' said Jeri with a forced smile.

'What are you going to do about it?' said Max.

'Well, I'm sitting the exam, so maybe promotion. Failing that I'll maybe look for an intel job. It can't go on like this. All the covert work, and the occasional UC job is taking its toll. I need something new.'

'I thought you'd aged,' said Max.

'Get fucked.'

'More to life than work, Craigie,' said Katie, winking.

'Aye, I guess.'

Max's phone buzzed on the table in front of them. He looked at the display, and saw it was DI Ross Fraser, Max, and Janie's boss.

'That's ominous on a Sunday afternoon,' said Max, holding up the display to Janie.

'And ironic,' said Katie, shaking her head.

'Ross?' said Max, standing up and walking across the garden out of earshot.

'Craigie, why is it that I'm in the fucking office on my bastard own?' he blasted down the phone.

'Possibly because it's Sunday afternoon and all right-thinking people are not there?'

'Aye well, you're paid to anticipate my needs and right now I need you bastards here. Something's come up. Is Janie with you?'

'Aye, just having a barbie with a pal from London.'

'Where the fuck was my invite, you snidey bugger?'

'Well, Janie just turned up uninvited, and I thought you and Mrs Fraser would be busy.'

'We were, as it happens, but I got called in. Someone's dumping on us from a great height, and I need you here to clear it up,' he said.

'Really? I've friends around.'

His tone lowered a touch. 'Look, pal, I wouldn't be calling if it wasn't urgent, but it is, so can you come?'

Max raised his eyebrows at Janie who gave a resigned nod.

'On our way,' said Max.

'Well, bloody hurry up.' Then he was gone.

'Really?' said Katie, with a resigned expression.

'Sorry, babe. Sounds urgent.'

'Just like in London. It's always urgent,' said Jeri, looking at Niall.

34

'When will the bosses learn that when everything is urgent, nothing is urgent, eh?' said Niall, smiling at his old friend.

'Sorry, man, I'll just go and get my bag and jacket, and then we'll head,' said Max, nodding at Janie, who just shrugged.

Max stood and went into the house and grabbed his work bag and jacket from a cupboard in the hallway. When he shut the door, Niall was standing there.

'You okay, bud?' said Max.

'Aye, I'm good. Thanks for having us to stay, we needed a wee break – it's been tough lately with all the hours,' said Niall, holding out his hand, which Max took, and they shook.

'Always a pleasure. Sorry I have to dash, but you know how it is.'

'Ach, go on. We'd better be off to the airport in an hour or so anyway,' said Niall.

'I know, but I feel bad. You know I'll not forget what you did in London that day,' said Max, nodding at the vivid scar on Niall's forearm.

'Best you don't. The thing itches like buggery every day, but I've forgotten all about it,' said Niall, grinning.

'Aye, of course, you never mention it, do you?'

'Well, not much anyway,' and they both laughed, before hugging, briefly.

'I'd best go, my boss is a great guy, but he's also a foul-mouthed tyrant.'

'Best kind, at least you know where you stand.'

They both walked out.

*

Max pushed open the door which bore a simple laminated sheet of paper. POLICING STANDARDS REASSURANCE, it read. There were three people in the office when Max and Janie arrived. Max deposited a small bag of brownies Katie had made earlier on his desk. Within seconds, the smartly dressed form of Norma, the team analyst, leaped to her feet. Her hand dived into the bag and pulled out a brownie, and she took a big bite.

Ross, Max, Janie and Norma were part of a small team that reported directly to the Chief Constable of Scotland on matters of all types of corruption that impacted on law enforcement in Scotland, although that was not their official role. The title of 'Policing Standards Reassurance' was something of a misnomer. Their published remit was to perform 'thematic reviews of covert and overt policing to ensure stakeholder satisfaction,' chosen because it was so spirit-crushingly dull that no one would want to know any more. However, Ross and his team had the chief's ear, and their true remit was to go wherever and do whatever was necessary to prevent and detect corruption that others couldn't.

'Afternoon,' she said through chocolate-coated lips. Norma loved a cake, biscuit or doughnut more than any cop Max had ever met, and she wasn't even a cop.

'Afternoon, Norma,' said Max. Norma replied with a thumbs-up. She chewed away, returning to the three monitors on her desk.

'Nice of you two lazy sods to join us, and sweeties won't excuse your tardiness,' said DI Ross Fraser.

'You won't be wanting one, then?' said Max.

'I didn't bloody say that, did I? Mrs Fraser will give me gyp for eating one if she finds out. Get the kettle on,' he said, his hand disappearing into the bag. He regarded the sweet treat with relish and took a big bite. Janie and Max shared a look and both watched Ross's off-white shirt with interest.

They were right. A lump of chocolate soon hit his chest.

'Ah, for fuck's sake,' he blasted, wiping at the stain, predictably making it worse. 'She'll go bastarding mad.'

'Do you need a bib?' said Max, laughing.

'Fuck you,' said Ross, trying in vain to remove the stain.

'Anyway, we aren't late, you only called twenty minutes ago,' said Janie.

'Aye well, Calder, things bloody change, and we have to react.'

'We are reacting. We're here.'

'Enough of your cheek. Something's developing. I'm not happy about a series of coincidences, and the chief wants us to research the background and see if there's anything in it. You heard of Shuggie Gibson?'

'Aye,' said Max. 'Freelance journo and blogger, who makes a big deal of police corruption and links to organised crime. He's not that popular in law enforcement circles. What's he been saying?' said Max, whilst pouring boiling water into four mugs.

'I know Shuggie well enough from our encounters over the years. He's not as anti-police as many think, and in this instance, he's worth listening to,' said Ross, accepting a mug from Max.

'Are you going to enlighten us?'

'Body of Scott Paterson found at Ravelston Golf Course this morning – heard about it?'

'What, Scott "The Axe" Paterson, acquitted of murder last week?' said Max.

'Not proven. Aye, that's him, you've not heard?'

'Can't say I have,' said Max.

'Bloody hell, don't you listen to the news?'

'Not today. I was forced to listen to some ear-bleedingly bad jazz that Janie played in the car.'

'Philistine, that was Critters Buggin, they're game-changers in fusion jazz,' said Janie, feigning offence.

'Well, whatever, it was crap. Ross, we failed to listen to the news as Janie insisted on listening to Bogging Critters whatever. So, what's occurred?'

'Snitches get stitches,' said Janie under her breath.

'Dog walker found him, looks like he'd been cuffed to a tree and his throat cut.'

'Well, that's not unexpected – he was hardly popular, was he? Gangland enforcer, suspected contract killer and all round scrote. He must have had loads of enemies,' said Max, chewing on his brownie.

'He certainly did. He had no allegiances, would work for whoever paid him, and he was the kind to enjoy his work a little too much,' said Norma, scrolling through an intelligence database. 'His advocate managed to destroy the only major witness who wasn't corroborated, give the SIO an absolute battering when he gave evidence, and swing a "not proven".'

'Aye, and three days later the bugger is dead. Want to know what is worse?' asked Ross, looking concerned.

'I take it that's a rhetorical question?' said Janie.

'Obviously, but of course, being the contrary Mary you are, you asked the bloody question, anyway. Okay, so Axe Man gets acquitted, and three days later he's dead, throat cut in a muddy bog on a golf course. What makes this a little more notable is that early this morning, his advocate in that trial, a slimy shite called Fergus Grigor, known in the trade as "Get You Off" Grigor, was found dead at the bottom of the cliffs at Dunnet Head.'

'Shit,' said Max.

'Indeed.'

'Anything to suggest foul play?'

'Well, he was on his honeymoon, so suicide doesn't seem likely, does it? Unless he was having regrets, like *really* early. I mean, there have been times I've felt like chucking myself off a cliff when Mrs F has been in a particularly irascible mood.'

'Inspector, is that entirely sensitive?' said Janie, shaking her head at the typically blunt remark from Ross.

'Fair point, well made, sorry. Anyway, there's more to it than that. Maybe it's best if I let Shuggie tell you himself. He's in the conference room.'

6

Alfa-Secure

SCOTT PATERSON WAS just too easy.

The target thought he was untouchable, but he found out the hard way the adage is true — bad things happen to bad people.

He thought he was the hardest man in Edinburgh, but he still pissed his pants like a baby when he knew what was going to happen.

He was the worst of the worst, so he had to die. Watching his smarmy, arrogant face on the steps of the High Court was enough to seal his fate.

He ran like a coward, but not fast enough. The look on his face when his throat was sliced open.

Justice was done.

Burn in hell, Scott 'The Axe' Paterson.

7

SHUGGIE GIBSON SAT in the conference room, a mug of tea in front of him. He looked up as Ross, Max, Janie and Norma entered the room, and his smile was genuine and warm.

'Shuggie, this is Max, Janie and Norma, who all work for me,' said Ross.

'*With* you,' said Norma.

Ross sighed and raised his eyebrows at Shuggie.

'Fine. Shuggie, this is Max, Janie and Norma who work *with* me. Happy, Norma?'

'Thank you, Ross-Boss.' Norma nodded with satisfaction.

Ross gave Norma his hardest stare before continuing, 'Shuggie and I have known each other for a few years. He kept a couple of things out of the press that he didn't need to, just because I asked him. Suffice to say, I trust him, and I trust his judgement, despite him being a pain in the arse. He's on the side of the angels, if you get my drift,' said Ross.

'Too kind, Ross, and unexpected, since you usually refer to me as a "scumbag, gutter-sniping, parasitic shite". Pleased to meet you all.' His deep blue eyes sparkled with amusement.

'Aye, well. You have that capacity, so I like to keep you on your toes, man. Anyway, you have the floor, Shug.'

Shuggie's eyes darted around the room.

'Well, as you all know by now, Scott "The Axe" Paterson was found dead, but more of a worry to me right now is the horrible coincidence of his advocate's death. I understand that when he failed to return, his wife used a mapping app that doesn't need internet which suggested he was still up by the lighthouse at the top of the cliff. The poor wee wifey went looking and there was no trace of him. She called it in, the search and rescue helicopter was despatched, and there he was, a hundred feet down, battered to bits on the rocks.'

A cloying silence suddenly descended on the room.

'Jesus,' said Janie, under her breath.

'Aye, that's what I thought. Helicopter winched a paramedic down, but it was no good. Massive injuries.'

'You're well informed,' said Max.

'I've my sources.'

'Carry on,' said Ross, flatly.

'I'm told there were no witnesses – tourist season being over, and it was blowing a hoolie at the top – so the duty officer is thinking that he either got too close to the edge or he topped himself.'

'And?' said Ross.

'Well, I'm not buying it, are you?'

'You all know my attitude to coincidences?'

'Well, he went over by the viewing point, by one of the seabird information boards. He'd have to climb over a wall into the danger zone next to the cliff edge. Seems odd, right?'

Max shifted in his seat. 'I get that it's a nasty coincidence, but why tell us? No offence, Shuggie, but surely the MIT should be looking at family and friends of the guy that Paterson allegedly killed, right?'

There was a pause in the room whilst Ross and Shuggie exchanged a silent gaze.

'The SIO for Paterson's murder is DCI Donnie Watson. He was also SIO for Paterson's recent trial,' said Ross.

'And?' said Norma.

'DCI Watson and his team were responsible for investigating a culpable homicide case five years ago. A young boy was mown down and killed in Perth by a singularly unpleasant, pissed-up driver called Chick Wilson. Wilson got a "not proven" after his trial at the High Court, some morally questionable jiggery-pokery was done by his advocate who pulled a few strokes, managed to cast enough doubt, and Wilson walked. It was made far worse by the fact that Wilson's driving history was shockingly bad. Multiple drink-drive convictions and he was disqualified at the time. Three days later, he's found hanging from a tree in a park in Perth, with marks on his wrists. They could never prove anything and there was nothing to go on. It was ruled as unlawful killing, but the murder team got nowhere with it and it remains unsolved. That's not the interesting bit, though.'

'I've a feeling what you're going to say next,' said Max.

'Aye. Fergus Grigor was Chick Wilson's advocate.'

Silence gripped the room again. The only sound was the officer's deep, regular breathing.

'Copycat, maybe?' said Norma.

'The handcuff marks on Chick Wilson's wrists weren't made public, and they instigated reporting restrictions. Basically, nobody outside of the core roles on the investigation team knew about them. They didn't want it leaking, for all the usual reasons.'

'So, how do you know about it?' said Ross.

'I was told by a concerned party,' said Shuggie, his face impassive.

'We possibly have a killer seeking revenge against acquitted defendants and their advocates,' said Janie.

'That's three dead. That makes this a serial killer case,' Shuggie said.

'Shite,' said Ross.

Shuggie sighed. 'It's worse than that. If my theory's right. I'd say it's not just a serial killer, it's something much worse.'

'Meaning?' said Ross.

'My source has recently reported concerns about Donnie Watson's MIT. He says there have been others.'

'Others?' said Janie.

'I've never spoken to the person. All I have are a couple of anonymous emails, and a few interesting comments.' He looked at his notepad. 'Being unsuccessfully investigated by DCI Watson's MIT is a dangerous position to be in. Someone on the MIT at Leith doesn't take failure well.'

'Well, that could be anyone. Lots of people have grudges in the wake of a serious crime investigation,' said Max.

'Aye, that's true, but the source is clearly a cop.'

'How can you be sure?'

'They just sound like a cop. I know enough about cops to recognise one. There's something else, as well.'

'Come on, just bloody spit it out, man!' Ross blasted, his normally beetroot face darkening.

'He or she immediately knew about the handcuff marks and Fergus Grigor's death. I got the email within an hour of him being found dead at the foot of the cliffs. Only someone closely connected to the police could know about it all and be able to join the dots that quickly. The killer is either a cop, or he has a cop feeding him information. Whatever, Ross, something is rotten at the heart of the Major Investigation Team at Leith, something very bad indeed. You've a vigilante, and I think he's one of yours.'

'Could your source be the killer?'

'No idea. I've never spoken to him, or her. All I have is a Gmail address and that's it.'

'How would you feel about us seeing if we could trace the email?' said Ross.

'Well, I'd normally never reveal a source, but they contacted me and I don't know who they are, so I don't see why not.' Shuggie took out a piece of paper from his pocket and handed it over. 'That's the email. I'll be honest, Ross, I want this story, but really, I just want whoever is doing this stopped. They're going to kill again, of that we can be sure. Serial killers don't just stop.' He sat back in his chair, a worried frown on his face.

Ross looked at the single sheet of A4 paper and handed it to Norma. 'Can you do whatever weird shit it is you do to trace that?'

'I'll need authorisations from above, but yeah, leave it with me. It could just be a burner email. I could set up a similar one in seconds,' she said, looking at the sheet.

Ross sat back in his chair and rubbed his face with his shovel-like hands.

'I'd better speak to the chief,' he said.

8

CHIEF CONSTABLE CHRIS Macdonald was standing in his office, hands behind his back, looking out of the window as Ross recounted Shuggie's story. When Ross finished, he turned, strode over to his coffee maker, and poured two cups. One he handed to Ross, the other he took a sip from, and sat.

Ross had managed to prise his way past the haughty staff officer with a little huffing and puffing and veiled threats of reprisals that always seemed to occur whenever Ross wanted an off-the-record meeting, referred to as a 'meeting without minutes'.

'What's your feeling about this, Ross?' said Macdonald, sitting up, his focus back, his eyes sharp.

'Shuggie is a good journalist, and he definitely has a conscience. I know Donnie Watson, as well, and he's straight as they come, but it's hard to ignore the facts here. Three murders all inextricably linked to the MIT at Leith. Wilson, Paterson and Grigor all connected to them with bastard verdicts. It's too big a coincidence.'

'And Shuggie thinks his source is a cop?'

'Aye. I've seen the anonymous email, and I agree. It sounds

like a cop. Norma is looking into the address to see if we can maybe trace it – oh, by the way, I'll need some authorities for that,' said Ross almost as an afterthought.

'Whatever you need. Shite, this is bad. Is Shuggie going to keep quiet?'

'He's a decent enough hack, and he knows if he publishes, he'll screw us over. He just wants an exclusive on whatever comes out of it.'

'Seems reasonable. What do you think we should do?'

'How about we just start poking around?'

'I've heard that before, Ross. It never ends well.'

'Aye, right enough, but maybe we do another of our "thematic reviews".' Ross waggled his fingers miming quotation marks. 'I'd like access to the HOLMES account and PM results for all, once they're done, and we can look at all three investigations with fresh eyes. I mean, it could just be a series of coincidences. One thing's for sure, though …' Ross paused, his bushy, unkempt eyebrows bristling as he fixed his boss and old friend with a steady gaze.

'What?'

'No one on MIT 6 can know about this. They get an inkling of it and anything that we can use to corroborate Shuggie will be lost. If we are dealing with a cop willing to kill – whether it's out of a warped sense of justice or just for kicks – then we have a big problem. He knows what we know, and he could derail us.'

'Okay, we'll call it a thematic review arising out of press interest and the factors linking them together, I'll speak to DCC McVeigh – he's just taken over serious crime and terrorism – and have the review ordered by him. He'll no doubt push it to

Miles Wakefield. You'll get whatever access you require, but fact-finding only at this stage. Any authorisations you need, come straight to me; we can't let this get away from us, Ross. If someone connected to MIT 6 is involved in these events, I want to know about it, urgently.'

9

DCI DONNIE WATSON was chewing at a torn fingernail, as he paced the wooden floor of the meeting room at Leith Police Station and thought about all the scrutiny this case would attract. Despite his many years of experience in investigating murders, he had to admit that this had him rattled. It felt like a lead weight was resting in the pit of his stomach, and it wasn't a pleasant sensation. He wanted to be away from this, but the retirement date was set in stone, and to go early would cost thousands. He wondered for a moment if it was a price worth paying.

The preceding twenty-four hours had been a blur of actions, requests, CCTV parameter requests, house-to-house strategy and the scene examination which had taken almost all of yesterday's daylight to complete. Then there had been all the activity following the closure of the scene – the activity that is rarely seen on the 'Real CSI' programmes on TV. The painstaking documentation of evidence seized from the small copse of trees, and the wider search area. The cataloguing of all the photographs and video clips, the packaging of the victim's clothing in brown paper bags, sealed top and bottom with tape, and signature seals. Bloodstained clothing had to be dried in forensic lockers prior to packaging and submission to the laboratory, or it would rot, tainting or even destroying any trace evidence.

This was a massive inquiry now, and the shout had gone out to the other teams for some backup, meaning that at present, close to thirty officers were sitting waiting for them in the MIR.

'What, nothing from the scene?' asked Donnie, looking at Fagerson incredulously.

'Nope. Well, obviously we have all of Paterson's clothing, shoes and the like, but we'll know nothing until they're fully dry and the lab has had a chance to process,' said Fagerson, looking at his A4 book.

'No weapon?'

'No.'

'No cuffs?'

'No.'

'Footmarks?'

'Only one, almost certainly made by Paterson's shoe after a visual examination. CSI has imprints of his trainers, and they lifted the shoe mark. Not conclusive. There's a flat depression in the loose dirt by the tree, but no ridge marks to indicate a shoe, and nothing to lift. If I was a guessing man, I'd say they were wearing flat-soled shoes with no tread pattern. Or …' he hesitated.

'What?'

'Overshoes?' Fagerson's eyebrows rose.

'Damn,' said Watson, scratching his thin hair.

'Aye. That's what I thought. Whoever did this has a very good sense of forensics.'

'Marnie?' said Donnie, looking at his deputy SIO.

'Nothing from house-to-house – as expected, bearing in mind no bugger lives nearby. The CCTV situation you know about already.'

'Aye, and I don't bloody like it, seems too convenient.'

Marnie said nothing, just shrugged.

'So, we can rule out robbery. He still had an Omega watch on, which is a six-grand piece, and his wallet with almost a thousand quid in it was untouched. I haven't seen mention of a phone?'

'He didn't have one,' said Fagerson.

'That's not right. No flash gang man walks around without a phone. Doesn't happen. This means our offender took it, but that still doesn't make this a robbery. How about a car?'

'He owned a fairly old BMW X5, although it was registered to his wife. It was found abandoned, keys still in it, outside a scrappie's in Coates.'

'So, the killer probably drove it there? Who owns the scrapyard?' said Donnie.

'Jackie McLennan,' said Fagerson.

'What, *the* Jackie McLennan?'

'Aye.'

'This complicates it. One of Edinburgh's biggest gangsters, and a murder victim's car ditched outside his yard. What do we make of that?'

'Sounds amateurish to me,' said Fagerson.

'Agreed. Why would anyone do that? Has McLennan been spoken to?'

'Out of the country in Spain.'

'Since when?'

'Four weeks. He owns a place there, and we have him on border targeting leaving the UK, so he's bulletproof.'

'Where's the car now?'

'At the forensic pound. Next on the list of things to be examined,' said Jimmy Duggan, looking at his clipboard.

'Needs doing quickly, Jimmy.'

'When we're ready, not before,' said Jimmy in his typical blunt fashion.

'John, what intel have you got?'

DS John Lorimer was a big, beefy-looking middle-aged man in jeans and a crumpled shirt with a heavy stubble covering his face. Lorimer ran the intelligence cell on the team and was responsible for developing all the background information on the victim and likely suspects. 'The FLO got a current number for him when they informed his family. I've put that in for urgent call data and cell sites, but still waiting. It's a priority, but you know how it goes.'

'Any theories?' said Donnie, yawning.

'I'd say he was lured to the location by phone call or message; which may explain why we haven't found a phone on him. There's no other explanation. Whoever killed him didn't want us to find something on the handset. They lured him there, killed him and then drove off in his car and dumped it.'

'Won't billing and cell sites give us that?'

'Yes and no, boss. If they called him or messaged him using standard GSM phone minutes then the number calling and the cell sites would be on the data, but if they used a secure messaging app that just used 4G, then we wouldn't see it. We'd need the handset, and if he was using Wickr, Telegram, or similar, the messages will irretrievably self-destruct. Or even worse, if it was an encrypted phone …' Lorimer left the sentence hanging.

'ANPR?' said Donnie.

'Only hits were hours before in Stockbridge.'

'Nothing between Ravelston and the scrapyard?'

'Nothing, and I know for a fact that there's no CCTV by the scrapyard. I was looking for some not long ago to deploy against McLennan, but *nada*,' said Lorimer.

'Anything from the snitches?'

'Nope, the jungle drums are singularly and unusually silent, but Paterson had enemies everywhere,' said Lorimer.

'So, we have the square root of bugger all, then?' said Donnie.

'Forensics on clothes, the victim's person and his car may give us something, unless they've been very careful. And there's always the Wicker PM,' said Marnie.

'Do we have a time for that, yet?' asked Donnie.

'Two p.m.'

Donnie nodded. 'You and I both there, Marnie, plus productions officer. Who do we have for that, Mark?'

'Doreen Urquhart, she's all set to go, systems in place, but she's not overly busy, since it's such a clean scene.'

'Doreen's excellent, and we'll need our A game here. How about Paterson's alleged victim's family, has anyone spoken to them? They have the most obvious motive,' Donnie said, referring to the family of the man that Paterson had been cleared of murdering.

'FLO went yesterday afternoon. The alleged victim's family are his old dad, and an alcoholic brother,' said Marnie.

'How did they take it?'

'Pissed themselves laughing.'

'Any suggestions they could be involved?'

'I can't see it. The old man is late eighties and the brother barely knows what day it is. Witnesses put both in the boozer the night before, and both had to be knocked out of their beds late morning yesterday. Neither of them, not even together, could overpower a steroid-addled Scott Paterson, and neither has a pot to piss in. No one would take a contract on Scott "The Axe" Paterson without serious wedge changing hands. We can do more digging, but I think it's a blind alley.'

'And the wrist marks?'

'PM will give us more, but to the naked eye, they look like metal cuff marks. I hope to God that the press doesn't get hold of it, particularly as Chick Wilson had cuff marks as well,' said Marnie.

'Don't bloody talk shite. The MO is totally different, and Chick died five fucking years ago. It could be a copycat. Anyone could get hold of handcuffs.' Donnie rubbed at his temples with his fingers, feeling a pulse beneath them. His mind swirled with the enormity of this task.

'It wasn't released.'

'Aye, well, things leak. Look, it makes no bloody difference. We do our jobs: secure and preserve the evidence, locate witnesses, get onto the snitches. Someone knows why Scott Paterson was killed. We do what we always bloody do. Key actions, gather the evidence and be thorough.'

'How about their lawyer, "Get You Off" Grigor?' asked Fagerson.

'I don't think it can be connected. I mean, look at the circumstances. He was killed after the dog walker found Paterson.

How could the same killer make that five-and-a-half-hour journey? People die all the time at Dunnet Head, and there are no other similarities. Grigor was a daft bastard who got too close to a notorious cliff when it was blowing a bloody hoolie, but we still must make sure we cover all the bases, so we'll need a team to get up there. Also pull the file for Chick Wilson. I'm not convinced they're connected, but we proceed as if they could be. Marnie, I want you to fully review the file, literally line by line.'

No one in the room said anything.

Donnie let out a long sigh and scrubbed at his unusually lined face with his hands. He looked up at his team, his eyes red and rheumy before continuing. 'What I really want to know, is how that bastard Shuggie Wilson got to know about this?'

'You know what these journos are like. Shuggie's an anti-cop crusader chasing his tail. No one listens to him,' said Marnie.

'Well, he has masses of followers. Don't write him off,' said Lorimer.

'Screw bloody Shuggie. Doesn't change what we do. Come on, the team's waiting and there's still shitloads to do.'

They stood and filed out into the main conference room. It was packed with tired-looking cops. Many of the faces Donnie didn't recognise, because they were from MITs and CID offices all over the city. They knew that a long day of routine actions were waiting for them. Contrary to homicide investigations on TV, this was all about routine inquiries done to a high standard. House-to-house, CCTV, phone intelligence, forensics and witnesses. Murder investigations are team efforts, with every member playing their part in securing and preserving the evidence that would help them catch the perpetrator.

A familiar face swam into view across the packed room. The beefy, shambolic form of DI Ross Fraser smiled as he caught his eye.

'Ross, to what do we owe the pleasure?' Donnie said, suspicion nipping at him. He knew Ross of old, but thought he was in some shiny-arse role at the chief's office.

'Morning, Donnie. DSU Wakefield asked the chief for our support with a thematic review. He's worried about the press interest. Don't worry, I'll stay out of the way,' Ross said, with a grin.

'Sure you don't fancy watching some CCTV?'

'Thanks, I'll pass. Chief wants a full report, and the bugger's lumbered me with it. I suggested you do it, but he thinks you may be a little busy. Can't see why – you normally delegate everything anyway, unless you've changed since we last worked together,' Ross chuckled, scratching his belly.

Donnie stared at Ross, narrowing his eyes. The chief's man suddenly wanting to know all about the investigation could only spell even more bloody pressure and scrutiny. He forced down the feeling of doom.

'You know me well. Anyway, let's get going, we've a lot to cover. Good morning, ladies and gents, and thanks to those of you who've been drafted in. The eyes of the world are going to be on us all, so we need to be cooking on gas. Do we all understand?'

No one said anything, but the hard eyes, and grim nods of determination told their own story.

10

Alfa-Secure

DCI WATSON IS an incompetent fool who was promoted way over his abilities. Police promotion processes throw up idiots like him all the time.

Listening to him droning on in that tedious meeting, it was plainly apparent that his abilities as SIO have been reached.

The biggest threat to the objective is that he gets replaced by someone competent.

11

THE ATMOSPHERE IN the autopsy suite at the Royal Infirmary of Edinburgh was as it usually is. Pensive and anticipatory.

Donnie Watson, Jimmy Duggan and Doreen Urquhart, the productions officer, all stood at the side of the room dressed in scrubs, trying not to look too hard at the corpse on the polished metal gurney in the centre of the room.

'You ready for this, Doreen?' said Donnie.

'I hope so,' said Doreen, who was a short and stout middle-aged woman, with a kind face. Her job was to seize and catalogue any physical evidence found during the procedure. PMs were always unpleasant for productions officers, as the items seized tended to be body fluids, tissue samples and nail clippings. She had a clipboard, and a case of bags, tubes and containers, ready for whatever the pathologist found that would be deemed relevant.

Scott Paterson's muscles, normally so pumped and intimidating, were slack and empty, his open eyes clouded and vacant. The grimace that he had worn at the golf course had been replaced by a relaxed expression. Donnie's eyes were irresistibly drawn to the vivid slash that bisected his neck, a bloody and dark gorge across parchment-coloured flesh. Rigor mortis had mostly departed, but residual stiffness could be seen in the partially bent angle of his legs and arms.

The officers spoke in whispers to each other, as if Scott Paterson could still hear them. Death is a strange affair, and no matter how many years of police service they had, its impact never lessened.

The tang of disinfectant filled the room, and every surface gleamed, but the underlying scent of death still hung in the air like a creeping, pervasive fug.

A sudden noise made them all look up at the viewing window. A lean, shaven-headed man dressed in jeans and a checked shirt walked in, sat on one of the chairs, steepled his fingers in front of him, and surveyed the scene. An ID tag with the word VISITOR hung around his neck. He nodded at the three of them.

'Who's that?' said Donnie in a hoarse whisper.

'No idea. Are we expecting anyone?'

'We sometimes have observers,' said Doreen.

'I think I recognise him from somewhere,' said Donnie.

Suddenly, the doors burst open, and a huge man clad in scrubs swept into the room.

'Donnie, good to see you, man,' he bellowed, in a rich, sonorous voice that almost made the tray of surgical instruments rattle on the metal trolley next to Scott Paterson.

'Baz, how's it going?' said Donnie. Baz was the mortuary technician – or more correctly titled, the anatomical pathology technician – who had been working at RIE for as long as anyone could remember. His bushy dark hair, full-sleeve tattoos and avuncular personality was a little at odds with his occupation.

'I'm grand, pal. Jimmy, you want to get the general photos done now? You can take any close-ups, or injury photos, once we've got all the normal angles done and we're underway.'

'Elsa not coming?' said Donnie.

'Aye, on her way. She knows how important this bugger is with everything going on, but she's happy to get the main photographs taken before we start slicing and dicing,' Baz boomed, yawning, and scratching his stubble.

'Can I start shooting now?'

'Just give me a second, fam. I want to get the equipment sorted, so we're ready as soon as Elsa comes in.'

'Suits me,' said Jimmy, opening his metal case and pulling out a professional-looking camera.

Baz then adopted a routine that they'd all seen before. With total focus, he went to various drawers in the equipment cupboards, and pulled out scalpels, saws, kidney bowls and the circular saw used for removing the top of scalps. Wordlessly, with quick economical movements, he arranged all the equipment on a stainless-steel trolley, with almost millimetre-perfect accuracy. He stood back and admired his handiwork, with a nod, and then looked at Jimmy. 'Over to you, geezer.'

Donnie suppressed a smile. This was typical for Baz. He referred to almost everyone by some kind of nickname. You could be a dude, homie, geezer, bloke, fam, cuz and on certain occasions and for reasons no one knew, shag. No one ever asked him why.

Jimmy took several shots of Paterson, from all angles, including some close-ups of the neck wound. Once happy he nodded at Baz, who turned the corpse onto his side as if he were rearranging cushions on a sofa.

'What's the wee mark on his arse?' said Jimmy, pointing at a small puncture wound surrounded by a vague suggestion of a bruise. He snapped away at it.

Baz took a step closer and squinted. 'Hard to tell, shag. We'll know more in a bit, but it looks pretty innocuous.'

'Injection?' asked Donnie, his eyebrows raised.

'Possibly. You thinking he was drugged?'

'Well, look at the size of him. His only injuries are cuff marks and a slashed throat.'

Baz shrugged. 'Need tox for that. I'd say it's a bit big for an injection, unless it was a seven-gauge needle for a glute intramuscular.'

'Well, somehow, someone overpowered him.'

'Aye well, I'm sure Elsa will have an opinion. Done with your shots, Jimmy? I know I'm a chunky monkey, but this fella is heavy.' Baz looked at the crime scene manager.

'Aye, set him back.'

Baz carefully rested Paterson on the gurney with a grunt, settling his huge skull on the resin support.

Jimmy showed the camera screen to Donnie and scrolled through the images.

The swing doors opened again and Elsa entered, smiling, her scarlet-lipstick-framed mouth wide. She was wearing scrubs as well as a thick, heavy, rubberised apron, her hair secured in a paper head covering.

'Afternoon, folks. Ready to rock and roll?' she said.

'As ready as anyone ever is to see a body dissected, I guess,' said Donnie with a rueful smile.

'Initial photos done?'

'Aye.'

'I take it we're recording?' she said, eyebrows raised at Baz, who just nodded.

'Feelings on the cuff marks?' she said, leaning closer to Paterson's wrists. She stared at the faint bruises.

'You're the celebrated and esteemed consultant forensic pathologist, Elsa. What the hell do I know?' said Donnie, a smile evident in his voice.

Elsa laughed, her eyes shining. 'Reminds me of an old Kosovan proverb, *Those who know how to praise also know how to lie.*'

'Can't say I've heard it. I'm from Kilmarnock, and I've never been further than Spain.'

Elsa grinned. 'Well, with the width of Paterson's back and size of his biceps, the cuffs would have been tight, and I think that you can see evidence of the pressure they put on the carpal bones on both sides.' The pathologist gently lifted the huge, limp hand. 'See here,' she said, pointing. 'There's a double indentation on the exterior face of the wrist by the carpal bones, but just a single line on the inside. Hold up a second.' She walked around the gurney and lifted the other hand. 'See, single line on the inside, double over the carpals. Has anyone got any handcuffs with them?'

'In my case,' said Doreen, reaching into a leather shoulder bag and bringing out a pair of rigid handcuffs. Elsa took them.

She examined the straight, metal cuffs, with black plastic covering the middle portion. One half of the wrist restraint was a double-curve piece of steel, the other a single. Elsa pushed the restraints, which clicked as they passed over the locking ratchets. She gently held the open cuff against Paterson's wrist without allowing it to touch.

The pathologist frowned. 'I'm going out on a limb here, but I'd say he was handcuffed, behind his back with his palms facing outwards. I'd also say it was a pair of restraints very similar to these. The injury marks match these cuffs. How common are they?'

'Almost universal. Every cop in the land has a pair and you can pick them up on eBay,' said Doreen, accepting the handcuffs and replacing them in her bag.

'I'll want full close-ups on all sides of those cuff marks, Jimmy,' said Donnie, his voice low and tight.

Jimmy exhaled, his cheeks puffed out. 'Aye. Rigid cuffs used to secure – that's a bit too close to home,' he said.

'Okay, let's get cracking, then,' said Elsa, moving without hesitation to the corpse. She walked a slow circle around it with a look of intense concentration on her face and a clipboard in her hand.

'Initial survey of subject, Scott Paterson,' Elsa said, speaking into her dictaphone. She talked through the preliminaries and listed everything they knew so far. 'Subject has a significant injury to the throat that begins from the area just below the left ear then travels inwards and downwards, severing the carotid artery and the trachea. Evidence of catastrophic haemorrhaging from the incision, which is clean and seems to have been caused by a very sharp clean-edged weapon. Angle of cut is suggestive of a left-handed attacker, unless they used a back-handed technique, which would be unusual. Everything suggests a front-facing attack.' She paused, and her brow creased with concentration as she looked at Donnie.

'I'm confident about this, Donnie. You're looking for a southpaw, and somehow they managed to subdue the victim long enough to be able to inflict this injury whilst up close and personal.'

'Not from behind?'

'If I had a mortgage, I'd bet this was front-on. Rear-delivered cuts tend to be far longer. This was calculated. Carotid to windpipe. The bugger had no chance and would have been dead in a minute.'

'Christ.'

Elsa looked at Donnie and shrugged before raising her dictaphone again. 'Injuries on both wrists suggestive of restraint, by hard restraints, certainly not rope, or zip ties, but further examination will make this clearer.'

Elsa smiled behind her mask, her eyes twinkling. 'Primary survey is now complete. Previous X-rays have shown NAD so I am now ready to begin further examination.'

She picked up a larger scalpel, its blade glinting in the harsh overhead light.

'Ready?' she said.

'I was born ready, fam,' said Baz, offering his gloved fist to Elsa, who gently bumped hers against it.

No one replied. There wasn't much to say about a human body being reduced to its components, reassembled like a gruesome jigsaw, and then destroyed.

However, this body contained answers. Within the collection of skin, muscle, fluids and organs lay the information as to how – and possibly why – Scott 'The Axe' Paterson died. They were here to witness that process. Death was their business.

A creak from behind the viewing window made them all glance around as the visitor stood and left the room. They all shared a puzzled look.

'Who was that?' asked Elsa.

'Wasn't he with you?' asked Donnie.

'He's a cop. I thought you would've known about it. Some review team have been authorised. Didn't you see the email, Elsa?' said Baz.

'Don't think so.'

'What's his name?' asked Donnie.

'I can't remember, but he had a warrant card and that,' said Baz.

'Anyway, can we get on?' said Elsa.

There being no answer, Elsa nodded, almost to herself as she wielded the scalpel at the top of Paterson's ribcage, just below the injury which presumably ended his life. As the wickedly sharp blade travelled downwards, carving through the marble-coloured skin, a line of a Rod Stewart song popped into Donnie's head. He could never fully remember it, but it was something about cuts being deep.

12

MAX JOGGED OUT of the blindingly white frontage of the hospital, pulling his phone from his pocket. He slowed to a fast walk and dialled Ross.

'Craigie, that was quick.'

'It's only just getting started, but I don't think there's much we can't learn from the report. I also saw something that I think I'd rather get straight on with.'

'What?'

'Just a theory. Do we have access to the crime scene photos and the pictures of Paterson's clothing?'

'Aye, we're copied in on everything. Did anyone ask who you were?'

'Just the lab tech, and he didn't seem that arsed. He looked like he was from a death metal band. I hung about in the viewing gallery. It's pretty cut and dried, massive blood loss from a severed carotid, left-handed assailant from the front.'

'That throws up all sorts of other questions, though.'

'Aye, plenty, which is why I've buggered off. I want to visit the scene, but I want to see the photos first. I'm heading back to the office – is Janie there?'

'Yes, she's fannying around with the Fergus Grigor case. She knows someone who was there and she has the photos and early reports.'

'When's the PM?'

'Tomorrow at Inverness, you want to go?'

'Maybe, but first I want to see both scenes.'

'Sure, but why?'

'Do we have the Chick Wilson files?'

'Not yet, but I've requested a full copy from archives, and we have HOLMES access.'

'Cool. I'll be back in an hour.' Max hung up, his mind whirring. The wound on Paterson's backside didn't look like any injection site he'd ever seen, but it did look familiar.

Janie, Ross and Norma were all tapping away at their terminals when Max arrived at the office just over an hour later.

'You took your fucking time, Craigie. No doubt swanning around giving it Charlie big spuds whilst we do all the bastarding work,' said Ross as he raised his mug to his lips. He took a sip and grimaced. 'Tea's bloody cold. Make us a new one, since you've finally graced us with your presence,' he added.

'And hello to you too, inspector,' said Max.

'Aye, anything to report?'

'As I said on the phone. Not until tox comes back, and it really doesn't matter for our purposes, does it?'

'I guess not. So what do you think we should do, always remembering that I'm the boss, here.'

Max recounted what Elsa had told them about the handcuffs.

'Why is that concerning?' said Norma.

'That method of cuffing is textbook technique, and it's awkward to do at the best of times. Whoever applied those cuffs either knew what they were doing or got very lucky.'

'Shit,' was all that Ross said, massaging his temples.

'Indeed.'

'So, cop cuffs and cop technique,' said Norma.

'Yes, but there are a million pairs of those cuffs out there, and anyone can learn the technique, so it's not conclusive, especially as more and more security companies are using them and training on them. A pal of mine runs training courses for security operatives, and handcuffs is part of it,' said Janie.

'Also, it's not like the security industry is free of scrotes, is it?' added Ross.

'Can we get the photos up of Paterson's clothing?' said Max.

'I have them here,' said Janie, tapping at her keyboard. 'Switch on the projector.'

Max reached and flicked a switch on a ceiling bracket and Janie's screen splashed across the screen at the end of the room.

'What do you want first?'

'Jeans, front and back.'

Two images appeared. Firstly, the front of a pair of heavily bloodstained navy-blue Hugo Boss jeans, the second of the back. Max studied them for a moment.

'Enlarge the backside right pocket.'

Janie fiddled with her keyboard and the image zoomed in on the embroidered pocket. A small rip was visible. It was just a nick, and you had to look hard to see it.

'Okay, now the back of his leather jacket.'

Janie tapped at her keys and a new image appeared, the back section of an expensive-looking leather jacket. It appeared brand new, although there were long scratch marks from the collar down to the waistband.

'Enlarge the shoulder section, right-hand side,' said Max, his face blank.

'What the bloody hell are you looking at?' said Ross.

'There's a small scratch and rip in the leather about where his shoulder blade would be. It's not big, but it's definitely there, almost exactly in line.'

'What are you getting at, Max?' asked Janie.

'His clothing was pierced by something in two places, about the same size hole. He had a small puncture wound on his buttock, but nothing on his torso. Maybe it didn't pierce the jacket.'

'Janie, can you arrange the two photos vertically, as if we were looking at Paterson wearing them.

'Hold up,' Janie typed and adjusted the images until the back of the jacket was above the jeans.

Max moved closer to the screen. His forehead creased in concentration.

'I reckon the holes are about twenty, twenty-four inches apart.'

'Spit it out, you obtuse nugget,' blasted Ross. Max paused, then turned to his colleagues.

'The big issue is how can someone the size of a silverback be taken out without a gun and without a struggle? We can assume his murderer didn't have a gun, or they'd have just shot him, and I doubt it's drugs. I think Scott Paterson was shot with a taser before he was murdered.'

13

'**A POLICE TASER?**' said Ross.

'I think so. In fact, I'm sure of it.'

'But surely there'd be burns and shit like that?'

'Not necessarily. You ever trained with a taser?'

'Joking, aren't you? They barely let me have a bloody truncheon.'

'It adds up. We know what Paterson was like – he'd always fight, and even if he was drugged, how did his killer get him there without a fight? As I understand it, his phone is missing, so I'd say he was lured there on some pretext and then zapped. You can see the scratches on his jacket, so I'm betting that once he'd been tasered he fell against the tree and slid down into the sitting position. Once the probes are in, any attempt to resist and the killer would hit him with another burst of electricity.'

'Aye, 50,000 volts in your arse and your day is ruined, right enough,' said Ross.

'It's the amps that get you, not the volts,' said Janie.

'Eh?'

'Seriously, think of the volts like a lorry where its sole purpose is to deliver the amps to the target. The amps cause massive muscle spasms, and Paterson's bulk means that it would be even more effective against him.'

'Jesus, Calder. You can even geekify a cool thing like a taser,' Ross muttered.

'But if it was a taser and the top probe didn't pierce his skin, would that still work?' said Norma.

'Aye, it would. The volts drive the amps into the jacket, they then jump the gap and cause the neuromuscular incapacitation without touching the skin.'

'Well, I have to say you've sucked all the fun out of it, but it's just a theory, right?' said Ross.

'Best we have.'

'How can we corroborate it? On its own, we've a couple of holes in clothing and a second hole on the victim's arse,' said Ross.

'AFIDs,' said Max, his face impassive.

'Craigie, yer' pushin' me over the line, man. Will you just tell me what the pissing hell you're on about?' said Ross, his rough Highland accent strengthening and his face flushing an even deeper shade of purple.

'As Max says, anti-felon identity tags. Every time a taser is deployed – certainly one issued to Police Scotland – it shoots out about thirty bits of paper, like confetti. Each one has a unique number on it, making it traceable.'

'Aye, I know that it shoots shit out, I'm not clueless. But I didn't know that they were named after bloody greenfly. Isn't it the older models that have ladybugs?' said Ross.

'Yep, the X26 second variant had AFIDs but was only issued to firearms teams in Scotland. Once normal cops started being issued with them, they were given the more up to date X2, with double-shot capability, but no confetti,' said Janie.

'You're well informed,' said Ross.

'I trained on the X2, but never actually deployed with it, although I did write a paper on all of this as part of my accelerated promotion process. So, how can we be sure he used a taser, and what type?'

'We can't. But we can make a good guess that it's a dart weapon, and Axon are by far the biggest manufacturer. Maybe the first question is whether any are unaccounted for?' said Max.

'I'm on it. My networking and negotiating skills are far better than you heathens. Piss off to the scene and get a feel for it. You never know, the search team may have missed one of your bloody greenflies.'

'They're not—'

'I know, I know. Bugger off and make yourselves useful, there's sod-all daylight this time of year,' Ross said. 'Mrs Fraser is always moaning about it being depressing.'

14

RAVELSTON GOLF COURSE car park was nearly deserted when Max and Janie pulled in. They stepped out of the big Volvo and set off towards the clubhouse and the open grassy expanse of the course beyond. The autumnal sun was already beginning to lower in the sky, casting deep shadows across the sweeping green fairways.

'Ghost town,' said Janie.

'A well-known gangster's body turning up on your favourite course is a bit off-putting,' said Max.

'I guess, plus it'll be dark soon, I hate autumn. Surprised they're not charging extra to play a shot from a puddle of congealing gangster blood. Is the scene closed?'

'Aye, processed it quick, which is why I want a look. They may have missed something.'

'Whether deliberately or accidentally.'

'Well, quite.'

'You ever play golf?' asked Janie.

Max raised an eyebrow at her.

'No, thought not. You're far too scruffy. Golfers wear expensive slacks and shite jumpers in pale lemon or magenta. You look like you buy your breeks in a charity shop.'

'Charming. Look out, here comes the staff,' said Max nodding at the man striding towards them. His face was red, his branded sweater and smart, colour-coordinated attire screamed, 'club captain'.

'Can I help you?' he barked, his eyes a little glassy. Max immediately suspected that he had been availing himself of the nineteenth hole.

'Afternoon. DS Craigie and DC Calder,' said Max, smiling and proffering his warrant card.

'I thought you lot had finished. The course was handed back to use, and we agreed to keep the cordon tape around the copse.'

'Aye, we just want a look,' said Max.

'Really, it's just too much. We agreed not to open until tomorrow, and this is a huge inconvenience to our members who pay a lot of money for these facilities,' he blustered, his moustache quivering.

'Sorry, I didn't catch your name, sir,' said Max as politely as he could. He desperately tried to hide the smile that was creeping across his face.

'I am Crawford MacDougall, chair of the greens committee,' he said with his chest puffed out, and thin lips pursed, as he surveyed them with disdain.

'Well, Mr MacDougall. We won't get in the way, we just want to check something out, then we'll be off,' said Max carrying on past MacDougall towards the copse.

'Making friends again?' said Janie, shaking her head.

'Aye, folk like him are the reason I never play golf.'

'What are you hoping to find, then?'

'I won't know until I see it, but I'm not buying that there was no physical evidence at all. It's always there, you just have to look properly. Do you have the scene photos on your smartphone?'

'I do. I'll bring them up.'

They walked into the small copse of birch trees, all with yellowing leaves that cast thick shade onto the muddy ground. The amount of activity that there had been was obvious by the churned-up, drying mud to the left of the tree where Paterson had been found. The light was struggling to permeate the trees, and it was several degrees cooler under the branches.

'This place is cold and bogging, and it bloody stinks,' said Janie as she picked her way around the sticky mud.

'It's not particularly pleasant, is it?' said Max as his trainer slipped.

The remnants of the blue-and-white plastic police cordon tape fluttered in the gentle evening breeze.

'Here,' said Janie, handing Max her smartphone. He looked at the lurid colour photo of Scott Paterson slumped against a thin tree trunk.

Max wordlessly scrolled through the images, his brow furrowed. He handed the phone back to Janie after a moment and then stood in front of the tree that had supported the body of a Scottish gangster, dead as the fallen leaves that littered the floor around him.

Max could detect where arterial spray had spurted away from the body and darkened the ground to the left of the tree. Attempts to clear the stain had been made, but it had mainly been left for the insects to feast on.

'What were the weather conditions like when they found the corpse?' asked Max.

Janie looked at her phone and swiped across the screen.

'CSI initial report says that the weather was cold but not raining, with almost no wind. This place was sticky and muddy, so they set the common path of approach through it to preserve the drier path the deceased would have taken. Fortunately, we can avoid it. There was an early morning mist when the responding cops arrived.'

'Anything recovered from the scene?'

'Soil samples and some leaf litter from the bloodstains and several other areas. Footprints were found, but almost certainly belonged to Paterson. Suggestion of overshoe prints, but nothing clear,' Janie read from the report.

'Who did the fingertip search?'

'PolSa. Nothing found, apart from a couple of ancient fag butts. Almost like the killer was forensically aware.' Her voice dripped with sarcasm.

'No shit, Sherlock,' said Max as he circumnavigated the tree, his eyes scanning the ground. Once completed, he turned his attention to the trunk. He raised his hand to the fragile bark, some pieces of which were peeling off like thin flakes of parchment. Looking at the base of the tree he knelt. There were a few fragments of the shed bark within a cluster of roots. He stood, his back against the trunk and stared outwards and down. The ground had been disturbed in two faint but visible lines, directly in front of his feet.

'Hard to say what happened here. It could be that he was leaning against the tree, but why was he here at all? Was he meeting someone or was he chased into here? I can't see why anyone would choose to come to this shit-hole in the middle of the night, but somehow our killer managed to get behind and zap him with a taser. He slumped, or possibly was pulled backwards, stiff as a board, then when the charge was released, he slid down the trunk, scraping his jacket on the bark.'

'Just a theory, though.'

'Of course. It's just me supporting a hypothesis.'

'That's bad practice, right?'

'Terrible, but we're not trying to do the murder team's job for them. We're looking at the possibility that the killer has police knowledge and forensic awareness. One interpretation is that Paterson was tasered. Let's look for AFIDs, although I'm not hopeful. I'm sure PolSa would have found them. We also have to consider something else.'

'What?'

'If our killer is forensically aware, and they used a taser, they could have retrieved the AFIDs.'

'At night?' said Janie.

'Actually, it would probably be easier at night to find them. There's only about thirty of them, the weather was still, and they spray out in a predictable pattern.'

'But it's dark, you know, light is a really good medium for finding shit,' said Janie.

'Now, my devastatingly sarcastic friend, for once your study into Taser that you did for your accelerated promotion portfolio doesn't help you. AFID tags fluoresce under ultraviolet light. A simple UV torch would have lit them up like beacons in the grass.'

'I admit I did scan read the paper – my assessor knows

less than me – but again it proves nothing. They're not here and I know what you're going to say next—' Janie paused.

'Go on, then,' said Max

Her voice deepened in an approximation of Max's soft Highland accent. 'Absence of evidence isn't evidence of absence.'

'Worst. Impression. Ever. There's no point us looking, not after a whole team of PolSa officers picked over it for hours. I know the team leader is as methodical as they come. If there were AFIDs to find, they'd have found them, but I know where we should look.'

'I've a nasty feeling about what you're going to say.'

'It'll be a nice trip, Janie. I know how you like a good road trip.'

'No, I don't. Every time we take a road trip up to the wilds of the Highlands bad stuff happens.'

'Dunnet Head is stunning, mate. You'll love it.'

'It'll be dark when we get there.'

'Mate, it's almost always bloody dark, but I know, and I agree. I also don't fancy clumping around up there in the pitch black. Come on, I'll drop you home and pick you up in the morning. We'll get there early, same time as Fergus Grigor went flying off the top.'

'I've a better idea. I'll drop you and take the car home. No point you driving into town to pick me up, and there's the other reason.'

'What?'

'You're a shite driver,' Janie said, smiling.

'This is so you can clean the car, isn't it?'

'No, it's because you drive like my grandad.'

Max opened his mouth to argue, but then realised that Janie was probably right. One of her many talents was her prowess behind the wheel, even if she was a little OCD about cleanliness.

'Fair point, well made. Pick me up at about four?'

15

MAX STOOD OUTSIDE his cottage at just before four. He shivered and zipped up his jacket against the autumn chill. He'd managed to creep from the house without waking Katie, but Nutmeg had bounded out with him, clearly hoping for a walk. She'd slunk off when he'd told her it wasn't happening, a forlorn expression on her scruffy face, as she headed back to the warmth of the bedroom.

Max yawned, his mind alive with the case, trying to slot the pieces together, but he couldn't come up with a cogent theory. It was all supposition, with nothing solid to hang those feelings on. Shuggie was clearly convinced, and Max's first impression of him had been a good one. He was missing something. Was there a killer cop out there? He shuddered at the prospect.

Headlights pierced the darkness and the low note of the Volvo grumbled as it drove slowly up the track.

'Morning,' said Max as he got into the passenger seat.

'I'm acutely aware it's morning, Max. Thanks to you, I didn't sleep a wink,' she said, her face unusually pale and drawn.

'Why?'

'I never sleep before an early start. Does anyone?'

'Slept like a baby, pal.'

'That's because you're a bloody weirdo. I always get too stressed about sleeping in and you giving me a row about it.'

'Ach, not my style, you know that. When did I last give you a row?'

Janie just grunted, disconsolately.

'Want me to drive?' asked Max, already knowing the answer.

'Obviously not, but I want you to buy me a bloody coffee for the trip, which – I am very annoyed to learn from the satnav – will take over five hours.'

'Five hours of lovely countryside, and my sparkling conversation,' said Max.

'Sparkling, my arse. There's a twenty-four-hour garage around the corner, so get your wallet ready,' she said, driving away, her shoulders hunched, but with the slightest trace of a smile forming.

Within a few minutes, Janie was pulling into a petrol station. She began to fill up whilst Max took the vehicle's fuel card into the kiosk. A lone elderly woman looked at him as she knitted, muttering, her eyes narrowing at the intrusion.

Soon after, Max had paid, collected the two coffees and was back at the car.

'She was a charmer,' said Max, getting in and handing Janie her coffee.

'Just because you're so bloody cheery for some reason, doesn't mean that normal people want to listen to your chirpy shite. Now don't bloody spill any of that. Milky coffee is a bugger to clean up,' said Janie, taking a sip of the scalding liquid.

'Let's get moving, I'm bored of this journey already.'

Janie took a sip and grimaced, slotted it in the cup holder in the centre console, then started the engine and moved off.

They drove through the dark streets of Dunfermline and headed north. The more Janie sipped from her coffee cup, the more her mood magically began to lift. Even so it was still almost twenty minutes before either of them spoke.

'So, what are you hoping to find?' said Janie.

'Cheering up already?'

She narrowed her eyes at him.

'Well, it wasn't treated as a proper murder scene, as far as I can tell, so who knows what was missed?'

'Aye, that's true enough. Apparently, his wifey said that he had been running up there each morning, and she'd told him not to stray too close to the edge. She has a fear of heights, but he doesn't. Seems to be that the duty officer didn't call it in as a murder, and no one from CID went. Half-arsed springs to mind.'

'She's not still there, is she?'

'I don't think so. I'm sure I heard that she'd headed home, and the MIT family liaison are looking after her.'

'Hence, I want to see it myself, plus, we have information they didn't at that time.'

'Fair enough.' Janie drained her coffee cup and handed it to Max. 'Litter bag under your seat,' she said.

Max pulled out a small plastic bag in which he deposited both cups.

'Why else are we heading north?'

'PM this afternoon in Inverness, I want to go.'

'Really?'

'Yes, really.'

'Body's a terrible mess. I've seen the photos. A hundred-foot fall, hitting every rock on the way down.'

'I know, but photos don't tell the whole story, and I know what I'm looking for. Do you know who else is going?'

'Well, Donnie Watson isn't, apparently. MIT are sending a representative, and a productions officer is going from Inverness, but the HOLMES account still seems to think there's no evidence of links between the two cases,' said Janie, yawning.

'Who handled the scene?'

'Duty officer, and they sent a lone detective from Inverness up there for oversight, but there wasn't much to do.'

'But no PolSa?'

'Nope.'

Max said nothing, just raised his eyebrows.

'I hate PMs,' said Janie, after a pause.

'I'm not exactly a fan,' said Max.

'Are we not announcing our presence a little to the MIT?'

'Thematic review. No one'll ask any questions. It's just too dull for words, and shite like this happens all the time.'

'I guess. Anyway, mind if I put on some music?'

'Depends what it is.'

'You're so uncultured.'

'How about The Cure?'

'Dirge.'

'Mogwai?'

'Mogwai are too loud. How about some classical?'

'Okay, but nothing "difficult".' Max waggled his quotation-mark fingers around.

Janie quicky fiddled with her phone and soon some strings eased out of the speakers, soothing and gentle.

'This is actually quite nice.'

'Vaughan Williams.'

'I like it, in fact, wake me in a bit and I'll take over the driving.' Max sat back in the leather seat and closed his eyes.

'You've got a bloody nerve,' said Janie, but like all ex-soldiers when presented with an opportunity to sleep, Max was instantly gone.

16

THE JOB WAS on. Jesus, it was happening now.

Max was sitting in the passenger seat of a BMW X5 when his ear radio sparked into life. They roared along the tree-lined West London street, his Glock 17 pressing tightly into his back.

'From Charlie Alpha, standby, standby. Trojan units advance, repeat advance, we're on. Subject one is out of the vehicle's passenger seat and onto the pavement – dark jacket, jeans and a beanie, hands under jacket. Driver remains in the Subaru. And, wait one. Confirmed, he's armed. Sawn-off shotgun. It's on. He's holding up the bank now.'

The observer's voice was tense. They were watching from the local authority CCTV centre that covered the front of the bank. It wasn't supposed to happen yet, but they'd lost the subject, a career criminal called Jerry Finnegan, during the follow when his unidentified wheel-man pulled an outrageous manoeuvre in the stolen Subaru and left the team in his wake. Max had deployed a man to the CCTV centre to train a camera on the bank that was suspected of being Finnegan's target, but it wasn't supposed to happen today. The bloody snout had properly fucked up and got his dates wrong.

Max spoke into his concealed mic talking to the specialist firearms team who had been shadowing them. Max and his team from the Flying Squad were all armed, but defensively, only with Glock 17 pistols. The SFO team were the experts. 'Trojan 975, what's your ETA? We're code red now,' Max barked into his mic.

'From Trojan 975, we're running on blues and twos, seven minutes. We were blocked by traffic but making progress now.'

'Jesus, that's no good. Niall, are you ready?' said Max to his driver, DC Niall Hastings.

'Seven minutes is too long. Subject one is on the pavement now and in the bank. We're going to intercept. All units, strike, strike, strike!' Max bellowed into his mic.

'Niall, pull over short, and be ready to cover the driver, yeah? I'll take the door, and I'll take Finnegan, and you get the driver. Whatever you do, don't let the bastard drive off. Ram him if you have to.'

'Yeah, let's fucking do this,' Niall said through gritted teeth.

Max dived out of the car, and strode, ostensibly relaxed, onto the pavement to the left of the door and up to the bus stop. He stood there, looking at the timetable, his peripheral vision fixed on the gaping door of the bank. He was thankful that the streets weren't too busy.

There was a sudden lull in the traffic, and Max could actually hear birdsong from the trees that lined the street. The sudden peace, after the high tension and intensity of the follow was eerie. There was no suggestion that there was an armed gunman currently pointing a sawn-off, double-barrelled shotgun at a terrified cashier. Max breathed steadily, and spoke again, in a whisper. 'I have control, exit is covered by me and Niall has the getaway vehicle. Trojan, any update?'

'Five minutes,' came the stressed-sounding voice, almost drowned out by the howling sirens.

'Any other units nearby?'

His earpiece crackled with responses from the rest of the surveillance team, but no one was close enough. Shit, it was just him and Niall.

Too long, thought Max. They were going to have to do this themselves.

'Niall, you in position?'

'Yes, mate. I'm ready.' The voice in Max's ear was tight.

Then it happened. Jerry Finnegan marched out of the bank, a duffel bag slung over his shoulder. Not that Max could tell it was Finnegan. A skull-emblazoned mask covered his face. He strode confidently towards the parked Subaru.

Max reached into the pancake holster in the small of his back and pulled out the Glock, the familiar weight and heft of the weapon comforting in his grasp. He pointed it at Finnegan's back and bellowed at the top of his voice.

'Armed police! Drop the weapon, Finnegan!'

Time stopped. It was no longer linear. It no longer existed. Max's arms were ramrod straight as the Glock pointed directly at Finnegan's centre mass. As slowly as if he were encased in treacle, the bank robber began to turn, the shotgun rising as he moved in a slow, deliberate arc towards Max. The wide bore of the barrels yawned inexorably through the air and swung in a slow, lazy arc.

Max could see the whites of Finnegan's eyes flashing with

shock, fear and pure, unadulterated hatred. Max knew at that moment that he was going to have to shoot.

'Drop it, Finnegan!' screamed Max.

The shotgun kept swinging, steadily, unstoppable and deadly.

Max knew. He knew that from now on, nothing would ever be the same again.

The Glock bucked twice in Max's hands and Finnegan's eyes widened in shock as the bullets smacked into his chest and he fell, like a puppet whose strings had suddenly vanished. The shotgun clattered harmlessly to the floor. Momentarily, there was total silence.

Then suddenly Max could hear people screaming. A car hooted, someone shouted. He ran towards the mortally injured man, his firearm still raised. He was still a threat, the shotgun being just inches from his fingers. Max kicked it away, and it spiralled across the cracked pavement.

'Shots fired, shots fired, ambulance urgently,' Max shouted into his mic. Finnegan's dark jacket flapped open, revealing a white T-shirt soaked black with blood. Terror flashed across Finnegan's eyes as he stared at Max, unable to speak. Max lowered the pistol, a sick feeling rising from his stomach, his face burning and legs weak.

Max knew. The two bullet holes in the T-shirt were smack bang over the man's heart. He was going to die on that pavement.

Then from nowhere, a howl of fury was audible and there was a crackle from Max's earpiece, 'Max, the driver's out, watch out!' screamed Niall.

Max turned, only to see the driver sprinting towards him,

gaining ground at a terrifying speed, a machete raised high, his face twisted in fury, 'You fucking bastard!' he screamed. Max began to swing his pistol, which felt as though it had doubled in weight. He was going to be too late.

Then, a shape flew out of nowhere, and suddenly Niall appeared and bodychecked the man, in what would have been declared an illegal tackle had he been playing rugby. The blade of the machete glinted in the sun, just as Niall grabbed the driver in a headlock and dragged him to the ground, roaring in fury ...

Max gasped, sucking in a sharp intake of breath as he jolted awake in the soft leather of the Volvo.

'Jesus, you scared the shite out of me,' said Janie as she drove, her eyes flicking from Max back to the road.

'You okay?'

Max looked at her, his thoughts scrambled as if a cog had come loose in his brain. He took another rasping breath, his eyes wide. He felt sweat on his brow, and his back was clammy.

'I'm fine, a dream. Sorry I startled you.' He wiped the beaded sweat from his face with his sleeve.

'Shit, are you sure?'

'I'm fine. Just a weird dream. Happens sometimes, you know.'

'Afghanistan?' asked Janie, her face full of concern.

'No, the other one.'

'I thought they'd stopped.'

'Sometimes it comes back, kind of inevitable having just seen Niall.' Max began to regain control of his breathing.

'How's that?'

'Niall was there at the time. He was my driver on that day. The robber's getaway driver came at me with a machete, but Niall took him on unarmed, got a nasty wound on his arm.'

'Jesus.'

'Aye,' was all that Max said, trying to get rid of the heavy feeling in his gut.

Janie's jaw was tight. 'Are you getting any help with this?'

'No, I'm fine. Sorry, not your problem. It's because I haven't run for a few days. I'm thirsty, can we stop for some water?'

'We're almost there, I've a bottle in the back.'

Max reached over the seat and found the sports bottle.

'Can I have some of this?'

'As long as you're cootie-free, knock yourself out. You're not going mental on me, are you? Mum's the word, I promise, but maybe you should speak to someone?'

Max drank deeply, his throat parched, as it always was after the dreams. He had them sometimes. Afghanistan or London. PTSD. He had been diagnosed in London, but he had been living with it for half a lifetime.

'I've tried that. It's cool, as long as I keep exercising, and stick to drinking cranberry juice rather than malt whisky.' He smiled at her.

'And you think I'm a weird bugger?' said Janie.

'Takes one to know one,' he said.

'Only reason I keep working with you.'

Max looked at his surroundings for the first time since waking up, his composure returning fast. They drove smoothly over the well-made single-track road through the vast Sutherland landscape and past a loch that sparkled in the morning sunshine. He looked at his watch, it was almost 9 a.m. Perfect timing.

They swept around a bend, and there it was – Dunnet Head lighthouse surrounded by a low stone wall. It rose from the treeless landscape, painted stark white against the green and grey of the heather and tussock grass. The sun shone, further highlighting the structure against the cobalt-blue sky.

They crossed the cattle grid and pulled up in a small, empty car park by the lighthouse.

'Look at the grass, it's blowing a bloody hoolie. He really could have been blown off the top.'

'No chance.'

'How?'

'Because the wind was coming in from the sea when Fergus Grigor went over the edge. In fact, it was a thirty-five-mile-an-hour southerly wind, gusting up to fifty.'

'How'd you know that?'

'I checked.'

'Not as stupid as you look.'

'He went over that cliff, but he didn't get blown off it. He jumped, or he was pushed.'

17

MAX AND JANIE stood in the shadow of the lighthouse and stared out at the boiling Pentland Firth as it raged in the distance. The wind tore in from the south-east, buffeting their clothes.

'Similar wind to when Fergus took a plunge. See what I mean?' said Max.

'Aye. Wind could almost blow you back up the bloody cliff. Tell me again why we're here? Any evidence of a taser has probably been blown all the way to London by now. Ravelston would have been better.'

'It was still at Ravelston, no wind at all. If there were AFIDs to find, the PolSa team would have found them. I'm telling you, the killer is forensically aware, they'd have recovered them.'

'But not here. Not in this wind.'

'And not in daylight when they couldn't use a UV light. Come on, I want to see where he left the cliff,' Max replied, already walking off. Janie followed, the wind whipping her hair into a frenzy. Max being almost completely shorn didn't have this problem.

They walked through the empty car park, around the

lighthouse and onto a well-made path. It led to a five-foot-high rough stone wall designed to keep the public away from the cliff edge.

The only evidence that anything untoward had happened was a lone police appeal board, in bright yellow, appealing for witnesses for an 'incident' that had occurred a couple of days ago. A blue plaque mounted on a sloped path next to the sign listed the common seabirds of the area, including gannets, guillemots and puffins.

'This is where he went over, right by the sign,' said Janie, looking out at the vast expanse of iridescent-blue sea, one hand trying to keep her hair in place.

'Why did he climb the wall?' said Max.

Janie shrugged. 'Not a clue. His wife said he had paused here to look at the seabirds and drink his water before coming back to the cottage.'

'So, he either made a conscious decision to climb in order to jump, or something prompted him to do so.'

'Like what?'

'No idea – come on,' said Max, hoisting himself to the top of the wall.

'What, are you bloody mad?'

'No, it's safe, there's about twenty feet of grass before the edge.' Max dropped onto rough, windswept grass. The wind was even stronger here, at least 25mph, he thought.

Janie landed next to him, fear written across her face.

'Heights?' asked Max.

'A posting to Benbecula is getting more and more bloody attractive. Now can we get this over with?'

'You have the scene photos?' said Max, smiling.

Janie sat on the grass, and thumbed through her phone's gallery, before handing it to Max.

Max took it and scrolled. Some shots of Fergus Grigor's battered body taken with a zoom lens, presumably from almost where they currently stood. The next were images that had been captured by the search and rescue helicopter as it approached. The high-resolution shots were startling in their detail.

'We're in exactly the right spot,' said Max, inching forward to the edge of the cliff.

'You'd better be right, I don't want to bloody move anywhere else,' said Janie, pulling her knees tight to her chest and pushing her back against the wall.

Lying on his stomach, Max crawled to the precipice and peeped over the top, taking in the rolling, crashing waves of the Pentland Firth almost a hundred feet below. He looked again at the screen.

'Yep, this is it, no doubt about it. I bet they didn't search at all. Come on, let's look. Hands and knees, inch by inch from the cliff edge to the wall.'

'Are you taking the piss – shouldn't we have harnesses, or something?' Janie's face was paler than normal and her brow was creased with stress.

'You want to wait here in this wind for those to arrive?'

'Do I buggery. I want to spend the bare bloody minimum time here. It's shite.'

'I'll start here, you can do from the bloody edge.'

'Hold up, if we're actually doing this, at least let's do it properly. None of your slapdash nonsense.' Janie reached into her jacket pocket and extended her hand to Max, clutching a pair of blue nitrile gloves.

'This is why I need you with me, pal. I never remember stuff like this,' said Max, snapping the gloves into place.

'Aye, well. I only want to do this once, so let's bloody get on with it,' said Janie, pulling on her own gloves.

They both began searching, brushing the turf as they swept between the edge and the wall. There was nothing. Nothing could resist the constant wind.

'Okay, now the wall. All of say about ten feet each side from our position, into the nooks and crannies, at the base, all of it, inch by inch.'

They started next to each other, shoulder to shoulder and inches apart, pulling the rough grass away from the bottom, sweeping the line with their hands. Again, nothing, apart from an occasional lone seabird feather, and a great deal of gull shit.

They pored over the cracks in the wall, tracing the joins and the crumbling mortar that had been torn apart by the Scottish elements. Millimetre by millimetre, they searched. After about fifteen minutes, Max straightened up, easing a kink in his back.

He let out a sigh. 'I think we're barking up the wrong—'

'We're not,' interrupted Janie, a glint in her eye. Something was clutched between her thumb and forefinger, pressing so tightly together that her fingertips were white.

'You've found one?'

'Pass a bag. If the wind takes this, we're buggered.' Her face was triumphant.

Max reached into his jacket pocket and pulled out a small self-seal bag. It flapped wildly in the wind, but he turned to face the wall, shielding it with his back.

'In here,' he said, holding it open.

Janie put her whole hand inside the bag until she was sure

the wind wouldn't be able to whip the precious article away. She then released it, and Max snapped the bag shut, peeling off the sealing strip and fastening it tight.

'Come on, let's get out of this wind.' They both jumped the wall and sat with their backs to the other side. The wind suddenly stopped and they both looked at each other. Max lifted the bag and looked at the contents.

A small, circular piece of yellow paper, about the size a hole punch would produce when it bit through a piece of A4. It was stamped with a number – A78823 – that was repeated across its surface repeatedly in tiny, but just about legible characters.

'We got one. I had a feeling the wind would blow it inland. We got lucky, Janie. An AFID. Proof,' said Max, breathing hard.

'Shit, so this proves that Fergus Grigor was murdered and that he was tasered before he died,' said Janie, also out of breath.

They both stared at each other, knowing what this meant. This was now more than just a hunch.

This was evidence.

Hard facts.

This wasn't just a vigilante serial killer. It was most likely a cop.

18

'**YOU'VE FOUND A BASTARD** greenfly? Shite, well done, you know I don't like blowing smoke up your arse, but that's a good find,' Ross's voice blared out of the speakers as Janie steered the car around the single-track roads away from Dunnet Head.

'Aye, well, Janie found it, but it's a break. It proves Grigor was murdered.'

'It's compelling, but we need something from the PM as well. Are you going?'

'Aye, what time is it?'

'Two p.m. at Raigmore Hospital. You're expected there, but I'm not sure how welcome you'll be,' said Ross.

'How?'

'Donnie's getting proper scunnered with me shoving my big fat beak in. He thinks I'm interfering and he basically accused me of being a snitch. He thinks something's going on.'

'Reckon he knows what we're actually doing?'

'I doubt it. It's too bloody unbelievable, right, I mean a cop … Whatever you think about "Get You Off" Grigor, he was mostly just good at his job. Whatever the motivation, we're moving hard on this, and I've a job for you before the PM.'

'Go on,' said Max.

'It's something nice, don't worry. No need to sound so nervous.'

Max and Janie shared a look.

'Norma worked up the email address that Shuggie gave us,' Ross continued, 'and we think we know who's using it. He's on your way back.'

'How'd she manage that?'

'Well, she told me at length, clearly expecting praise, but I didn't fucking understand a word of it. So, I'll put you on speaker and she can explain.'

'Hi, Max,' rang out Norma's voice, slightly echoey as the speaker phone was engaged.

'Nice work. Go on then, dazzle us with your genius.'

'Simples, mate. Chief authorised the works with the phone companies. Luckily Shuggie's source wasn't using a VPN, so I found the IP address that accessed the web-based email server. It's linked into a mobile 4G account from an iPhone.' She paused for dramatic effect.

'And?' said Max.

'From that I managed to back-trace the handset IMEI number. Then a historic IMSI search got me the phone number.'

'See what I fucking mean?' Ross's voice chimed in.

'Carry on,' said Janie.

'The phone is registered to an Angus M Fraser who lives in Inverness. Want to know the interesting bit?'

'I'm listening,' said Max.

'I did a financial profile on him, and he gets a monthly pension from Police Scotland. He was a DS, who took early retirement two years ago, and for a while, he served on Donnie Watson's team.'

'Shit.'

'That's what I said, once she told me the interesting bit,' Ross chimed in. 'I zoned out during all the other shite. Right, Max, Angus Macdonald Fraser runs a crazy golf place down by the river, next to the skate park. He bought it out with his lump sum and it has a coffee and tea stall there. Gets busy by all accounts.'

'Golf – what is it with this job and golf courses. I've played at that crazy golf place a few times when I was young, I know it well.'

'Well, it's hardly bloody Gleneagles.'

'Do you know him?'

'What, because we share the same clan name? No, he was a legacy Northern Constabulary man who spent most of his service in Inverness and Dingwall, but he also spent some time with Donnie Watson, doing intel support. I don't know much about him. Get down there and scope him out.'

'Aye, Norma can you send me the profile you've got? We'll be a couple of hours.'

'Almost ready. I'll finish it off and it'll be with you when you get there.'

'Is there a photo?'

'Which one do you want – passport, driving licence, website or his old warrant card?' said Norma.

'Whichever one you'll be the least smug about,' said Max, chuckling.

'Cake. Harry Gow's is up there, isn't it?'

'Aye, all over the place.'

'Then I'll take a dream ring,' said Norma, referring to the sweet cakes sold by the popular Highland baker.

'On it.'

'Tread carefully, Max. He had a reputation, from what I heard,' said Ross.

'Who, Harry Gow? He only makes cakes,' said Max. Norma could be heard giggling through the speakers.

'Stop being a smart-arse.'

'What kind of reputation?'

'Short-tempered, a bit handy with his fists, but the feelers I've had out suggest that he was mostly straight. Rumour is he had a major fall-out with management over something and ended up going off sick with stress. He was let go a bit early with a full pension.'

'Can I make a point?'

'I'm sure you will anyway, so go on,' said Ross.

'Can we be sure that he isn't the killer? I mean, how would he know all this if he wasn't involved in some way?'

There was a pause on the line for a beat before Ross spoke. 'I guess we can't be, but it'd be a funny old double-bluff grassing to a journo?'

'Wouldn't be untypical for a psychopath, though, would it? You know … self-aggrandising, arrogant, narcissist, and all that?'

'Well, that's why you're going, and you spend so much time punching things, you can clearly handle him, particularly with your kung-fu expert sidekick. I need someone smart to assess the bugger, just tread carefully. None of your usual fucking bull in a bastard china shop, man.'

'Ross, with the deepest of respect, you're a right cheeky bastard. I'll call you—' but Ross had hung up.

'So, we know who Shuggie's source is, but who is Gus Fraser's source?' said Janie.

'Gus?'

'Aye, I've met him once or twice.'

'Did he strike you as a murderer?'

'Can't say he did, but who can tell? Everyone calls him Gus and I had him pegged as a nice guy, very outgoing and ebullient. He'd been put out to pasture from paedophile squad and into a shite intelligence management role for a few months before he retired. I got some intel packages from him when I was working vice.'

'Ebullient?'

'Aye, ebullient, you know. Adjective, meaning cheerful and full of energy,' said Janie.

'Couldn't you just have said cheerful or chirpy. Maybe even chipper?'

'You'll see when you met him, ebullient is more accurate.'

'Wow, you really are a posh bird, aren't you?'

'It's called an education, you imbecile.'

'Imbecile is also a posh bird's term of abuse. Why not use a proper Scottish insult like nugget or fud?'

'All right, awa' and bile ya fuckin heid, ya wee fannie. That better?' said Janie, her cultured Edinburgh brogue suddenly becoming harsh and coarse.

'You're learning. Come on, let's get weaving, and go and see your "ebullient" friend.'

They both laughed.

'I'd best call Shuggie. If we're going to doorstep this guy, he may need to vouch for us,' said Max, picking up his phone and dialling.

Shuggie answered almost immediately.

'Yeah?'

'Shuggie, it's Max Craigie. We've located your source.'

'Aye, Ross told me a wee while ago.'

'Has he acknowledged?'

'Not yet. What are you going to do?'

'Just talk to him. Janie's met him in the past, so that may help.'

'Tell him to call me and I'll speak to him if there's a problem. You'll keep me in the loop, yeah?'

'I will, but nothing on your blog or the papers yet, you understand me? We don't know anything about this bloke, and we have to wonder about his motivation. I mean, how does he know all this?'

'Of course, man. I've been doing this thing a while, and I want answers, but I'd rather work with you than against you. We all want the same thing, so maybe I should have a little poke about too?'

'That's a bad idea. I know you want to make a splash but doing it before we've got any evidence will destroy our chances.'

'I know. I'm not daft.'

'Remember one more thing, whoever this is has killed at least three times. If he thinks you're a problem, he'll kill you.'

Max was surprised at the strength of feeling evident in his voice, but he was genuinely worried. They had a serial killer on their hands, he was certain of it.

19

IT WAS ALMOST midday when they pulled up a few metres down from the crazy golf course. It was situated slap bang in the centre of Inverness, the capital of the Highlands, right on the tree-lined banks of the River Ness. The water surged from Loch Ness, through the middle of the city, and out into the Moray Firth a few miles north.

The sun was low in the clear sky, which was an unusually clear, opalescent blue studded only with a few wispy clouds, and the roads were busy with cars parked on both sides. Long shadows reached towards them from the trees that lined the riverbank. Walkers and late-season tourists mingled with skateboarders and BMX riders heading for the nearby skate park. Max shivered in the shady chill as he thought about the many occasions he'd been here, having grown up just a few miles away on the Black Isle, and his elderly aunt still loved a Sunday morning walk along the river and a coffee.

It was a perfect place not to be noticed. Somewhere people came to unwind, to sit by the river, to fish or to drink at the riverside pubs. One could just hang about and not attract any attention at all. It's not being on the street that attracts attention. It's activity that isn't typical for the environment. Max remembered the gruff words of the instructor during his surveillance course: 'You've as much right to be in public as anyone else. Just act like you belong there, and you're invisible.'

Max scrolled through the typically detailed profile that Norma had managed to put together. Name, address, current vehicle, National Insurance number and all the usual stuff.

His police complaints record showed a couple of unproved allegations of violence, although details were almost non-existent. Something tickled at the nape of Max's neck at the sight of the complaints summary. It wasn't what was written. It was what was missing. He composed a text to Ross.

Request Gus Fraser's full complaints file.

The reply came back immediately. *What am I, your fucking lackey?*

Then a few seconds later, another text came through from Ross. *Done.*

Max sniggered. 'Ready?'

'How'd you want to play it?' said Janie.

'Will he recognise you?'

'Maybe.'

'How much interaction did you have?'

'Not that much, just collected a few dockets off him.'

'Do you have sunglasses?'

'Aye, here.' Janie pointed to the door pocket.

'I think we need to check if he has that phone in his hand first, just on the off chance that the intel steer was wrong. Let's have a walk by and see what's what. Sunnies on.'

They walked past the skate park along a hedge and through an open gate flanked by fluttering banners. INVERNESS

CRAZY GOLF was emblazoned in multicoloured letters on either side of the gate, and a queue snaked from a wooden shack.

A lean-looking middle-aged man stood behind the counter of the shack, a broad grin splitting his face as he handed coffees over to a couple. They returned his smile as he chatted away, clearly in no rush to clear the queue. A short, white-haired lady stood next to him wiping a counter-top with a cloth.

Max recognised Gus Fraser, even though he wore dark Ray-Bans. He seemed happy and jolly and was clearly revelling in his work. The white-haired lady was restocking the shelves with packets of crisps from a box.

'I'll give it to you, Janie. He does look ebullient. Coffee?' said Max.

'What, from here?'

'Why not, what better way to watch a man serving coffee than from a coffee queue?'

'I guess, and I could do with one. Some bugger made me get out of my bed at three this morning.'

Max grinned as he picked his phone from his pocket and dialled.

'Max?' Shuggie's voice was tight.

'Shuggie, I'm about to go and see your source. Send him another email right now and tell him to expect me and that I can be trusted, okay?'

'Max, you sure? This could backfire,' said Shuggie.

'It won't. Send the email now, right now. As in as soon as you've hung up from me, yeah?'

'Okay, if you say so.'

Max hung up. 'Okay, if he's doing what we think, he'll look at a new email from Shuggie.'

The couple with the coffees and golf putters moved away towards the centre of the course.

As the next customer – a mother with three small kids – approached, Gus looked down and picked up a smartphone, his forehead creasing in a frown. He looked at the screen for a moment, before glancing up, his head swivelling. He stopped when his eyes locked on them. The smile disappeared, and he looked pensive for a few moments, as the family moved away, clutching ice creams and golf clubs. He said something to the white-haired lady, and then disappeared out of the side door of the shack.

The next customer approached, and was greeted by the white-haired lady.

'Where's he gone?' said Janie.

'Maybe the email was a bad idea.'

'Shit. Is the course fenced in?'

'Yes.'

'So, he can't get out then. Shall we follow him in?'

'No. We don't want a scene in there. Come on.' Max turned on his heel and retraced their steps back towards the car.

'Where are we going?'

'Keep your eyes open. He clearly doesn't want to chat.'

'Shall I get the car going?' said Janie, frowning with confusion.

'No. Follow me.' Max picked up the pace and turned right into the skate park. They walked along the footpath that ran adjacent to the fence that separated it from the golf course. Shrubs, trees and bushes obscured the course, so they couldn't see a thing, but Max fell into a light jog until he reached the top corner of the fence line where there was a bench against it. Max sat down and quickly looked behind him at the fence posts.

'Max?' said Janie.

'Just sit, quick,' said Max, looking again behind him at the fence, where there was a small gap between the posts.

A few moments later there was a rustling in the shrubs behind them. Max looked at Janie and winked. A second later, Angus Fraser McDonald squeezed between the gap in the fence, his face pale and drawn, his movements hurried.

'Hi, Gus,' said Max, looking straight at the ex-detective.

Even with the sunglasses on Max could see the eyes widening in shock. He looked around, his features frozen, before exhaling, resignedly.

'Max Craigie, I presume?'

'Aye. This is Janie, we work together.'

'How did you know about the gap in the fence?'

'I grew up around here. Used to come to the skate park when it was the old shitty one. We used to sneak into the golf course through it,' said Max.

'I guess legging it wasn't the best of ideas.' He sighed again before sitting down on the bench next to them.

'Who's minding the stall?'

'My mum. I'll catch hell for disappearing.' He shook his head.

'I can imagine,' Max chuckled.

His eyes turned to Janie. 'I recognise you. Were you on vice a few years ago?'

'I was. Hi, Gus.'

'I'm ex, you know. As in retired. As in not a cop anymore.'

'We need to talk,' said Max, his voice low and even.

'Bloody hell. I wanted away from this shite. Bloody Shuggie. I thought I could trust the wee bastard.'

'You can. We need to stop what's happening, and you can help us. Your name will be kept out of it. Come on, man. You obviously want this to stop, or you wouldn't have sent that email.'

Gus Fraser massaged his temples with his fingers, earlier ebullience nowhere to be seen.

'You've got ten minutes,' he said, looking at the skateboarders, all of whom appeared to be playing some kind of game, each taking it in turns to see who could complete the most complex of tricks.

'Why'd you leave the police?' said Max. He glanced at the ex-cop whose eyes were fixed on the skateboarders.

'It was time to go, and I'd made myself a little unpopular.'

'Why?'

'I take it we're off the record?'

'Totally.'

'Neither of you are wearing a wire, or shite like that?'

'Gus, let me say one thing, okay. I'm not part of MIT 6. I've only been in Police Scotland for a year or so and really don't know anyone. Me and Janie are part of a very small team that looks at corruption and malpractice in the cops and other law enforcement. We've brought down bent cops and we've brought down bent customs. We just want to get to the bottom of whatever it is that made you break cover and contact Shuggie,' Max said, firmly and seriously.

'I didn't know I'd broken cover,' said Gus.

'Aye, I get that.'

Gus said nothing, just rubbed his face with his hands. His shoulders were hunched, his face pale and furrowed.

'Some members of MIT 6 thought they were like gods,' Gus said eventually. 'You understand me?'

'Why don't you enlighten us?'

'I was just the intel DS for a while. I'm a proud Highlander and when I went down there after the amalgamation, I was an outsider. A teuchter, you know? I wanted to be accepted, so I joined in with some shit that maybe I shouldn't have.'

'I'm a Black Isler who went to the Met, so yeah, I know what it feels like.'

'Love the Black Isle. My favourite place to go is Eathie beach, you know it?'

'Aye, of course. Used to go looking for fossils there as a kid.'

'Me too. So peaceful. Space to think. I'd spend ages there, sleep in the bothy when things were difficult.'

Max just nodded.

Gus took off his sunglasses and his eyes looked tired and muddy and full of shame.

'Right, you've not cautioned me, so this would go nowhere anyhow. I was running intel on the paedophile squad for Donnie Watson when he was a DI, a few years ago. We had an investigation running on a bad bastard called Danny Macallan. He was a real piece of work, Max. A proper kiddie fiddler with a long history, who'd been meeting kids from the internet whilst pretending to be a thirteen-year-old boy. You know the drill. Stalked in chatrooms and struck up conversations with wee girls, some as young as eleven. Persuaded one of them

– a poor wee girl of thirteen called Lily – to send him nude pictures.' The ex-detective stared at his trainers and sighed.

'Carry on,' said Max, gently.

'Well, her parents found out about it and called the police. There wasn't enough corroborated evidence on her computer, so we needed to find it from Macallan. The raid went down and he was arrested, but ...' he hesitated.

Max said nothing, feeling no need to fill the uncomfortable pause.

Gus took a deep, shuddering breath, his eyes brimming with tears. They trickled down his face and spilled onto the grass at their feet. 'I made a mistake. A dreadful mistake. They nicked him, at his home and seized his computer and phone. The computer went to the lab for examination, but they got me to do the download of his smartphone. I used the standard download machine, but I screwed up. When I switched the phone back on, in order to start the process, I didn't enable safe mode, and a remote programme the bastard had activated, completely corrupted everything on it. Totally overwrote the whole device and made anything on it irretrievable.'

There was a long silence again, as Gus stared at the skateboarders, his eyes clouded and wet.

'And?' said Max, softly, knowing what was to come.

'He walked. They charged him, but there wasn't enough. He walked out of the High Court with a smug, shit-eating grin right across his face. I was devastated, but some on the team were spitting with anger.'

'Where's this going?' said Janie.

'I haven't told you the worst bit. Poor wee Lily was distraught. I mean, properly distraught. She'd been self-harming, you know, cutting herself and that, but then ...' He paused and rubbed his eyes with his fingers. 'She took her own life.' The tears returned, trickling down his tanned cheeks. He wiped them away with his cuff.

'How?' said Janie, her voice catching in her throat.

'She went into the woods near her home and hanged herself. That poor wee toot took her life because I didn't do my job properly.'

The silence was almost palpable.

'I'm sensing there's more,' said Max after a full minute.

'Aye, there is. The team were raging. They threw it all my way and I was properly shunned. I was carpeted by Donnie Watson, but he had to accept some of the blame. I shouldn't have been given that phone to interrogate. It should have gone to an expert in the bloody lab, but they were penny-pinching with the forensic budgets. In the end I had a breakdown, and I went off sick.'

'I'm assuming that wasn't the end of your involvement?'

'I was broken. Broken with guilt that my mistake had led to that poor lassie's death. One of the team came to me and said that we couldn't just leave it. That we needed to sort out Macallan, properly, but no one could find him. He'd fled and changed his name, and no bugger knew where he was.'

'What happened?' said Max, a sense of dread rising in his stomach.

'I found him. I wasn't the greatest cop in the world, but I was good at intelligence, and I knew how to flush out a paedo. This time, Macallan screwed up. I knew his methods on the chat-rooms, so I created an unofficial and unsanctioned false profile. I pretended to be a wee girl, and lo and behold, he contacted me. A bit of back and forth and we had a meeting arranged. The things he was going to do to me. He was a fucking animal.'

'And?'

'I told someone on the team. He said he'd sort it for good.'

'Who?'

'His name is DS John Lorimer, Max. A massive, dangerous bugger who now works for Donnie on MIT 6.'

There was a long pause as the three cops sat motionless.

'What happened to Macallan?' said Max, knowing the answer.

'He disappeared from the face of the earth. All his belongings left behind, bank accounts untouched, car parked outside his house, and no one has heard anything from him since.'

'So why contact Shuggie after all this time?'

'It was something Lorimer said to me that I first thought was bullshit. I thought Macallan was a one off, but when I heard about the link between Paterson, Grigor and Chick Wilson, I knew that I had to do something. I'm not sad about Macallan – that bastard deserved whatever happened to him – but cops can't be judge, jury and executioner, or the whole bloody world will fall down. Lorimer once said something whilst pished that made me think.'

He paused, and scratched vigorously at his scalp with his fingernails.

'What?'

'He said that Macallan wasn't the first, and he wouldn't be the last, and you know what?'

Max raised his eyebrows.

'He laughed when he said it. I didn't believe it then, but I do now.'

20

RAIGMORE HOSPITAL IN Inverness was like any city hospital, sprawling, busy and almost impossible to navigate around, unless you had the type of brain that could interpret a multicoloured hospital map.

Fortunately, Janie seemed to have one of those and they were soon outside the pathology department just before 2 p.m.

Max's phone buzzed in his pocket, just as they were getting close to the autopsy suite.

'Ross?'

'When were you going to bastarding call me, you gobshite?' Ross's Highland accent was stronger than ever.

'Now?' said Max tentatively.

'Aye, coincidence much, you cheeky bugger? So, what happened with Gus?'

Max told him.

'Ah bollocks, the chief will go bastard doolally when he hears this. What do we need?'

'A little time. We've actually no firm evidence that Lorimer has done anything wrong, and even if Gus goes on record, which he won't, he'll get ripped to bits as being malicious, particularly as he crashed a serious case.'

'Aye, you're probably right, but we need to come up with something before some other bugger who escaped justice gets topped. Any suggestions?'

'All options open, but let's get the guvnor on standby. We'll be going intrusive. We need something we can use.'

'Guvnor, fuck's sake, you've been back from London for ages, so stop the *Sweeney* bullshit. Right, consider it done. Are you popping into the PM?'

'We're here, now.'

'You may encounter some petulance. That tall bint DI Marnie whatshername is representing the MIT and they think we're interfering busybodies. You ready for that?'

'Aye, can you smooth things over? Maybe get someone above to read her horoscope for her, if you get what I mean?'

Ross chuckled down the line, and belched. 'I do indeed, Maxie-boy. In fact, I know exactly who to call. Right, go and make your presence felt, then get your arses back to the office. We need to plan shit.' The click in Max's ear indicated that Ross had gone.

'That sounded almost polite and chirpy for our dear leader,' said Janie.

'Borderline charming. Come on, let's go and shake a tree or two.'

Max pushed the double doors open and walked into the wide-open space of the pathology department. Another set of doors were directly in front of them, with a foreboding sign above that read POST-MORTEM SUITE.

Standing by the reception desk, talking to a scrubs-clad

man, were two smartly dressed women, both wearing Police Scotland ID badges on lanyards around their necks.

All eyes turned to Max and Janie as they entered and approached the group.

'Afternoon, I understand we're expected. DS Craigie and DC Calder,' said Max. They both proffered their warrant cards. One of the officers, whose name tag read DI Marnie Gray, leaned forward to read them. She was very tall, lean, smartly dressed in a business suit, with dark hair tied up in a ponytail. Her eyes were hard and suspicious, and they flicked between Max and Janie for a full heartbeat before she spoke.

'I'm DI Gray, deputy SIO and this is DC Doreen Urquhart, productions officer. Can I ask who authorised you to attend?' The green eyes bore into Max.

'My boss, DI Ross Fraser,' said Max, smiling.

'Well, I only just heard of this, and it's not really in order that unnecessary officers are present at a PM. We have the next of kin to consider, and it doesn't seem appropriate that others are here just to gawp. It's not entertainment, sergeant.' She was well spoken, and her delivery was soft but assertive.

'Well, all I can say, ma'am, is that we've been asked to come. Policing Standards reassurance are performing a thematic review of the inquiries to provide reassurance, bearing in mind the media attention and ...'

'I know why you're here, and I don't like it, neither does DCI Watson. We're running these murder inquiries, and we're the subject matter experts. I don't want you here. You're not required. You can have sight of PM reports once they're complete. There's no reason for you to be at this PM, in the same way that there was no reason for you to be at Scott Paterson's

PM. Do I make myself clear?' Her eyes seemed to blaze, despite her calm voice and neutral body language.

'Crystal, ma'am. Maybe check in with your boss. I understand that our presence is authorised,' said Max, gently.

DI Gray's eyes narrowed, and she tilted her head to the side. 'Sergeant, I will do no such—' Her words were interrupted by a piercing trill from her jacket pocket. She pulled out her phone and looked at the screen before putting it to her ear.

'Marnie Gray?' she said, efficiently. A tinny voice could be heard from the handset. After a moment, her face fell, crestfallen.

'Yes, sir … I appreciate that, sir, but I just didn't feel it was necessary …'

The tinny voice increased in intensity, and DI Gray's face reddened even more.

'I understand. Of course, sir. Yes, of course, every courtesy will be extended.'

The call was ended, and DI Gray looked at Max with renewed interest.

'It seems you have powerful allies, DS Craigie. That was DCC McVeigh's staff officer. Apparently, we're to extend every courtesy to you.'

'Oh,' said Max, his face impassive.

'So, you're staying then. Well, I need you to keep out of the way. It's bloody ridiculous,' she said, puffing out her cheeks.

'You'll not know we're here, ma'am,' said Max, desperately trying to prevent a smile forming.

DI Gray turned and moved away, all interest suddenly lost.

'That was fun,' whispered Max to Janie.

'I could tell you didn't like her,' she whispered back.

'How?'

'You called her ma'am. You never do that.'

'Do you know who the pathologist is?' Max asked Doreen.

'Elsa Morina. She's up from Edinburgh, our usual man is away,' said Doreen Urquhart, looking at her clipboard.

'Didn't she do Scott Paterson's as well?'

'Aye, handy really. She'll spot any similarities, if they're there to be seen, but I think it'll be hard to spot anything on poor old Fergus Grigor. Have you seen the photos?' said Doreen Urquhart, looking down at her productions log. Her accent was soft and lilting and redolent of the west coast.

Suddenly, the double doors from the PM suite burst open, and the huge form of Baz emerged.

'Yo, dudes,' he almost shouted as he strode into reception, dressed in scrubs, scratching at his arm, which was partially wrapped in clingfilm.

'New ink?' said Doreen, pointing at the clingfilm.

'Aye, fam, another three hours last week, filling in all the colour. Looks cool, but it's scabbed like a bastard. We ready to go?'

'Yep,' said Marnie.

'Cool. Although I'm not sure what we're gonna learn. The poor bugger looks like he's partially inside-out. I hope you've got strong stomachs.'

They all looked at each other, grimly. Only Baz was still grinning, clearly revelling in it.

'You're a real weird bugger,' Doreen said to him.

'Come on then, dudes. Elsa's waiting.'

They all filed into the stark, clinical space, not so different from the PM suite at RIE that they'd been in yesterday. There was one noticeable difference, however. Whereas Scott Paterson had only one visible injury this was certainly not the case with Fergus Grigor, who lay ready on the gurney in the centre of the room.

Cops are used to seeing death. It goes with the turf, and most detectives – particularly homicide detectives – are used to PMs.

As they all looked at the battered, torn and mutilated corpse of Fergus Grigor, they all realised this was going to be different. His legs were smashed and lacerated, the stark white of the bone visible and chunks of flesh torn away. His skull was smashed and compressed inwards, with the grey of his brain peeking through shards of shattered bone. Revulsion surged in Max's mind, accompanied by unwelcome memories of that fateful day, years ago, in the dusty heat of Helmand Province. The smashed bones of Dippy, visible through his shredded combat trousers, stark and visceral. When Max served in Afghanistan, his friend Dippy had been killed by a roadside bomb. Dippy was the source, and the subject, of many of Max's nightmares.

Max stared, cold and numb inside as the image of his friend's face burned into his memory, began to fill his vision. He swayed on the spot, swallowed.

'Let's get out of here,' he said quietly to Janie and turned to walk out, leaving the horrors of Fergus Grigor behind him.

21

'MAX?' SAID JANIE, concern in her voice as they emerged into the sunshine from the reception of Raigmore Hospital.

Max just carried on walking, his face set firm, not looking back, breathing deeply, trying to find the calm that the square-breathing technique brought him. Slowly exhale, slowly inhale, hold, slowly exhale. He focused on nothing but the breathing technique, once taught to him by a counsellor from the Met occupational health. It was about the only thing he'd found useful in talking therapy. That, not drinking alcohol and running with Nutmeg was his therapy. His mind raced and whirled as he grasped, mentally, for something to cling onto.

'Max?'

They arrived at the Volvo, which Janie unlocked, and Max got into the passenger seat. He slammed the door shut, his eyes fixed straight ahead.

'Max, talk to me, yeah?'

Max barely heard Janie. His mind felt like it was overflowing with random images. He breathed evenly and steadily, willing the images away.

'Max?' Janie's voice was soft.

He opened his eyes and exhaled deeply. Relief started to sweep through him as calm began to overpower the panic.

'I'm okay. Just give me a moment,' he eventually said, his voice raspy.

'Jesus, you had me worried, are you okay?'

Max turned to his friend, smiling weakly for the first time in a while. 'It's fine, now. I'm not crazy, I promise, but don't mention this to anyone.'

'What caused that? I mean, I know it was grim, but you've seen that stuff before.'

'Afghanistan.'

'Ah.' Janie's eyes softened.

'I was a corporal in charge of a section in Afghanistan, years ago. One of my guys, who we called Dippy, was hit by a roadside bomb. Blew him to bits, and I watched him die.'

'Oh …' Janie's eyes were wide and full of emotion.

'Just sometimes, things jolt me back to that day, and poor old Dippy … I'll be fine in a wee while.'

'I don't want to sound like a stuck record, Max, but are you sure that you don't need to talk to someone about this?'

'Not for me.'

'Cranberry juice, boxing and running with your wee doggy, right?'

'Something like that, come on. Let's get out of here.'

'Sure, you don't want to go home, you know, run with Nutmeg?'

'What and incur the wrath of our foul-mouthed leader? Nah, we've sneaky shit to plan. Whoever is responsible for this thinks they're untouchable. We're going to prove them wrong.'

22

'SO, AFTER ALL this pissing about, what do we know?' said Ross, dunking a biscuit into a large, chipped Ross County FC mug, with a look of intense anticipation on his face.

Max, Janie and Norma watched with interest, knowing what was about to happen. Ross pulled the tea-soaked digestive from the mug and raised it to his open mouth.

The soggy biscuit broke in mid-air and half of it landed on his pale-blue shirt, instantly disintegrating into a brown paste.

'Oh, Jesus suffering fuck,' he muttered, wiping at the mess that was now all over the front of his shirt. The rest of the room giggled like naughty schoolkids. 'And you buggers can stop pissing yourselves, as well. Mrs Fraser will go bastard doolally. I'm not supposed to be eating biscuits. I've got to eat these fucking things.' He held up a small Tupperware pot that contained what looked like small balls.

'What the hell are they?' asked Max.

'Baked and spiced fucking chickpeas. Mrs Fraser thinks they're a more appropriate snack, but they taste like ball bearings covered in curry powder. They're bastard bogging.'

He threw the pot down on his desk with a clatter. 'Anyway. Enough of my dietary needs. What's happening?'

'We know someone's used a taser on at least one occasion, up at the top of a cliff. We can't prove it was used on Grigor, as his injuries are so terrible. He's ripped to pieces,' said Janie, trying desperately to stop chuckling.

'But you found a greenfly there, which I am impressed about,' said Ross, scratching at his belly. A button was missing, displaying some hairy, pale flesh.

'Aye, but it's circumstantial. If I was a defence lawyer, I'd be suggesting that it came from one of the cops clumping about during the investigation,' said Max.

'So, we've no bloody proof against any individual, just a cop who retired under a cloud pointing the finger at John Lorimer. He'd get torn up for arse paper in the witness box, particularly as he broke the law himself in setting a trap for Danny Macallan. We need more,' said Ross.

'Anything from the taser manufacturers?' said Max.

'Well, with my expertise in getting shit done,' said Ross, 'I tracked down a cockney sergeant who's the national lead on less lethal weapons for NPCC. Font of all knowledge on shit that doesn't kill you but really ruins your day. Turns out that a few tasers have gone missing over the years. You know what cops are like, can't be trusted with shiny toys. Also, the older generation holsters had a habit of becoming detached from the belts, particularly when jumping over fences, and the like. I've a list of locations and where and when.'

'How about cartridges?'

'Well, some forces are more careful than others. Once the cartridges have expired, they should either then be retained for training purposes or returned to the manufacturers. Controls vary across the country, but there're no reported thefts, or any major losses. The cockney expert's opinion is that a number could have gone missing over the years or been listed as used in training, when in fact they'd just been tucked away.'

'So not a lot of help. How about the AFID number we found?'

'Cockney geezer's waiting for the manufacturer to come back with where that one was issued. They get sent over from the manufacturer in batches, then they're distributed within the forces to training units and operational teams. There are controls, and the cartridges have to be booked out when cops take them on the street.'

'We need to look into where the tasers went missing, and maybe compare that to where John Lorimer has been – possibly other members of MIT 6 too. Maybe we'll get a lead?' said Max.

'Already on it. I have Lorimer's file,' said Norma.

'What do we know about him?' asked Janie.

'Been in twenty years, decent service record, well regarded as a thief taker. A few too many complaints of excessive force, though, including one where he supposedly broke someone's jaw, but the complainant pulled out and refused to cooperate,' said Norma.

'How about the Danny Macallan incident?' said Max.

Norma removed her glasses and polished the lenses on a cloth. 'Surprisingly little information out there. Seems like they tried to hush it up. Gus Fraser shouldn't have been asked to download the phone, it should have gone to a forensics lab. Words of advice all round and new guidance drawn up.

A few people were transferred out of the paedo squad, though. Donnie Watson and John Lorimer to name just two.'

'But surely the missing person was investigated?' said Max.

'Not really. It seems that Macallan had been totally disowned by his only surviving relative, an older brother living in the States, so there was no one pushing and it just withered on the vine. His flat in Glasgow was cleared by his landlord and all his shite ditched or sold. Seems like there was no appetite to look for him, and a number of anonymous reports came in saying that he'd got a new identity and fled to the Far East somewhere,' said Norma.

'I've looked at the log, and it's a shite-show. I've not seen a less proactive misper inquiry. It's almost like they didn't want to find him,' said Ross.

'Were any enquiries sent overseas?' asked Janie.

'Interpol messages sent, no dice. No one has seen or heard from him since.'

'Sounds like a bloody whitewash, to me,' said Norma.

'Aye, that's what I thought. No one came out of it looking good. The only thing that saved heads from rolling was that the wee girl's family didn't press. They were far more magnanimous than I'd have fucking been,' said Ross.

'This is all very interesting, but none of it helps us right now,' said Max.

'Meaning?'

'Well, all this history and background is just that. We have to be proactive. Macallan has been missing for years. I doubt we're going to get far with that, and there's not enough of us to explore every single lead, cross reference postings, cases and locations. We have to go live and operational on our best lead.'

'Max, as fucking usual you're moving your mouth but making no pissing sense,' said Ross, his red face deepening a shade.

'Lorimer. He was on the Paedophile Squad at the time of the Macallan disappearance, he was on the MIT when Chick Wilson died, and he's on the MIT now. He has a motive, he had the opportunity. He's our lead. We'll find nothing out about Macallan, or Chick Wilson. Those cases are too old, and he's had too much chance to cover tracks. We need to know where he's been, and importantly where he's going right now. MIT 6 is a closed shop – a tight team – and we need to breach that before someone else gets killed.' Max almost surprised himself with the strength in his words.

'So, let's get the surveillance team primed, then?'

'We go proactive, but not with a conventional team – he'd spot them, as good as they are. We use all the tools we have at our disposal to look at his movements over the last few weeks, but we must tread carefully. You've seen his file, Ross. He's good, he's a thief taker, he's surveillance-trained himself. He knows what we know, so we need to be cleverer than him.'

There was a pause and they all looked at each other, the ticking wall clock sounding almost deafening.

'What do you suggest, then?'

'Is the chief ready to do the necessary?'

'Aye. I have an appointment with him tomorrow afternoon, and you're coming.'

'Okay, I need to make a couple of calls. Is Barney available?' said Max, referring to their technical surveillance expert.

'He will be.'

'Good. We'll need him. We need to be seeing what Lorimer's

doing now, and more importantly, what he's planning in the future. We need all options exploring.'

'Make your calls then, and we have to be ready with a plan to present to the chief tomorrow afternoon. Full tactical options, okay? He's open to anything, as long as it's legal.'

'It will be.'

'Right, folks, let's all get home and be ready to get going first thing tomorrow. We're going to start shaking trees and see what falls out. You all know how these things go. We could be in for a long one. If there is a bent cop topping bad guys, we need to be all over it before they kill again. We're putting a stop to this, and we're doing it now.'

23

PREDICTABLY, IT WAS the Afghanistan dream that tore Max from a deep, uncomfortable sleep, his eyes snapped open and he gasped, his heart pounding. He lay there, breathing heavily, the smell of hot Afghan earth and the coppery tang of Dippy's blood all around him. Looking at the clock he saw it was 5.30 a.m.

Nutmeg whined, and moved closer, her tail twitching. She flicked her tongue at the cold sweat beaded across his face.

'Babe?' said Katie, her voice thick with sleep, as she turned to look at him in the gloom of the dawn light that was filtering through the curtains.

'I'm fine, love. Go back to sleep. I'm heading to the office. I'll take Nutty out first,' he said.

'Dream?' she said, reaching a hand to touch his face.

'No, I'm good,' lied Max.

'You sure?' Her eyes full of concern.

'Aye, go back to sleep.' Max reached over and kissed her warm face.

'You're sweaty. Sure it wasn't the dreams?'

'I'm good, I'll see you later.'

Katie snuggled into the thick duvet. 'Love you, be careful,' she said, her voice already succumbing to sleep. One of Katie's notable skills was her ability to sleep. Max knew from bitter experience that sleep was impossible once the dreams had struck.

He threw back the covers and climbed out of bed, picking up his clothes and padding softly out of the bedroom, Nutmeg at his heels.

'Run?' said Max to the little cockapoo, whose tail instantly went from a small twitch to a thrashing metronome.

Ears cocked forward, her face was the picture of anticipation as Max pulled on his running gear, desperate to be pushing his body out in the chilly air.

'Come on, then,' he began to run, steadily at first before picking up the pace.

The Nietzsche line came to mind as he ran, almost like it was being branded on his brain.

Whoever fights monsters should see to it that in the process he does not become a monster. And if you gaze long enough into an abyss, the abyss will gaze back into you.

Max drove his body hard, punishing it, forcing the dreams away and making him feel better.

Not all better. Just a bit better.

24

MAX WAS STARING at his computer screen when Ross and Janie walked into the office, both clutching coffee mugs in each hand. Ross had a Tupperware box jammed under his arm.

Norma didn't look up from the complex chart on her screen, her fingers quietly tapping away at her keyboard, her glasses perched on her nose.

'I should be impressed with your industry in getting in early, but I can't just help thinking that you're both job-pissed freaks,' was Ross's opening gambit.

'And a good morning to you, too, Ross-Boss,' said Norma with a smile.

'I bought you coffees, so don't say I don't look after my people,' he said depositing a cup at Norma's side.

'No doughnuts?'

'I'm watching my figure, and if I'm not eating sweet and tasty treats, neither are you two buggers.' He placed his Tupperware box on his desk, and Max was almost certain he could detect a sneer.

'What's in there?' said Janie.

'My bastard lunch,' said Ross, eyeing it with suspicion.

'You made it yourself?' said Norma, trying to hide a grin.

'Fuck no, it's a bastard couscous and mung bean fucking salad that Mrs F made for me last night. Now, I don't want any sarky arsed comments from any of you buggers, either. My body is a temple, you know.'

'More of a cathedral, I'd say,' said Max.

'Fuck off,' muttered Ross, booting up his computer.

'Or a broken-down church,' added Janie.

'How I long for the times when the DI was spoken to with respect. Now can we all stop blethering and get to work, please.'

Janie handed Max a cup.

'Thanks, any news from anywhere?' said Max.

'Nope,' said Janie. 'Last update I had was the briefing for DCC McVeigh. MIT 6 are getting nowhere with the murder of Paterson. No intel steers, nothing from forensics, PM had nothing, nothing from the snitches. They've already released a load of bods back to their other teams.'

'Fergus Grigor?'

'No evidence to link, and we've not shared the ladybug find with them, for obvious reasons. But no witnesses, obviously no CCTV and the PM was inconclusive owing to the catastrophic injuries,' said Ross, reading from his computer screen.

'Is Barney coming in today?' said Max.

'Aye, he should be here soon. I also have a reply from the cockney taser expert, here. Looks like the greenfly number was from one of the first batches of cartridges issued to Police Scotland in 2015. They'd be well out of date now.'

'What about internal records? We must know where they went,' said Max.

'Into the training pool, is all I have. Shite recording, as it was at the very early stages. I don't think we'll get too far with them.'

'Shite. Inspectorate would go mad if they knew.'

'Well, loads of the bloody things got shot off during all the early training courses. Firearms teams got them first and you know what those buggers are like with a new toy. They'd have been shooting them off all over the place.'

'So, there's no link to Lorimer?' said Janie.

'Nope,' said Ross.

'I wouldn't be so sure about that, guys,' said Norma, looking at her screen.

Everyone turned to face her.

'I have a potential link.'

'Spit it out.'

'Lorimer was on the Paedophile Squad in 2015 at the time that Macallan went missing.'

'We know this already.'

'Aye, but did you know that John Lorimer's wife, Iona Lorimer, was a firearms instructor at that exact time. She was also one of the first to be trained on taser and had access to all the kit.'

The only sound was the ticking of a clock on the wall.

'Where's she now?'

'Passed away shortly after.'

'How?' said Max.

'Car crash. Two cars in a head-on collision that ended up in a big fireball. No one walked away alive. Three dead, both occupants of the other car, and Iona, who was alone,' said Norma, her voice quiet.

'I remember this now,' said Max. It had been big news, and the death of a serving police officer always sticks in the memory.

'So, what are we saying? Does this change anything?' said Janie.

'It gives John Lorimer possible access to tasers and cartridges and it gives him something else, as well,' said Ross, his voice flat.

'What?' said Norma, her face puzzled.

'A motive. Put yourself in his shoes. You've just buried your wife and then you have to watch a scumbag drunk driver, like Chick Wilson, walk free from court, grinning like an idiot.'

'So, what's next?' asked Janie.

'Max?' said Ross, eyebrows raised.

'I've a plan. We're going to have to work non-stop to get everything in place, and we'll need some help.'

'Whatever you need.'

'Norma, what do we know about Lorimer's home?'

'He lives alone, as far as we can tell, in an apartment in a converted school in a nice bit of Portobello. There're ten apartments, and he's number 7. Smallish mortgage on it and he seems financially well set. A significant insurance payout after his wife's death set him up comfortably. Flat has an alarm registered with it, but no CCTV.'

'Does the block have CCTV?'

'No. I've managed to access the building profile here from the crime prevention officers' database. They did a survey a few years ago, after a couple of break-ins. It was converted in the early 80s. It has voice intercoms only, but the doors are heavy and recently upgraded, one at the front and one at the back, accessible with magnetic fobs. There's a fire brigade key slot, which is required by law.'

'So, a technical attack on his house will be tricky, what with close neighbours, particularly in this timeframe. How about his car?' said Max.

'Flash Audi SQ5. Just a year old, on a PCP thing. Costs him four hundred a month.'

'Registration?'

Norma told them.

'Have we run it through ANPR?'

'Aye, hits around the city, which I'll map when I have a moment.'

'How about the night of the murders?'

'Only between Leith cop shop and his home. No activations on the obvious routes, around Ravelston or going north to Dunnet Head.'

Max paused for a moment, thinking. 'You have the VIN number?'

Norma handed a sheet of paper across. 'PNC printout, it's all on there.'

'Cool, thanks. Does he have much of an online presence?' said Max, scribbling into his A4 notebook.

'Not particularly active on social media, although he does have a Facebook profile. He's clearly really into share trading. Lots of money moving around in share accounts.'

'How about phones?'

'Well, he has his work phone, which we have all the details for, and he pays for another phone with O2. I'll forward you the info, but I've submitted all the data requests for itemised billing and cell sites.'

'I'll get them hurried up,' said Ross, writing on his pad.

'Anything else notable?'

'He clearly likes a drink. Lots of purchases in bars in Leith and others close to his place in Portobello.'

Max nodded. 'A very security-conscious detective, but he has weaknesses we can exploit. He likes his car. He likes a drink, maybe there's an angle there.'

'You've got that look on your face, Max,' said Janie.

'What?'

'One that means bad shit's about to happen and no one's going home early today,' she said.

'What time are we seeing the chief?'

'As soon as you stop talking. He wants to accelerate the timescales,' said Ross.

'Well, let's go and see him, then.'

25

THE MIT 6 supervisors' meeting had been a little terse right from the start. It always happened like this. A murder breaks, and it's all hands to the pump during the golden hour, and onwards searching for and collating the evidence, particularly the type that tends to deteriorate with the passage of time. They'd been full-on, collecting the CCTV, smashing the house-to-house enquiries, working the scenes. The team was all tired and jaded.

DCI Donnie Watson looked over his spectacles at the other supervisors, Marnie Gray, Mark Fagerson, John Lorimer, Jimmy Duggan and a new face, DS Billy Bruce. They all stared back at him with tired eyes. His phone buzzed on the table, a message from his wife. *Are you going to be home today, or will I be eating alone again?* He didn't touch his phone, deciding that he'd deal with that situation later. His wife was getting more and more fed up with the job and was putting on pressure for him to retire. He looked up and put her out of his mind.

'Jimmy, anything from the forensic submissions? Give me something, please.'

'Sorry, I can't. Literally not a bloody thing. Not a fibre, not a hair, not a sausage. Couple of nicks in Paterson's clothing, but scientists think it is likely from the bark of the tree.'

'What about the minor injury to his backside?'

'No idea. Maybe from the tree, as well. Pathologist won't commit herself.'

'Toxicology?'

Jimmy shook his head.

'Shit. So, no witnesses, no CCTV, no forensics. How about source intel, John?'

'Well, an anonymous Crimestoppers message came in via the website saying, and I quote, *Scott Paterson was killed by one of McLennan's boys over drugs debts. He owed forty grand for some coke that was lost.*'

'Is that it?'

'Aye.'

'No name, number, email address?'

'No. I tried to backtrace, but it looks like a VPN was used. Unless they come back to us, we're knackered.'

Donnie stroked his chin and stared at the ceiling, as he tried to quell the frustration that was threatening him. His face began to flush, so he breathed, deeply. 'Keep looking into this, John. If there's a chance this is McLennan, we need to be all over it. Last thing we need is retribution and one of Jackie's boys getting topped.'

Lorimer nodded.

'Still nothing on phones?'

'Nope. The number we had for him was switched off around the time we suspect he died, and it's never been on since. No calls or texts that are of interest. Only calls into him are from family or friends, all of whom have been

TIE'd,' said Lorimer, using the acronym for 'trace, interview, eliminate'.

'Any data usage?'

'Nothing relevant.'

'I'll bloody decide on relevance, John. Just fucking tell me.' Donnie's face began to darken to an even deeper shade of red and he felt the skin on his neck prickle as he always did when anger or frustration began to bite.

'Plenty, but without the handset, it's meaningless. Cell site puts the phones in or around the golf course, but that's not a lot of help. We can't find any obvious social media accounts in his name either.'

'For fuck's sake, this is shite, guys. Probably my last case, and it's almost unsolvable. What the fuck is going on and what the hell are you lot doing? You're supposed to add something to this fucking investigation and all I'm hearing is, "Nothing, boss." It's not fucking good enough!' Donnie bellowed at the officers in front of him, his face contorted.

A tense silence filled the room for a full thirty seconds, before Donnie exhaled, forcefully, then rubbed his face with his hands. A vein pulsed at his temple.

'Boss, we're doing everything we can, but we can't make leads that aren't there,' said Marnie.

Donnie slumped back in his chair. He said nothing, just stared at a point a few inches above all their heads, feeling his insides churning.

'Boss?' said Marnie.

Donnie just shook his head again, before sitting upright, 'Fergus Grigor?' he asked, looking at Marnie Gray with tired-looking eyes.

'Literally not a shred of evidence to be had.'

'PM findings?'

'Died of multiple injuries. Nothing from tox, nothing in injuries to suggest that anything happened before he went over the cliff.'

'So, we can't link them beyond the fact that Grigor was Paterson's advocate?'

'Nope,' said Marnie.

'How're the team?'

'As knackered and pissed-off as we are, boss,' said Fagerson.

'Aye well, it's 4 p.m, now. Let's go and have a beer together, you know, bonding and that. I'll give them a lie-in tomorrow. No one in before midday, okay?'

There were nods and smiles all round.

'Also, I know some of you have met him already today, but just in case, can I introduce DS Billy Bruce, who's just transferred in from MITs in West Midlands Police. He's plenty of homicide investigation experience. As he's been in England for bloody years, he's off the streets until he's done his conversion course, to bring him up to speed on our wonderful Scottish way of doing things. I've given him the bonnie job of CCTV coordinator, which he's delighted with.'

Billy nodded and smiled showing even, white teeth. 'Aye, thanks, boss, love a bit of CCTV, me.' His accent was a soft central belt, not harsh, presumably blunted by years away from Scotland.

'When's your course, Billy?' asked Lorimer.

'Next month, three weeks at Tulliallan,' he said with a grimace.

'Okay, let's go for a pint and piss off home, okay?'

'You buying, boss?' asked Marnie.

'Am I shite. DSs who earn the overtime can put their hands in their bloody pockets.'

'New boy rules, Billy, first pint's on you,' said Lorimer, chuckling.

'I would, but I've gone and left my wallet at home,' said Billy, returning the laugh.

'Okay, okay, let's get everyone to the boozer, but we've plenty of work still to do, so I want everyone back here fresh tomorrow and ready to graft. I want to do an appeal, and I want an anniversary press conference at the scene. We also have the DCS visiting tomorrow, and I'm going to have to convince him we're on top of this. So, a few beers only, and then home. And yes, I'm looking at you, John.'

'Why me?' said Lorimer, a sparkle in his eyes.

'Because I've worked with you for bloody years, and I know what you're like. No getting on the pish and showing up here in a shite state tomorrow.'

'Understood,' said Lorimer, innocently.

'Right, come on, let's get this over with.'

26

'HERE THEY GO,' said Max into his covert mic. He was sitting in the small café opposite Leith Police Station on Queen Charlotte Street.

Leith, once a working-class port, was undergoing the evolution of gentrification, possibly since the film *Trainspotting* had hit the screens, which was ironic, bearing in mind the subject matter of the film. Old traditional pubs were being torn down and replaced with gastropubs and Michelin-starred dining. Even the fish and chip shop on the harbour felt posh.

The group of about fifteen or so cops, dressed in suits with slack-knotted ties, left the large Georgian building and headed away. The big figure of John Lorimer was at the front, his smart suit struggling to contain his powerful bulk.

'Why not go to the Compass across the road?' said Janie in his ear.

'Because it's more of a restaurant. They'll go to the Port O' Leith, that's the cop pub around here,' said Max, under his breath.

'You sure?'

'Cops always go to cop pubs.'

'Received. You want me to come and get you?'

'Not yet. I'll shout when I do. Is Barney with you?'

'Aye, sat next to me and eager to crack on.'

'I hope he's prepared for all eventualities.'

'He says piss off.'

'Charming. Anyway, I'm going mobile. I'll shout if I need you.'

Max finished his coffee and left the small café. He remained about fifty metres behind the crowd of ambling detectives as he followed them for the three-minute walk to the Port O' Leith.

As expected, as soon as they crossed Constitution Street and into Maritime Lane, they all filed into the small, nautical-themed pub, presumably to be met with a delighted smile from the publican, seeing a load of overtime-rich detectives hitting his pub at the quiet time of mid-afternoon.

'They're inside. I suspect they'll be a while, the first few pints after a bit of hard graft can get a bit ugly. Hopefully he'll get pished.'

'You know the type. First in last out, CID's full of them.'

'Is his car still where it was earlier?'

'Yep, tracker's still on. He must have a relationship with one of the business owners on Mitchell Street, just behind the nick. Parking's shite round here, and he'd have been clamped if he just left it there.'

Max smiled. The last twenty-four hours had been a blur of activity, authority applications, technical liaisons, and planning, just to get to this stage.

None of them had slept, but they were ready. They had no way of getting eyes and ears in his home, but they could get onto his car. A simple tracker had already been planted, but they had bigger plans. If Barney the tech guy was on his game, they may get their break tonight.

But right now, all they could do was wait.

27

IT ALWAYS HAPPENED this way.

One pint led to another. Then another, and then a little more. A round of shots were necked, followed by a few others, until the less hardcore team members began to drift away.

Detectives had changed, thought John Lorimer, and he wasn't sure why. It used to be that drinking together was as much a part of being a detective as working together.

He'd always been a fair drinker, even before Iona passed away, but since then, he'd got worse and worse, or better and better, depending on your point of view.

'Another beer, John?' the face of Billy, the new DS, swam into view through the alcoholic haze, the result of several hours of hard drinking.

'Fucking damn right, mate. I'm glad to have someone who values the team-bonding affairs of a good evening on the pish. Is it just us, now?'

'Aye, Donnie was giving us daggers when he left.'

'Ach, fuck him,' he said, accepting his pint of lager from Billy, and taking a deep draught of the cold, crisp beer.

'So, what brought you back to Scotland, then?'

'Usual shite. Women. I got cleaned out in a divorce, pal. My parents had left me their old place in Craigentinny which I'd had rented out, but once the bitch took everything, I came back. Applied to Police Scotland, and I was in. Wish I didn't have to do this shite course, though.'

'Aye well, there's no good jobs on this bastard of a murder. Nae bloody leads, and nae bugger gives a fuck about Scott Paterson. He had enemies all over the place. No bugger'll miss him.'

'Ah well, screw him, John. It's tequila time,' roared Billy, laughing.

'Jesus, you're an animal. I'm gonna regret you coming on the team,' said Lorimer, tipping the remainder of his pint down his throat and slamming the empty glass on the table.

'Ach, don't be a pussy. We must keep the tradition going, or it's all falafel and beetroot juice. I don't know what the world's coming to, pal.' Billy stood and walked back to the bar, staggering slightly as he did.

Within a minute he was back with two more pints, and two clear shot glasses, some limes, and a salt cellar.

'Oh man, you're gonna be the death of me,' Lorimer said as Billy handed him the salt cellar and a slice of lime.

Billy licked the back of his hand, necked the contents of the shot glass, and then sucked on the lime, screwing up his face afterwards.

'Your turn,' he said, nodding at the glass.

Lorimer followed Billy's lead without hesitation, licking the salt, downing the fiery tequila, and then sucking the shite out of the lime.

'Jesus, man, that's boggin,' said Lorimer, grimacing as the liquid burned a path down his throat.

'Soothe it with a beer, boy. Soothe it with a beer.'

They both drank from their pints, and laughed, slapping each other on the back, a bond forming already that only really exists amongst the drunk and newly acquainted, short-lived though it normally is.

'We best do these and get out of here,' slurred Billy, 'it's only my second day tomorrow, and I don't want to get on the boss's wrong side.'

'Ach dinnae be a Jessie, man. One for the road, aye?'

'Mate, I really need to get my head down, I've hardly slept,' Billy said, laughing.

'I thought I'd found a kindred spirit, like. Come on, then,' said John, gulping the rest of his beer.

They both stood and staggered out of the pub and into the crisp air, breathing it in deeply after the dense fug of the crowded, sweaty pub.

'Cab?' said Billy.

'Aye,' said Lorimer, patting his pockets. His face fell. 'Ah shite. House keys are in my car. I need to walk back and get them, or I'm sleeping on my bloody doorstep,' he said, his face flushing an even deeper red.

'Ya daft nugget. Where's your car?'

'Just behind the nick. You get home, man. I'll get a cab once I've got my keys.'

'Mate, you're not planning on driving, are you?'

'As if?' Lorimer said, mock offended.

'No way, come on. Let's get your keys and we'll share a cab. You can drop me on your way to Portobello.'

'Ach, you're no fun. We're the polis, man. Nae bugger will stop us.' He swayed slightly on the spot, as the cold Edinburgh evening air cut right through him.

The journey to the deserted street behind the police station only took a few minutes, despite the level of intoxication. Lorimer reached into his pocket and eventually found the black oblong plastic and metal key fob. He pressed the button and the Audi blipped, its indicators flashing away in its parking space.

'Lucky parking spot, man?' said Billy.

'Owner of the unit there's a pal. Lets me park for nothing.' He belched as he opened the door and drunkenly sat behind the wheel, putting the key into the slot on the dash. The car sprang to life.

'John, no way man. No way,' said Billy.

'Ach, don't be daft. Only a short trip, I'll drop you on the way.'

'No way. I'm not letting you drive.' Billy reached in and snatched the key out of the lock and pressed the ignition switch, killing the engine. He tucked the single key in his pocket.

'You're a bloody square, man. Whit's the use in being polis if ye cannae drive home pished.' He giggled as he fumbled for a bunch of keys which he tucked into his pocket.

'Come on, let's get you in a cab,' Billy also chuckled, and hiccupped.

Defeated, John hauled himself out of the car and slammed the door.

'You English cops are boring, haud up,' he said, yawning deeply before opening the back door and pulling out a slim attaché case from behind the driver's seat.

'I need to put this in the boot, man. If I take it now, I'll lose the bastard and I need it tomorrow.' He quickly opened the boot and slid the case under the carpet and into the spare wheel space. 'Full of fucking thieves, this place,' he mumbled.

'Come on, man. We need to be back here before you know it.'

Exhaustion suddenly hit Lorimer as they walked back to the main road. His previous long strides had deteriorated to more of a shuffle and relief flooded through him when a passing cab stopped in response to Billy's outstretched arm.

'Get this pished reprobate home to Portobello, will you?'

'Is he gonna whitey in ma cab?' said the driver, frowning.

'Nah, he's an old campaigner. How much?'

'Depends if he hurls. If he doesn't, it's twelve quid.'

'Here's twenty, keep the change. Come on, in you go, John.'

'Whit about you?' he said, collapsing into the back seat.

'I'll get the next one. You need to get to bed. I'll give you an alarm call, and I'll pick you up in the morning,' Lorimer barely heard him as he began to drift off into an alcoholic slumber.

Billy watched the cab roar away into the Edinburgh night, relieved to have John out of the way, and pleased at the opportunity that had presented itself.

He picked his phone out of his pocket and dialled.

'How'd you get on?' said Max Craigie.

'All good. In fact, better than expected. He's pissed as a fart, asleep in a cab on his way home and I have his car keys. Are you ready?' said 'Billy Bruce' also known as DC Niall Hastings.

'Aye we're coming up now, we'll get the keys off you and get cracking. How pissed is he?'

'Steaming. Fell asleep as soon as he got in the cab.'

'How come you're still standing?'

'A mix of non-alcoholic lager and water in shot glasses. His short-hands-deep-pockets routine of letting me pay for most of the beers worked nicely for me, and the pot plants have been well watered with Tennant's when he did deign to buy me one. My expenses are going to be a bit tasty, though, Maxie-boy.'

'He say anything interesting?'

'Not really. Said no one would miss Paterson, but that's about it. I wasn't going to press him. Far too early for that.'

'Agreed. Be there in a couple of minutes.' Max rang off.

Niall stood on the pavement and yawned. He was exhausted after a whirlwind of activity following Max's call. The under-cover deployment had been authorised in double quick time, and he was soon on a plane and into a bungalow. It was owned by Police Scotland, although there was no paper trail to show that. It was registered to an anonymous trust fund in the name of the late Mr and Mrs Bruce. The property had already been dressed as if a divorced man had just moved in. Old furniture that would look like it could have belonged to his parents, a few old photos and just enough clothes. An anonymous, ageing Peugeot on the drive to suggest someone struggling for funds after an expensive divorce.

The Scottish covert operations team had worked a miracle to make the place authentic, and Niall already had a backstopped legend in the name Billy Bruce, ready to go. The legend was always a work in progress, and it was now being tweaked and developed. A service record had also been speedily created with West Midlands Police, just in case any suspicious individuals decided to check.

They'd find nothing untoward. Covert operations were good, they had to be. Lives depended on it.

Within a couple of minutes, a dark Volvo swept into view and turned into the side road just off Commercial Street. Niall walked into the dimly lit street, wordlessly opened the back door, and took a seat behind the driver.

'Maxie-boy?' said Niall, and they bumped fists.

'Nice work,' said Max, smiling into the rear-view mirror at his old colleague and friend from London.

'I know. Jeri is bloody fuming that I agreed to do this, particularly as I was moaning to you about it the other day.' Niall shook his head.

'You love it really, and I just couldn't come up with anyone better than you at short notice with a legend that would fit. Hopefully it won't be too long. What did Jeri say – does she hate me?'

'She doesn't know. I decided to be a little ambiguous about what I was doing. I prefer she doesn't know too much. You know the score.'

'I do. Katie has learned not to ask. How's our friend John Lorimer?'

'All good. He's a right old piss-head. I had to relieve him of his car key to stop him driving away.' Niall handed over the Audi key which Max took gratefully.

'Now that's a stroke of extreme luck. This is Barney, by the way, our tech guy.' He nodded to a silver-haired man who seemed to be in his sixties seated in the front of the car. An unlit hand-rolled cigarette dangled from between his lips.

'Now then,' said Barney in a broad Yorkshire accent.

'Now then, indeed,' said Niall.

'Barney's an elderly ex-spook who does our tech surveillance for us.'

'Bloody cheeky beggar, I'd outrun you any day,' he said, his grin widening, his cigarette bobbing up and down.

'What you planning?' asked Niall.

'Eyes and ears inside the car, a proper wired-in tracker, and see if we can download the internal GPS,' said Max.

'There's a laptop in there. In the boot's spare wheel space. He moved it there when I refused to let him drive.'

'That's worth some thought. Anything you can do with that, Barney?'

'Laptop or Mac?' said Barney.

'It was in a case, so I couldn't see.'

'I can have a look, for sure. I've some kit with me,' Barney said.

'Excellent, despite how he looks, Barney's hot on tech and he loves his job.'

'I do now that you've got me the key. These late-model Audis are buggers to get into without going noisy. Means you can cancel the low-loader,' said Barney.

'Aye, minimum of street disturbance. Right, get yourself back to your place and get some kip. I'll pop the key through your door when we're done. You've work to be at tomorrow with MIT 6. Eyes wide open, pal, yeah?'

'You got it. Speak tomorrow.' Niall nodded, and then he was gone, striding off into the night.

28

'JANIE, WE'RE GOING in now. Ready to follow us?' said Max into the covert mic.

'I'm ready,' came the immediate response.

Max put the Audi in gear and drove along the streets behind the police station. They turned into the deserted road that housed a number of industrial units.

Max handed the key to Barney and pulled over just short of the Volvo. 'Is the garage ready?'

'Aye, Ross is waiting. I reckon an hour, tops, to get this done.'

'Okay, let's go. Street's clear, Janie has the other end blocked and it's one way.'

Barney nodded and stepped out of the car, pressing the key fob. The Audi blipped and the lights flashed. He opened the door, climbed in and almost immediately the engine started, and the big car moved off along the street and out of sight.

'Okay, Janie,' said Max into his mic.

Within a few seconds, headlights flashed into Max's rear-view mirror and an identical Audi SQ5 swung into the street and passed Max, parking in the space that Barney had vacated seconds ago.

Not only was the Audi the same model, age and variant, but it had the same stickers, and number plate. An identical vehicle that they had procured from an Audi dealership earlier that day and false-plated with Lorimer's vehicle registration number.

Janie jumped out, locked the car and within seconds, they were driving off together in the Volvo, leaving the street exactly as it was before. Now any friends, acquaintances or colleagues of Lorimer wouldn't see anything different, because there wasn't anything different to see. Same car, same registration, same parking space, and all the time the real car would be on a hydraulic hoist, being fitted with intrusive surveillance kit, in a lock-up garage on a small industrial estate in nearby Bonnington, less than a mile away.

'Good work,' said Max as Janie settled in her seat and snapped the seatbelt in place.

'How long do we have?'

'Plenty of time. Barney practised on the dummy car, so we know the kit will fit perfectly. It's the same model and year, and he's already built the unit.'

'How about the GPS?'

'Easy, he reckons.'

'Luckily he doesn't have a dashcam.'

'Aye, for someone so security conscious, that's a little surprising.'

'Nice. I hope there's coffee at the garage.'

'We'll make a stop, otherwise Ross will be bloody impossible.'

29

ROSS WAS – as expected – in an irascible mood as they used the pedestrian door within the roller shutter of the lock-up garage.

He glared at Max and Janie from the front of the Audi as he held some wires in place that were connected to a laptop. Barney was almost upside-down, contorted into a tight space, fiddling in the engine compartment.

'You two took your bastarding time,' was his snarled greeting.

'We bought coffee,' said Janie, holding a slotted tray with four Costas inside.

'Your most significant contribution for a while, DC Calder,' he muttered. 'Come and hold these fucking wires whilst this old codger does whatever he's doing. I'm knackered.'

Janie placed the coffees down on a workbench and took the wires and laptop from Ross.

'What's he doing?' asked Max.

'Downloading the GPS. Lucky he's only skin and bones. No chance I'd fit in there, not even after a year on this bloody diet. I wouldn't be surprised if the sneaky ex-spook bastard is just playing for time to get his overtime rates up,' said Ross as he snapped the lid from his coffee and took a sip. His face screwed up in a grimace.

'I have to say, Ross, amazing work getting all this sorted in just a day,' said Max.

'Aye well, you can keep your toadying to yourself. Let's get this done and get the car back on the street. It's doing no good here. How's the UC?' he said, referring to Niall.

Max told Ross what had happened.

'Has he gone back to Craigentinny?'

'Aye. He's a good guy, and his legend is tight, which is a miracle in the time we had.'

'Not a fucking miracle. A result of my bridge-building, negotiation, and sweet-talking. You've no idea how many cakes I had to get to the flat dressers to get them to do it so urgently, and don't talk to me about the bloody audit trail.'

'Well, credit where it's due. Maybe you're as good as you constantly tell us you are.'

Barney suddenly appeared from the Audi's bonnet, sweat on his face. 'That's the GPS on the satnav downloaded. It's on the laptop and I'll transfer it to a flash drive once we're away. Not sure what state the data is in, but Norma should be able to do something with it.'

'Cool, what's next?'

'I'll get the probe in, won't take a moment. It's prebuilt.' Barney went to his bag and pulled out what looked like a small monitor with his gloved hand.

'What's that?' asked Ross.

'The display screen. I've hidden a pinhole camera and microphone in it, and I'll secrete a 4G SIM down in the dash. Easy as anything to fit.'

Without another word he was in the car, the seat covered with a protective plastic sheet. He took a screwdriver and fiddled for a few moments, before pulling out the existing, identical screen and handing it to Max who was standing by the open driver's door, watching.

A few minutes later, he pressed the ignition switch and the display burst into life. The Audi symbol flashed up on screen followed by map mode.

'Perfect,' he said.

'Same display as when he parked it?' asked Max.

'Aye. It's just like unplugging a computer monitor and reconnecting with another. The data's in the chip, not the screen. When you drive back it'll move the map naturally to the location you park in. He won't know it's moved, unless he goes into the GPS, which I've just done, and it's a right fiddly bastard. We're perfectly safe – just don't touch anything you don't need to. Last thing is to switch it from Radio 1 to Radio 4.'

'Is that the car done?' asked Ross.

'Let me just check the feed.' Barney got out of the car and went to his laptop, which was on a workbench nearby, and began tapping away at the keys. 'Get in,' he said to Max. Max took the driver's seat, the door remaining open.

Barney tapped and swiped on the screen for a moment, before nodding. 'Bingo, we're live.'

He swivelled the screen so Ross could also see. Both seats were visible, Max was as clear as a bell.

'Say something?'

'I heard that Ross is a hen-pecked husband,' said Max in a flat tone but with a smile on his face. His voice was tinny but clear out of the laptop's speaker to the extent that it echoed around the garage.

'You can fuck off and all,' said Ross, trying to stop a smile creeping across his face.

'Okay, Max, I videoed the insides of the car before I started faffing about. Can you check it's all identical before we finish? I'll drive it back, as I know the exact position of the steering wheel and the handbrake. Someone show me the laptop.' He passed Max his phone, which displayed a paused image of the car's interior.

Ross handed the simple laptop case to Barney who opened it carefully, noting the zip's position and the leather strap that was secured to a buckle. He pulled open the flap, unzipped the top and removed an ordinary-looking Lenovo laptop.

'What do you want from this?' asked Barney.

'What can you give us?' said Ross.

'Well, safely I can image the hard drive. Riskily I can boot it up, or really riskily I could insert some spyware.'

'I'm voting for safety first,' said Max.

'You always were a boring bastard,' said Barney.

'Well, if it was a democracy, maybe you two would get a vote. But I'm the bloody gaffer, so it's my decision.'

'Well?'

'Safety first, obviously, but not because of anything you've said, Craigie. Stay in your bloody lane.'

'You two bickering is a bit like listening to Hinge and Bracket, or summat,' said Barney, chuckling, as he rolled a cigarette which he duly lit and sucked on with evident pleasure, the tip glowing.

'Typical for a man of your vintage to use an ancient cultural reference. DS Craigie gets ideas above his station. Download the laptop, Barney,' said Ross, puffing out his cheeks.

'Past your bedtime, boss.'

'First sensible thing you've said all day. How long?'

'Couple of minutes, no longer for the laptop, then probably another five for me to access the car's odometer and take off the mileage we've put on it.'

'You can do it that quickly?'

'Piece of piss. That's why I'd never trust the mileage on a second-hand car.'

'Probably why Mrs Fraser's car is always smoking like a bastard. Scummy car dealers. Right, folks, let's start getting packed up, and let's get the hell out of here.'

30

NIALL HASTINGS PULLED up outside John Lorimer's flat. It was on a nice street in Portobello, in what looked like a converted school. It was only a couple of miles away from his far less grand cover house in Craigentinny. He'd phoned Lorimer first thing that morning, and after three attempts, a gummy, thick voice had answered.

Niall sent a message to Lorimer's phone. *I'm outside.*

There was a brief pause before his phone buzzed.

Come up. Struggling. Apartment 7.

Niall jumped out of the car and ran up the steps to the front of the large building. He buzzed the bell for apartment 7. The door clicked and he pushed it open. The staircase was sweeping and impressive, with a long, dramatic banister rail, wrought-iron fixings, all finished to a high specification.

He jogged up to the first floor and along the marble-floored corridor, following the sign for Lorimer's flat.

A minute later he found the door and knocked. It was answered by a dishevelled-looking John Lorimer. His hair was bushy and unkempt, his jaw covered in bristles, and his eyes were red-rimmed and hollow. He was still in last night's clothes and a wave of alcohol fumes hit Niall like an express train. Lorimer said nothing, just beckoned him in with a nod of the head.

The open-plan space was bright, modern and spacious. It looked like there was just one living area, a large kitchen, diner and sitting room, in which an enormous flatscreen TV was playing the news.

'You're a bastard,' muttered Lorimer, hitting Niall with another waft of stale alcohol. 'It was the bloody tequila. I need a lightning shower and coffee, then I'm good to go. Coffee's on and in the pot. Help yourself, I'll be three minutes.'

'Looking a bit peaky. You suffering?'

'Aye. Head is shite, guts are churning and I think someone shat in my mouth. And it's your fault.' A painful-looking smile played at the corners of his mouth as he turned and shuffled out of the kitchen. Soon Niall could hear the hum of a power-shower from down the corridor.

Niall looked around the airy room, noting the tasteful prints on the wall, the expensive units with high-spec white goods. He went to the shiny granite worktop where a sleek-looking drip machine stood beside a couple of cups. Niall poured himself one, nodding appreciatively at the rich liquid. His eyes continued to sweep the room in a practised fashion.

There was a photograph on the wall of Lorimer, standing with his arm around a blonde woman. They were both tanned and smiling, standing on a tropical beach in front of coconut palm trees. Niall took another sip of coffee.

'A good brew, right?' Lorimer's voice rang out from behind him.

He was dressed in neat, clean trousers and a crisp, white shirt. His previously wild hair had been combed and tamed.

'Really good.'

'I get it from a website. Regular deliveries, better than all the shite in the supermarkets.'

Niall nodded, 'Pretty woman, the missus?'

'Aye,' was all that Lorimer said.

'You still together?' Niall knew the answer, but he wanted to see what Lorimer's reaction would be.

'No. She passed away,' he said, his eyes tired but impassive.

'Man. Sorry, long ago?'

'A few years, yeah.'

'Can I ask how?'

'Car crash.'

'Shit, mate. I'm so sorry, and I was moaning about my ex last night.'

'Nae bother. No way you'd have known.'

'Aye. I know. Life is shite, right? Especially with the scum we deal with breathing in and out.'

Lorimer paused a beat, his eyes fixed on Niall. After a moment, he shrugged, and poured himself a mug of coffee, sighing as the rich brew hit his senses. 'Coffee, eh? Makes everything a little better. Come on, we'd best get into the incident room, or Donnie'll be well scunnered with us and you'll never get away from CCTV.'

31

MAX AND THE rest of the team were all crowded around Janie's desk, looking at the screen of a tablet computer. Max's phone buzzed. It was a message from Niall.

Just dropped JL at his car. He's in a shit state.

'Here we go. Are we listening?' said Max.

'Yep, kit's on and working, from what I can see,' said Janie, looking at the tablet computer.

There was a click and then a clump from the tablet. On screen, the door opened and Lorimer flopped down on the driver's seat with a sigh. His hand went up, and he stuck out his tongue, as he examined himself in the mirror.

'Ah, jeez, I look a fucking mess,' he muttered. The quality was excellent. His hand reached down and he threw something into his mouth and sucked.

'Mints. There were breath mints in the car,' said Barney.

Lorimer disappeared and the door slammed shut.

'Good work, Barney. Quality lump-up, that,' said Ross.

'Is this praise from the mighty Ross?' said Barney as he pulled out his trusty pouch and swiftly rolled a cigarette.

'Aye, don't get bloody used to it, Grandpa.' Ross moved away and sat at his own desk.

There was another clunk from the car, and light streamed in as the Audi's hatchback opened. The covert camera in the satnav screen could just make out Lorimer, bending into the boot space. He appeared again as he stood and slammed the boot shut. There was a muffled *clunk* as the car was locked.

'Laptop retrieved. I take it there's no trace of our presence on it anywhere?' said Max.

'Nope. All I did was image it. I'm keywording it now, as it goes.'

'Anything?'

'Nope. Not a bloody thing. He deals in shares quite extensively and seems to be making a fair go of it. Decent money coming in. Neighbours in the block on the same floor so a short notice tech attack would be very tough without knowing their movements. Last thing we want is Mrs Miggins catching our old codger of a tech man about to burgle Lorimer's place.'

'Quite frankly, I don't give a flying fuck about his finances. No one's killing these scumbags for moolah,' said Ross, massaging his temples. He looked particularly shattered today. His shoes were unpolished and scuffed, his chin was dark with bristles and his hair was wild and untamed.

'What keywords are you using?' asked Max.

'All victims' names, taser, Ravelston, Dunnet, cliff, lighthouse, golf, throat, UV, ultra, violet. Want me to go on?' said Barney.

'No. You're very dull. How about the GPS data from the car, Norma?' Ross's voice was laden with sarcasm.

'I'm on it, but it's really bloody complicated. Every journey recorded, but it's hard to extrapolate the timeline because of the way it's backed up on the car's internal systems. It's going to take me a while to plot on a map,' said Norma, her cheeks flushed.

'How about his phones?'

'I've had a reasonable look at the times of both murders, his work and personal phone were hitting a mast near his home. I need to do more, but I only have one pair of hands,' she said with a sigh.

'So, we've fuck all?'

'Ross, I say this with the deepest respect, but can you fuck off with the accusatory tone? I'm doing the work of three analysts, here.'

Ross opened his mouth to argue, then stopped and closed it again. After a moment, he twisted his face into something approaching a soft expression.

'I'm tired and grouchy and getting shite from above. I know you're doing more than you should.' His tone was genuine.

'Apology accepted,' said Norma.

'Who said I was bloody apologising?' said Ross, but his tone was conciliatory.

Norma chuckled, and turned to her computer screen.

Max spoke up. 'One step at a time. We've some good circumstantial evidence against him, even if we could do with more before we arrest.'

'Fine for you to say. You don't have the bloody chief chewing you a new one every five minutes. What happens if Lorimer kills someone? What happens if some nasty piece of fucking work gets acquitted at a trial, and he thinks that justice hasn't been done, eh? Max, we have someone on the inside, who's most likely killed on four occasions at least. There sure as shit can't be a fifth, not on our watch.' Ross's eyes blazed.

'We'll get the evidence. We just need time.'

'Well, we don't even know if we have any bastard time. We have to watch him like a bloody hawk.'

The tension in the room was palpable. They all knew what was at stake.

'We have to be cool, Ross. Cool like the Fonz. We'll get the evidence.'

'Aye, well we'd better and fucking soon!'

32

THE MIT 6 supervisors meeting had been ugly.

Donnie was angry at the state of half the team after the 'few beers' he'd encouraged had descended into an almighty piss-up. He raged at them, clearly suffering the effects himself and ordered everyone back to the golf course to revisit the scene, canvass for further witnesses and hand out leaflets. The team now amounted to fifteen officers only, so they had all tramped out of the front of Leith Police Station into the cold, buttoning up coats, ready to get in the cars and head off. They all knew that a leaflet drop and extra canvassing was pointless. No one liked doing an onerous task simply to appear proactive. It was a waste of everyone's time.

Donnie and Marnie left the station together and were about to get into their car when a diminutive figure appeared on the pavement, holding up his phone, clearly filming them, a microphone attached to it by a wire.

'DCI Watson, Shuggie Gibson. Is there any progress on the murder of Scott Paterson and the unexplained death of Fergus Grigor?' he said, his eyes sparkling.

'Not now, Shuggie, we're busy.'

'Surely a progress report? The public have a right to know.'

'Nothing further to add. Please submit any requests to the press office, you know the drill.' Donnie smiled, keeping a lid on the frustration that surged in his chest.

'How is it that all of these unexplained deaths and murders have you and your team at the centre of them? Why aren't you catching these killers?'

'Come on, Marnie, let's get out of here. It's bloody Baltic in any case,' said Donnie, looking at the rest of the team, all staring at Shuggie Gibson. 'Right, everyone, get going.' He slammed the door of the Mondeo. 'Fucking Shuggie Gibson. Someone needs to read that bastard his horoscope. Let's go.'

As they all drove away, Donnie watched Shuggie in the rear-view mirror. He just stood there, on the pavement, filming the departing cars, a half-smile on his sharp face. His mission was clearly complete. Donnie knew that all the footage would soon be uploaded onto his blog and twitter. Within hours more hashtags would be trending about Police Scotland inaction, all of which would only lead to one thing. More shit from the DCC. And everyone with an interest in policing knew that shit always rolled downhill at a ridiculous rate of knots. Donnie sighed; he really didn't need this.

33

Alfa-Secure

I'VE ENCOUNTERED A MINOR risk to the operation. It is only minor at the moment, but failure to deal with it could lead to escalation.

One thing is for certain, it can't be ignored. I have learned that a small, insignificant problem left unchecked will grow and grow until it threatens the operation.

DCI Watson is still nowhere near me; he doesn't have a clue, what – or more likely who – they are dealing with.

But it's time to act.

34

TIME WAS PASSING and they were getting nowhere. This was always the case with major crime investigation. Long periods of routine screening of data, watching surveillance feeds, and reviewing seized intelligence product only occasionally punctuated by short, intense bursts of high-stress activity.

Max was continuing searching the keyword data that Barney had pulled from Lorimer's computer, Janie was glued to the feed on the laptop that was tuned into the surveillance footage on the Audi, whilst also looking through the phone data, to try to extrapolate if there was another burner phone in existence. It didn't make any sense that the phone didn't seem to move at the times of the murders, so there must be another phone out there. Any rogue and unexplained numbers would have to be cross-checked, which started a whole new raft of forms to be completed, authorised, and submitted to the phone companies. This then produced more data to be dug into, more applications and yet more authorisations, all like looking for a needle in a haystack.

It was frustrating in the extreme.

Ross had been called down to update the chief, and he had

been gone a while, so Max was sure he'd be in an even worse mood when he came back.

Suddenly, there was a scream from Norma's desk.

'Got you, you bastard, I've nailed you. Max, I have it. I've got the break!' Norma yelled, pushing back her swivel chair and punching her arms in the air.

'Calm down, pal. What do you have?' said Max, trying to stop the rising tide of excitement in his stomach.

'The GPS data from Lorimer's Audi. I pushed it through a program, and I have it: date order, locations, the lot. It took bloody ages, as I had to use an external laptop, and piss around with it from all angles, but I have it. It's all here.'

'And?'

'It's him. Not a doubt about it. Look, these are the movements of his Audi on the night of the murders. She pointed to a map on her large screen. It showed a time and date-stamped trail that traced the directions travelled by the Audi on the night in question. It was clear.

There was no doubt.

Lorimer killed Paterson and Grigor.

And they could prove it.

35

'**WHERE'S LORIMER NOW?**' said Ross, after Max and Norma had briefed him, shown all the mapping and explained it in painstaking detail. He took a large bite from a green apple and chewed with relish.

'I've just had a message from our man,' said Max. 'The whole team is out canvassing at Ravelston Golf Course, handing out leaflets. Lorimer is with Donnie Watson, who's apparently in a shit mood after everyone went out and got pished last night,' said Max.

'Do we know timings?'

'Not really. The feeling is they'll be there for a while. They want to cover until the authorised clubhouse closes, to catch anyone who was there at closing time on the evening Paterson died.'

Ross sat back in his chair and stroked his chin. He finished chewing and swallowed. 'So, opinions required on what we do next?'

'We have him under control. His car's lumped and tracked, and we don't know for sure the location of the taser or anything else that may be relevant. We want to give ourselves the best chance of getting him along with the evidence. We have the GPS data, but on its own it's not conclusive, is it? We haven't put him in the car that night. Still nothing on ANPR?' said Max.

'Nothing. He didn't hit any cameras at the relevant times, and certainly nothing heading north to Dunnet,' said Norma.

'So, we really want some other hard, physical evidence. Juries struggle with stuff like this and if it's just the mapping, it's not enough. Not gonna lie, the prospect of him killing someone on our watch concerns me more than if Mrs Fraser caught me eating a big fish supper right now,' said Ross, tapping his fingers on the desk and studying the half-eaten apple.

'It'll come. It's somewhere in his computer, or his phones, or CCTV. We'll find it,' said Max.

'We can't leave him out there. We have him under some degree of control, but what if he has another car? What if we lose him, the equipment fails or is discovered? He's a smart boy. He's also a cop with bags of experience. We need to take him off the street and get him remanded. He'll have something incriminating at his house, I'm certain of it,' Ross said.

'I'm with you, but let's give him a little more time. Lorimer is with the team until late, then we can follow him with the surveillance kit and track his phones. We don't leave him until his lights go out, and then his door goes in, okay?'

'Fuck me, Max, I hate this level of risk. What if we lose him? What if he sneaks out when he's on our watch and tops some poor bastard?'

'We won't lose him,' said Max.

Ross let out a sigh. 'Okay, we nick him first thing in the morning.'

'We'll need some backup,' said Max.

'We can't justify armed. My pal is an inspector on OSU – they can door bosh and secure entry. The bugger only has a taser that we know of.'

Max nodded. OSU would be perfect. They were specialists in rapid entry, search operations and public order. 'What time are we going in?'

'Early. Four a.m., let's get the bugger in bed, preferably with a hangover – you reckon our man can persuade him to have a few pints tonight?'

'One thing I know about Niall is that he's an expert at persuasion, particularly when getting a man to go out on the piss,' said Max.

'You sound like you have experience of this,' said Janie.

'One of the reasons I don't drink anymore.'

'Right, I'll call OSU now and get it sorted. Then I'll speak to the chief. Four a.m. through the door. In the meantime, we watch the bugger as closely as we can until he hits the sack, okay?'

The whole office nodded.

'Let's do this,' said Ross, standing up and putting his phone to his ear.

36

NIALL SHIVERED AND pulled his coat tight against the evening chill. It had been a long day at Ravelston, handing out leaflets to passers-by, completing questionnaires and essentially hanging around.

Donnie had spent most of the day scowling and staring at his laptop in the car, or with his phone clamped to his ear.

'He's been a right grumpy bugger today,' said John Lorimer who had walked across from the copse of trees surrounded by the scene tape.

'Is this his default attitude?' said Niall.

'Well, he's usually pretty dry, but a combination of the fact that this case looks like a sticker, together with his own hangover has taken his mood to new levels of irritability. Probably not helped by the fact that we all massively abused his trust and got blootered last night.' Lorimer's face was lined and drawn, his eyes red with fatigue, but he still managed a weak smile.

'Well, there is that. This is bloody pointless, though. The only people here are a few golfers giving us daggers from the nineteenth hole. How long is he going to punish everyone for? It's getting dark, it's miserable and it's fucking freezing.'

Lorimer yawned. 'He can be cussed, but he's also hungover, so I suspect he'll break sooner or later. We'll be getting into overtime territory. He still has a budget to manage.'

'Feeling it?'

'Aye, your bloody fault as well.'

'Fancy a swift one after this?'

'No chance. I'm headed to see a man about a dog, like.'

'By man, you mean bird, right?'

'No comment.'

'Who was the wee rat of a gadgie outside the station with the camera?' said Niall.

'Shuggie Gibson. Freelance blogger, journo, and all-round pain in the arse. Making accusations all over the place.'

'Like what?'

'He thinks there's someone on the team who knows more about the murders than they should.'

'Meaning?'

'Fuck knows. Look out, here comes Donnie.' Lorimer nodded to the car park where Donnie was walking across the tarmac towards them, dark shadows lining his face.

'Right, get everyone away. I'm not paying overtime to you two or your bunch of piss-heads. In the office at eight tomorrow.' He turned on his heel and stomped off back towards his car. After he got a few strides away, he turned, his face still set in a grimace. 'And if I find that even one of you has been out on the piss again tonight, you're on bloody traffic duty by lunchtime. Do I make myself clear?'

'As a bell, boss,' said Lorimer, smiling as the DCI stormed

off. They could see Marnie sitting in the passenger seat of his car, her eyes closed.

'Sure I can't tempt you with a pint?' said Niall.

'Not a chance, you bloody animal. Firstly, I feel like absolute shite. Secondly, I have an errand to run. Third, I'd rather not incur the wrath of our dear leader. This job isn't perfect, but it's a sight better than directing traffic in the middle of Edinburgh, particularly when it's brass-monkeys Baltic. C'mon, let's get these boys and girls away to their beds.'

37

MAX WAS SITTING in the office, still ploughing through case notes and phone cell sites, when his phone buzzed. It was Niall.

We've been stood down. Everyone going home from here, just dropped JL off at his car, says he has to see a man about a dog. He'd been making a few calls.

Max looked at his phone seeing that it was almost 7.30 p.m. He read out the content of the message.

'Moving now, then?' said Ross.

'Yep, standby for movement, anything on his phones, Norma?' said Max.

'Not on the two numbers I have for him.'

'Making calls, and yet nothing on his call data, so he has a burner?' said Ross

'Sounds like it. Door unlocked and opening now, and he's in the car,' said Janie, looking at the screen on the laptop.

'On his own?' asked Max.

'Looks like it.' Tinny sounds erupted from the speakers. 'Not surprising given his poor taste in music,' she added just as a moody vocalist began to warble. 'Jeepers, Coldplay? What is he, eighty?'

'Mrs Fraser loves Coldplay,' said Ross in a mock-offended voice.

'Case. Rested.'

'Cheeky mare, just because it's not Ukrainian bloody pipe music or whatever it is you listen to,' he added.

'Okay, he's moving. He's south on Duncan Place, pretty sedate from what I can see, about thirty. Now right onto Salamander heading south-east, still thirty, and it's a right onto Duke Street, heading north. He's not going home, is he?'

'Nope, wrong direction, shit,' said Max, standing up, and taking a swig from his coffee mug only to find that it was empty. Max felt that familiar gnawing sensation in his gut. Where the hell was Lorimer going?

'He's picking up speed but not deviating, still heading north.'

Janie kept the descriptions of the route up for about ten minutes: clearly, concisely and accurately, as if it was a surveillance operation and she was in a car behind him.

'Okay, he's passing Goldenacre Playing fields on his nearside and he continues on, same speed, no hurry.'

There was a long pause and the tension in the room almost crackled like static electricity.

Ross eventually broke the impasse. 'Where the hell's the bastard going?'

'This is why we should have a team on him,' said Janie.

'He'd blow out a team in a bloody heartbeat,' said Max.

'Okay, he's turning left, and he's onto Easter Drylaw Drive, and he's stopping. Yep, that's him stationary, and engine off, and thankfully, so is Coldplay. Seatbelt undone. I can't see, but it looks to me like he's sending a text or buggering about with a phone.'

There was a pause of about thirty seconds which was then broken by a single *ping* indicating a message. A deep sigh was audible over the speakers.

'Nothing on the phones we have, definitely a burner,' said Norma.

'Bastard,' said Ross.

'He doesn't look happy,' said Janie. Another pause. 'He's getting out, and he's out.' The door slammed shut and there was a blip as the car was locked.

A thick silence descended over the room at the realisation that John Lorimer was out of the car and out of their control.

'Shit,' Ross said.

38

SHUGGIE WAS DRUNK. Pissed as a fart at eight in the evening. Not good.

In fact, scrub that. He was *really* pissed. He staggered out of the Ferry Boat Bar in Drylaw on the edge of Edinburgh. He hiccupped and belched as he tried to negotiate the door, his head spinning. Stepping onto the pavement, he relished the cold air as it hit his lungs. He shivered and pulled his old pea coat tight around him. Nausea welled up, the result of the shots that he'd been persuaded to neck alongside his usual pints of heavy. A lot of his success was down to his conviviality, which, of course, was often accompanied by booze. Alcohol and journalism, particularly his brand of investigative journalism, went hand-in-hand. Particularly when investigating bent cops, politicians, lawyers or anyone in power. If you wanted to get close to the corrupt and loosen their tongues, you needed to be generous with your drinks. This had certainly been the case tonight.

He'd met an ex-stripper who called herself 'Kenzie' even though she was clearly from Russia. She had some information on an MSP that had frequented her establishment for a few years. According to her, he was an unpleasant creep who often went a little further than the 'no touching' rules allowed. When she complained about him being a bit grabby, she got fired by the owner who really wanted the MSP 'looked after'. She was understandably furious now that her main source of income was gone, and she wanted to drop the dime on the pervy politician. She'd been a whole load of fun, but Jesus, could she drink. Added to that she'd persuaded him to partake in her gram of coke and so, unwisely, he'd done a couple of lines in the toilet before coming back to even more beer and shots.

Shuggie doubted her story would be picked up by anyone, being uncorroborated, but he'd had a right laugh of an evening, and he had to admit, he'd hoped 'Kenzie' might take things further. Shuggie was a good journalist, but he was lousy with women. He had been more than a little disappointed when a big, nasty-looking Russian picked her up from the pub after a tense-sounding call.

He was glad that his dingy flat above an unoccupied kebab shop was just fifty yards away, desperate as he was to climb into his bed and sleep off the booze and coke. The street was deserted at this time of night. He was struggling to walk straight as he meandered along the uneven pavement, when a strange noise permeated the alcoholic fog in his brain. He stopped, straining to listen. Had he heard a scratch on metal? Was it a cat or a fox in a bin somewhere nearby? The street was quiet and everything seemed normal, so he shook his head to clear the dizziness and continued his unsteady walk towards his flat, suddenly desperate for a piss.

He wobbled on the front step, struggling for his key. It took three goes to slide the bastard thing into the lock. He opened the flat door which was at the side of a newsagent's and stepped into the pitch-black hallway. He swayed on the spot and then stumbled forward to the steps. Another horrible wave of nausea gripped him.

It was then that Shuggie realised the door had never closed behind him. He'd let go of it, but there had been no reassuring click of the latch engaging. He stopped in his tracks and listened, suddenly too scared to turn around. Could he hear someone breathing in the dark hallway?

He reached for the light switch, missing it several times before the single, unshaded bulb burst into life, flooding the depressing space in a yellow light. Just as he was about to turn, what felt like a sledgehammer smashed into his back, and there was a crackle of electricity. A wave of agony gripped his whole body. He went stiff as a board, his vision failing as he toppled, like a felled oak and hit the staircase, face-down, with a thump. Everything went black.

39

'YOU REALLY OUGHT to be more careful, Shuggie,' I said, watching him with amusement as he gasped on the floor like a beached fish. 'You've made it easy for me, which is a shame, because I like a challenge.' This bit is fun.

He slid down the grimy staircase, gurgling as he began to rouse, gasping for air as he let out a low, guttural moan. I pulled the trigger again and he stiffened as the two probes that were buried in his coat conducted the electricity into his muscles – the scream unable to leave his body. His face was locked tight, and a thin, strangled cry finally left his mouth.

I released the trigger and he began to relax. He retched violently, probably a mix of the taser and the alcohol he'd been consuming. A gush of liquid escaped from his mouth and he spat and coughed. The stink filled the hallway, but I barely noticed it.

I grabbed his feet with my gloved hands and pulled him down the stairs, his head bumping rhythmically on the stained carpet. I grabbed his shoulder and turned him onto his back. He opened his eyes and looked at me, wide with fear, as he vomited again. I smiled and shocked him once more. His limbs stiffened, and his back muscles fused, trapping him like a tortoise, unable to move, and unable to spit the vomit from his mouth as the muscles in his neck spasmed, and prevented him from swallowing. I imagined the acidic liquid travelling into his lungs, his diaphragm choked with electricity. The taser crackled, keeping his body in a state of paralysis.

I chuckled, looking at the panic in his eyes, aware even through the fug of blinding agony and intoxication that you knew. You knew your time was coming.

Death was approaching. I saw it in his eyes.

I released the trigger, and he slumped, his muscles exhausted and spent, his brain scrambled. I know what electricity does to a human body. He managed to cough, but it was too late. Vomit had already hit his lungs, clogging his trachea, and his chest was heaving in the desperate, if forlorn, search for air.

I pulled the trigger again. He locked up with a strangled, wet gurgle, as the amperage totally overwhelmed his synapses, and all resistance vanished.

I released the charge, but he didn't move. There was just a wet, raspy rattle from the back of his throat.

This is what I had come to see. This was the moment. The fascination. Right there.

Being alive is dull, being dead is tedious.

The transition is what counts. Watching him die made me feel more alive than I could ever describe to anyone.

His eyes were wide open, the light was still there, but it was fading fast. I could almost see the lack of oxygen hitting his brain. It wouldn't last long, only a few more seconds, the vomit in his lungs and trachea made sure of that. Hypoxia awaited, soon to be followed by death.

Then it happened, the final gasp. His eyes moved from panic and fear, to confusion, and then to nothing.

Flat and empty. Just dead, now. Nothing more than a pile of skin, muscle and organs, already beginning to break down and decay.

I let out a sigh and stood up, already moving onto the next thing in my busy schedule.

Now that the fun was over, the real work started. I couldn't make it too easy for the investigation team. They'd suspect foul play, but really, I knew that the PM would just find that Shuggie died, whilst drunk after choking on his own vomit. How fortuitous that he had indulged so heavily and vomited so copiously. I now didn't need to inject him with the insulin that I had in my pocket. He died because of his poor choices, that's what they'll say. The drunkard journalist.

I pushed his dead weight onto his side, and a quick tug on each of the barbs pulled them free. I suspect that they hadn't even touched his skin, so any marks would be barely visible. I removed the cartridge from the taser and slotted a fresh one in place, just in case. I wound the wires up and tucked them in my pocket. I let him fall onto his back and clicked off the light in the hallway. I reached into my pocket, and switched on my torch. Flecks of white fluoresced bright purple in the inky darkness as the ultraviolet light hit the small tags – like disco lights – in that putrid space

I knew I'd get them all, as there was no rush now. I knew that he lived alone and that his neighbour the other side of the wall was drunk, slumped in front of the TV.

I'd done my research.

I began to pick up the AFIDs, counting each one as I went, and tucked them into a small plastic tub.

I didn't look at him any longer, he was nothing more than a blank slate to me now. Death is interesting only if the life remains. Once the light goes out, the rush of adrenaline goes as quickly as it arrived.

I felt like we were so close tonight, me and Shuggie. Maybe next time.

40

'STANDBY, STANDBY. HE'S back. In the car, door shut, seatbelt on and engine starting,' Janie blurted.

'How long was that?' said Max, breathing a sigh of relief which was matched by everyone else.

'Twenty-two minutes,' said Norma.

There was a pause, the only noise in the room the tinny hum of the Audi's engine through the speakers on Janie's laptop.

'What's he doing?'

'Staring into space.'

'No more. No more,' came the voice over the speakers, barely a whisper.

'Ah, fucking hell. What's the bastard done?' said Ross, rubbing his temples, his eyes wide.

'In twenty-two minutes? Any known links around here?'

'Not that I know of,' said Norma.

'Right, he's woken up, into gear and he's moving off, back the way he came. Speed thirty again. He's right onto Ferry Road and retracing his route.'

'Going home?' said Ross.

'I bloody hope so.'

'Should have had a surveillance team,' said Ross, shaking his head, worry etched on his lined brow.

'Too late for that now.'

'Okay, he's picking up speed, completely retracing his previous route.'

Janie kept the commentary up, simple and clear, but the rest of the team was barely listening now. They all knew it. He was going home.

There were no further deviations on the half-hour journey, and soon he was pulling up in Portobello.

'Okay, that's him parked up by his block of flats. Shame we can't get on his front door, but we have his car under control.'

'Good work. We're all set to go through the door at 4 a.m. OSU are meeting us there – they have building plans and have already recce'd the place, so we leave the rapid entry to them. How do you all feel about sloping off for a few hours' shut-eye?' said Ross.

'I don't think I want to,' said Max.

'Why? We have him under control?'

'We don't really. What if he moves suddenly? We have his car, but that's not enough if he decides to go and kill someone. We'd be too late. We can't ask anyone else to do it, we can't be sure it wouldn't leak. I'll go and park up nearby and be ready to follow if he moves. At least then if anything happens, I'll be able to intervene. It's nearly ten, now. A few more hours won't make any difference.'

'You sure?' said Ross.

'Yep. I can kip once he's nicked, I take it we'll be handing this over to PSD when he's in custody, anyway?'

'You'd be right. Chief has a small team of trusted individuals ready to go, even though they've been kept in the dark. Once he's safely in custody, we hand everything over and then disappear as normal, free to fight another day.'

'Well, I'm staying on, then. I'll park up with a view of the block's communal entrance. If he leaves, we'll see him, even if he doesn't use his car,' said Max.

'I'll join you, at least we can take turns with the eyeball,' said Janie.

'On one condition,' said Max.

'What?'

'None of your shite music.'

41

JOHN LORIMER LET himself into his flat and threw his rucksack on the leather sofa. He made straight for the fridge and pulled out a beer. Twisting off the cap, he took a long pull on the cold lager, feeling it calm his raw throat. His hands trembled, as he took another swig.

He was still hungover, but that wasn't the cause of his splitting headache and his shaking hand. It always happened when he was stressed like this. When things happened.

Sometimes there was euphoria, sometimes there was a sense of having done right. Macallan, Wilson, Paterson and even Grigor had deserved to die. They were scum, and why the fuck should they have been allowed to keep breathing in and out when his Iona was in the ground? His eyes flicked up to the picture of his beautiful, smiling wife.

They'd all deserved to die. It was justice. He'd dispensed justice when the courts and the system had failed.

But tonight had been different.

Lorimer looked at his hands, big, meaty, and calloused, his stomach churning with a mix of fear and loathing.

He drank his beer in one swig and set it back down on

the granite work surface. He opened the kitchen cupboard and pulled out a bottle, grabbed a glass from the drainer and poured a big slug of the pale, straw-coloured Port Charlotte whisky. He downed it in one, relishing the peaty, smoky bite of the raw spirit. He immediately poured again and repeated the action.

The hit of the neat spirit was almost immediate. His eyes watered as he stared at his reflection in the polished granite.

This had to stop.

'No more,' he said, pouring another measure of whisky.

42

MAX CLIMBED BACK into the passenger seat of the Volvo, handing a coffee to Janie.

'Nice, thanks. Any sweeties?' she said hopefully.

Max threw a packet of chocolate buttons into her lap.

'Even nicer. Glad I came now. Anything?'

They were parked on the drive of a house clearly undergoing major renovations, about thirty metres from the communal front entrance of the block of flats. It was a perfect spot, not being overlooked by anyone, and well back from the main road in the dark shadows. They had a clear view of the front door, and Lorimer's car in one of the allocated bays to the front of the building.

'His place is at the back of the block – literally no chance of getting a view of it from anywhere with it backing onto the railway line. His light is out now, so I assume he's hit the hay,' said Max, sipping the scalding coffee he'd just bought from a twenty-four-hour garage.

'Well, it's almost one, so I'm not that surprised. Just three hours before he gets his wake-up call by the team with the big red key,' said Janie, referring to the red-painted enforcer ram used for breaching doors.

'An unpleasant way to wake up. I hope to God there's an extra nugget in the flat. All we have right now is the word of a disgruntled former colleague and the GPS on the car. We still haven't put him in the car at the relevant times.'

'I'm bothered by that.'

'Me too. Why no ANPR activations? That's a long way to go without hitting some.'

'Has to be false plates,' said Janie, throwing some chocolate buttons into her mouth.

'Aye, but where are they? Not in the car, that's for sure.'

'In the flat, I hope. He's knackered if they are.'

'Same with the taser.'

'Do you wonder why?'

'What?'

'Why he does it?'

'I'm no psychologist, but the mix of his wife dying in such terrible circumstances, and the injustice with Macallan could have tipped him over. Loss and grief can do that to some people.'

'Didn't happen to us, though, did it? We both lost people in horrible circumstances.'

Max just shrugged and sipped his coffee.

'How about Gus?' said Janie.

'How'd you mean?'

'Is he at any risk?'

'I can't see why. He left a while ago, and he's living a whole new life,' said Max.

'Have you heard from him?'

'No. I'm not sure I trust him, completely. Do you?'

'I don't know, but we need to see him again. He's part of

this.' Janie sipped her coffee. 'Jesus, have they heated this by nuclear fusion or something?'

'Not sure what I think – this is all new,' said Max. 'This isn't corruption, is it? This is something wholly different.'

'Noble cause corruption?'

'No, it's not even that, is it?'

'Well, what is it, then?'

'It's Lorimer playing God. Simple as that. He thinks he's above everyone else and can make life-and-death decisions. He thinks he's judge, jury and executioner, and we have to stop the bastard, now.'

43

THE APPROACH WAS the same as always in raids like this.

Slow, quiet and deliberate.

Until the door went in, that is. Then it was noise, shouting and overwhelming force.

The OSU officers were all dressed in flame-proof overalls, body armour, Kevlar gloves and NATO public-order helmets with the visors down. The lead officer approached the communal door in a white helmet. He reached up to a slot on the intercom panel and jammed in a fire brigade access key. A quick twist and the door mechanism clicked. He eased it open and nodded.

They advanced in total silence, all eight of them moving carefully and deliberately up the stairs, to the first floor. Another nod, and the internal door was noiselessly eased open. The team filed along, halting four each side of Lorimer's stout-looking wooden door, with the brass number 7 in the middle. Max, Ross and Janie kept well back, but with a view of the team. Only once the OSU had gained entry would Ross, Max and Janie advance.

The team leader raised a thumb at them, and Max nodded.

He counted down from five with his fingers.

The door exploded inwards with the enormous kinetic energy meted out as the enforcer ram smashed into its central lock. The officer wielding it immediately stepped to one side to allow the remaining seven officers to rush in, screaming shouts of 'Police officers, stay where you are!'

The officer with the ram dropped it and rushed in to join the fray. Continuous screams and shouts of 'Police, stay where you are!' echoed from the open door, as the officers used shock and awe – standard procedure to overwhelm any occupants.

Then the noises stopped dead, as if a switch had been flicked, only to be replaced with an all-encompassing silence that was almost as deafening as the shouts and crashes of the team.

The team leader appeared, removing his white helmet to reveal a deathly pale face. He nodded at Ross.

'You'd best see this,' he said, a slight tremble in his voice, as the other team members began to file out, all removing helmets, or flipping up visors as they did, shock written on each of their faces. 'Back to the van, guys, and wait there. No one's going anywhere for a while,' he added.

Max, Janie and Ross all looked at each other in turn.

'What is it, Joe?

'Best see for yourself.'

They knew what they were going to find.

44

Alfa-Secure

JOHN LORIMER WAS weak.

He'd outlasted his usefulness.

45

LORIMER'S FLAT WAS immaculate.

The sink was clear of dishes, the surfaces gleamed, as if the whole open-plan space had been professionally cleaned in preparation for something.

His laptop lay open on the breakfast bar, the screen blank.

Two keys on a Hibernian FC fob sat neatly on the worktop next to three mobile phones. One an iPhone, one a Samsung, and one a cheap-looking Nokia. The Nokia screamed 'burner phone'.

'Let's suit up first,' said Max.

Ross nodded and they all went back out into the corridor to don white forensic suits, overshoes and nitrile gloves. Masks were secured over faces and hoods pulled up.

'Come on, let's get this fucking over with. We'll need the on-call SIO down here, and the chief will want a full briefing, so we best be able to give one. Janie, can you have a very quick visual scan of each room, just to make sure there isn't something that requires an urgent action.'

'Sure thing,' said Janie, moving into the flat.

'Come on, Max. Let's go, heads round the doors only, yeah?'

They knew John Lorimer was dead before they even got to the bathroom. Its door was wide open, the fresh, coppery smell of blood permeating the hallway.

John Lorimer's massive form was slumped on the toilet, his legs stretched out in front of him. His white towelling robe had fallen open, revealing white boxers.

Max assumed that the garments were once white, but now they were both saturated in dark, congealing blood. There was a long, deep gash on his left wrist, and a further smaller but equally deep hole at the top of his thigh, close to his groin. Lorimer's skin was almost as white as the towelling dressing gown had once been.

Blood.

There was just so much fucking blood.

The bathroom looked like an abattoir, with arterial spray up the walls, on the ceiling, covering the mirror. There was an old-fashioned razor blade lying in an enormous black puddle on the floor, glossy and mirror-like. It was a scene of utter horror.

A word popped into Max's mind, almost from nowhere.

Exsanguination. Noun. The action of draining a person of blood.

Lorimer's eyes were open wide, clouded and empty, his face frozen in a mask of shock.

'We don't need to go in any further,' said Ross, his own face sombre.

'Suicide?' said Max, his voice quiet, feeling the familiar, but unwelcome darkness starting to bubble in the recesses of his mind. He breathed slowly, quietly and evenly, holding each intake for five seconds.

'Has to be. He died in here, and no one else was in here when he did. They'd have been drenched in the stuff. No way can that be cleaned up. The door was locked tight and keys on the side.'

'No one checked for signs of life?' said Max, looking at the blood on the floor and noting the absence of footprints.

'Joe's an old campaigner. He could see from six feet that this bugger breathed his last some time ago. Scene's intact. Fucking hell, this is a shit situation, the press will go fucking ballistic. Serial killer cop commits suicide whilst cops plan arrest.'

'It's too convenient.'

'Is it? This bastard killed a number of people in cold blood on some daft quest for justice. He knew the net was closing. It seems almost likely that he'd want to finish himself before we got him. I mean, what did he have to live for, eh?'

'It feels staged to me.'

'Aye, well. Not our problem anymore. The MITs will have to sort out this pile of shite. Our suspect is dead at his own hand. We found the killer on MIT 6, just a couple of hours too late, that's all. Come on. Let's get this scene sealed and a log started.'

Ross moved away from the door back into the kitchen, his steps weary, his shoulders hunched.

Max looked again at the slumped corpse of John Lorimer, his hand trailing down by his side, almost touching the tiled, blood-drenched floor. Max focused on the razor blade. It was the type found in old-fashioned safety razors. The type he remembered his father using, years ago.

Staged. Too perfect.

Max looked at the minimalist open shelving unit that was

lined with toiletries, mouthwash, an electric toothbrush, toothpaste and a modern Gillette Mach 3 razor that was sitting on a new box of blades. All the items were covered with fat drops of blood that clung, thick and glossy. The harsh spotlights shone on the wickedly sharp triple-edged razor blades. Something tickled at Max's subconscious.

'Max.' Janie's voice pierced his reverie.

Max took a last look, his eyes moving between the razor barely visible in the pool of dark blood and the Gillette on the shelf.

'Yeah?' he said, quietly.

'Check this out.'

Max turned back into the kitchen. Janie had the top of a dark rucksack open that was on the large leather sofa.

'What?'

'Look inside.'

Max moved closer and peered into the dark recess of the bag. Already knowing what he was going to see.

'Straight-edged, razor-sharp, bloodstained. We're missing the weapon for Paterson. Want to bet this is it?'

'I'm not taking that bet. This is staged. This isn't right, guys.'

'Looks just like a suicide to me, Max.'

'Aye. It does. Far too much like a suicide. As if someone googled what a suicide scene looks like and recreated it. Door locked, decent locks, as well. Keys on side, burner phone. No bloody note, though, I see.'

'Could be on the laptop. In fact, I bet it is.'

'Whatever, it's the MIT's job now. We're done here, unless the chief has other ideas,' said Ross.

'There's someone else,' said Max.

'How?'

'Keys left for us to find. Phones left for us to find. I'm putting next month's wages that the burner phone on the counter is cell-sited up at Dunnet Head and Ravelston. In fact, I'll go further, I'll bet it matches the journey taken by Lorimer's Audi, and I'm going to dazzle you all with my foresight now.' Max paused.

'Go on, then,' said Ross, his face reddening with anger.

'I'll give you even odds that we'll find even more evidence in this bloody flat, somewhere. Just the final piece of the puzzle to let everyone be absolutely sure that John Lorimer was the serial killer cop who killed himself. All too bloody convenient and I'm not buying it for a second.'

'Wait a minute. Are you saying Lorimer was innocent?' said Janie.

'No, I'm not saying that at all. I think Lorimer has been party to these murders, but I don't think he did them on his own.'

'What are you saying, then?' said Ross.

'Lorimer wasn't alone. There's another killer and you know what's even worse?'

'What?'

'I think they killed Lorimer.'

46

ROSS EMITTED A DEEP, depressed sigh.

This was bad. This was very bad, and for once, he had no idea what to do. They wouldn't be investigating this much more, that seemed obvious. There was going to be a big debrief here, and he needed to be ready with the answers and wasn't sure he had them all.

He had to concede that his friend did have a point – it was too easy and far too convenient. Feelings didn't matter, though. Evidence was what mattered and, as it stood, this looked just like a suicide. He could hardly argue against that conclusion by saying, 'It can't be suicide, it looks far too much like suicide.'

Within an hour Lorimer's flat had been a hive of activity. The flat had one route in or out, so they quickly secured the scene by stationing a young cop on the door with a log. Blue-and-white tape was placed across the entrance, just to reinforce what they had here.

Not just a supposed suicide, but potentially the death of a serial killer cop.

There was a different sort of tension in the air and it told in the faces of the cops attending. The duty inspector went pale when Ross explained what they had and what was required of him. No cop wanted involvement in a situation like this that could hang around anyone ambitious like a bad smell.

Ross's phone buzzed as they all stood in the corridor outside the flat. He looked at the display and raised his eyebrows at Max. 'It's the chief,' he said. 'Morning, sir.'

'Ross, I don't like what I'm hearing. DCC McVeigh has just been on with a message from Miles Wakefield. Can I hear it from you?' Chief Constable Chris Macdonald said, without preamble.

Ross told him. He told him everything.

'Shit. So, on the face of it, a clear suicide?'

'On the face of it, yes.'

'I'm sensing something in your voice.'

'Max isn't happy.'

'Why?'

'He thinks it looks staged. He reckons it's too perfect. Keys on the side, mysterious burner phone with it and a bag with what looks like a murder weapon in it. The place hasn't been fully searched but I've a feeling that everything found will point to the fact that Lorimer is guilty of the murders of Grigor and Paterson.'

'What hard evidence is there?'

'Well, we had the GPS on the car, which is really damning, we now have a burner phone to work on, and of course, a bloodstained knife.'

'I assume that we're thinking it's the murder weapon for Paterson?'

'That's what we're clearly supposed to think.'

'You don't sound convinced?'

'You know, boss, if I was the SIO turning up on scene now to take over, I'd peg this as a suicide, but Max has me thinking.'

'I'm listening.'

'It really is too easy. Why would an experienced cop keep a murder weapon? Why set it all out like that for us?'

Macdonald was silent for a moment. 'Right, here's what I want. A whole new team is coming out to deal with the scene and I want every bloody resource used to go over his flat millimetre by millimetre. If there's anything to suggest that anyone else is involved, I want it found.'

'Fine. Who's coming?'

'Hughie Johnson. He's scrambling a team now and he'll be along soon. Hand the whole thing over to him – lock, stock, the whole lot – then get your guys out of there and to the office. We'll reconvene once they've broken the back of the scene processing. If I even have the merest trace of a doubt that this is a suicide, I want you guys on it, okay?'

'Fine. We still have an asset within MIT 6.'

'Which is why I still want you watching and listening. Any press there?'

'Nothing.'

'Not even Shuggie? Surely he's heard about it.'

'Now you come to mention it, no. I'd have expected something by now. He obviously has a source, and this is far too juicy for him not to be sniffing around.'

'Well, let's keep it away from all of them for as long as we can. I'm going to have to brief them later, but I really want the full facts. This is going to be so bloody damaging.'

'Aye. Of course, sir.'

'I have to go. I'm going to have to refer this to the Police

Investigation Review Commissioner, as well. Shit, last thing I need. Speak later.' He hung up.

'Chief okay?' said Max.

'Worried, I'd say. This is bloody dynamite. Have you heard anything from Shuggie?'

'No, why?'

'I can't believe he isn't sniffing about with all his sources. This is too big. Do you know where he stays?'

Max shook his head.

Ross picked his phone out of his pocket and dialled, listening to the tone, voicemail kicked in. '*Hey, it's Shuggie. Leave a message.*'

Ross frowned. 'He always picks up. Always.' He dialled again. Same result.

'Janie, can you call up control and get an address for Shuggie?' He stared at his handset.

Janie nodded and dialled.

Ross muttered to himself, anxiety beginning to nip. Then it hit him.

Drylaw. His meeting with Shuggie in a pub a few months ago in Drylaw. His mind flared at the thought of Lorimer's twenty-two-minute stop in that neighbourhood.

'Janie, please don't tell me he lives in Drylaw?' said Ross.

'Aye, he does.' She read out an address, pausing as she got to the postcode. 'Shite, that's where Lorimer paused last night before coming home.'

'We need to get there. Now.'

47

MAX, JANIE AND Ross passed the Ferry Boat Pub and pulled up in the Volvo outside the small parade of shops in Drylaw.

'I met Shuggie in that pub, once for a chat, like. It only just occurred to me when he didn't answer the phone. Fuck, I should have called it when Lorimer parked up a street away from here. Fuck, fuck, fuck,' said Ross.

'His place is there, flat above the kebab shop,' said Janie.

'Any CCTV?'

'Nothing obvious. Although there may be as there's shops about.'

'Come on, let's go.'

The three of them got out of the car and went to the battered-looking wooden door. There was no number, no bell, no cameras. Just a rundown, neglected flat above an abandoned kebab shop. The shop window was plastered with peeling posters of local bands and it was clear that it hadn't been open for business for some time.

Ross banged on the door with a clubbed fist and tried the lock. It was shut tight, but only on a single Yale. Janie bent down, pushed open the letterbox and peered inside.

'Pitch black.' She gagged, put a hand to her mouth. 'Shit, it stinks.'

'What of?'

'Piss, booze, shite and puke.'

Janie produced her phone and activated the torch. She held it up and shone it inside.

There was a long, agonising pause.

'Oh, Jesus. Get the door open, now. Someone's collapsed on the floor.' She stood up, and a split second later, Max's right foot shot out and the door splintered inwards. The early morning light flooded the dingy hallway and staircase. The smell hit them like a wave.

Shuggie Gibson lay on his back, his vomit-covered face the colour of bread dough, eyes open, but devoid of even a vestige of life.

They all stood in total silence, looking at the scene, the tension in that dingy hall so thick that even Lorimer's razor couldn't have cut it. Ross held up his hand, covering his mouth and nose, his face suddenly pale.

'We should have stopped him. We should have arrested Lorimer yesterday. Fuck, fuck, fuck,' muttered Ross.

'No visible injury. Looks like he choked on his own vomit. How did Lorimer manage this in the twenty-two minutes he was gone? It's a solid five-minute walk to get here from where he parked his car,' said Max.

'Eight minutes, to be precise,' said Janie, looking at her phone's map application.

'Not enough time. No chance. He can't park his car, walk all the way here, at the exact moment Shuggie arrives home, murder him by some mysterious means, and then walk back.

No way. He wasn't even out of breath when he got into the car.'

Ross just stared, his eyes full of sorrow, at the small figure of Shuggie. He was lying on his back, his arms stretched out by his sides, keys still clutched in his right hand. His head was tipped backwards and his mouth full of thin, viscous vomit.

'Poor Shug. He was a decent man. I'll call it in.' He swivelled on his heel and walked out into the street.

Max continued to stare at the body, his mind whirling, and the dark clouds forming, as he tried to organise his thoughts.

'All wrong.'

'Aye, I don't like it, but it's not going to be our problem much longer. You know what they're like. They'll want it wrapped up all neat, like.'

'Shuggie was murdered, Lorimer was murdered and they were both killed to protect whoever's behind all these fucking revenge killings. They've been careful and they know how to stage a scene. Shuggie dying from inhaling vomit, and Lorimer killing himself. They know what we look for, and they've given it to us. The MIT team will swallow it hook, line and sinker, and they'll move onto the next murder.'

Ross appeared in the doorway. 'Right, team's on the way. Get out of there, you two. We'll keep it secure until CSIs arrive.'

They both backed out of the hallway, grateful to be in the fresher air of an Edinburgh morning. Max eased the door closed and they stood in silence for a long moment.

'Will we be taken off this?' asked Janie after a full minute had passed.

'Maybe. Depends on the scene exams and the post-mortems, I guess.'

'We have to stay on it. We've found what the killer wanted us to find.'

'Aye, well, that's as maybe, but we have to follow the evidence, work the clues. We go where the evidence is.'

The street was getting a little busier, with the early morning commuters beginning to make an appearance, and their presence on a splintered door was causing a little attention.

A man paused, a sheaf of newspapers under his arm. He was broad and fat, with a whiskered face and rheumy eyes full of concern.

'Is Shuggie okay?' he asked in a thick, heavy accent.

'You know Shuggie?' said Janie.

'Aye. You the polis?' His broad face screwed up with suspicion.

Janie held out her warrant card, and he squinted down at it.

'Aye, I'm the landlord of the Ferry Boat. He was in last night. He's a regular. A good lad is Shug.'

'What time did he leave?'

'About eight, I guess. He was pretty blootered, mind. Is he okay?'

Janie looked at Max and Ross. 'Was he alone?'

'Well, he'd been with a lassie. A right bonnie bird, as well, Russian by her accent. You know the type, blonde, short skirt, looked a bit like a stripper, ken?'

'Did they leave together?'

'Nah, she was picked up by a big dangerous-looking Russian bastard. Shug meets loads of folk in the bar, almost his office, ya ken? I hope he's all right.'

'What's your name, pal?' asked Ross.

'Bobby.'

'Well, someone'll come to see you in a while. We're just sorting a few things out and once we know we'll be along.'

Bobby nodded and went on his way.

'Timing's work, but he was alone and pished, which is borne out by the smell of booze in there. I don't like the sound of a big Russian. What d'you reckon?' said Ross.

Max said nothing. He stared at his feet, the cogs not connecting in his sleep-deprived mind. He was missing something.

'Okay, if Shuggie has been murdered, what's the motive?' he said after a pause.

'He knew too much? He was asking too many questions?' said Janie.

'This could be a misadventure death, couldn't it? Gets blootered, falls and chokes on vomit. It's hardly an uncommon way to die,' said Ross.

Then Max realised what had been bothering him. It hit him like a punch from a heavyweight.

Gus Fraser. He reached for his phone and dialled, feeling his heart beating in his mouth.

The phone went straight to voicemail.

'Shit,' said Max, redialling.

'What is it?' said Janie.

'Gus Fraser. He told Shuggie all this. He was his source. If our killer knew this then he's at risk. We have to warn him.'

The phone went to voicemail again.

'Phone's off,' said Max.

'I'll make the call to the locals, get him checked on.' Ross dialled and stepped away, his phone clamped to his ear.

'You think Gus is at risk?'

'I hope not, but he was once a part of this. He knows

something, and if the killer is being careful, maybe they'll want to close that risk down. Shit, why didn't I think of this earlier?' said Max.

'We had no idea. How could we?'

Ross turned to face them, his expression betraying what he was feeling.

'Just spoken to the control room. They set up a message to call on Gus, but there's something else,' he said.

'What?'

'He didn't come home from work last night. His wife has reported him missing.'

48

CSM JIMMY DUGGAN pulled his surgical mask down and lowered the hood on his forensic oversuit. He stepped back into the corridor outside and took a deep breath. It had been a painstaking initial survey, getting the step plates in place and having the first sets of photographs taken.

'Early impression?' said DCI Hughie Johnson, standing, similarly attired, an A4 hardbacked book in his gloved hand.

'Well, I'd not want to stake my mortgage on it, but certainly suicide seems the most likely. Pathologist has already been. Her view is the wrist looks like a classic hesitancy cut, before he plucked up the courage to go for the leg. No trace of any external interferences in the bloodstains, and the arterial spurts seem to be uninterrupted. I'd wager there was no one else in the bathroom when the cuts were opened. If they were, they'd have been bloody covered and there's no way that it wouldn't be reflected in the rest of the flat. We'll luminol it once we're done, but there's no evidence of heavy cleaning; in fact, the floor has a tiny bit of dust.'

Hughie pursed his lips in thought.

'I'm told that the door was secure and double-locked and that the keys were on the breakfast bar?'

'Yes. Along with a burner phone. You seen the knife in the bag?'

'I have. Best get it to the lab, particularly with the blood as it is. I won't even remove it from the bag, as there'll be transferred staining inside. I'm assuming we're considering this as a possible murder weapon for Paterson?'

'Seems so.'

'It's straight-edged, looks bastard sharp, so it's not beyond the realms of possibility. Elsa will have a clearer view. What's the objective here, Hughie?'

'Number one. Any reason to believe this isn't a suicide. Also, any evidence that someone else was in here at the relevant times.'

'Fine. It'll take a good while with all this claret in the bathroom. We'll want a pattern analyst here. How's the forensic budget on this job?'

'As much as you need. Chief himself is watching closely on this one. Serial killer cop is going to drive the press bloody mad.'

'Fine. I'll make some calls and get some other staff here. I see there's a computer as well. Are you gonna deal with that?'

'Aye. I've a man waiting to receive it for a speedy imaging, just in case he wrote a note or confession on it.'

'Fair enough. We're gonna be here a while. Are you going to stay?'

'No. Lots to do. I'll leave you with a productions officer and a uniform for the security.'

'I hear there's another scene close by. We're thin on resources, but I have some people on standby and I'm borrowing and begging from wherever I can.'

'Aye, Shuggie Gibson has been found dead by Ross Fraser and his team, close to where Lorimer was last night in Drylaw. Early indications are that he was pished and choked on his sick.'

'Shite, that's a bit of a coincidence. Hasn't he been doorstepping cops?'

'He has, aye. He confronted Donnie Watson at Ravelston, and he was also at Leith a couple of days ago, accusing them of all sorts. There's another team going to deal with the scene, we don't want any cross-contamination, do we?'

'Nope. We'll take all the usual precautions. Productions from the other scene can go to Drylaw Mains, and everything from here will go to Leith. I'll make sure none of my people will work both addresses until we're sorted, okay?'

'Perfect. Jimmy, you know why I've been brought in, right?'

'Aye. MIT 6 have a bad smell about them, and it looks like the poor, late Detective Sergeant Lorimer was some kind of vigilante. Press dynamite. I feel bad for Donnie, though. He's a good cop, and he's a man under pressure. I'm not sure he's coping well.'

'The chief wants nothing left to chance. Get this wrong, Jimmy, and we're all screwed. We have to conclusively prove that Lorimer killed Paterson and Grigor, and rule in or out any involvement in Shuggie's death. This is going to be on the front of every newspaper in the bloody country.'

49

MAX AND JANIE had barely spoken on the journey up the A9. Firstly, because there was just too much tension and worry about what had happened to Gus, but mainly because the decision had been taken to travel the 150 plus miles as quickly as possible. The weather was horrendous, with driving rain lashing down, the wipers barely able to cope as they crossed the Cairngorms.

Max couldn't be sure of the average speed that Janie had driven the big, powerful Volvo up through Edinburgh and onto the A9, but he was sure that Ross would have a lot of work to do, writing off the speeding tickets that they were collecting.

As always, Max was in awe of Janie's proficiency behind the wheel, even with the typically Scottish weather. She propelled the big car at some tremendous speeds, but somehow never seemed to be rushed, and even managed a big yawn, as she overtook a lorry at speeds well in excess of 100 mph, the covert blue lights flashing and siren wailing. She was the picture of unhurried calm as the car hit 130 mph on the final approach to Inverness, just two hours after leaving Edinburgh.

'Nice work, you shaved off ninety minutes, although I reckon

I could have lost a few more,' said Max as she slowed on the approach to the outskirts of Inverness.

'Yeah, right. We'd still be waiting to pull onto the A9. Bloody drive like my gran. Where d'you want to go?'

'His home. His wife's there. It's not far from here.'

Max directed Janie to a pleasant, leafy suburb on the opposite side of the river from the crazy golf course. They approached an attractive riverside villa, fronted by a tall rhododendron hedge and a well-cared-for garden. Janie swung the Volvo onto the drive alongside a marked police car.

'Nice place,' said Janie, yawning as she unbuckled her seatbelt.

'Aye. Looks like crazy golf is a lucrative business.'

A young female officer opened the door as they approached.

'DS Craigie?' She nodded at them. Her name badge announced that she was Constable James.

'That's me, this is Janie Calder. How's the wife?'

'Step inside, the weather's really turned,' she said, looking beyond them at the driving rain bouncing off the paved drive. 'She's scared, I'd say. He's never done this before. He's well respected around here, I know him pretty well, and he's always good for a complimentary tea.'

'How long's he been gone, PC James?'

'Brenda, please. He didn't come home from work. The golf course and coffee stall were all closed and locked up as normal, but he didn't come home.'

'Car?'

'Aye, a Mitsubishi 4x4, that's gone as well.' She read out the registration which Max noted.

'Any phone work been done?'

'Waiting for it, but his phone hasn't been on since the wife started trying, about nine last night. I think someone called Norma at your office has taken the further work.'

'Aye, that's grand, thanks. We'll handle that. How about CCTV?'

'Checked it at the course. Nothing abnormal, he just closed up at about nine. He was looking at his phone, though, and he didn't look happy.'

'Where's the footage?'

'They've opened up the course. One of the staff members showed it to us on the system. They'll be there now if you want to look, or it'll have to wait until later when we can get the disc back to the nick.'

'It's fine, we'll go and take a look.'

They walked down the tiled hallway and into a large, open-plan kitchen. Gus Fraser's wife was sitting at the table in a pink tracksuit. Her dark hair was tied up in a ponytail, her face puffy and blotching, her eyes red.

'Sarah, this is DS Craigie, who's assisting on this,' said Brenda.

Sarah turned to look at Max, her lips curling up in a smile that didn't reach her eyes.

'Hi, Sarah. How out of character is this?'

'He's never disappeared before. He had some issues in the police, but he's been really happy since we took over the course. Well, until a couple of days ago.' She paused to wipe at her eyes.

'What happened?'

'He went to work all fine, but when he came back, he was moody. Barely spoke to me and wouldn't tell me what was wrong, other than someone had been to see him and it had brought back bad memories from his police days. I was a bit worried, but just got on with it. We're so busy, what with the business and teenage kids.'

'Any other changes in him?'

'He got really security conscious. Always double- and triple-checking the locks, and he installed one of those doorbells. You know – the ones that send video from your front door to your phone.'

'I do. Did he say anything else, anything at all?'

'Just that he needed some headspace and time to think. He broke down yesterday morning, I couldn't get through to him at all.' The tears welled in her eyes and she dabbed at them with a tissue.

'Look, Sarah, this sounds like he just needed away for a bit. I'm sure he'll be back. We'll have a look about, check the CCTV and Brenda here will keep you abreast of any changes.'

Sarah nodded, sadly, and Max and Janie left the room, followed by Brenda.

'Is that it?' she said.

'Pardon?' said Max.

'I thought you were taking this over, or am I still dealing?' the young cop looked confused.

'You stick with her for a bit. I've a feeling I know where Gus is, but I don't want to raise her hopes.'

'You do?' said Janie.

'Only maybe, worth a punt. Come on, let's check the foot-age.' Max nodded at the slightly put-out Brenda and they got in the car, reversed off the drive and drove away.

It was only a ten-minute drive to the crazy golf course, and

Janie was soon reversing into a parking bay. Thankfully the rain had eased from its previous stair-rod-like state to a much softer hazy drizzle.

'So, are you going to enlighten me?' said Janie, looking at Max as she switched off the engine.

'Let's look at the footage first. Just that thing she said about him needing headspace. A hunch I want to check out.'

They walked through the swirling, misty rain and approached the coffee stall. A white-haired woman nodded at them, her pale, lined face shot through with worry. 'Help you, folks?'

Max produced his warrant card. 'DS Craigie and DC Calder, looking into Gus's whereabouts. Can we see the CCTV?'

'Aye, I'm so worried and I'm so glad you're here. Any leads? I'm Bet, by the way, Gus's mum. I have to say that he's not been himself recently. Come in and I'll show you. Hopefully it's still in the right spot. I'm not good with this camera thing,' she said, fiddling with a computer keyboard.

Max and Janie went to the side and into the small cabin. There was barely enough space for the three of them as Bet brought up the images on the screen. A little adjustment and a freeze frame appeared. Max noted the time on the display. It showed 21.10 hrs.

Gus had paused outside the coffee shack, reaching up for the hatch.

'Spin it on,' said Max.

Bet pressed a key, and the excellent-quality picture came to life. Gus reached up and pulled the hatch down, securing it with a padlock. He then went and locked the side door as well. Suddenly, he reached for his pocket and pulled out a mobile phone, staring at it intently. His demeanour changed almost palpably. His free hand came up and began to scratch frantically at his scalp. He scrubbed at his face; the stress evident. He tucked the phone back in his pocket, and began to pace, his mouth moving as he spoke to himself.

'Wind that back a bit where he looked at his phone,' said Max, reaching for his phone.

Bet did as he asked, pausing it from before he got the phone call. 'Okay, play it again.' He held his phone up to the screen and began to record with his video camera.

Suddenly, Gus's body language changed and became more business-like. Firstly, he returned to the shack and let himself in again. He disappeared inside for a few moments before returning with a thick blue coat and a carrier bag that seemed to be full of bottles and packaged sandwiches. He locked the door again and turned away from the shack and closed the big metal gates, securing them with a padlock and chain. Without a backwards glance he strode over to a big Mitsubishi. He got in, reversed out and was gone.

Max stared at the screen, his face blank.

'Thanks, Bet. We'll keep you informed via Sarah, okay?'

'Promise me you'll find him? He's had some problems, but he's a good man, you know.' She clutched at Max's forearm, her eyes brimming with tears.

'I promise we'll do everything we can, Bet.'

'I know you will. Now cut along, you'll not find him here.'

Max nodded and they left, getting back into the car.

'Where are we going, Craigie?' asked Janie.

'I think I know where he is.'

50

'SO WHERE, MR ESP?'

'Black Isle. I want to drop in on Elspeth very quickly and then on to somewhere else. Gus mentioned it, and I'm thinking he may have gone there.'

'If I was your auntie, I'd be offended if the only time you visit is for some lip reading.'

'She'll be grand about it.'

'I'd be pretty pissed off if I was her,' said Janie as she headed towards the Kessock Bridge.

Within twenty minutes they were pulling up outside Elspeth's tiny fisherman's cottage in the pretty seaside village of Avoch.

'Nice wee place is Avoch,' said Janie.

'Careful no one hears you say that, pal. You'll get nowhere. It's pronounced "Och",' said Max.

'Really, a silent "Av"?'

'Really. Locals would piss themselves if they heard you.'

'Highlanders are weird.'

'Not so much as you bloody Sassenachs,' countered Max.

They went around to the back of the house and stood beside the wide-open back door.

'Still no sense of security from Auntie E, then?'

'Nope.'

'Not even after Tam Hardie tried to kill you and her in there,' said Janie, referring to an incident in the recent past.

'She views that as a reason to not be security conscious. Her fatalism is something to behold. Her opinion is that the chances of anything happening at her place is zero now that something bad has actually happened.'

'She probably has a point.'

As they were on the path, the small compact figure of Elspeth appeared from inside the property, a watering can in her gardening-gloved hand. Despite the rain, she was wearing a floral dress, a straw hat and Wellington boots. Her face broke into a wide beaming smile as she saw Max and Janie.

'Max, darling, you never said?' She hugged him.

'Just passing, Auntie Elspeth,' said Max, looking directly at her face as he spoke.

'Janie, lovely to see you again. You still hanging with my favourite nephew?'

'Only nephew,' said Max, but as Elspeth was focused on Janie she didn't react.

'Tea?'

'Not right now, literally on our way somewhere on a job. Can you look at a bit of imagery and give a lip-reader's opinion for me?' said Max.

'Expert opinion, I think you'll find. I'm now certified by the Deafness, Cognition and Language Research Centre at a posh university, don't you know? Nice little side business when the work comes in,' Elspeth said proudly. Elspeth had been profoundly deaf since birth and had learned to lip read as a child. It was only when she was called on to provide Max with an opinion on a piece of surveillance footage that she had decided to get properly assessed and become qualified to lip read for legal proceedings.

'I know, I've seen the certificates plastered all over the cottage, Auntie E.'

'Well, if you're not stopping, I've things to be doing, so show me,' she said, unable to conceal her excitement.

Max swept at his phone screen and handed it over. Elspeth parked her spectacles on her nose and pressed the screen, watching the short clip three times over.

'He mostly says "no" repeatedly. He looks very stressed.'

'Just "no"?'

'Well, he then finishes with "No, you fucking bitch", although I can't be sure of that. Why do you always bring me foul-mouthed lip reads?'

Max and Janie looked at each other in silence.

Ten past nine at night.

'We need to find Gus, now.'

51

Alfa-Secure

GUS FRASER HAS become a serious liability.

He was always weak, and now he has become a threat.

He doesn't have long to live.

52

'STOP HERE,' SAID Max at the layby just by a farm gate with a footpath sign that led to what looked like a well-made track.

His phone buzzed. 'Norma?'

'I've some phone records,' said Norma without preamble.

'Go on.'

'Gus's phone was last on the network at 21.12 last night. No call received on the GSM system, but it was active on the 4G network, which means that it could have received a message on an app like WhatsApp, or if he was being really cagey, like Wickr or Telegram. The phone went off immediately after that and it hasn't been on since.'

'Thanks. Anything else?'

'Nope. He's dropped off the face of the earth, as far as I can see. Nothing on his car, no PNC checks, no bank activity, no ANPR activations. Where are you?'

'Black Isle. Something he said to me when we met and I've a hunch he's here.'

'Okay, best of luck and stay in touch.' The phone clicked.

'Nothing?' said Janie.

'Nope. He's gone off-grid.'

'Shit,' said Janie, rubbing her face.

'You saw the video – he went back for his coat and took provisions. Food and sandwiches, he's keeping his head down. Come on, we've a short walk to the beach.'

'Are you going to tell me why we're at the beach?'

'He loved the Black Isle and came here to Eathie for head-space. He said to his wife he needed headspace. I'm betting he's here. Come on, it's a wee walk and we need to move.'

It was beginning to rain again, a heavy mist that swirled and danced in the brisk easterly wind coming in off the North Sea.

'Glad I've a coat, then. That muddy path is going to ruin my gutties,' Janie said, pulling on a Gore-Tex jacket and pointing at her Converse sneakers as they rounded the gate and onto the path. It skirted around a wide-open field in which a flock of sheep grazed.

The path firmed up and wound down a steep hill, traversing from side to side into thick woodland. Before long the sky disappeared behind the canopy and they were totally enclosed by dripping undergrowth.

'Look at the state of these. I only bought them last week,' said Janie, looking at her mud-encrusted footwear.

'Ach, overtime will pay for a new pair.'

They continued for about forty minutes, before the path widened out and they heard the distant whisper of the sea. They emerged from the thick woods and onto a rocky shoreline. The only sound was the calm waves, gentle and soft.

The low sun was beginning to emerge from behind the clouds, despite the soft curtain of rain. They trudged along the beach towards a tumbledown old bothy.

'Crazy weather up here. Sun starting to blaze and it's still pissing down. He's not staying in that, is he?' said Janie from under her hood.

'All four seasons in a day, pal. Typically Highlands. You should leave the city more often. There's two bothies on the beach, but the first one is a bit wrecked. The one to use is much further down. I stayed in it a few times myself. Look out for fossils.' Max began to pick his way along towards a small, stone fishing bothy, close to where the beach met the trees.

The place was deserted other than a few seabirds that picked at the shoreline.

They walked up over the rough stones and onto some muddy grass before approaching the cracked and peeling door. Max crept to the window at the front of the structure, the glass splintered and broken and patched with an animal-feed sack. He looked at Janie and held his fingers to his lips, as he eased a finger in and slowly created a gap between the plastic and the wooden frame.

Gus Fraser lay still on the rough concrete floor, his face partially obscured by a fur-lined hood pulled over his head.

53

'GUS?' MAX SAID.

The prone figure didn't move.

'Gus, it's Max Craigie, we're coming in,' said Max, louder this time.

Still there was no movement.

'Ah, man, don't be fucking dead. No more death, please. Let's get in there – you have any signal, in case we need help?' Max's heart was pounding, his stomach tight.

'None,' said Janie, looking at her phone.

Max pushed the door open and entered the rustic bothy. The room smelled of smoke and whisky, but the fire in the hearth was long dead. Max shivered; it was freezing.

Max knelt, his heart in his mouth, and pulled down Fraser's hood, revealing a pale, unshaven face. He pressed his fingers to his neck, searching for a pulse, dread gripping him. As his cold fingers touched the pale, cold skin, Gus flinched, just slightly, a snore escaping from his lips. Max exhaled and relief flooded through his body as he found a steady pulse from the carotid artery.

'He's not dead, thank God.'

'Definitely not dead, but most certainly pished,' said Janie, holding up an empty bottle of White Horse whisky.

Max sniffed. The acrid stench of whisky mixed with wood smoke and the sour tang of body odour.

'Gus.' Max shook the ex-detective's shoulder, gently at first, then more vigorously.

A low groan escaped his lips, his eyes fluttered open then closed again, and the snoring resumed.

'Shit, we don't have time for this,' Max muttered. He extended his thumb and jammed it just under Gus's earlobe into the mastoid nerve.

Gus's eyes flicked open as his survival instinct took over. Alarm, fear and pain suddenly washed over him like a bucket of icy water.

'Fuck,' he shouted, pulling away from the source of the pain. His eyes met Max's, and the fear turned to confusion.

'Gus, it's Max. You're okay, pal.'

Gus's eyes widened again, red and bloodshot. His brain struggled to catch up with what he was seeing.

'Max, what the fuck …' He shook his head, trying to clear the fug, the breath escaping in gasps as he looked at Janie and then back to Max. 'How'd you find me?'

'Your wife said you needed headspace. You'd mentioned this place, so I took a guess.'

He paused, sitting up and pressing his fingers into his temples.

'Shite, my head is fucking banging, man.'

'I'm not surprised. That's a whole bottle of whisky.' A clear plastic bag lay on the floor with a few bottles of water in it. Max picked one out and cracked the top open. He handed it to Gus who accepted and drank deeply.

'How's Sarah?'

'Worried about you. You didn't think to tell her?'

'I couldn't. It's too dangerous.'

'What is?'

'I'm scared, you know, not just for me, but for Sarah and the kids.' He drained the bottle of mineral water and crushed it in his fist.

'You need to tell us the truth, Gus. We have to stop all this and you're the one who can help us.'

'Lorimer is dangerous. He'll stop at nothing.'

'Not anymore, he isn't.'

Gus's head snapped around to face Max, as if he'd been slapped.

'What, you've arrested him?'

'No. He's dead. The evidence suggests he killed himself.'

Gus's mouth opened and closed several times, like a beached fish. 'What?'

'Just that. He apparently cut his wrist and leg open last night.'

Gus closed his eyes, and just sat there on the rough stone floor, breathing deeply.

'No way. No way did that bastard top himself.' His voice was low.

'Tell us. This doesn't end with Lorimer's death, does it? The killing has to stop.'

His eyes snapped open. 'What's happened?'

'You tell us. Tell us fucking now, Gus. No more bullshit, no more excuses. Right this minute, or so help me God, I'm taking you in for conspiracy to murder, and you can fight it out in the High Court.' Max's voice was low, even, and his meaning was utterly unambiguous. Gus's face fell. He knew it was all over.

'It was five years ago. It started five years ago.' His eyes were closed again.

'What did?'

'This is all down to one person, and I got bloody wrapped up in it, because I was weak. I managed to get away from her, but John Lorimer couldn't. She's every man's bloody nightmare. She's evil.'

'She?' said Janie.

Gus paused for a full minute, staring at the inert fireplace. He took a deep breath and spoke. 'DI Marnie Gray, or to be more accurate, when I knew her, DC Marnie Gray. She got us both – me and John – like a spider reeling in a couple of flies. She's not stopped. No way has she stopped.'

54

'MARNIE TURNED UP on attachment to the Paedo Squad as a young DC. I was DS on Intel and John was running one of the teams. She was a good-looking lassie and all the guys fancied her. Accelerated promotion, so just hopping from squad to squad, picking up experience. She was competent, but also, she had something about her. Kind of a magnetism.'

'So, what happened?'

'We had an affair.'

There was a pause as this sank in.

'Go on,' said Max.

'I'm not defending myself. No marriage problems, no "my wife doesn't understand me" bollocks. I just fancied her, and then at drinks after work one time, she came onto me and I couldn't say no. We ended up in a hotel room together. She had something. I just couldn't resist her. She was everything my wife wasn't. Mad, reckless, adventurous. She was fun, and I was weak.'

'How long did this go on for?'

'A few months. You know the drill. Long hours, time away, it was too easy to keep Sarah in the dark. It was a wild and fun time. We took drugs, we drank, we partied and went to raves. It was like being a teenager, but …' He paused to sip some more water, moistening his dry lips.

'She liked pain. She liked being slapped, she liked being tied up and if you didn't play along, she'd go wild at you. She really wanted to be dominated, and it wasn't what I wanted. She'd threaten to tell Sarah and if I got angry with her, she'd just piss herself laughing and dare me to hit her. I tried to end it loads of times, but she always drew me back in, it was like I was powerless. Then it happened.'

'Go on.'

'John's wife died in the accident. It changed everything.'

'How?'

'She abandoned me, completely. Almost like I'd disappeared and she turned all her attention onto John. It's like she could smell his vulnerability and they were at it almost straight after her funeral. He was like a bloody puppy dog with her, fawning over her, and doing anything she wanted.'

'You didn't feel jilted?'

'Not in the slightest. She was a nightmare. Her temper was something to behold so, if I'm honest, I was glad to get her out of my life and make things better with Sarah.'

'Where's this going?' asked Max.

'Well, shortly after this the shite with Macallan happened. He disappeared off the face of the earth, and then a while after that, Chick Wilson was killed in Perth. All within a month of them getting together. She's the arch manipulator, and he was her blunt instrument. They killed them together, I'm certain of it.'

'Was it well known that they were an item?'

'No. Not at all, the same as when we were together. She was adamant that no one could know. It was the same with John. We were the only two who knew what was going on; she was an expert at separating work from the relationships.'

'Do you have any evidence of her involvement in the killings?'

'Nothing that would stand up, no corroboration, no chance of a guilty.'

'Forget about that. What do you know?'

'John asked me to find Macallan, which I did, as I told you before. We met up to pass the information over – nothing electronic, you know. I handed the slip of paper with all the information on to John in the pub one afternoon. He went off with it all cock-a-hoop and that. I followed him out of the pub and he gets straight in the car. Guess who drives off?'

'How about Chick Wilson?'

'I've got nothing, and I'd gone on the sick by then, anyway. Marnie was shifted to the MIT at the time and was actually working on that investigation team as the next phase of her accelerated promotion process. She had access to everything, and she had John's muscle to help her.'

'This is a big leap of faith, Gus.'

'She's evil. Pure evil, I'm telling you, but she's bloody clever. She'll have covered her tracks.'

'Why, though? Why is she like this?' said Janie.

'She had a shite childhood. Her dad was a bloody monster and he abused her and her mother systematically. She hated him with a passion. Maybe something to do with that. I remember something she said about him.'

'What?'

'Said she danced on his grave when he died, or something. Danced with joy when she knew he was being eaten by worms.'

His words hung in the bothy for a long moment.

'You haven't told us about the message that made you run here,' said Janie.

Gus sighed and reached for his phone in his pocket. 'It's on flight mode so it can't be traced. I enabled it as soon as the message came in. Learned my lesson on that years ago.'

'Was it from a phone number?'

'No, just some weird configuration of numbers and letters that flashed up on my messages and then disappeared as soon as I opened it.'

'What did it say?'

'Nothing. It was just a picture of a bottle of whisky.'

'Well, that's hardly a threat,' said Janie.

'It was a bottle of Macallan.'

'Ah, right. That is a threat, I guess.'

'I saw something else before it disappeared.'

'What?'

'The zip-mouthed emoji. The meaning was clear enough.'

55

NIALL HASTINGS SAT in the MIT office at Leith and looked at Acting DCI Marnie Gray as she surveyed the assembled officers. Everyone in the room looked shattered, and the gloomy air hung around them like a thick fog.

She looked at the twenty or so officers, her iridescent green eyes somehow managing to catch everyone at the same time. An instant personal connection.

'Okay, folks. This is a "clear the air" session. It's a bad time, and we're all shaken up by John taking his life, and the news filtering through about what he'd been doing is startling, to say the least. Now DCI Johnson has his team on John's activities, and as I understand it, the evidence against him is overwhelming. The knife found has been confirmed as the murder weapon for Scott Paterson. John's prints are on the handle, and it's Paterson's blood on the blade. The burner phone's cell site movements clearly show it travelling between Ravelston and Dunnet Head at the relevant time. The fiscal is content that were John still with us, he'd be charged. He's also content that there is no evidence of any other individual's involvement.'

She paused and looked around the room, once more, her gaze firm and calm, the picture of control. Her eyes rested on Niall for a moment.

'Where does this leave us, boss?' said Fagerson.

'Well, obviously we are off the case for Paterson and Grigor. Detective Superintendent Wakefield reasonably considered that with John being the main suspect MIT 6 couldn't be anywhere near it. I've carried out a full and detailed handover to DCI Johnson and in the next day or so, all the officers with key roles will hand over in a similar fashion. I want everyone today to ensure any material you have is in tip-top shape. We must be above reproach, do I make myself clear?'

'Are we going to be redeployed?' asked a voice.

'Yes. Once the handover is complete, we have a new case ready for us. A linked series of sexual assaults across a wide area and over a number of years. We're going to be busy.'

There were nods all around the room. This was new territory for everyone. One of their own was responsible for the murders that they had been investigating.

'Now I am assuming that you've all heard about the sudden, unexplained death of Shuggie Gibson?'

There were more nods.

'As I understand it, at this stage it's being treated as unexplained rather than suspicious. Working theory is he collapsed drunk and choked on his own vomit. No speculation, okay? It's not our job, it's being adequately investigated elsewhere, and the PM is later today.'

'Anyone linking it to John?' asked a voice.

'Not as far as I know. The MO is totally different and there are witnesses who have him leaving a pub very inebriated. Not our problem, guys. Look, this is hard. We all feel let down and we now have the eyes of the world on us. It's going to be uncomfortable, but we have to be professional and get on with our jobs.'

'How about the press?' said Fagerson.

'DCC McVeigh is holding a press conference this afternoon.'

'Shit, they'll go doolally,' said Fagerson.

'They probably will, Mark. Nothing we can do about that, but we're still professionals and we'll hand this case over in the best possible shape it can be. We need to be transparent and open.'

'How about Donnie?' asked Niall.

'DCI Watson is currently on leave, Billy.' She had an edge in her voice at Niall's use of the DCI's forename. 'I understand that he will remain without a portfolio for some time pending the outcome of the Police Review Commissioner's investigation.'

'Shit, PIRC?' said Niall.

'Of course. A serving cop is a strong suspect in a double homicide, so PIRC referral is mandatory. We will all no doubt be interviewed in the future, and they're going to be shadowing all handovers. It's imperative that we support this investigation, so confidence can be regained in us as a team, and as individuals. Okay, everyone. There's lots to be getting on with, on you go.'

There was a rumble of muted conversation as everyone rose to their feet.

'Remember, guys. No short-cuts. No cover-ups. If mistakes were made, we own them. This is a sticking plaster that needs ripping off and ripping off soon. Only from there can we start to heal, do I make myself clear?'

There were mumbles of assent as everyone made their way to their desks, yawning and stretching.

Niall left the incident room and went into the toilet, quickly checking each of the cubicles to make sure he was alone. He took out his phone from his shirt pocket and cancelled the live feed on the app that Barney had installed. Every word of the meeting should have been broadcast to Max and the team. He dialled Max.

'Niall?'

'Did you get it all?'

'I did, clear as a bell. She almost convinced me,' said Max.

'She's actually quite impressive. What's next?'

'Can you get away for a bit?'

'Probably. All the CCTV's in order, so there's not much left for me to do. Where are you?'

'Nearby. Just find a reason to pop out and then call us, yeah?'

'Sure, I'll say I'm going to the bank. Give me ten, or so.' He rang off and pocketed his phone. He quickly used the facilities and washed his hands and then left the toilets, heading back to the main office.

'The boss about?' he asked Fagerson.

'Donnie's office.'

'Shite, that's quick to jump in Donnie's grave,' said Niall.

'Ambitious, that one.' Mark shrugged, tapping at his keys.

The DCI's office was just along the corridor from the main incident room. The door was wide open and Marnie sat behind the desk looking at a laptop, a pair of reading spectacles balanced on her nose. She had a phone clamped to her ear. Niall noted that it was a Samsung, similar to the one he had been issued. She beckoned Niall in as he stood at the threshold and waved at a chair in front of the desk. Niall sat.

'One second, Billy. Just on hold.'

Before he could answer, Marnie spoke, 'Hi, sir, yes. All sorted. Team's clearing everything for a handover. Should be ready by close of play today. Fine. Yes, thanks.' She looked at the handset and replaced it on the desk, next to an iPhone.

'DCC McVeigh wants updates constantly. Everything okay?'

'Aye, fine, I just need to pop to the bank if that's okay?'

'Is CCTV all up to date?'

'Yep, all fine. Schedules completed, stills taken and all viewing records up to date. I assume everything will be reviewed again?'

'Who knows? Hughie Johnson is particularly thorough at the best of times, and he has the eyes of the DCC all over him. How are you settling in?'

'Aye, fine enough.'

'I wanted a word, actually. Now it won't come as a surprise to learn that DCI Watson is unlikely to return so close to retirement, so I've been asked to step up as SIO in the medium term.'

'Congratulations, boss.'

A voice sounded out from the open door. It was Mark Fagerson. 'Boss, Hughie's on the phone in the incident room. Wants a quick word.'

'Can't you transfer it?'

'I've no idea how to do it, sorry.'

'God, you're useless.'

'Shite old phones. Can't see why he doesn't try your mobile.'

Gray sighed and raised her eyebrows. 'Give me a minute, Billy. I still need that word, so don't dash anywhere.' She stood suddenly and angrily causing the swivel chair to rotate making the arm collide with the desk, juddering it. An expensive silver pen began to roll across the surface. DCI Gray smoothed her skirt and left the office, heels clipping on the floor. Niall watched the silver pen continue its path until it rolled to the edge and fell with a click onto the floor.

Niall swivelled and looked behind him, sensing an opportunity. Undercover work is all about thinking on your feet and not passing up an opportunity if one presents itself. He looked at the two phones side by side, one clearly an issued phone, the other – he guessed – her personal iPhone. He glanced behind him again and pressed his finger to wake up the handset. A photograph of DCI Gray holding a small terrier appeared on the screen. Niall immediately discounted this. He checked the coast was clear again.

He pondered for a second, recalling Max's description of the covert message that had been sent to Gus Fraser's phone with the bottle of whisky on it. He made a split-second decision.

He walked around to the back of the desk. A small, leather Mulberry messenger handbag sat on the floor. His eyes flicked to the pen beside it, and he stooped to pick it up, quickly and smoothly flipping open the soft leather flap and peering inside. There was just a small purse, a set of keys and a compact. Niall stood, the pen in his hand, and turned his attention to the desk. He paused, listening hard for any footsteps outside the door. Hearing nothing, he continued, his heart pounding in his chest.

He looked at the blank screen on her computer and touched the track pad, waking up the screen. It was set to the BBC homepage and the usual cavalcade of bad news, a major fire in Dumfries, rising inflation and a disturbing-looking man who had been released on appeal after a rape conviction in Durham. His gaze went from the screen to the drawers.

He opened the first, his eyes flicking from the door to the desk and back again. A scratched and battered Samsung smart-phone sat inside the drawer, its screen black and ominous. A burner. Niall put his finger on the home button and the screen lit up. There were just a handful of apps visible on the screen.

One had a logo he hadn't seen before. It had a padlock icon and the words 'Alfa-Secure' underneath. Niall frowned, unsure what he was looking at. Maybe a banking app?

Footsteps in the corridor made him start. Quickly he replaced the phone and slid the drawer shut, moving back towards his chair, just as DCI Gray appeared in the doorway. She walked into the office, a surprised expression flickering across her face when she saw Niall standing at the side of her desk.

'Billy?' Her raised eyebrows quickly dropped and narrowed. Niall felt the hairs stand up on the back of his neck.

'Your pen fell on the floor, boss. Didn't want anyone tread-ing on it. It looks expensive.' He held it up to show her and laid it back on her desk.

She paused for a moment before her face relaxed. 'Ah, thanks, it was a gift. Sit down again. Look, we now find ourselves in a position of not having an intelligence DS. How d'you fancy it? It's a good job.'

'Sure, I'm up for that, once I'm up to speed and done with my course,' he said.

'Sure you're okay with this? You and John had clicked, right?'

'Aye, he seemed a decent guy. It's a bit of a shock.'

'It's a terrible shock. We're all dumbfounded by it, but we have to crack on – you understand that, right?'

'Of course,' said Niall.

'That's great. I'll speak to the intel manager and get your access levels raised, so you can get up to speed. Anything else?'

'No, I'm good. I'll pop to the bank now, then,' said Niall.

'Everything else okay, though?' she said, concern on her face. 'It must be a bit overwhelming, a new force and a new life and of course recent events. Must leave a mark?'

'It's fine, boss. Just need to get the house sorted. Still looks like an old folks' home, and it's suffering the effects of being rented.' He smiled.

'Tell you what. Why not go home? CCTV is sorted, and there's little else you can do until you're on all the systems and you've finished your course. I'll be sending everyone else home in an hour or two, anyway. They need a break.' She smiled, her face lighting up like a beacon, her eyes sparkling.

'Well, if you're sure, boss.'

'I'm sure. Before you know it, we'll be knee deep in a long-term job, and time off will be at a premium. Get going,' she said, picking up the issued Samsung which had begun to buzz on the desk. 'Oh, God. It's the super again, I'd best take this.'

Niall nodded, stood up and left the office. As he went, he felt her eyes on him all the way out into the hall. He walked quickly and picked up his coat from the rack, then descended the marble staircase. As he hit the street, he withdrew his phone and dialled.

'Yes?' said Max.

'I'm out. She's got a burner in her desk. Oldish-looking Samsung with some weird app I didn't recognise.'

'What type?'

'I think it was called Alfa-Secure, or similar.'

'Shit, that was risky,' said Max.

'It's fine. Where are you?'

'Where did you say you were going?'

'Bank, but she's released me for the day.'

'Okay. Head for the RBS on Baltic Street and we'll pick you up nearby. This is an opportunity, Niall. Good work.'

56

DCI MARNIE GRAY couldn't shake off the uncomfortable feeling that sat in her gut after Billy Bruce had left the office and she'd finished the call with Superintendent Wakefield. She twirled the pen in her fingers, looking at the Montblanc logo. It had been a gift from John a few years ago. She smiled at the thought of it all. He had been such a softy under all that bravado, eager to please, but so easy to control.

Something about DS Billy Bruce made her uneasy, though. He seemed smart, competent, but there was also something not quite right about him. She could usually get a handle on men very quickly, but Billy was harder to read. She opened the drawer and looked at the burner sitting there inert and dark. She frowned: was that how she'd left it, or had it moved a touch?

She stared at it intently, her mind turning over. She'd survived as long as she had by listening to the instinctive part of her brain, and it was telling her right now to be careful. Their recent activity had raised the stakes, and the resources being thrown at the investigations were getting bigger by the day. A smile stretched across her face. It wouldn't matter. They'd never get anywhere even close to her, the incompetent idiots. They were too fucking stupid.

Her attention turned to her laptop; she woke the screen by touching the track pad. She navigated to the BBC newsfeed, to see if anything about the cases had hit yet. Even though a conference was planned by the DCC things often leaked ahead of time.

There was nothing about the case but the story she'd been reading yesterday caught her eye again.

BREAKING NEWS. CONVICTION OF CUMBRIAN LEON
BLACK OVERTURNED ON APPEAL.

She read the brief description about how a disclosure failure by Cumbria Police had led to the conviction of alleged multiple rapists being ruled unsafe. A smile played across her lips as she read the article and looked at the smug, grinning expression on Leon Black's face as he left the Court of Appeal in London, flanked by his barrister. She reached for her burner, twirling it around in her fingers, as she stared at the screen of the computer.

Cumbria was perfect. Things would be too hot in Scotland for a while, and whilst the buffoons in Police Scotland were nowhere near them, there was no point in making it too easy. Cumbria was close enough, and yet because of the vagaries between the Scottish and English forces, she'd only have to tweak her methods slightly and no one would connect the cases. They really were that stupid. She smiled as she closed the drawer and locked it, tucking the keys in her handbag.

She looked at the shit-eating grin on Leon Black's face, the contempt in his piggy eyes and the familiar tingle in her gut began to stir again. A new operation was about to begin. Maybe not right away, but soon. It would be absolute child's play.

57

NIALL LOOKED ALL around him as he approached the bank, just a short walk from Leith Police Station. However, anyone watching would have just seen a man walking in the streets, apparently unaware of his surroundings. Niall was an experienced surveillance operative, so he used shop windows, mirrors in window displays, and visible camera monitors to watch for a tail. His training equipped him with tactics for evading surveillance as well as carrying it out. All tradecraft honed on the streets of London and beyond, so when he arrived at Baltic Street, he was confident that he didn't have a tail.

He went straight into the bank, ignored the assistance of a helpful member of staff and walked to one of the ATM machines with a clear line of sight of a bank of monitors. He produced his recently obtained bank card in the name of WJ Bruce and checked the balance, pleased to see that it contained just over a thousand pounds. A mini statement showed several deposits and withdrawals, including one from West Midlands Police. He nodded, impressed at the efforts of the covert teams to create a financial legend. Anyone checking would only find what would be expected of a man who had been in Birmingham until recently.

He withdrew fifty pounds and tucked it into his wallet. After a final check on the monitors, he dialled a number on his phone.

'Go on,' said Max.

'I'm in the bank.'

'Okay, come out and cross over Baltic Street. There's a narrow street opposite – Maritime Street – walk down fifty metres and we're in our Volvo in the car park on your right. We need to get our heads together.'

'On my way.' Niall hung up and crossed the road, heading down the narrow cobbled street. It suddenly popped into his head that cobbles were known as 'setts' in Scotland, although he couldn't really think why that felt important. He saw the big Volvo, walked up to it, and without hesitation, got into the back.

Max swivelled in the passenger seat, smiling. 'Hey, bud.' He offered his fist and they touched knuckles.

'Shite, am I glad to get away from that office. Gloom and bloody doom, you know?'

'I can imagine. What's been occurring?'

'Marnie's now acting DCI. She's a little smug about it, and wants me to run intel. Now that Lorimer is no longer with us.'

'You should be flattered.'

'Oh, am I ever,' Niall said with maximum sarcasm. 'Where are we heading?'

'A satellite office close by here. Tulliallan's a little too far, so Ross found us a temporary home, and boy, is he proud of it. We need to get our heads together and plan what we do next.'

'Aye. There's something unsettling about Marnie, and that phone is definitely a burner with a secure message app installed. That's not normal,' said Niall.

'It's not, but it may be an opportunity. We need this, as we have sod all hard evidence now that John has left the building.'

Within a few minutes they were by the harbour in Leith, once scruffy and neglected, now with new-build estates and artisanal bakeries. Even the fish and chip shop served prosecco and craft ales.

Janie turned into a new-build estate and pulled over into a numbered parking space in front of a monochromatic modern block of apartments.

'How did Ross pull this off?' said Janie.

'You know our illustrious leader. He probably stamped his feet like an overgrown toddler until they did what he wanted. Come on, we're top floor.'

They left the car and were soon in the immaculately maintained block, riding up in a lift that smelled fresh and clean.

'Last time I went into a scheme lift in Leith I had to step over the puddles of pish,' said Niall.

'It's called gentrification.'

They continued along the corridor until they came to number 46. Max tapped and the door immediately opened. Ross's big, meaty face greeted them with a broad smile.

'Come on in, motherfuckers, and bask in my brilliance at getting this sorted in twelve hours.'

Max and Janie shared a look and trooped inside. They had to admit, it genuinely was impressive. The apartment would have been well furnished, but most of it had been shoved to one side to allow for several desks, covered in laptops and large monitors. A projector screen was situated where the TV would have been.

'Ross, Niall, Niall, Ross,' said Max as the Met undercover officer and Ross shook hands.

'Fuck me, more Met cowboys on my bloody turf. You'd better not have shown up with your MEET THE MET stickers. Last time we had a Met team up here they bloody plastered half of the cop shops with the things.'

'Sorry, I forgot them, guvnor,' said Niall with a smile.

'Shite, more "guvnors", and I get enough of that from this bugger,' said Ross, pointing at Max.

'Norma over there is our black-belt ninja analyst,' said Max.

Norma waved from behind three large monitor screens, her spectacles slightly askew. As always, she was immaculately dressed in a business suit, matched with an incongruous pair of trainers and thick socks.

'Barney there is our elderly tech guy.'

Barney was at the open window, puffing on a roll-up and trying to direct the smoke out of the window. He grinned widely as they came in, a few flakes of ash falling on his cardigan.

'Right, I've even made coffee.' Ross nodded to a drip machine on the sleek work surface.

'I'll pour,' said Barney. He tossed out his roll-up, shut the window and went to the machine.

'Jesus, Barney, you're bringing that stink back in and there's a perfectly good balcony over there. You need to buy a bloody air freshener.'

'You should be grateful I'm sharing my Golden Virginia,' said Barney.

'Aye well, I'll be bloody banning you, pal. A man of your

advanced years shouldn't be smoking anyway. Best put another pot on, we're expecting visitors,' said Ross, looking at his watch.

'Who wants a drink?' said Barney.

'No coffee for me, Barney,' said Ross.

Barney stopped what he was doing and stared at Ross, open-mouthed.

'There's some green teabags there,' Ross said. 'Can you bung one in a mug with some boiling water?' His face registered a little distaste.

'Green tea?' said Max.

'Aye. Mrs F is worried about my blood pressure, so I'm not allowed coffee. Green bloody tea. Actually, it's not as bad as I feared.'

'You're beginning to scare me. Mung bean salad, apples and now green tea,' said Max.

'All for the good of my health. You should try it. You drink too much coffee. Explains why you sleep like shite.'

Max just stared at Ross, his eyes wide.

Ross sat and looked at a sheaf of paperwork in front of him. 'Ah, Niall, whilst I've got you, can I get your moniker on these forms? All part of the health and safety bullshit I have to do,' he said, handing a sheaf of forms to Niall, who accepted them, sat down and began scratching away with a pen.

After a moment, Niall looked at Max and winked, a half-smile on his face.

There was a soft rap on the door. Ross walked over and looked through the spy hole. He pulled the latch and swung it open.

Chief Constable Chris Macdonald walked into the room,

casually dressed in jeans, trainers and a hooded sweatshirt. He wore a Hibernian FC baseball cap. Closely following him was a middle-aged man, with a bushy moustache, glasses and swept-back silver hair. He wore a well-fitted suit and carried a briefcase.

'Jesus, boss, you look like mutton dressed as bloody lamb,' greeted Ross, an enormous smile across his face. The Chief Constable and Ross were old friends, and rather than being affronted he simply smiled.

'I felt a low-key approach was probably useful today. For those of you who don't know, this is DCI Hughie Johnson. Hughie and I also go way back.'

Everyone nodded.

The chief summarised the current state of play.

'So why are we all here, now?' asked Max.

'Quite simply, this. Hughie's going to run the inquiry as normal. He's going to use his team and leave no stone unturned, to seize all the available evidence and satisfy the fiscal as to how and hopefully why these individuals have died. Hughie's team has been expanded but run strictly on a need-to-know basis. Hughie will continue with his inquiry, whilst you guys develop new, proactive strategies to identify anyone else that may have been acting with Lorimer. Hughie, can you give us the latest?'

Hughie smiled and spoke in a deep resonant voice. 'Thanks, sir. Well, in very short order, everything's pointing to Lorimer. The weapon found at his apartment has Paterson's blood on the blade and Lorimer's fingerprints on the handle. The burner phone clearly demonstrates the route of travel from Ravelston Golf Course to Dunnet Head. The timings are tight, but I'm confident the journey could have been made. This tallies with the GPS download that you guys very usefully obtained. In short, the fiscal's advice is that there would have been more than enough to charge Lorimer with both murders, were he still with us. We also have something else.' He paused to accept a cup of coffee from Janie and take a sip.

'Go on,' Ross said.

'His laptop. We've imaged it, and there are some very interesting internet searches, including Dunnet Head and Ravelston Golf Course. Searches on how to commit suicide by cutting wrists and on the murders of Paterson and Grigor.'

'Whoa, back up there a minute.' Norma spoke for the first time.

'Norma?' said Macdonald.

'We covertly imaged it a few days ago. I've the results here, and he never searched anything like that. All he used his computer for was share trading. Why did he suddenly get all slack in the couple of days since then and search historic murders, when he was working on the inquiry team? What could he possibly learn from the bloody BBC that he didn't know from the incident room? Someone else did those searches.' Her voice was firm.

'Can your covert imaging be shared with me?' said Johnson, his face registering that this was all creating more work for him.

'Of course, we'll share everything, but your eyes only, yeah?' said Ross.

'How about Gus Fraser?' said Hughie.

'What do you know?' said Max.

'Just what the chief told me. He suspects DCI Gray – based on her past behaviour during their brief affair which moved on to Lorimer – but has no actual evidence, beyond an admission that he was potentially a party to the murder of Macallan several years ago.'

'That's not provable either. Not without a body, anyway. There's a trail of breadcrumbs suggesting he left the country,' said Ross.

'Gus is clearly terrified of her. He and his family have gone away for a bit. Staying with a friend on Orkney,' said Max.

'Is he credible?' asked Johnson.

'I'd say so,' said Max. 'He didn't need to tell us any of this.'

'So, we have basically nothing evidential against Marnie Gray?'

'Nothing corroborated that would be enough for the fiscal. We have to keep this covert until we can develop it into something admissible,' said Ross.

'What do we know about her?' asked Johnson.

'Norma?' asked Ross

'I've a profile on her which I'll share with everyone. In very short order, there's not a lot known. She's thirty-two, grew up in Edinburgh. Only daughter of a well-off family and went to a fee-paying school. She then went to university in England where she got a first in psychology and criminology, before joining the police on the graduate programme. She's financially solvent, owns a nice Lexus and lives alone in Linlithgow right by the small loch. Nice-looking place, no mortgage.'

'No mortgage?'

'Parents' place, mother moved overseas, father died a few years back and the house is now in her name.'

'Any information on how father died?' said Max.

'Cancer. Mother moved to Spain a few years ago. It's all in the profile.'

'How about phones?'

'One in her name. I've billing and cell sites. Nothing notable. In fact, there's nothing notable about her, full stop.'

'So, she seems clean as a whistle, and we've nothing beyond the suspicion of a disgraced ex-DS who played away with her. That'd go nowhere,' said Johnson.

'She's dirty, all right. We just need proper, corroborated evidence,' said Max.

'But it's thin. Will we get this past the investigatory powers commissioners?' said Johnson.

'I'll be supporting them, and we'll get them. I'm seeing his lordship personally. How about the PMs. Both were today, right?' said Macdonald.

'They were. I attended Lorimer's, whilst my deputy went to the one for Shuggie Gibson. Pathologist found no evidence of anything to disprove the assertion that Lorimer inflicted those cuts himself. She feels that the wrist cuts were most likely hesitation ones, and then he plucked up the courage to go to the femoral artery. Blood spatter examination makes it fairly clear that it's almost impossible that anyone was in the bathroom with him when the cuts were made, particularly as there's no blood at all outside of the bathroom. Scene was treated with luminol, but there was nothing. We're waiting on toxicology.'

'And Shuggie?' asked Janie.

'My colleague tells me that cause of death was definitely asphyxiation after inhalation of vomit. Still waiting for toxicology, but stomach contents were alcohol-heavy and he

281

apparently stank of the stuff. This ties with witness accounts of him being shit-faced when he left the pub, and before you ask, no there was no sign of taser injuries.'

'Was it mentioned to the pathologist?'

'No. Elsa Morina seemed unconcerned by the bruises. As he seems to have fallen down the stairs and onto his back, injuries would have been inevitable.'

'I take it nothing found on the search?' asked Max.

'PolSa went through the scene with a fine-tooth comb. Literally nothing,' said Johnson.

'We need to make our own luck here, boys and girls. Hughie, you carry on as normal. Leave the irregular stuff to Ross and his team. If Marnie Gray is connected, they'll find it. I take it you guys have a plan?'

'We do, boss, particularly now we have DS Billy Bruce at the heart of the inquiry,' said Ross.

'Well then, over to you. Whatever resources, whatever authorities you need, you'll have.'

'We're on it,' said Ross.

'When?' asked Macdonald.

'Tomorrow. Barney, will you be ready by tomorrow?'

'Pretty much ready now. I just need to check my software, but essentially I'm good to go.'

'Right, in that case I suggest you all go home and be ready to rock and roll. Niall, what does Marnie have in store for you tomorrow?' said Macdonald.

'We've a briefing at eleven about the new series rape case and then there's a load of intelligence and planning work to do. I think we'll be busy,' said Niall.

'Everyone present?' said Macdonald.

'Yep, three-line whip.'

'I've had a briefing on this case. It's a big one, so it'll be busy, which is perfect. We need Marnie Gray's mind on her work, not anything else. In fact, I can probably ramp up the pressure a little. Right, everyone, get home and be ready tomorrow.'

They all stared at each other in silence. Something seemed to pass between them. A sense of determination and a knowledge that they were doing the right thing.

58

THE RAIN HAD arrived with a vengeance as they emerged from the apartment block and into the car park.

'Want me to drop you home?' said Max to Niall.

'Nah, I'm good. Just drop me back at my car in Leith and I'll drive back myself. I need the car in the morning. After the meeting, I have to go to Gartcosh for some input on the intel system, because I'm now intel manager for MIT 6.'

'Glory days, pal. Before you know it, you'll be transferring to Police Scotland.'

'Fat chance of that. Jeri would never move. Her massive, crazy family would hit the bloody roof.'

'Fair. Quiet night in for you, then?'

'Aye, I imagine so. Kids want to speak to me on FaceTime, then it'll be a couple of cans and whatever fast-food delivery I can get my hands on in Craigentinny. I'm knackered, man.'

'All high life this UC work, right?' said Janie as they got into the Volvo.

'Oh aye. Champagne and hookers, man,' laughed Niall as Janie drove off, heading back to Leith.

The journey only took five minutes despite the torrential

rain bouncing off the road's surface with the wipers struggling to keep up with the deluge.

'This is another reason I won't be moving back to Scotland any time soon,' said Niall.

'No bad weather, just inappropriate clothing,' said Max as they pulled up just around the corner but out of sight from the station.

'And to think I left my coat. What time do we reckon tomorrow?'

'Can't be exactly sure, but probably to coincide with the meeting. You'll get a text from a betting company ten minutes before, and then we go as planned.'

'Cool. Right, be lucky, dudes,' said Niall. He got out of the car and jogged away, his collar turned up against the rain.

'He's a good guy,' said Janie, watching him dodge the rapidly expanding puddles and disappear into the back street where his car was parked.

'He really is, and we need him now. He's our eyes and ears. You want a lift home? I can pick you up in the morning. It's on the way.'

'Can I choose the music?'

'How offended would you be if I said no?'

'Mortally. Okay, you pick.'

'The Jam?'

'Whatever, Grandpa,' she said as she drove off, and the speakers burst into life.

59

MARNIE GRAY WAS sitting in the café with her laptop open and a latte in front of her. She often did this when the office got busy and she wanted to work in a different environment. She looked up from her screen and watched a big Volvo pull to the side of the road and a lean man jog away, his collar up. She couldn't see who was in the car, owing to the bouncing rain, but she was pretty sure that she recognised the man who got out of it, even with the deluge.

Billy Bruce.

She looked at the Volvo sitting in the now heavy rush-hour traffic and scrawled a note of the registration number. She frowned. Why hadn't Billy gone home, and who had he met?

She pulled out her mobile phone and dialled a number.

'Roads policing admin, Di speaking.'

'Hey, Di, it's Marnie. You okay?'

'Yeah, I'm fine, boss, what can I do for you?'

'Can I get a vehicle check? Some bugger's blocked me in. I know it's not totally proper use, so can you log it as a traffic camera violation or something?'

'For you, anything. How you been, I heard you got temporary promotion.'

'I did – in unfortunate circumstances – but it's progression.'

'It is. Right, what's the number? I can disguise it, just don't give the owner too much of a row in case they complain.'

'You know me, Di. I'm diplomacy personified.' Gray told her the registration.

'Okay, dark Volvo V90, keeper since new is Macpherson Asset Management, 229a Shelton Street, London, WC1.'

'Oh damn. No Edinburgh address?'

'No, sorry.'

'Ah well, no matter. I'm sure someone will be back soon. Thanks, Di.'

'No bother, meet up for a wine or two soon?'

'Sure thing, bye.' Gray rang off, and opened Google on her laptop. She tapped Macpherson Asset Management into the search bar. No result.

She checked the address. There were multiple results, hundreds of companies registered there. She put the address into Google Maps and searched. Looking on Street View, she found the building. It was a small, shabby-looking office that looked badly kept.

Why was a new officer – a transferee – getting out of a car registered to what appeared to be a shell company registered hundreds of miles away?

She sipped her now cool latte and pursed her lips, wincing at the cold, bitter liquid. Her thoughts on Billy handing her the pen and the phone that she was sure had moved.

The lizard part of her brain was itching.

Something was wrong with DS Billy Bruce.

60

AS MAX PULLED up at Janie's tenement in Stockbridge, his phone began to buzz.

'Ross?'

'Is that fucking joker Met twat Hastings with you?' Ross's voice exploded out of the speakers.

'No, he's made his own way, why?'

'He drew a small cock alongside every bloody signature he did on my health and safety forms. The cheeky bastard. I'm sick of bloody Met cowboys with their stickers and crudely drawn phalluses on official forms. Tell him I'm after him.' The phone clicked.

Max and Janie both laughed uproariously.

'Good to see old Met traditions haven't gone away. You could never leave anything alone in a Met station. Leave a hat, pocketbook or important document around for even a minute and someone would draw a cock on it,' said Max, smiling widely.

'My respect for Niall has just soared,' said Janie, still laughing.

'I'll pick you up in the morning. You ready for it all?' said Max.

'Yeah, I guess. We need a big dollop of luck and for Niall to be on top of his game. We've basically sod all evidence against Gray.'

'Not right now, but I'm convinced it's down to her. You know what they say. The harder we try, the luckier we'll get.'

'Aye, I suppose so.' Janie yawned.

'Look out, you've a welcoming committee, pal,' said Max, nodding towards her front door. Melissa was smiling and waving excitedly whilst jogging down the path. She was dressed in joggers, a rugby shirt and fluffy bunny slippers. She almost skipped to the car and yanked the door open. 'Babes.' She threw her arms around Janie's neck and hugged her.

'Hey, Max, I'm amazed you've brought her home and it's still light. It's normally midnight or worse. I was thinking today that I don't like you much, but now Janie's home in time to eat the fabulous food I've created, I've forgiven you and now like you again. How's your gorgeous wife?'

'She's fine, and I'm glad you like me again.'

'I do, but keep her at work too late, too often and I'll go off you again. Come in for a drink?' she said.

'I'd love to, but I've promised Katie I'll come home with food,' he said.

'Well, then get away, man. You need to look after her. You're definitely batting above your average with her.'

'Right, I'll do that. See you tomorrow morning, Janie.'

Melissa had thrown her arms around Janie's neck again, hugging her tightly.

Max was pleased that after years of dating disasters with both men and women that Janie seemed to be genuinely happy.

He had a feeling that things were about to get busy at work

for a while if the plan came to fruition, so he was looking forward to a nice meal at home with Katie and Nutmeg.

Tomorrow would bring challenges – the stakes were high and the consequences of failure didn't bear thinking about. He engaged the gear shift and drove away, his mind on DCI Marnie Gray.

He remembered their confrontation at the PM suite at Raigmore Hospital. There was something in her jade-green eyes that was hard to read. They were disconcerting and disturbing.

Were they the eyes of a killer?

61

THE DREAM RIPPED Max from a deep sleep.

It was Afghanistan, the stench of the desert, the cordite, the blood and the desiccated, scorched earth. The scent remained in Max's nostrils long after he had gasped awake. As always, he was forced to see Dippy's eyes glaze over as he passed from alive to dead, but this time there was a disturbing difference. Instead of the usual muddy brown, pain-filled eyes of his friend, Dippy's eyes were jade-green, cruel and glittering.

Max lay there, trying to control his breathing, the sheen of sweat on his body cold against the sheets. Nutmeg whined, and nestled into him, flicking a tongue at his forehead. A feeling of dread clutched at his stomach, and dark clouds began to rise in his mind.

Max looked across to his wife, who was sleeping peacefully, her soft breaths regular and even, her beautiful face lit by the moon. The digital clock on his bedside table told him it was five thirty. No point in trying to sleep again. He slid silently out of bed, and crept from the bedroom, Nutmeg padding in his wake, her tail twitching in anticipation. She knew what was next.

Max pulled on his shorts, a scrappy old hoodie and his trainers. Nutmeg's excitement rose as she saw exactly what footwear he was putting on. His Asics trainers meant one thing. She slobbered at his face as he bent down to lace them up.

'Come on then, girl. Five miler and I'll be good to go,' said Max as he opened the door and stepped out into the dark morning chill. Autumn was in full swing now, with a promise of the dark winter detectable in the air. Max shook his head to clear the fog and set off, at a hard, punishing pace, Nutmeg galloping at his side. The worse his dreams were, the harder he ran. The pain would chase the darkness away. Temporarily, at least.

As he ran, he began to feel better. Not perfect, but as the endorphins cleared his mind, they took away some of the darkness too.

An hour later Max opened the door, sheened in sweat, his breath ragged. Nutmeg's tongue lolled as she buried her head in her water bowl, slaking the thirst of a hard run.

'I'm thirsty too, pal.' Max filled a pint glass and glugged it down, as his breathing began to return to normal.

'Morning, good run?' said Katie, appearing at the door, wearing a towel around her head and her big fluffy robe.

'Aye, not bad,' said Max, draining his water.

'You were up early. Dream again?'

'Aye, coffee?'

'Of course. Which dream?'

'Afghanistan,' was all that Max said, not really wanting to be drawn in further.

Katie walked up close to Max, and kissed him on the cheek,

gently, wrinkling her nose. 'Phew, I'll make coffee, you go and get a shower.'

'You sure?'

'Of course, I may even join you.'

'You've just had a shower,' said Max, a slow smile stretching across his face.

'I know that. Go on, Craigie,' she winked, her eyes sparkling mischievously.

62

MAX PULLED UP outside Janie's tenement just before eight. He dialled her number.

'You here?' she said.

'Yep, come on. Places to go, people to see, serial killers to catch.'

'Two minutes,' she said and rang off.

Max yawned as he looked at his phone. A message from Katie.

Sex-God, with a cheeky wink emoji after it. Max smiled, and his stomach softened at the thought of his beautiful, kind wife who was probably already working hard at her desk at the solicitor's office.

'Yo, dude, want me to drive?' said Janie, jumping in next to him.

'Morning, I think I can manage. Have a nice evening?'

'It was better than nice,' she said, waving at Melissa who was standing on the doorstep in a pink tracksuit, waving back extravagantly.

'Sounds like someone got lucky,' said Max.

'Very. She's such fun, almost makes up for all the duds I've met over the years. You ready for today?'

'Aye. Shouldn't be too challenging, but it's important. Right, to the secret office in Leith. Norma and Barney are there already.'

'How about Ross?'

'On his way, apparently.'

'Oh great, that'll mean a load of abuse from Ross when we go in. How about Niall?'

'Already in at the incident room, Gray's at her desk. He's ready to go as soon as the time's right.'

'Cool. This music is crap, by the way. Can I change it?'

'It's Radio 2, and I was enjoying it.'

Before he could say anything else, Janie had fiddled with the controls on her phone and Genesis was blasting out of the speakers.

'Genesis?'

'*Early* Genesis. Peter Gabriel days when thankfully Phil Collins was just bashing drums. Classic prog-rock. This is *Foxtrot*, their fourth, and some would say best, studio album. So complex and intricate and ground-breaking. Did you know that their longest ever track is on this album? Twenty-three minutes long, so cool.'

'Not sure cool is the right word. Maybe self-indulgent. It's the kind of thing your dad would listen to.'

'Ach, you're a philistine.'

'I can tell you're happy. You're all enthusiastic and overly talkative.'

'Shush. Anyway, let's get going or the abuse and swearing will be worse than normal. I'll pick up cakes on the way,' said Janie.

*

'You fuckers took your bloody time. I've been in here bloody ages, putting in the hours and grafting like a bastard to get this job going, and then you two swan in like you're here for a fucking spa day,' Ross blasted, looking harassed, two fingers poised over his laptop keyboard. His face was unusually red and there was a sheen of sweat on his forehead.

'Ten minutes,' said Norma whilst affecting a cough.

'Aye and you can mind your lip, you cheeky mare, or you'll be back at Gartcosh with all the NCA buffoons again.'

'You look hot and sweaty, Ross,' said Max.

'Grafting, mate. I cycled in,' he said proudly, nodding at the cycle helmet that was displayed prominently on a chair.

'What?' said Max.

'Yep. Six miles. You should try it. It might even make you less of a stressed bastard. I'm feeling good. Mrs F is very impressed with my attitude, I have to say.' He smiled.

'I have no idea who you are anymore, Ross,' said Max turning to his screen.

Norma giggled, not taking her eyes from her monitor.

'I bought carrot cake,' said Janie, proffering a box.

'Carrot cake? What fresh hell is this? What's next, beetroot cake, fucking sardine cake?'

'You won't want any Ross, then?' said Janie.

'I didn't say that, did I? It's practically health food, so Mrs F couldn't complain. Coffee's made.' He nodded at the machine, then took a sip from his cup. Max noticed a string dangled down the side of his mug.

'Still on the green tea?'

'Most definitely. Coffee causes all types of stress. I'm a changed man.'

'Are we all set?' said Max.

'Aye, and no thanks to you two,' said Ross, biting into a large chunk of cake. A big blob of icing predictably fell from the corner of his mouth and splatted onto his keyboard.

'Quite nice, for hippy food,' he said.

'I'm all set, and ready to go,' said Barney, roll-up behind his ear. Unusually, he wasn't wearing his customary cardigan, but sported a fleece with an embroidered chest logo saying NTS ALARM SERVICES.

'How long will you need?' said Max.

'I won't know till I get there. Hopefully just a few minutes.'

'Okay, well, Niall is in position, and Marnie Gray's at her desk, and has been since early. Do we have a time?'

'That depends. I'll send the coded text and once he's replied, we're good to go.'

Ross slurped at his coffee and dusted some carrot cake crumbs from his tie. 'Okay, this has to work, boys and girls. We need to light a candle in the darkness.'

Everyone turned to look at Ross and then flashed each other wide-eyed glances.

'What? I'm profound as fuck. It's a Mark Young song.'

'Strangest thing you've ever said,' said Barney, putting his roll-up in his mouth and walking towards the balcony.

'Ah well, piss off, you old codger. I was being inspiring. Everyone stand by, make sure kit is checked and double-checked and we need to be ready to move at a moment's notice, okay?'

63

MARNIE GRAY CAME into the busy incident room, looking smart in a grey business trouser suit. She was accompanied by a dour-looking middle-aged man in saggy suit trousers and a jumper.

'Okay, everyone. Five minutes and into the conference room, Phil here from force intelligence is going to brief us on the new operation. It's big and complex and is going to mean a lot of work, so everyone needs to focus, understood?' There was a general murmur of agreement and people started to stand and gather their things.

Niall Hastings checked his phone. There had been no update since the dummy text purportedly from an online betting company indicating that they were ready.

Niall quickly composed a one-line reply. *Now*. The prearranged signal that the meeting was about to get underway. He deleted both the received and the sent text messages and tucked his phone into his shirt pocket, having first enabled the livestream app.

He tried to shift the uncomfortable feeling that was developing in his stomach. Something about this job was making him more and more anxious. He tried to pin down what it was, but nothing would come. His thoughts turned to Jeri and the kids, and his heart lurched. He was missing them so much and not for the first time he wondered if he'd made the correct decision in accepting Max's offer. He sighed and shook his head. He couldn't afford this, not now.

The whole team filed into the conference room and settled in the chairs dotted around the long central table. A projector screen displayed the Police Scotland crest with OPERATION JUPITER emblazoned below in prominent letters.

'Looks like we have a planetary theme for operation names now,' said Fagerson.

'Interesting to see what they do when they get to Uranus. What do you reckon, boss?' said a voice from the back of the room to accompanying sniggers and guffaws.

'Predictable and obvious from you, Chas,' said Gray, a smile on her face, before continuing, 'Right, guys, can I introduce DS Charlie Wright, from the National Intelligence Bureau? He has kindly come to give us a full briefing on Operation Jupiter. I've had a preliminary read of the document. It's a high-profile, and very serious case where several stranger rapes have been linked. These traverse several years but there are a number of similarities. It now seems a single offender is responsible. I appreciate this isn't homicide, however we are a major inquiry team, and this is a major inquiry. So, we'll be giving this our all. We'll be in an intelligence development phase for a while before moving operational, but there'll be plenty for everyone to do. So, without any further preamble, I'll hand you over to Charlie.'

Charlie stood and pressed a button on a remote control.

The slide changed to a map of Scotland, marked out with a number of lines and pins.

He cleared his throat and opened his mouth to speak.

At that moment, a shrill squeal suddenly erupted from unseen alarms, deafeningly loud and at a pitch designed to irritate.

'We're not due a drill, are we?' asked Gray.

'Only had one last week,' said Doreen Urquhart.

Suddenly, the door burst open, and the small portly form of Ben, the building manager, appeared. He looked flustered and panicked.

'Everyone oot. It's no a drill. Well, no one I bloody organised, anyways, not that anyone tells me anything, ya ken. Every bugger doon into the yard and wait until I clear the building. Come on, fire could be afoot, there's nae time to waste. Fire could be ragin', and we'd ken nothin aboot it. Fire brigade are on their way,' he said.

'Bloody hell. Come on then, let's get out of here,' said Gray, shouting above the piercing squeal. 'The superintendent got very pissed off after our last poor performance during a drill.'

'Aye, quick as ye like. Nae time for coats, be thankful it's no raining. All form up outside and fire marshals take roll calls,' said Ben, opening the doors and ushering everyone out.

There was a lot of groaning and mumbling, but most made their way quickly to the door.

Niall held back just a touch, until he was at the rear of the throng as they descended the broad marble staircase. Marnie Gray was side by side with Mark Fagerson, her phone in her hand, seemingly composing a message.

They hit the ground floor, and Ben ushered them towards the back yard like a panicky sheepdog with a clipboard.

They all stood and scowled as Ben returned into the building to check that it was now empty.

'Are we all here?' said Gray to Fagerson.

He looked at the clutch of suited detectives in front of him. 'Everyone but Billy Bruce,' said Fagerson.

'Where's he, then?' said Gray, looking about her, her jaw tight.

'He was coming down the stairs with us, I saw him.'

Gray dialled a number and held the phone to her ear with a frown.

Niall appeared from the door and into the yard, clutching a phone in his hand.

'Where'd you go?' asked Gray to Niall when he joined them in the line.

'Left my phone on my desk. Christ knows how long we'll be out here,' he said.

Gray just shook her head and stared once again at her phone. 'Bloody DCC will be giving me a row if this meeting doesn't happen, and I'm due elsewhere after lunch,' she grumbled, looking at her watch.

Ben appeared at the door, now in a hi-viz vest. 'Building is clear,' he said, nodding with satisfaction.

'Now what?' said Gray.

'We wait for the fire brigade. They should nae be long,' he said, ticking a box on his spreadsheet.

64

BARNEY EASED THE side fire door open and entered the police station, closely followed by Max. He was thankful that Niall had managed to crack it open before joining the rest of MIT 6 in the yard. Both wore latex gloves and fleeces bearing the NTS alarm logo. Barney had a small rucksack on his back.

'How long?' asked Max, having to speak loudly because of the squealing alarm.

'Not long. Building's clear, but once the fire brigade arrives and the alarm's reset, everyone will be back in,' he said, removing the unlit roll-up from his mouth and tucking it behind his ear.

They jogged through the building and ascended the stairs, Barney barely out of breath as they went up, two steps at a time. They went along the corridor towards the incident room and halted outside the office of Acting DCI Marnie Gray. The door was wide open.

Max produced his phone and activated the camera, taking a snapshot of the room exactly as it was before they entered.

Once inside, Barney went to the drawer and pulled. It was locked. Within a second, he had a pick wallet in his hand and was pulling out a small sliver of metal. Within two seconds he was opening the drawer. The battered and scratched Samsung lay inside. Barney produced a pad of Post-it notes and quickly stuck four around the phone marking its exact location.

Barney reached into his rucksack and pulled out a battered-looking laptop festooned with Leeds FC stickers. He picked up the phone and pressed the home key. It lit up and asked for a passcode.

'Be nice if we had the pin. I could extract more from it,' said Barney.

'Hand it here,' said Max, holding out his gloved hand.

Barney passed it to Max who looked at the screen from an oblique angle. He put his mouth close to it and breathed close to the screen, as if he was polishing it. The faint outline of a square was temporarily visible in the fog on the screen. Max drew the circumference of the square and the phone sprang to life. He handed it back to Barney.

'Nice work, mucker,' said Barney, who took the lead from the box and plugged it into the phone. He then began to tap away at the laptop, his face set in a mask of concentration. Max squatted and looked on the floor, noting the small leather handbag under the table. He photographed it before flipping open the top and photographing the contents. A solitary lipstick, a hair brush and a Lexus car key on a ring, alongside a fluffy toy and what looked like a door key. A house key.

'Barney, can you do anything with a house key?' said Max, over the wailing alarm.

Barney looked at the key, fished inside his bag and handed over a small oblong box. 'Press it in there and shut the box tight to get an imprint,' he said, before turning back to the laptop.

Max opened the box, which contained a grey putty-like

compound. He isolated the modern-looking key and pressed it in. He closed the lid of the box and clamped it tight. Opening it back up he saw a millimetre-perfect impression of the key on the inside of the lid. He carefully eased out the key and gently closed the box. Checking there was no residue on the key, he replaced the bunch back in the bag, comparing its position to the image on his phone's screen. He then flipped the flap back and pocketed the key impression box.

'How you getting on?' said Max, loudly. His volume was unfortunate, as just as he was finishing the short sentence, the alarm suddenly stopped. His utterance of the word 'on' was deafening in the now utterly overwhelming silence. They both looked at each other. Max risked a peep out of the window. The fire fighters were all walking away from the yard, clearly satisfied that there was no fire.

'Barney, how long? I think people are about to come back inside.'

'Couple of minutes and I'll be done.'

'We may not have that.'

'Mate, you get out of here. I only need two minutes, then it's drawer locked and I'm golden. You can't get seen in here, no one knows who I am. Go on, piss off and take the back stairs.'

'Barney ...'

'Piss off, I'll be fine. I've a reason to be in here. Sod off.'

'What if she comes back?'

'Mate, I used to put bugs in under the noses of IRA hitmen. I can handle this.'

There was a pause, as Max looked at Barney. He opened his mouth as if to argue, but then closed it again. Barney chuckled, his eyes twinkling. This was his business, and he loved it.

'Right, no risks. Get the job done and get out.'

'Max, will you fuck off. I'm almost there.'

Max nodded and left.

Barney continued, watching the progress bar move across the screen as the operation inched towards completion.

Installation successful. Finalising, read the text on his screen.

Footsteps on the marble staircase were audible, along with the hubbub of conversation, growing louder and closer.

Complete, unplug device.

Barney breathed a sigh of relief and unplugged the wire from the phone. No rush, no panic. His decades of experience came to the fore. He tucked the laptop into his bag and shouldered it. Replacing the phone in its original place, he carefully removed the Post-its, screwing them up and jamming them in his pocket. He then gently closed the drawer, and within a few seconds, he had locked it with the pick, which he returned to his pocket. The voices were almost upon him, as he left the office, checking behind him to ensure it was as they found it, and went into the corridor. Now the footsteps were almost on him. He had nowhere to go. He was going to be seen. His eyes fell upon the alarm-control pad halfway down the corridor.

Calmly and unhurriedly, he walked to the panel. It was secured with a simple cam-lock, the type you might find on a locker at a gym. He pulled out the pick, and quicker than if he'd had the key, he got the flap down and accessed the control panel. He looked at the row of lights, just as a knot of detectives walked into view, chatting and laughing.

They all stopped at the sight of Barney. He now had a screwdriver in hand and was unscrewing a small panel at the bottom of the control unit.

'Who are you?' said DCI Gray.

'NTS alarm services. I'm doing a system check before resetting,' he said, pulling out the ID that had been created for him by covert support just yesterday.

'Hmm, well can you make sure it doesn't go off again? We've work to do,' said Gray, her chin raised and nostrils flared.

'All sorted now, just an earthing problem. I'll do checks on each floor, then I'm away,' said Barney, cheerfully. Screwing the panel back up, he began to whistle, tunelessly.

65

'THAT WAS TOO bloody close,' said Max as Barney climbed into the Volvo's passenger seat beside him.

'Judged perfectly, mate. Getting her house key copied is a major bonus. Let me see it?'

Max handed over the key box which Barney took and opened, looking at the impressions with a practised eye. 'Looks good, and these locks are bastards to defeat without a key.'

'Excellent. Too bloody close though, Barney,' said Max, engaging the gears and pulling away.

'I've had closer shaves. Hopefully it'll be worth it – we've lit a candle in the dark, to use Ross's strange metaphor.' Barney plucked the roll-up from behind his ear and lit it with his battered Zippo.

'Did you get seen?'

'Yeah, but with a good reason to be there. It was fortunate there was an alarm panel in the corridor.' He exhaled a blue cloud of smoke with obvious pleasure.

'What if there hadn't been?'

'Smoke alarms, heat detectors, whatever. There's always a reason to be somewhere.'

'Everyone's waiting for us at the flat. Did you get what you wanted?'

'Difficult to say. I'll do some tests when I get back. I'll have to sort the data and work through it with Norma, but the speed of the download suggests that there isn't much on it.'

'That's not great.'

'Well, I've an ace up my sleeve. Let's get back and we'll go through it.'

The first thing that was evident when Max and Barney entered the office was the smell. Norma was busy in the kitchen frying bacon, and a pile of Glasgow rolls lay buttered and ready on the breakfast bar, next to bottles of sauce. A large pot of coffee was bubbling in the machine.

'All smells awesome,' said Barney as Norma slapped several rashers in a roll and handed it to him.

Within a few moments, Max, Janie, Norma and Barney were all tucking into thick bacon rolls. They all ate in silence. Ross scowled at them as he picked at a Tupperware box that contained a mixed fruit salad.

'How's the fruit salad, Ross?' said Norma.

'Piss off. Cured meat takes bastard years off your life,' said Ross, with a wistful glance at the bacon.

'That was bloody tremendous, Norma. The bacon was perfectly crisp, the rolls fresh, and the brown sauce set it all off beautifully,' said Max.

'Get fucked, Craigie. Now can I please have an update, if it's not too much trouble?'

'I'll let Barney fill us in,' said Max.

'All went according to plan. Niall came up trumps and

opened the fire door. I managed to download the burner phone, but I doubt there's a great deal on it. Might've been some aftermarket updates to the handset. I couldn't locate the camera for one, but I managed to install the malware. We also have an impression of Gray's house key.'

'That was fortuitous,' said Janie.

'Yep. Luckily, I had a key impression kit with me. I'll get a copy made as soon as I've worked out what's the deal with this phone.'

'What malware have you installed?' said Norma.

'Screen sharing. All we'll get is what she's actually seeing on her screen. We can't activate the camera or microphone, as the pathways to those have been corrupted somehow. GPS is deactivated, as well. I'll dive deeper and update when I'm done.'

'Get on with it, then. Stop with your blethering, man,' said Ross.

'I'll crack on, but I'm having a tab first,' he said, pulling the rolled cigarette from behind his ear and moving towards the balcony. He lit up as he opened the door and stepped outside.

'Okay, folks. So, we need to give Barney some time to work the data and get the key cut. I'm open to ideas about what we do next,' said Ross.

'Can I make a suggestion?' said Norma.

'You made tasty rolls, so yes.'

'We still have no explanation as to why Lorimer's car never appeared on ANPR, and yet we know from the GPS download what route he took between Ravelston and Dunnet Head.'

'Anything that can be done with the data?' said Janie.

'We could possibly overlay the timings with the route and

manually search each car that went through the checkpoints at the relevant times. A number are linked to traffic cameras, and the images will be stored. We may capture who was in the car,' said Norma.

'Good idea – you crack on with that. Any observations?' said Ross.

'Just one. Do you have the forensic reports on the examination of Lorimer's Audi?'

'We've got it all on our shared drive,' said Ross.

'Anything notable?'

'Hold up.' Ross tapped at his screen and scrolled on his track pad.

'Aye, it's here. Lots of prints lifted, almost all were Lorimer's and there were a few unidentified that weren't on the database. No significant DNA, no suggestions of blood. Seats were all taped, but they're leather, so not much found. It wasn't given the highest of priorities, as it looked like a slam dunk that Lorimer was guilty. It's his car, his fingerprints and DNA. Where are you going with this?'

'What if someone else was driving?'

Ross opened his mouth to answer, but then closed it again.

Max continued, 'It's not beyond the realms of possibility, is it? I'm still not convinced that the same person could have committed both murders within such a short period of time. Can we be sure they didn't split resources?'

'But we think taser was used for both,' said Janie.

'Maybe there are two tasers?'

There was a long silence as everyone turned over the idea.

'A theory. One of our murderers tasers, restrains and then secures Paterson to the tree and cuts his throat. The other travels to Dunnet in the Audi, tasers Fergus Grigor and heaves him off the cliff. We need to find some imagery of the Audi travelling north, and see if one or two people were in the car.'

'He's right,' said Janie.

'Aye, and I fucking well hate it when he's right. So, what do you suggest?'

'Where's the Audi now?'

'Mitchell's in Lochrin,' said Ross, peering at his screen.

'I'm going to take a look at it. CSI may have missed something. Come on, Janie.'

'What do you think you could find that they couldn't?'

'Ross, it wouldn't be the first time I've found crucial evidence that CSI has missed. They were looking for evidence to put Lorimer and anyone else in that car. They weren't looking for how it managed to evade ANPR.'

'Maybe leave it to Hughie's team?'

'Hughie's not going to do it, is he? Can we be sure how far Marnie's influence stretches? If Gus Fraser is to be believed, she can wrap men around her little finger.'

Ross's eyes were hard, his jaw tight.

'Get on with it, then.'

66

NIALL SIGHED AND stifled a yawn. The meeting had been as dull as dishwater. Operation Jupiter, whilst serious and high profile, was going to be long-term data analysis, suspect screening, and probably major DNA trawls. And once his involvement was no longer required, a reason would be constructed to withdraw him from this deployment. It couldn't come soon enough, as far as he was concerned.

Undercover policing could be exciting, enthralling and dangerous. Now he was just doing a tedious computer-based job, whilst keeping his eyes open and his ear to the ground.

DCI Gray had wrapped up the meeting and dished out a load of research portfolios on several possible suspects, several of whom were already in prison. One or two were actually dead. She'd then disappeared into her office and closed the door.

Niall looked at his phone and noticed a single message from a tooth-whitening company. A code meaning contact was required.

Niall looked at his watch. He'd need to leave soon to get to Gartcosh, anyway.

He grabbed his jacket, pocketed his phone, and went to Marnie Gray's office. He knocked and popped his head around the door.

'That's me off to Gartcosh, boss.'

She looked up from her laptop, a frown etched across her fine features. 'Sorry, Billy, what's that?'

'Gartcosh. Training on the intel and open-source systems?'

'Ah right, yes. Fine, when are you back?'

'Well, training is the rest of the day. You want me back after?'

She looked at him, her jade eyes holding his for a moment. 'No, go home and back in tomorrow ready to go. You've a core role, here. Intel is going to be front and centre on this operation.' Her gaze flicked from his head to his toes, and she smiled. 'Sit down for a moment,' she said. Her eyes were now wide and engaged.

Niall sat down in front of Gray, a tickle of nerves in his stomach.

She stood up and walked past him to shut the office door. As she returned, her hip brushed against his shoulder. Her perfume was light and floral. Billy swallowed.

As she sat back down, she fixed him with a gaze, her head cocked to one side. 'Settling in okay?' she said, her smile widening, her white teeth even.

'Aye. Not so bad.'

'And where is it you're living?'

'Craigentinny.'

'Your parents' old place, I think you said.'

'Aye. It's not so bad. Funny coming home after all these years in England.'

'I hear it was a marriage break-up. Detective's curse, right?'

'Something like that. It's fine, all for the best.'

'Do you get lonely?'

Billy paused for a moment, his mouth suddenly dry. 'Maybe a little, but I'm okay. Work keeps me busy,' he said, his throat tight.

She looked directly at him; her brilliant green eyes bored into him. She ran a hand through her ponytail and tossed it over her shoulder. He felt his stomach tighten.

'Billy …' she hesitated for a moment, flicking her eyes down momentarily. 'I'm really impressed with your performance and support. You're clearly a cut above the others on the team. I just wanted to let you know that I appreciate it.' She looked straight at him.

Billy paused a beat, his mind working overtime. He'd been married to Jeri for so long he had absolutely no idea how to flirt.

'Er, thanks, boss,' was all that he could think of to say.

She continued to watch him. 'When it's just us Billy, Marnie will be fine.' Billy began to understand the effect that DCI Marnie Gray had on men.

She was intoxicating.

67

JANIE PULLED UP the Volvo outside the vehicle compound in Lochrin and switched off the engine.

'So, what are we looking for?'

'Whatever we find,' said Max.

'Want a sweetie?' said Janie, handing over a bag of boiled sweets.

'Nice. Keep the blood sugar up,' said Max, picking one out, peeling off the wrapper and popping it in his mouth. 'Somehow, the Audi managed to travel hundreds of miles through Edinburgh, up the A9 and along the main arterial route from the central belt to the Highlands. They must have done something with the plates.'

'No mention of it in the CSI report.'

'Which suggests they didn't check. Wc handed this over, so we're in the hands of someone else's forensic strategy. Come on, just a quick lookie.'

They got out of the car and held up their warrant cards as they went through the big metal gates.

'Help you?' said a big, meaty man in stained overalls and a baseball cap.

'From the police. Just want to have a quick look at the Audi over there.' Max nodded at the powerful-looking Audi SQ5 in the far corner of the compound.

'Knock yourselves out. You need the keys?'

'No, I think we're good.'

'Suit yourselves,' he sniffed and wandered off, wiping his hands on a rag.

They approached the sleek car. It was sitting on low-profile tyres, the sun glinting off the metallic paintwork. Certain patches were clouded where aluminium powder had been used by the fingerprint officers. White stickers with green arrows pointed to where prints had been lifted.

Max pressed his face against the tinted glass, noting the powder-covered dash and rear-view mirror. The seats were sleek leather, but you could see some slivers of tape on the carpeted floor, the results of seat and carpet tapings.

Janie squatted at the front of the car, fiddling with the number plate fixings. The plastic screws appeared to be new.

'I don't think the plates have been removed,' said Janie.

'Why?'

'No screwdriver marks on the plastic screws.'

Max went to the rear plate and squatted down to get a better look at the screws. Their edges were as clean and crisp as the day the plates had been attached. There were powder marks around the far edges of each side of the plate, presumably where the CSI had checked for any print marks that might suggest the plates had been removed.

Max pulled out his pocket-knife and slotted it into the left-hand screw. He twisted with a fair amount of force, and the screw gave, unscrewing in a dozen turns. A perfect circle of the plate was a lighter colour underneath the tightly fitted screw where dirt and grime had not managed to penetrate.

'Nope, not been removed,' said Max.

'How the bloody hell did they dodge ANPR, then?' said Janie.

Max sat back on his haunches and looked at the plate from an angle. The light seemed to be hitting it differently by the letter L. Max ran his hand over the metal, and it felt sticky. Excitement began to rise in his chest. 'Check the L, Janie,' he said.

There was a brief pause. 'It's sticky,' she said.

Max stood up quickly and went to the wheel arch of the car. He reached under and broke off a dried piece of desiccated, powdery mud. Rubbing it in his hands until it was a fine powder, he returned to the plate and threw the handful of earth at the L.

And he saw it.

The L had morphed into an E as the powdery earth adhered to the sticky residue. Tape had clearly been used to change the registration.

Crude yet effective and enough to fool the ANPR system.

Max reached for his phone and dialled.

'Maxie-boy?' said Norma's cheerful voice.

'I need you to run a plate for me.'

68

'**SO, THE CHEEKY** bastard used four inches of electrical tape to confuse the ANPR?' said Ross, when Max and Janie returned to the office.

'Aye. Just changed the L to an E,' said Max clutching the plates which had been secured with zip-ties into a box and placed in a bag.

'More than that. The fake plate was taken from an identical model of car. So, whoever put the tape on had to have access to PNC. The real car with that plate is registered in Newcastle.'

'Isn't that a coincidence – same make and model, like?' said Barney from his seat by the window. He took a drag of his roll-up and Ross shot him a venomous look.

'Not really. Manufacturers batch register vehicles with DVLA. It's totally feasible that two identical vehicles will bear similar plates. It happens all the time,' said Norma.

'So, any cop checking, or ANPR activations, would show it as a Black Audi SQ5 registered in Newcastle. And unless there was a reason to stop it, no one would know?'

'Pretty much,' said Norma.

'Were any prints recovered from the plates?' said Janie.

'Nope. Not a sausage,' said Ross.

'Shows some recklessness, doesn't it?' said Norma, tapping at her computer.

'Not so much of a risk, once out of Edinburgh, particularly in the early hours,' said Janie. 'Once you're north of Perth count how many cops patrolling you see. Road policing has been decimated with austerity, cuts and that. I'd say there was almost no chance of getting stopped if they drove carefully.'

'How about all the speed cameras on the A9. They use ANPR, right?' said Barney.

'Only focused on the plates. The data's encrypted and each activation is probably only stored for an hour or so before being overwritten,' said Norma.

'So, whilst it's nice to know, it's pretty much useless to us?' said Ross.

'I wouldn't go that far. It gives us a solid lead, and something else to look for. We can track other fixed ANPRs and extract the activations. So, for instance, many garages and service areas have ANPR. We can then check other CCTV systems to potentially identify the driver and/or passengers. It could be a clincher,' said Janie.

'Nice to have, but it's not number one priority. We need to go proactive on Gray and very soon. Anything from our contact in MIT 6?' asked Ross.

'Funny you should say that. He's just messaged. He's at Gartcosh doing some tedious computer training.'

'Nothing to report?'

'Nothing specific,' said Max.

'I'm not up for bloody nuance, Max. In fact, I'm not sure I actually know what nuance means.'

'He reckons that Marnie Gray was flirting with him.'

Everyone in the room stopped what they were doing and stared at Max.

'Shit. That woman is a fucking hellion. I take it that not getting too close to her was relayed to our friend. Pissing last thing we need is the UC shagging the target,' said Ross.

'He knows the score, but it's an insight into Acting DCI Gray, isn't it?' said Max.

'Yeah, but how? Is she onto him? Or maybe she's identifying her next patsy?' said Janie.

'Well, remind him what happened to the last bloke who was giving her one. She's like a spider, she eats her lovers. Now we need a plan to deploy on her. We need her movements controlled whilst we do the sneaky shit we're planning. Any observations?' said Ross.

'I'd say that using the surveillance team is risky. Two members worked with DCI Gray in the past, and one joined the force alongside her. And one thing links them all.'

'No amateur dramatics, Norma,' said Ross, yawning.

'All are men,' Norma said, simply.

'Aye. Too risky, it seems she can get under the skin of blokes. Any other ideas?' said Ross.

'A full technical attack. Home, office, phone, car. The works. If we can't follow her conventionally, we lump and track her. We need to get into her computers, her emails, her social media, the whole lot. We get into every bit of her life, and then we make something happen. We chuck a big rock into a pond and let her make a mistake.' Max's eyes blazed with determination.

'Yep,' said Janie.

'Damn straight,' said Barney.

'It's the only way,' said Norma.

'That's exactly what I was thinking. We light a candle in the darkness,' said Ross. 'I like it.'

Everyone rolled their eyes.

'Okay, then,' Ross continued. 'Go home, none of this is going to happen overnight. We can take it in turns to monitor her phone screen. Barney, can you share the link with everyone? We'll all need to be ready to deploy at a moment's notice. I don't need to tell you all just how serious this is, do I?' said Ross.

The silence in the room was answer enough.

69

Alfa-Secure

–We may have a minor issue.

–What?

–We need to meet.

–When?

–Usual place in an hour?

–Okay. Any news on Gus?

–He's disappeared. Gone misper.

–That's not ideal. He's a risk to us, he needs to be taken care of.

–He's being looked for. He knows nothing.

–Still a risk. Find him.

–I will.

–We still have that more serious unresolved issue.

–I know. I'm on it.

–Okay. Make sure you have auto-delete on the messages.

–Of course. I love you.

–????

–Have you gone?

–????

Messages deleting in 5-4-3-2-1. . .

70

NIALL LET OUT a huge yawn as he pulled onto the paved drive at the front of his depressing bungalow on Craigentinny Road. Instead of getting out of the car, he just sat for a moment, looking in his rear-view mirror, wondering why he felt so uneasy.

He sighed, trying to push the depression away. He was badly missing Jeri and his kids. He'd call them later with his personal phone he kept well hidden inside the bungalow. Carrying your personal phone whilst actively deployed was a risk he wasn't taking.

He also couldn't shake the uncomfortable feeling in his gut about his earlier encounter with DCI Gray. He couldn't entirely work out if she was genuinely flirting with him, or if she was trying to check him out. It was disturbing that in amongst it all, he had felt a tiny bit of pleasure at the attention. She was very attractive, after all, and had something that he couldn't put his finger on. It was disconcerting, and yet somehow exciting.

This was the general problem with covert work. Much of it was routine and tedious, but you never managed to shake the underlying gnaw of anxiety at the possibility of being blown. The severity of the consequences of exposure often caused that constant nag of uncertainty.

He got out of his car and slammed the door shut. Trying to shake the disquiet, he looked over his shoulder, but the street was empty, and routine, with soft lights escaping from his neighbour's curtains, and he could just imagine the domestic scenes from within.

He unlocked the uPVC door and entered the house. His stomach rumbled. He threw his coat on one of the floral-patterned, high-backed chairs and went through to the tiny galley kitchen.

Opening the fridge, he stared at the contents with a wrinkled nose. Niall considered himself a foodie and the prospect of a flabby microwave lasagne or a dodgy-looking chicken curry was not appealing. There wasn't even any beer.

He had seen a Chinese takeaway on his way back. Fuck it, off-licence for a pack of beers, and a Chinese takeaway in front of the TV. His mouth began to water at the prospect of kung-po chicken and egg-fried rice washed down with lager.

Undercover deployments could be fascinating, heart-stopping. Niall had posed as a successful drug dealer, drinking champagne at an exclusive nightclub in Mayfair whilst planning to purchase a million pounds' worth of cocaine. He'd travelled to Spain and been wined and dined by a notorious London criminal, whilst posing as a high-level money launderer. He'd even pretended to be a hitman for a very angry wife who wanted to have her multi-millionaire husband killed.

And here he was, in a 1960s pebbledash bungalow, with floral curtains, patterned carpets, and an avocado-coloured bathroom suite. He was miles from home, missing his family, with the prospect of a day's tedium in an office of detectives the next day. The least he deserved was a decent meal and a couple of beers.

Niall returned to the living room, picked up his coat and left the house, locking the door behind him.

After a ten-minute walk along the busy Craigentinny Road, he arrived at the Chinese takeaway in a small parade of shops set back from the main road. There was a pizza place, and two Chinese takeaways. He picked the one that looked the cleanest and went in and ordered kung-po chicken, fried rice, prawn crackers and a side order of lemon chicken. The smells were deliciously spicy and aromatic, and his mouth began to water.

'How long?' asked Niall.

'Ten minutes, hen,' said the grinning lady in a broad Glaswegian accent.

Niall nodded. 'Back in five.'

He walked a few doors down on the same parade and went into a small convenience store. It was a typical suburban shop that sold everything you needed and a good few things that you didn't. Within a few minutes he had selected two bottles of Singha beer, a large bar of chocolate, and a motorcycle magazine. He paid the taciturn cashier and returned to the takeaway at a leisurely pace. It was a pleasant evening, just a touch of chill, and the roads had quietened considerably in the past half an hour since he arrived back at the cover house. He'd get his food, walk back and eat, then he'd risk a call to Jeri. He was desperate to speak to her, having been away a few days now. He looked around at the grimy streets, and at that moment he decided that this would be his last undercover deployment. He'd had enough. He didn't want the stress and pressure anymore of having multiple identities, constantly on edge, always at work and putting his family second. That's it, he thought. It's over.

He went into the takeaway and paid for his food, pushing open the door with his shoulder and emerging into the chill air. He shivered, and he wondered for a moment if it was the weather, or the deployment that was making him nervous. He looked up and down the streets but saw nothing untoward.

He was just approaching the junction at the end of the service road when his phone buzzed in his pocket. With a bit of transferring of bags into one hand he answered it, 'Yeah?'

'How was the course?' said Max.

'Very, very dull. Trainer was a real computer-intel nerd and I didn't get out until five thirty. Took me bloody two hours to go from Gartcosh back to this depressing bungalow.'

'Anything from DCI Gray?'

'What after her eyelash fluttering earlier? No, thankfully. I've no desire to get too close to her. There's something very nasty in those eyes, I tell you. Anything from the burner phone?'

'Yes. Worrying messages. It seems likely there's two of them.'

'What?'

'I guess the only interpretation is that there's someone else involved.'

'What? So, you mean there could have been three killers before Lorimer got topped?'

'It seems possible, maybe even plausible.'

'Did the phone move?' Niall's gut tightened at the news.

'No, it was switched off straight after.'

'Bit odd, who the hell is on the other phone?'

'We can't tell as it's not going to a phone number but an encrypted messaging service.'

'Shit,' said Niall, switching hands between his phone and carry-out bags.

'Aye, keep your eyes open, yeah? What's Gray got for you tomorrow?'

'Intel screening. It's going to be seriously tedious. I'm not sure what I'm bringing to the party now? Plus ...' he hesitated.

'What?'

'Marnie scares me. I'm not contributing anything, and she's a fucking psycho. I really want to get home, and I'm just not sure this is gonna work.'

'Mate, not now. You disappear now and it's bloody game over and it'd blow the whole bloody shebang. Plus, you give us the control we so badly need. It's not long-term, we'll be closing in a few days, I'm certain.'

Niall sighed as he walked along the road, his bags heavy in his hand. 'I don't have the stomach for it anymore, but I'll stick it for a bit longer. I only agreed because it was you who asked.'

'Good man, you know it makes sense. I reckon we can wrap this up within a week. We can't leave her out there running unobserved. Just a few more days, yeah?'

'Aye, okay,' Niall said, suddenly aware he'd lost his appetite for the food he was carrying.

'You know the score, we're planning a full tech attack on her, and you give us an early warning system of what she's doing and where she is. Last thing we need is her and whoever she's operating with finding another target who's escaped justice for murdering, raping and pillaging, or something.'

Niall took a deep breath, trying to chase away the anxiety

that was nipping at him. 'I know, I know. Just missing Jeri and the kids, I guess. Not sure if this UC game is for me. This might be my last one.'

'You're doing great. If she's hitting on you, it means she likes you, and that may offer opportunities in the future.'

'Yeah, that doesn't relax me, there's something bloody scary about her.' Niall shifted his grip on the bags, the one with the bottles in was beginning to bite into his palm with the weight.

'Aye I guess, anyway. Enjoy your takeaway,' said Max.

'Cheers, bud,' and he finished the call, an uncomfortable feeling in his gut. Something Max had just said was making him worry. He stopped dead on the pavement, trying to extract it and join the dots. There was an image circling at the edges of his memory. Something he had seen.

Then it hit him like a slap in the face. Max's words just a minute ago. *Last thing we need is her and whoever she's operating with finding another target who's escaped justice for murdering, raping and pillaging, or something.*

'Shit,' he exclaimed. The BBC feed yesterday. The image of the creepy-looking man on Marnie Gray's computer, freed on appeal from a court somewhere. He quickly brought up the BBC app on his phone and scrolled until he found the story. CONVICTION OF CUMBRIAN LEON BLACK OVERTURNED ON APPEAL.

Niall stood in the pavement, rooted to the spot. That had to be it. That was their next victim.

He dialled Max, his hands shaking. 'Shit, shit, shit,' he said as he misdialled. He keyed in the numbers again.

'What's up, mate?' said Max.

'Max ...'

Niall had only a fraction of a second to recognise what was happening. Headlights suddenly blinded him, and a large Ford mounted the kerb. Bits of gravel spat from under its wheels. Someone screamed. The vehicle thundered straight towards him at speed, its engine roaring. His heart leaped with the complete and utter terror at what was about to happen, unable to move as if his feet were stuck fast to the pavement.

'Max ...' he yelled. At that exact moment the car struck him, the bumper shattering both of his kneecaps. He was tossed like a rag doll into the air, his head striking the windscreen, and his body continuing over the top across the roof and into mid-air. He hung there for a second before hitting the tarmac pavement in a heap. Strangely, there was no immediate pain, just a rush of colours and sounds, as the adrenaline took over. He managed to look back, feeling warm blood on his face. He tried to move, but his legs were dead. Totally inert. They may as well have been someone else's legs. The last thing he saw before he passed out was the Ford, screeching, bumping off the pavement and back onto the road, its wheels kicking up dust as it tore away into the night.

71

'NIALL?' SHOUTED MAX into the phone. He listened to the tinny silence, willing his friend to say something. Niall had shouted his name, there had been a loud clatter, and then the phone went dead.

'Niall?' he said, louder, and more urgently. Nutmeg whined and lowered her head, moving from Max across to Katie.

'What's up?' said Katie, who was curled up on the sofa in her pyjamas.

'Niall?' Max shouted, his jaw tight. There was no response, not even a dial tone.

'Max?' said Katie, her brow furrowed.

Max looked at his phone, dread clutching him like a vice.

'Something's happened to Niall,' he said.

'What, Niall Hastings? Jeri's other half?'

'Yes.'

'Sorry, Max. I don't understand. Where is Niall?'

'He's in Edinburgh, helping us on the case.' Max hadn't mentioned that Niall was up as he didn't want Katie to know that he was working in Edinburgh. It would have complicated things.

'What's he doing up here? Is he okay?'

Max ignored her and dialled Norma.

'No movements on the phone, Max. I assume that's why you're ringing me,' was her opener.

'Is your laptop open?'

'Yes, what's up?' she said.

'Can you check the current incident log for Edinburgh, urgently?'

'Sure, but why?'

'Are there any incidents in Craigentinny?'

'Hold up.' There was a tapping as she worked her computer.

'Just the one. Fail to stop. Injury accident on Craigentinny Road – literally come in just now – units on the way.'

'Shit, shit, shit. Any other details?' Max's stomach tightened, and his heart began to pound in his ears.

'Errm … one second …'

'Fucking, come on,' shouted Max, feeling his face burn.

'Jesus, I'm doing my best. It's a new call and information is still coming in. Informant is a passer-by. Ford Mondeo mounted the kerb and struck a pedestrian. Serious injuries, ambulance and cops on the way.'

'Fuck. Fuck, I heard it happen. I was on the phone to Niall when the car hit him. They've tried to bloody kill him.' Max screwed his eyes shut, and pressed his free hand to his temple.

'Max …'

'Okay. Can you forward the details to all our accounts and call Ross and Janie and let them know? Janie's the closest. I'm on my way. Keep me updated. I'm going to be driving on blues and twos.' Max hung up, feeling the clouds gather in his head, a sense of deep rage mounting, his blood rushing through his ears.

'Max, what's happening?' said Katie, her eyes confused.

'I think Niall's been hurt. I have to get there now.'

Katie covered her mouth with her hand and gasped, her eyes brimming with tears. 'Oh my God. He was only with us the other day. Can I do anything?'

'No. Just stay here. I'll call you later.'

'Max?' she said in a faltering voice, but she knew. She could see it in her husband's grim eyes and set jaw.

'I'm going now,' he said, lacing up his trainers and grabbing his jacket. He opened the door.

'I love you,' said Katie, but he was gone.

72

ROSS, MAX AND Janie were all standing in the silent waiting room at the Royal Infirmary of Edinburgh, their faces blank and shell-shocked.

A senior doctor in scrubs came in and beckoned them over. They followed him into a room marked RELATIVES.

'I'm Dr Carmichael, A and E consultant. Do we have a next of kin nearby for Mr Bruce?'

'His name is actually Niall Hastings. His wife is in the process of being informed, but she lives in Hertfordshire,' said Ross.

The doctor frowned. 'I heard he was an officer, but the police who came in with him said his name was William Bruce.'

'Long story, but I can assure you, his real name is Niall Hastings. Look, this needs to stay quiet, but he was on covert, operational duties. We need to tell you this as you'll be needing medical records, but it's essential that this information isn't leaked or made public. What's his condition?'

'He's in a very serious condition, and he needs emergency surgery. He has multiple lower-limb fractures, a nasty head injury, possibly a skull fracture and God knows what else.

He's going for a CT scan now, so we'll know more after that,' he said.

'Will he survive?' asked Ross, his face pale.

'Short answer. I don't know. He's lost a great deal of blood, he may have internal bleeding and we still aren't sure whether his spine is compromised. It's very serious, and I have to stress that next of kin should be here as soon as possible.'

'It's in hand,' said Ross.

'Is he conscious?' said Janie.

'He's heavily sedated, but we haven't fully put him under yet. He'll be going for surgery as soon as the scans are done.'

'Shit.'

'Indeed. Any news on the driver of the car?' said Carmichael.

'They made off. We're searching for them now.'

'There's something you should know …' Carmichael hesitated.

Ross raised his eyebrows.

'He was hit once, front side, head on which damaged the knees, and caused his head to collide with the windscreen before he passed over the car. But I'm told that the car mounted the pavement and was driven directly at him. This is clearly an attempt to kill. I take it you're aware.'

'Aye. It's being treated as such,' said Ross through gritted teeth.

'Okay, well take as long as you need in the relatives' room. I have an armed officer guarding his side room. Any reason for that which you can share?'

'Just being careful. In case whichever bastard did this to him decides to try and finish him off.'

'Is that a genuine concern?'

'We're treating it as such, yes.'

'Okay, fine. Look, I need to get back to it. Will someone be staying?'

'Yes, for the foreseeable.'

The consultant nodded and left the room.

'What's happening with Jeri?' asked Max.

'Locals are with her now. She's sorting childcare and then she's being driven up here on blues and twos. She'll be here in a few hours.'

'Where's Gray?'

'Norma is doing the work, but it looks like DCI Gray is at home. Phones haven't moved.'

'Any activity on the burner?' said Max.

'None.'

'This is down to her, you know that, right?' It was a statement, not a question. Max's eyes were clouded, his jaw tight and the muscles in his neck were corded with tension.

'I don't doubt it. On call MIT is despatching and it's being properly dealt with. There's one witness, but he didn't see the driver and we've yet to locate the car, although I'm sure it'll turn up,' said Janie, looking at the messages on her phone.

'It's her. No doubt about it. We have to sort this out.'

'We have no evidence, beyond motive, and even that's pretty thin.'

'We need to get her bugged up. Everywhere, everything, the whole lot. She shouldn't be able to bloody fart without us knowing about it. It's my fault that Niall is in that state.'

'Max, don't be bloody—'

'No, Niall is in that state because of me.' Max almost growled at his boss, his eyes blazing. 'He's my friend, he saved my life in London, and I brought him into this. His wife is my friend, I know his kids. I asked him to come, Ross. I invited him to my house for a fucking BBQ and then persuaded him to get himself killed. A few seconds before that car smashed into him, he was telling me he wanted out, but I persuaded him to stay. It's. My. Fucking. Fault.'

'Max ...' said Janie.

'We're finishing this. I'm waiting here for Jeri to turn up, so I can look her in the eye and accept responsibility for putting Niall in this position. Then we go after Marnie Gray.' Max's voice was as hard as tempered steel, his face rigid.

They all shared a knowing look.

'Anything I can do in the meantime?' said Janie.

'We need to get feasibility studies on all the options for the tech attack. Hook up with Barney and let's get ready for tomorrow. Her car and her home, anything. We need to think out of the box here,' said Max.

'On it.' Janie moved closer to Max and reached out to grab his hand with hers. 'You couldn't have known. Only one person is to blame.' She looked him straight in the eyes.

Max said nothing.

Janie nodded and left the room.

'What are you going to do?' asked Ross.

'I'm staying until Jeri gets here. You go and start getting all the shit in order that we'll need. The chief will want to know chapter and verse, so you'd best get up to speed with what's happening at the crash scene.'

Ross's phone pinged and he glanced at the screen.

'Niall's wife is on her way now. She'll be here in a few hours. Why not go home for a bit?'

Max shook his head. 'I'm staying here. What if he wakes up and wants to talk?'

'You heard the doc. It's unlikely he'll be awake for some time.'

'I'm going nowhere. I owe it to him and Jeri, and the doc wants someone here, I think.'

'I know that look. You're a stubborn bugger. Right, I'll go, then. Try and get some rest. We're going to be busy.' Ross nodded and left.

Max sat on one of the chairs and closed his eyes, his thoughts raging like a tumultuous sea. Dark clouds began to form in his mind, and he took a breath. In, hold for five and slowly release. In, hold for five and slowly release. He sat like that for a full five minutes before his eyes snapped open. He left the relatives' room and went through into the resus ward. Dr Carmichael nodded at him. 'Everything okay, officer?'

'Any news? His wife is on the way and I'd like to be able to update her. She's going to be going out of her mind with worry.'

Carmichael sighed. He looked shattered. 'He's just back from a CT scan. He has multiple leg fractures, a fractured skull, and a small bleed on the brain, which we're worried about. Some internal bleeding that we need to stop urgently. The emergency surgical team are just getting theatre ready. He's a mess, but we have the best people on it.'

'Can I see him? Just for a minute.'

'He's deeply sedated.'

'Aye, I know, but I want to tell his wife that I've told him she's on her way.'

'It's highly irregular.'

'Please. He's my friend. His wife's my friend,' said Max, his voice low.

'Five minutes. I'll tell the charge nurse,' he said with a sympathetic sigh. He turned and pulled back the curtain, then disappeared out of sight into the cubicle.

Two minutes later, he emerged again, nodding towards the interior. 'Five minutes, okay?' he said.

Max nodded and followed the doctor inside, his heart racing at the dread of what he was about to see. Images of Dippy flashed in his mind in vivid colour but he forced them away. A nurse nodded at Max as he entered. He was a huge tattooed man with a rough face but kind eyes.

'I'll leave you to it, but five minutes only, okay?' said the doctor who nodded and left.

Niall lay on his back, his neck in a brace, tubes and wires attached to every part of him. A thick dressing obscured the right side of his face. He was covered with a thin sheet that had been elevated above his limbs by an unseen cage. There was the regular beep of the monitoring equipment and a screen flashed and blinked as machines measured his vitals. An oxygen mask covered his mouth and nose, hissing quietly.

'How stable is he?' asked Max.

'Blood pressure is low, heart is strong and oxygen sats fluctuating, but bearing in mind what happened, it's a miracle he's still with us,' said the charge nurse.

'Can I talk to him?' said Max.

'Aye, be my guest. He's looked at us a couple of times and squeezed my hand once. He's a fighter, this one.'

Max went to the bedside of his friend and took hold of his hand, being careful to avoid the oxygen meter that was attached to his finger. His hand was cold and dry, his skin pale, and there was a smear of blood on his exposed cheek. He breathed steadily and raggedly.

'Niall, pal. It's me. Max Craigie.' There was no response. Not even a flicker from the one eye that wasn't covered.

'Jeri's on her way and the kids are being taken care of. I'll be waiting here for her and I'll look after her, I promise.'

Nothing. Just the same rasping, regular breaths. The monitor beeped frantically, and the charge nurse silenced it with a jab of his finger.

'It's fine,' he whispered at Max's concerned expression.

'Niall, you fight this, pal. We're gonna find who did this, I promise you that. We'll find them, but you keep fighting. Jeri and the kids need you …' Max's voice cracked as he looked at the broken form of his friend. Tears began to well in Max's eyes and one spilled, carving a path down his cheek. He breathed deeply, trying to regain his composure.

'You fight this. You get better.' Max's voice cracked again and the tears spilled onto both cheeks.

Niall's eye fluttered, and the lid parted a fraction. The deep blue of his iris shone. The pupil like a pinprick thanks to the opiates he'd been given.

It sparkled, a brief parting in the clouds. Niall's hand tightened in Max's, an almost imperceptible increase in pressure.

The oxygen mask moved, and the corner of his mouth twitched with the merest suggestion of a smile.

'That's enough now,' said the charge nurse.

Max nodded and let go of Niall's hand.

'See you soon. Keep fighting.'

Niall breathed evenly, his eye fully closed, his face relaxed, any trace of consciousness now gone.

'Thanks,' said Max to the charge nurse and left the cubicle, everything now clear and focused.

One thought dominated his mind.

'I'm coming for you, Marnie Gray.'

73

MAX WAS HALF-SNOOZING in the relatives' room when the door opened. A young officer wearing the white shirt and insignia of the Metropolitan Police entered and nodded at Max.

'DS Craigie?'

'Aye, is Jeri with you?' said Max, standing and shaking the proffered hand.

'Just in the loo,' he said.

'How is she?'

'Scared and upset, mate, as you'd expect,' he said in a broad cockney accent.

'Aye. Thanks for this. Are you sorted for accommodation?'

'Yeah, hotel booked from your side. Some foul-mouthed geezer phoned me and said we had a place nearby. I'm bloody knackered, a five-hour blue-light run.'

'I appreciate it. Thanks, mate.' Max looked over the officer's shoulder and saw the diminutive, red-haired Jeri Hastings come out of the toilet. She saw Max and her face just dissolved. She strode up to him and threw her arms around his neck.

'Max, I'm so glad it's you. What was Niall doing up here?

He just said that he was going on a deployment, and I didn't ask. I mean, I never do.'

'He was doing some work for us, and then last night someone deliberately ran him over in Leith. We're investigating how and why right now.'

'Where is he?' she said, her cheeks damp with tears.

'In theatre. I'll see if I can find a doctor to talk to you.'

'How serious is it?' she said, her hand clutching at his forearm so tightly that her knuckles were white.

Max opened his mouth, and then stopped. He had no idea what to say, or how to say it.

'Max?' Jeri repeated, her chin trembling.

He took a deep breath. 'It's serious, Jeri. He has broken legs and a fractured skull. There was some internal bleeding, which they're sorting.'

'Oh, no, no, no,' she said, collapsing into Max's arms and sobbing uncontrollably. Max took her into the relatives' room, his insides churning. They just stood like that, under the strip lighting in the small room, holding each other whilst she sobbed.

74

IT WAS ALMOST nine the following morning when Max arrived home. Jeri was sitting next to him in the Volvo, tired and wrung-out.

Niall had remained in surgery all night. Max had sat next to Jeri as the surgeon explained the nature of her husband's injuries.

Niall was gravely injured, but he was going to live. The big question was what quality of life he would have. Wheelchair? Crutches? Mobility scooter? The unasked questions were uppermost in everyone's minds.

The fractures in his legs had been pinned and his internal bleeding had been staunched. More worrying was the subdural haematoma that they were closely monitoring and would possibly have to operate on if it got any worse.

'You okay?' said Max, unable to think of anything else to say.

Jeri turned to look at him, her eyes dark and circled. 'Not really, Max. I thought my husband was doing some boring work somewhere, expecting him to come home with presents for the kids in a few days. Instead of that, I find out he's been undercover at a police station in Scotland, and now is in traction and may spend the rest of his fucking life in a wheelchair, so I'm pretty bloody far from being okay,' she said, wiping her eyes.

'Cup of tea?' Even as he said it, he knew how stupid he sounded.

'Is Katie indoors?'

'Yeah. She's waiting for you.'

'In that case, I want a glass of wine. In fact, I want a fucking bottle of wine.'

'Come on. Let's go.' They got out of the car, just as the French doors opened, and Katie appeared, hair askew and her eyes wide. She ran to the Volvo and threw her arms around Jeri as soon as she stepped out of the car, Nutmeg circled their legs, barking joyously at the newcomer.

'Jeri, Jeri, I'm so sorry,' said Katie, tears streaming. Jeri buried her own face into Katie's dressing-gowned shoulder and they both stood there shaking for a long moment.

Max caught Katie's eye, and simply said, 'I'm off.'

'Where?' asked Katie.

'Back to work. I've things to do,' he said, his voice hard.

'But you need to sleep,' said Katie.

Max didn't answer. He got back in the car, turned it around and roared off, gravel spitting up in the Volvo's wake.

75

MAX ARRIVED BACK at the apartment in Leith to find Ross, Janie and Norma at their desks.

'Max?' Janie said. The question hung in the air as everyone stopped what they were doing to listen.

'He'll live, it seems. Although what his life will look like, who knows?' Max described Niall's injuries.

Max poured a coffee from the pot and sat down heavily at his desk. He blew out a sigh and took a long sip.

'Some sleep may be a good idea, no?' said Ross.

'I'm fine. We need to progress and finish this, guys. Who knows what she'll do next?'

'Aye, about that …'

'What?'

'Chief's coming under some pressure. Met want to know how Niall got into this position, and the IP commissioners are none too happy about the evidence we have to justify intrusive surveillance and property interference. They weren't too happy about the key imprint. I'm presenting again to them in the morning.'

'So, we're not signed off to do the tech attack?'

'Not yet. Gives us more planning time, I guess.'

Max's knuckles turned white as he gripped the mug. 'Ross, that's bullshit. Who knows what they could get up to in that time? It's twenty-four hours, for God's sake. All we have is fucking screenshot malware on her phone.'

'Anything on that?'

'Just the one message we all know about.'

'Anything from the accident inquiry?' asked Max.

'Not much. Only one witness made themselves known. Definite full-on attempt. Mounted the pavement, accelerated, and went straight into Niall. Captured on CCTV.' Ross paused. 'Want to see it?' he said after a moment.

Max wondered if he did. He thought about the stack of images already in his memory bank.

'Yes,' he said.

Ross nodded at Norma, who swivelled her screen around and clicked on the keyboard. The CCTV was local authority.

The image seemed to have been recorded from high up on a lamppost. It began with Niall, his phone clamped to his ear, bags in his other hand, crossing the road. A big Ford Mondeo then appeared, its headlights blazing. It sped up and swerved onto the pavement. They all stood in silence for a long time after the video clip had finished.

'Anything on the registration?' Max broke the impasse.

'Registered to an identical car with a similar registration in Bolton. I suspect the tape-on-the-number-plate trick again. Car's not been recovered, yet – everyone's looking for it,' said Norma.

'Replay it.' Max's expression didn't change.

Norma shuffled her mouse a touch and the image replayed.

'Focus on the driver,' said Max, concentrating intently on the grainy image.

'Can't make anything out. Whoever it is has a cap pulled down low and a scarf over their face,' said Ross.

'You can see one thing, though,' said Janie.

'What?' said Ross.

'I've met Marnie Gray. What's the first thing you notice about her?'

'Her height. She's almost six feet tall. No way is that driver that tall. Whoever drove that car at Niall, it wasn't Marnie Gray. We need to get the footage in for image analysis.'

'This won't help me with the IP commissioners, you know that, right?' said Ross, gravely.

No one said anything. The only noise was the whirring fan from Norma's computer.

'We already knew there's someone else involved in this. It changes nothing,' said Max.

'I'm not sure his lordship will see it that way.'

'How about the chief?'

'His hands are tied. If we don't have the evidence to present, he can do nothing without the say-so of the commissioners. I'm going to see him shortly,' said Ross.

'We're wasting too much time. We need to act now.'

'Aye well, that's as maybe, sergeant, but there's shit called the law, which we're encouraged to fucking adhere to, you get me?'

Max turned his eyes to his computer and started booting it up.

'Max?' said Ross.

'Aye?'

'I hope you're not thinking of doing anything daft. Remember there's still the small issue of an ongoing shooting in London, and things like this wouldn't help your cause, would they?'

'Naturally, sir.'

'Don't you fucking "sir" me. I know you only say that when you're being a sarky bastard.'

Max said nothing.

Ross glared at him, and then turned back towards his screen, muttering under his breath.

76

Alfa-Secure

—**Is it done?**

—Yes.

—**You're amazing.**

—It had to be done.

—**I think I've identified a suitable subject for our next operation.**

—Later. I have to go.

—**Can we meet later?**

—Maybe.

—**Please say yes.**

—**I miss you xox**

—**Are you there?**

—**Please answer.**

—**????**

Messages deleting in 5-4-3-2-1…

77

MAX, JANIE, NORMA and Barney pored over all the data and documentary evidence in a moody silence. Ross had not long left for his meeting with the chief at Tulliallan, glaring at them all as he went, his meaning clear.

'What's that message about?' said Janie, looking at the screenshot that had just popped up on the link.

'I don't like it one bit. The "next subject" bit makes me very nervous – sounds like they're planning to strike again. Shit we need to ramp up the timescales,' said Max.

'Definite master-and-servant relationship, there,' said Norma. 'It's cell-siting in Leith again, so she's at work. Do we know which is which?'

'We only know what's on the screen. Encrypted end-to-end, and it only shows up as data being used on her burner. It's of limited use, but better than nothing,' said Janie.

'Barney, is all your kit ready to go?' said Max.

'Yep. I've a vehicle tracker for her Lexus. We've got the house key and I have a couple of very simple wireless 4G bugs that can be rapidly deployed. I've also managed to secure keyless entry in her car, with a bit of jiggery pokery and help from a pal of mine, who's a vehicle security expert.'

'Define vehicle security expert,' said Max.

'Oh, he's a really good car thief. Box used to use him back in the day. The bugger can get into anything,' he said, using the old term for MI5, his eyes twinkling, his roll-up bobbing up and down.

'Only need a few minutes, then?'

'Yep. The bugs can be hidden anywhere – battery only, but they're voice-activated so should have plenty of life.'

'Are there any alarms at her house?'

Norma spoke up. 'None listed with any companies. No evidence on bank accounts of paying for any type of service, and I managed to get into her Amazon account and no sign of buying anything: cameras, alarms, door-bell activated surveillance. Nothing.'

'I've a jammer I can use, just in case. We should be good to go, once we get the okay from the bureaucrats. When Janie and me recce'd the place it looked a doddle.'

'Maybe we should go and have another look. What do you say? I've not seen it and it can't hurt to get ahead of the game, right?' said Max, his face innocent.

Everyone looked at him. '*Max?*' said Janie.

'Just a look, you know. Familiarise myself.'

'It'll be reet, Janie love. Can't hurt, eh?' said Barney, his accent strengthening, a glint beginning to emerge in his eyes.

'Okay, let's go then. I'd like to see what we're dealing with and once we get the nod from the IPC, we'll be ready to go.'

'You two must think I'm bloody daft,' said Janie.

'You sure about this?' said Norma.

'Sure, we're just going to have a wee lookie. Can you monitor phones?'

'You need to be careful,' Norma said.

There was a pause as Max's phone buzzed on the table. It was Katie.

'What's up?' said Max, answering the call.

'It's Niall,' said Katie, her voice thick with emotion.

Max felt the blood drain from his face, 'What?' he stammered, the words catching in his throat.

'His brain bleed has worsened. He's going in for emergency brain surgery to relieve pressure. I'm taking Jeri to the hospital now.'

Max opened his mouth to speak, but he couldn't find the words.

'Max?' said Katie.

'I'm here, what do you want me to do?'

'Catch the bastard. Catch them and lock them up.'

Max ended the call and stared into space, his head spinning.

'Max?' Janie's voice pierced the fog.

He told them what Katie had said.

No one spoke for a long moment, their eyes flicking between them.

'What shall we do?' said Janie.

'Hospital first. Then we're going to check out Gray's place. I want to know what we're dealing with.'

78

MAX FOUND JERI and Katie in the relatives' room. They were sitting in silence, hands clasped together, eyes red and bleary. Untouched vending machine coffees sat on the low table in front of them.

Jeri looked completely exhausted, her face drawn, deep circles around her eyes.

As she noticed Max, the exhaustion in her eyes was suddenly replaced with something darker.

'Any news?' said Max.

'He's about to go under. The pressure was building, so they're operating. They're taking a portion of his fucking skull off to take out the blood, so whatever you do, don't ask me if I'm okay,' Jeri glared at Max, her eyes glinting under the lights.

Max opened his mouth, but then closed it again, unsure of what to say. He felt crushing, all-enveloping shame. She was right. He'd brought Niall into this.

'I'm sorry,' he said, sitting down, trying to stop the tears from brimming in his eyes.

'Don't be, just do something useful. Catch the bastard.' She picked up her coffee in shaking hands and sipped at it, screwing up her face in disgust. 'Or at least find me a decent bloody coffee. That'd be a start,' she added, the tears beginning to well again.

Katie stretched her arm around Jeri and pulled her closer, rubbing her hair with her hand. Her eyes remained fixed on Max, and she shook her head almost imperceptibly.

'Jeri, I'm sorry. I'll never forgive myself for this, but I promise you, we'll catch them.' He tried to keep his voice steady, but it trembled with emotion.

Jeri buried her face in Katie's shoulder and sobbed. Katie looked at Max. 'I love you,' she mouthed, silently, as she rubbed Jeri's back.

Max nodded and turned to leave the room. Janie and Barney were sitting in the main waiting area.

'What's happening?' said Janie.

'He's going in for brain surgery. Come on, we're going.'

'Where?'

'Linlithgow.' Max looked at his watch. 'It's only three now, she'll be at work for a while yet, and I want a look in daylight, Norma can watch her cell site, but one way or another, we're doing this and we're doing it tonight.'

79

DCI MARNIE GRAY stood in front of her team in the conference room at Leith Police Station. The mood was sombre, heads drooped, shoulders slumped, and a gloomy atmosphere seemed to press down on them.

'Okay, guys, I just wanted to brief you all on the current state of play with Billy Bruce. As you've heard, he was the victim of a hit-and-run close to his home in Craigentinny last night at about 9 p.m. He's in a serious but stable condition at RIE with multiple injuries. The inquiry is being managed by MIT 4 who are treating it as an attempted murder inquiry. I'm told that the situation at the hospital is very tense, and no visitors from this team are to attend. A card is doing the rounds, so make sure you all sign, yes?'

'Aye, a card. That'll bloody help,' came a tight voice from the back of the room.

Gray flushed and brushed a lock of her hair behind her ear. 'Look, I know it's bad, but what can we do apart from support, and do our jobs?' she said with an attempt at a smile.

'It's bloody shite, boss. John Lorimer was working in our fucking team and that's a cloud that will hang over all of

367

us.' The voice came from an older-looking DC at the back. His arms were folded, his eyes fixed on Marnie. There were murmurs of agreement from around the room.

'Look, we're all shocked at what's happened, but we need to be professional,' she said. A strand of hair had come loose from her bun and she swept it back into place, trying to hide the tremor in her hand.

'Aye, professional doesn't help when we've got fucking rubber-heelers and the PIRC all over us wanting to find out who knew what, and who should have known. This will taint everyone's careers,' another voice called out, trembling with emotion.

'Look, we all just have to do our job ...'

'Aye, whatever,' a deep voice interrupted, full of sarcasm.

DCI Gray's face flushed, and she scratched at an itch with a painted fingernail. She swallowed before she spoke, her voice wavering. 'I'm still the SIO, and we still have to do our jobs. So, we continue, do I make myself clear?'

The silence in the room was long and uncomfortable.

'Any updates on the collision inquiry?' said Fagerson eventually.

'Nothing from SIO. No trace of the car, yet. It seems to be a cloned plate as the genuine owner is somewhere in England and has been ruled out of the inquiry. CCTV captured the incident, but identification of the driver isn't possible, and ANPR has no hits. Early days, but I know for a fact that MIT 4 are a great team with an experienced SIO, so we have to let them get on with it. Clear?'

No one spoke. No one moved.

'Now I know that this has come as a huge shock – particularly after the tragedy with John – but we have a job to do.'

'Any links to any of the recent events?' said Fagerson.

'None that have been relayed to me. I can't see how, can you? Billy was brand new to the team. I think primary focus is a drunk driver, but, as I say, I'm leaving this to the SIO.'

'But he was still one of us, boss. Makes you wonder, don't it, which one of us is going to be next? It feels like we're on a bloody cursed team. I for one don't want to be working any more overtime on these jobs. It's too fucking toxic,' said a voice from the back of the room. There were further murmurs of assent to this comment.

Gray looked up at them. 'That's an attitude we don't need. There are full investigation teams on both of these tragedies, and what they don't need is speculation and gossip. They'll do their jobs, and we have to do ours. Our involvement is now over in that inquiry and we now have a serious and complex rape inquiry and we need to focus. Right, it's just after three, I want a close of play report from supervisors on progress on your actions at five thirty and then we'll break for the day. All clear?'

No one replied. Arms were folded, eyes cast up to the ceiling, the mood of the team like a herd of truculent cattle.

'Right, crack on,' she said, standing as the team filed out of the room. Gray gathered her things and as she did so she dropped her pen onto the floor, the sound of it landing strangely loud in the silence. Everyone glanced down at it, but no one went to pick it up for her, not even Fagerson who was walking right past her desk. No one would look her in the eye. She swallowed, stooped down to pack the pen into her bag, and made her way back to her office.

Once there, she took a deep breath and wiped sweat from her brow. She stared at her laptop, her eyes not taking in the screen. She was losing the team. She could feel it, see it in her officers' shifting eyes and tense body language. She sighed, a tight sensation in her chest.

Taking out a small key from her pocket, she unlocked the drawer, sliding it open. She picked up the burner and opened the secure message app. She quickly composed a message, and pressed send, trying to ignore the flutter of nerves.

The reply came back immediately.

80

Alfa-Secure

–Tonight?
–Yes.
Messages deleting in 5-4-3-2-1...

81

DCI MARNIE GRAY'S home was a large, whitewashed cottage that backed onto Linlithgow Loch, with only a footpath separating it from the expanse of water. The weather had cleared and a watery, autumnal sun glinted off the water's surface. Max, Janie and Barney were parked up in a secluded spot along the road.

From there they could see that the neat front garden was shielded on all sides by well-tended hedges and a low wall. Through the gaps in the hedge, Max could just make out a footpath and gate that led to the lochside public footpath.

Max whistled, softly. 'Literally waterfront, must have cost a fortune. I'll dive out here, have a skulk about and check out what's what. You two head back up the top and use the parking bays opposite the entrance to this street. Get out and go into the Swan Tavern that's right there, get a drink and something to eat. We've no idea when we'll get another chance. You'll not stick out at all. The nice weather has brought everyone out for walks and early evening drinks.'

'What are you going to do? Like seriously, no bullshit.' Janie frowned at him.

'Just taking a look. I want to see if we can get a camera on the door, so we can sit away and observe from a distance. There's a gated drive that clearly gets used, so she'll enter and exit the house from the rear. We don't have to cover the front.'

'Nothing on your own, sarge. We're not authorised, yet.'

'Scout's honour,' said Max.

'No way were you a scout. Do you want some food?'

'Aye, whatever you're having. Last message from Norma was that all of her phones are still cell-siting at Leith, so we have a little time, even if she moves now, we can withdraw.'

'Okay, don't be long. What do I say if Ross calls?'

'Tell him the truth. We're doing a recce on her place ahead of the IPC authority.'

'Is that the truth, though?' said Janie.

'For now, yes. Barney, can I see your camera?'

Barney pulled the roll-up from his mouth, tucked it behind his ear and delved into his bag. It was a tiny base unit, no more than the size of a box of matches, with a wire that led to a tiny pinhole camera.

'How will you monitor it?'

'I'm wearing contact lenses I'm trialling where the feed puts up a display right into my frontal cortex. It's mint, lad,' said Barney, tapping the side of his head.

'Piss off,' said Max.

'Via an app to my laptop. Are you going to deploy it now?'

'I'm just going to see if anything jumps out at me.'

'Oh, here we go,' said Janie. 'Of course you are, we all bloody believe you.' She stared moodily out of the window, her voice thick with sarcasm.

'I used to manage to get cameras on front doors even in the

worst estates in London. Sometimes you just need to be a bit ballsy. I'll take it with me, just in case.' Max smiled.

'Aye, "just in case" my arse. We don't have authority for this,' said Janie, her jaw tight.

Max paused. 'I'll tell you something about Niall, guys. We worked together for several years and there is a significant possibility I wouldn't be breathing in and out without him. I owe him, and I owe Jeri. I brought him into this mess and now he's about to have bloody brain surgery. We need to make progress and Marnie Gray is the only lead we have. You guys can go and leave me here, if you like, but I'm staying.' His voice was firm.

'We're going nowhere. What's your plan?' said Janie.

'Here's a compromise. I'll find a suitable place for this tiny camera, for now, but we won't monitor until we get authority, right?'

'I believe you one hundred per cent, lad,' said Barney with a crooked grin and a chuckle.

'Bollocks, utter shite,' added Janie.

'Look, if you want out, then you can go. Seriously, guys. I'll take the risk, I'll take the responsibility. If it all goes tits-up, I'll fall on my sword.'

'Aye, that's what I'm worried about. I like you, despite you being a cowboy. Moreover, I like Katie, and I'm sure she likes living in a nice house which you'd lose if you got sacked,' said Janie.

'Seriously. If you want to go, I won't hold it against you. I mean that, but I'm doing this,' said Max, checking his pockets, and adjusting his jacket.

Janie sighed in capitulation. 'What drink shall I order you, sergeant?' she said, her tone clipped.

'Cranberry juice, I'll join you in ten minutes.' Max opened the door and got out of the car. It reversed away, swinging around, and driving back up towards Linlithgow.

Max didn't hesitate. He just did what all the other late-afternoon walkers did. He daundered out onto the lochside and turned right, walking in front of Gray's cottage. He glanced at the ancient front gate, which was covered in rust. The front path needed weeding and the paintwork on the front door was faded and peeling. It spoke of being an entrance that was rarely, if ever used. He sauntered along the lochside for one hundred metres, passing other late-afternoon walkers, before turning and doing the journey in reverse. This time he passed the better-kept vehicle gate. He noted the drive was block-paved and weed-free. The hinges on the gate looked clean and well used. Max continued, not looking back but taking in the houses on his right. The first one had a Neighbourhood Watch sticker on the kitchen window, and on the pedestrian gate, a note proclaiming that HAWKERS AND TRADERS NEED NOT KNOCK. The garden was immaculate, and an elderly gentleman was hand-washing a spotless Honda Jazz on the drive.

Max continued past the property, picking out his phone, and noting the name of the house, Lochside Cottage. He dialled.

'Max?' said Norma.

'Can you check out the following address, Lochside Cottage, Linlithgow?'

'Hold up.' There was the sound of tapping on her keyboard. 'What do you want to know?'

'Any reports from it?'

'Aye quite a few, mostly reporting local kids, alleging drug dealing lochside. Likes to mention he's Neighbourhood Watch coordinator a great deal, from what I can see,' said Norma.

'What's his name?'

'Major Charles Canning. Make sure you salute him.'

Max thanked Norma and hung up.

He spun on his heel and walked straight back to Lochside Cottage. Opening the gate, he went in, reaching for his warrant card.

'Major Canning?'

'Yes,' said the man, suspicion glinting in his eyes. He was clearly in his seventies, but looked lean and fit and was immaculately dressed, wearing chinos, a neat polo shirt and polished deck shoes.

Max flashed his warrant card. 'DS Craigie, might I have a word in private, sir? Sensitive subject, you know,' he said, gravely.

The major stared at the proffered card for a moment, then looked Max up and down, taking in his shaved head, jeans, trainers, and loose-fitting jacket.

'Plainclothes, huh?' he said, in an Edinburgh brogue softened by years away from the city.

'Aye, don't need the attention, you know?'

'I was in the Intelligence Corps, sergeant. I started out as a private and ended up a major. I do indeed know. Come in,' he said, nodding.

He led the way into an immaculate house, with polished wood floors and whitewashed walls that were richly adorned with military memorabilia. It reeked of single man.

'So, what can I do for you?' he said, his moustache bristling.

'You reported some lochside drug-dealing, yes?'

'I did. A little while ago. They meet up on the corner, down by the loch and they're always exchanging. Often, it's the same car that arrives, a scrappy old BMW.'

'Can I just take a look from your upstairs window? Maybe see if it gives a good view of it?'

'Ah, you'll be looking for a good OP, yes? By all means, sergeant. Civic duty and all that. Twenty-five years in the Int Corps taught me the value of good intelligence.'

He led the way up a carpeted flight of stairs and onto a small landing. The window overlooked the street outside, including a plum view of Marnie Gray's drive and back door. Max affected looking down towards the loch and nodded.

'This is perfect. How do you feel about me installing a small camera here? You know, intelligence-gathering, sir,' said Max respectfully.

The major's eyes narrowed. 'You look like you've served, sergeant.'

'Aye. Black Watch, sir,' said Max, straightening up, his heels coming together.

'See any action?'

'Iraq and Afghanistan, sir,' said Max, holding the major's gaze.

'Good man,' he nodded. 'I served in the Falklands and did many tours of Northern Ireland. Tough times, but I'm glad I did it. Yes, fix your camera, Sergeant Craigie. It'll be my pleasure to help. Do I need to do anything?'

'No, sir. It'll all be routed back to us wirelessly. I'll only need to come back when we recover it, you know, to minimise risk of compromise,' said Max, slipping into military vernacular.

'Indeed. A compromise wouldn't do at all. I'll leave you to it, then, keep up the pretence of washing my car, which I always do this time every week. Neighbours may think something's wrong, otherwise.' He turned to go downstairs.

'Thanks, this won't take long,' said Max, reaching into his pocket for Barney's camera.

He dug out his phone and dialled.

'Ayup,' Barney's broad northern tones rang out.

'I've a hide for the camera, perfect location. You ready to check?'

'Hold up.' He paused for a few moments. 'Right, tablet is up and running. Slide the base unit switch on,' he said.

Max slid a small switch to the right of the unit, and a small red light came on, the battery indicator showing a hundred per cent.

'All I can see is right up your bloody hooter, mate. Point it out of the window, at least.'

Max spotted a rubber plant in a small pot on the windowsill. He snaked the cable up and through the foliage, nestled the camera into the plant, and pointed the lens towards the gate.

'Down a bit,' said Barney. 'Bit more. Bit more. Now to the right just a nudge.'

'How's that?' said Max.

'Bang-on. I've a remote zoom facility, so can adjust that. Where have you got it?'

Max told him. 'Right, I'll be back in a minute. What's for tea?'

'Fish and chips.'

'Perfect. See you there.'

Satisfied that the small, cigarette-sized camera was secure

between the rubber plant leaves, Max wedged the main unit out of sight behind the pot.

He took one last look and then went downstairs and into the garden, where Major Canning was applying a coat of wax to the little car.

'All okay?' he said as he rubbed at the paintwork.

'Aye, all fine. You'll never know it's there, major.'

'Capital. Well, best of luck.' He reached into his pocket and pulled out his wallet from which he produced a small business card. Max took it.

'Anything you need from me, you only have to ask. I don't go very far and I don't miss much that goes on in this neighbourhood. Not much else to do since my good lady passed away,' he said without obvious sorrow.

'One thing, major. Do you know much about your neighbours opposite, in case we need to approach them in the future? In confidence, of course,' said Max, hesitantly. Int Corps spooks loved a secret, so this might be an opportunity.

A frown crossed his fine features. 'I'd avoid, if I were you. A young lady called Marnie has lived there alone for quite a few years. I used to know her mother Laurel, quite well. She was a charming woman. Moved to Spain, don't you know.'

'How well do you know the daughter?'

Major Canning paused, clearly uncertain as to what to say next. 'I don't know her well, but I've heard concerning things about her. Laurel did confide in me, you know. We were good friends.'

'All in confidence, sir, I assure you.'

'Well, I understand that her late father – Laurel's husband – was not a nice man. Abusive in the extreme to both Laurel and his daughter. Wouldn't let them out of his sight. She never said as much, but I know what some men are like. He was always coldly charming to me, but poor Laurel was clearly terrified of him. More than once, I saw her with black eyes, but she'd never discuss it. Laurel was relieved when he passed away a few years ago. It was like a new lease of life to her. But then as Marnie got older, she became rather difficult. She inherited her father's nasty side, I think.'

'Anything else about her?' asked Max.

'Laurel was a very meek and sweet lady, especially after her husband died. When I asked her why she was going to Spain, she said something that made me wonder, even though she'd had a drink or two.' He stopped and stared at the car, rubbing gently with his soft-leather cloth. 'Poor wee Laurel just said, "I have to get away from Marnie, Charles," and she wouldn't say anything more about it.'

82

THE SWAN WAS a traditional pub like many in towns across the country complete with chipped, dark wood, stained carpets and a taciturn barman polishing dirty glasses behind the bar. His smile and nodded greeting seemed genuine enough, as Max entered and joined Janie and Barney at a table in the corner. Barney had a beer, Janie an orange juice, and a Coke sat in front of the empty chair. Several bags of crisps were piled in the middle.

'No fish and chips?' said Max.

'Should've seen the look on the barman's face when we asked for food. Hence the crisps,' said Janie.

'Oh well, never mind. Plenty of takeaways about. No cranberry juice?'

'You think a place where the food options are salt and vinegar or cheese and onion will have cranberry juice? A drink for ladies of a certain age with waterworks issues, or summat like that,' said Barney, an amused look on his face.

'Shame,' said Max sipping his Coke and opening a bag of crisps.

'Footage is great, by the way. I'm impressed, not so bad

for a technophobe such as thee,' said Barney, his Yorkshire brogue deepening.

'Interesting chat with the gentleman who lives in that place.' Max recounted the conversation with Major Canning.

'Hmm, seems that our DCI Gray has another side to her. I wonder what a psychologist would make of that?' said Janie.

Max's phone buzzed in his pocket. It was Katie.

'Katie?'

'Max, Niall's had his surgery. He's stable, but he bled quite a lot. He's in an induced coma whilst he recovers.'

Max exhaled. 'How's Jeri?'

'As you'd expect. I'm going to take her home now and she can stay with us. When will you be back?'

'Not for a while. Things are about to get a bit interesting.'

'Okay. Be careful, babe. I love you.'

'You too,' said Max, but Katie had already gone.

83

Alfa-Secure

—I'm leaving soon.

—Great. No change for tonight?

—None. As we planned, so be ready.

—I will. I'm so excited, darling. I hope you are?

—?

—??

Messages deleting in 5-4-3-2-1...

84

'**WHAT'S THAT ABOUT?**' said Barney as he looked at his screen and popped another handful of crisps in his mouth.

'Well, she's clearly leaving the office, but what can that mean? What the hell do they have planned?' said Max.

'I don't like it,' said Janie.

'Nor do I. I'm calling Ross.'

Max dialled.

'Where the fuck are you bunch of fuds?' was Ross's gruff opening line.

'We're close to you know who's. Now don't go mental. We haven't gone in, we're just getting sorted and doing our feasibility studies, but something's come up.'

'What?' said Ross, his tone blunt.

Max described the contents of the last intercepted messages.

'Shit. I don't like the sound of that at all. What do you need?' he said, clearly a little deflated.

'Urgent authority to deploy a tracker on her car and mount a technical attack on her house. We have all the kit built and ready to go. We just need the chief to say that as a result of new, high-grade intelligence we need to do it now. It can't wait till tomorrow.'

Ross didn't hesitate. 'I'm on it. Stay put until I've had the chance to speak to the chief.' He hung up.

'That sounded unusually easy,' said Barney, twirling his roll-up between his fingers.

'He's not daft, and the chief trusts him. We'll get the authority. We need that kit in, but it's too early and there are far too many neighbours and passers-by.'

Max's phone beeped with a text from Norma.

All MG's phones are now moving west. Last cell is Craigcrook. Suggest she's on her way.

'That's her on the way here. Let's withdraw. I can't see that this is her local, but no reason to take the risk. She's probably about thirty to forty minutes away.'

They all pushed back their chairs and left the pub, crossing the still-busy road and getting into the Volvo.

'Where to?' said Janie, plugging in her seatbelt.

Max checked the map application on his phone for a moment. 'Head up to the railway station. It's only five minutes away and it's easy to not be noticed there. She probably knows people around here, so best to be off-radar.'

'Can we get chips to take with us? I'm bloody starving, and a packet of cheese and onion hasn't filled the gap,' said Barney from the back of the car.

'Why not? I could eat,' said Max.

Ten minutes later they were in the car park of the station in the east side of Linlithgow, all of them munching on paper-wrapped fish and chips from a chip shop in the centre of the village. The smell of vinegar and salty batter filled the car, and the only sound was the rustling of paper and the occasional satisfied sigh from Barney.

'I'd missed how hungry I actually was,' said Janie, through a mouthful of crispy batter.

'Aye, you know what I always say …'

'Eat when you can,' said Janie, 'because you never know when your next meal is coming, yada yada yada …'

'Same in Box. It's a wonder I'm not a fat bastard after all my years sneaking about in the shadows,' said Barney, chewing with relish.

Max's phone buzzed in his pocket. It was Ross.

'Aye?' said Max.

'Are you eating? It sounds bloody disgusting.'

Max mumbled through a mouthful.

'What is it?'

'Fish and chips.'

'Jammy buggers. I'm bloody starving. Just had another lentil fucking bake that Mrs F supplied. Some of us have been slaving like poor wee bastards getting everything sorted, whilst you three lazy toe-rags swan about in a car and stuff your faces. Norma and me carry this bloody team, you know.'

'I take it that there's a purpose to this call,' said Max.

'Aye. With my incredible powers of persuasion, I've spoken to the chief and he's authorised you on an emergency basis. Lump the car, bug the house, and survey the shite out of DCI Gray and anyone she meets with. Got it?'

'Yep. How'd he take it?'

'He's a little nervous about bugging up a serving officer, when we don't have a great deal of admissible, corroborated evidence, but he understands the stakes, and has enough bottle to run with it. He's spoken to the IPC, and they're on board, as well. Please don't fuck this up,' said Ross.

'We'll try.'

'He also wants a surveillance team with you. I've explained the issues about anyone connected to our target, but he insisted. I've had a chat with the team leader, and he's going to run a half team, excluding the three who have a past connection with her. As the car will be lumped up, it should suffice.'

'How long will they be?'

'At least four hours. They're way up north but are splitting and scrambling to you now.'

Max looked at his watch. It was almost seven. 'If she moves, we'll just do our best, but we need that car lumped first.'

'Understood. You heard any more about Niall?'

Max told him about the latest update.

'Well, fingers crossed, eh?'

'Aye.'

'Right. I must go. Me and Norma are still working on all the ANPR and phone data. We'll hit you up if anything develops.'

'No bother.'

'And Max?'

'Yeah?'

'Don't fuck this up.'

'You already said that.'

'I know, want me to say it again?'

'No, I get it. Speak—'

The line went dead.

'We're good to go on all fronts, and we're getting a half surveillance team,' said Max to Barney and Janie.

'How long?'

'Hopefully before midnight.'

'That could be too late. What happens if she goes out before then?' said Janie.

'We can hopefully sneak the lump on before then. Once that's on, we should be able to manage,' said Max.

Max's phone buzzed again. It was a text from Norma.

She's hitting cell at Queensferry. 10-15 to home.

Max relayed this to Janie and Barney.

'Come on, let's move up a bit and I need to make a stop,' said Max.

'Where to?' said Janie.

'There's a minicab office five minutes away, past her place.'

Janie moved off. 'Why do we need a cab?'

'We don't, but we need a reason to be here.'

'You're being cryptic. I hate it when you're cryptic,' she said as she steered the car through the thinning traffic.

Within five minutes they were outside the front of a scruffy-looking cab office with a peeling sign that read, A-B CABS, LINLITHGOW.

'Give me five,' said Max, jumping out of the car.

He walked into the faded office that doubled as a waiting area. Nylon-covered easy chairs crowded the space, partially covering the stained and threadbare carpet.

An elderly woman perched behind a screen, knitting furiously. She glanced up as Max entered and smiled, pulling aside the scuffed Perspex.

'Help you, pet?' she said in a kind voice.

'Hi, yeah, we're opening up a B&B on the outskirts of the village. Can I get some business cards to leave in the hall? Might be a few good fares in it for you?'

'Aye, pet, that'll be grand,' she said, reaching into an unseen drawer and coming out with a thick stack of black-and-yellow printed cards. She handed them over with a smile.

'Great, thanks. We often have guests asking for cabs, so it's nice to be able to give them these.'

'No problem,' she said as Max turned and left the office.

As he got back into the car, Janie eyed the cards suspiciously. 'I'm sure there's a good reason why you want those, Max. I just can't think of it right now,' said Janie.

'Never know when they'll come in handy. Head away from the main street, and we'll hold there until she's back. I want to get the lump on as soon as humanly possible, in case she goes out again.'

'Stop being a mysterious bugger. You treat me like a bloody kid, sometimes,' Janie grumbled.

'That's because you're barely old enough to buy a beer,' chuckled Max.

Max's phone buzzed. Norma, again.

Hitting a mast very close by. Suggest she's almost there.

'Eyes on the prize, Barney. She could be very close.'

'I'm on it,' said Barney, his eyes glued to the small tablet computer.

Janie drove until they came across a small supermarket with a decent-sized car park. She pulled in and turned off the engine. There was no one else around. The metal ticked and cooled.

'Okay. Standby, folks, we have movement,' said Barney, swivelling in his seat in the back so that the others could see the screen.

The camera showed the wooden gate swinging inwards. Marnie Gray suddenly appeared on the screen, wearing a smart business suit, and red court shoes, but her blouse was untucked and her hair looked somewhat dishevelled. She secured the gate with a bolt into the ground and once again disappeared from view. The Lexus then filled the screen as it passed in front of the camera before coming to a halt to the front of the property's rear door. She got out again, slammed the door shut and walked towards the door with a laptop bag over her shoulder. The indicator lights of the Lexus flashed as she locked the car. She had something in her hand, larger than a mobile phone, but Max thought he could see a screen, lighting up intermittently.

'What's she holding?' he asked.

'It's an Airwave radio. She bloody brings her radio home. That's not good,' said Janie.

Max considered this. If they needed to shout for help, she would hear it.

'Right. Nothing on unencrypted radio channels. I'll message Ross now to warn the surveillance team leader,' he said, composing a text.

'Why has she brought it home?' said Janie.

'Two options. One is legit, the other is very dodgy. If you're out and about doing bad stuff, the ability to know where the local constabulary are is a real bonus. Let's not forget, she can listen in to any force or area in the UK on that thing.'

'How about a third option? She's as job-pissed as you are.'

'Ha-ha,' said Max.

'It's a trunking system, right?' said Barney.

'Aye. GSM-based.'

'Hmm, let me think about that,' said the technician, grabbing a smaller tablet computer.

Gray continued towards her front door, but her bag fell from her grasp. She paused, looked at it on the ground, and vigorously scratched her scalp. Picking it up, she searched through it, presumably for her keys.

'She seems a little antsy,' said Janie.

'Not her usual ice-maiden self,' agreed Max.

She fiddled with the lock and a moment later the door swung open to reveal a light hallway. There was no sense of hurry – no sign of an alarm code – she just removed her jacket, and hung it on an unseen hook. She then stooped to pick up some mail from the tiled floor, flicking through the envelopes with minimal interest. She seemed to mutter something to herself and then dropped the post to the floor.

'No alarm there, Maxie-boy,' said Barney.

'Zero awareness. For a serial-killing cop, she doesn't seem to be taking her security seriously, does she?' said Max.

'I'd say she looks a little stressed, but there's something about her,' said Janie.

'What?'

'Psychopath. Self-aggrandising, arrogant. Clear as bloody day. It's almost if she thinks the world is too stupid for her.'

'Nah, she's just a bastard,' said Barney.

'Much as I'm enjoying your scientific analysis, Barney, fancy delivering a few business cards?' said Max.

'Why me?'

'A few reasons. Firstly, me and Janie have met her, and she didn't like us. You were just the oily rag fixing an alarm, so she's less likely to remember you. Second, you're better than both of us at snapping a lump on a car in the blink of the eye. And of course, the obvious third reason.'

'Go on, then, clever bollocks,' said Barney, his hands busy making a roll-up, his eyes focused on the tablet screen.

'You look like an elderly cabbie.'

'So predictable. Give them here,' he sighed.

Max handed the stack of cards over to Barney who took them. He rooted in his bag before coming out with a dark-coloured box about the size of a packet of cigarettes, covered in a thick bituminous substance, similar to that you'd find on the underside of a car. He reached into his bag and produced a greasy baseball cap which he fixed to his head. Next, he slotted on a pair of heavy-rimmed spectacles.

'Instant camouflage, team. Not my first time, you know. Drop us a bit closer,' he said, tucking the box in a cavernous pocket in his jacket.

Barney got out of the Volvo and slammed the door. He walked off without looking backwards, crossing the small car park at the bottom of the road that ran parallel with Gray's street. As he walked down to the lochside, he could feel the weight of the tracker pulling his scruffy jacket out of place. He strolled the ten metres to Gray's road where he turned right, walking uphill towards the pub. He went into the front garden of the first property on his right, walking to the front door. Without hesitating he popped one of the business cards through the letterbox. He returned down the path and onto the road again, walking at a steady pace, until he found himself opposite Gray's house. He crossed the road, whistling, as if he hadn't a care in the world, and without hesitating walked straight onto her drive and past her parked Lexus. It ticked away, still cooling down. He went to the door and withdrew a business card, tucking it into the letterbox. He spun on his heel and walked around the other side of the Lexus, placing it between him and the house. As he passed the car close to its boot, he stumbled on an invisible hazard, the whole pile of cards raining to the floor.

He muttered a curse and squatted at the rear of the car. Glancing at the house, he saw nothing. No movements, no glints, no twitching curtains. Without hesitating, he pulled the tracker from his pocket, reached underneath the valance and peeled off an adhesive strip, revealing a contact-adhesive coated pad. He jammed it against the plastic, feeling the glue bite as it attached itself.

Standing, the cards regathered, he walked off without any further hesitation, thankful for the time he spent practising yesterday on an identical model Lexus they'd found at a second-hand dealer's.

He knew the rule of seven Ps as well as the rest of the team. Prior Prevention and Planning Prevents Piss-Poor Performance. He lit his roll-up and inhaled with great pleasure, as he carried on up the road. Just a handful more cards to deliver, in case he was being watched.

Barney had few pleasures outside work. He liked an occasional flutter on the horses, enjoyed a pint, and loved watching his village cricket team play when he visited his hometown.

He knew, however, that nothing ever could, or would, replace the buzz of playing his part in bringing down bad guys, be they terrorists, criminals, or bent cops.

85

'NICE WORK. MAYBE now they'll finally let you retire,' said Max as Barney got back into the car.

'All those years you spent working with Kim Philby in the Cold War as a spook have paid off. You were smooth as silk, there,' said Janie.

'Cheeky whippersnappers,' Barney said, removing his cap and glasses and pulling out his tablet. He immediately started swiping and tapping.

'Bingo. We're up and running,' he said.

'Top man, that's two out of three objectives done. Camera on her door and lump on the car. She just needs to bugger off out, so we can attack the house,' said Max.

'Can we be sure she'll do that?' asked Janie.

'No, but we saw that message. Something's going to happen, it's just a question of when.'

'I guess. So, we just wait.'

'Aye, hurry up and wait as we used to say in the army. It's dark now, so I don't think we'll be waiting much longer.'

Max's phone buzzed with a text from Norma.

Surveillance team two hours away. All phones are still hitting local cell.

'Two hours is too long,' said Max after relaying the message.

'You're right. Her burner's active and she's browsing,' said Barney.

'Browsing on her burner? Why?' said Janie.

'Deniability, I guess. Okay, she's on a minicab page, and she's dialling a bloody cab. Shit, that means no tracker,' said Barney.

'Pass me the surveillance footage. Barney, you watch the burner.'

Barney handed over the tablet showing the camera feed of Gray's drive. The house was in complete darkness, presumably shaded by thick curtains. No movement. Max handed it to Janie. 'Keep an eye whilst Barney gets me up to speed.'

'Tell me she's not calling the cab office I visited?' said Max.

'No, different one but not far away,' said Barney.

'Thank Christ for that. What's happening?'

'Phone screen's blank. I assume she's getting a cab. What do we do?'

'Should we call Ross?' said Janie.

'No time, we need to do this now. How simple is the kit to deploy, Barney?'

'Piece of piss. As it's short-term only, these are simple, battery-operated and voice-activated. I've six prepared on a best-case option of what I'd expect to find in a typical home. I've a plug adapter one – magnetic option, and one that can be quickly put into a plug socket – plus a backup that can be put into the lining of soft furnishings. I also have one in an LED spotlight for a recessed light.'

'Does it matter which ones?'

'No. All the same frequency. I prepared loads, so I had plenty of options.'

'Could I fit them?'

'Well, unless you're an idiot, yes. But why can't I? I'm the bloody expert here.'

'I know, but the authorities always state that entry has to be gained by a cop. You're a freelancer. It could foul up the admissibility.'

'Then we both go in.'

'It needs both of you on a follow, though. If she stops and dives out of a cab, Janie can't just ditch the car in the middle of the road, can she?'

Barney opened his mouth to argue, and then closed it. He pulled a socket adapter out of his rucksack onto his lap.

'Right, if she has one of these, just swap them. Simple as that. In fact, first choice must be that you replace like for like, so bugged kit with an identical one.'

Max nodded.

Barney pulled out an LED spotlight, with a sucker attachment affixed to the surface – the type that goes in almost all kitchens and bathrooms. 'Just use the rubber sucker to pull the existing one out, then replace it.'

'Got it.'

Next, he pulled out three-gang and five-gang extension leads, with lengths of wire and plugs attached.

'Both of these are one-metre extenders. If she has one similar, you know what to do.'

'Aye.'

'Right, this one is simple. If she has a smoke alarm, just

pull off the cover and secure this on the back of it. It's self-adhesive. And replace the nine-volt battery whilst you're there. Spares are in the bag. Means she won't need to change it if it starts beeping at four in the morning.'

'Yep.'

'I also have about six very simple self-adhesive or magnetic bugs. If there's a cheap wall clock, or anything on the wall you can get behind, just stick the bugger on, and pull out the battery snib. If she's got a double radiator, just drop it down the gap and let it snap into place. You've loads of options. If you get two in, we'll be golden. Are you sure about this?'

'Dead sure. She's calling a cab from her burner, so she's possibly up to no good. We can't risk her being left, can we? Imagine if she kills someone on our watch.'

The car was silent for a few moments as the implications sank in.

'Everything you need's in that bag, mate, including enough tools for most jobs, but go for the simplest of the devices. They all work well,' said Barney.

'Movement at the door,' said Janie, holding up the tablet.

Barney picked up the burner. 'Yep, she's getting a message from the cab company, driver is called Ahmed, and here's the registration.' He read it out.

There was a shaft of light as the cottage door opened. As Gray closed the door behind her, she was illuminated by headlights of an unseen car.

'Cab's here, and look, she's carrying her bloody Airwave again. Shit,' said Janie.

'Stay off the net, then. We can handle this. It's a golden

opportunity. You follow the cab and whatever you do, don't lose it. You have the key to her place, Barney?' said Max.

'Yep, it'll work.' He handed over a single key on a Leeds Football Club fob.

'Leeds?' said Max, pocketing the key.

'Damn straight.'

'Okay, I'll walk down once you're well away. Best of luck, guys.' Max got out of the car, shouldered the rucksack, and walked off towards the loch without looking back. He heard the Volvo drive away.

Game on, thought Max, as he hit the footpath heading towards Gray's cottage. As he rounded the corner, he saw the cab, an anonymous Toyota. It was moving off.

He dialled. 'Yep?' said Barney.

'Cab's on its way.'

'We're here and waiting.'

86

MAX FOUND AN empty bench lochside with a partial view of the cottage's front door. He went through his plan in his head as he waited, imagining the cab making its way with Gray in the backseat.

His phone buzzed in his pocket. It was Barney.

Leaving the village. G2G

G2G, good to go.

Max stood, settled the rucksack on his back and felt for the key in his pocket. Breathing steadily and evenly, he walked into the road and turned towards the back entrance of Gray's property. He didn't skulk, didn't creep or hesitate.

Movements attract attention, so Max just walked straight up to the door. No lights came on. He paused for a moment, listening carefully for any sounds from within. There was only silence.

He pulled the key from his pocket, held his breath, and slotted it into the sleek, modern-looking lock. It went in as easily as if it had been designed by the manufacturers for that very lock, not made from an impression in putty. A quick twist, and the lock gave. The door swung silently inwards on well-oiled hinges. Max entered; his trainers soft on the tiled floor. He gently eased the door shut behind him, applying the snib, locking it in place.

He stood for a few moments, breathing silently, as he adjusted to the environment, straining to hear any sounds.

Only silence, and the gentle creaks of a settling house. Warming radiators, and the buzz of a distant fridge. There was a staircase directly in front of him, but his intention for now was focused on the ground floor. He padded along the hall to the back of the house, where the door was slightly ajar. He impressed upon his mind the angle of the opening, in order to make sure he returned it to its original position when he left.

The kitchen was dimly lit by plinth lights at the base of modern units and underneath high-level wall cupboards. There was a half-drunk bottle of wine in an ice-bucket on the scrubbed wooden worktop together with a lone glass. He reached into his pocket and snapped on a pair of nitrile gloves, the sharp sound almost deafening in the silence. He pulled out his mobile phone and tapped out a message to Barney.

I'm in.

The reply came back almost immediately.

Heading towards town.

Max sighed, safe in the knowledge that Gray was some distance away now. He enabled the camera function on his phone and selected video. Sweeping it around the room, he logged the position of everything so he could check before he left. Even a spoon out of place could be enough for Gray to sense that something was wrong.

Looking up, he was pleased to see LED recessed spots in the ceiling. He shrugged his rucksack from his shoulders, felt inside until he had located the bulb. He pulled it out using the rubberised sucker, which reminded him of the arrowheads on his childhood toy bow-and-arrow. He pulled the sucker surface away from the bugged bulb and pressed it against the bulb that was closest to the large island unit. He pulled it, feeling the resistance as he did. A sharp tug and it came away cleanly in his hand. He was just pulling the sucker free from the bulb when he froze. His eyes remained fixed on the kitchen counter. Horror gripped his stomach like a sudden icy fist.

There was another wine glass on the work surface by the sink.

It was almost, but not quite, empty and there was a faint smudge of scarlet lipstick on the rim.

87

SOMETHING IN HIS subconscious made him turn, but in his heart, he knew it was too late.

The blood turned to ice in his veins.

In a flash it all made sense as to how no one had ever linked tasers to the murders. How no evidence of a taser was ever found even during detailed post-mortems. There definitely hadn't been two serial killers.

There were three, and the third wasn't a cop.

Dr Elsa Morina, consultant forensic pathologist stood there, her arms outstretched, a yellow-and-black taser in her hands, her lips done up neatly with scarlet lipstick. Her face was twisted with hate, her dark, almost black eyes glittering in the harsh light.

The impact in his back was like someone smashing him with the flat blade of a spade. There was a crackle of electricity, and he froze stiff. His muscles locked, as his diaphragm contracted. He crashed to the hard tiled floor like an oak that had just been cut.

He gasped, as the charge was released and he was able to breathe again. Stars flashed before his eyes, as blackness began to creep inwards from the edges of his vision.

Through the fug, he felt his wrist being grabbed and something hard and metallic being snapped into place. His synapses were so fried that he simply couldn't resist. He felt his arm being pulled away and there was another metallic snap and a clanking noise as something was locked into place.

He sucked in another breath and tried to focus. The diminutive figure of Elsa Morina was looking down at him, her brightly painted lips parted in a sneer, her white teeth bared. Her deep brown eyes seemed to blaze with unmitigated fury.

He began to get control of his breathing as his vision cleared and his muscles relaxed.

It seemed incongruous to him that she was wearing a short, towelling bathrobe and her hair was loose and free around her shoulders. She looked small and child-like, but there was something horrifying in those dark eyes. Max's eyes focused on two curling wires that snaked from the barbs attached to his body to the weapon in Elsa's small hands. He began to move his free hand towards them, but she pulled the trigger again, her jaw tightening. A bolt of electricity flowed into him, locking his body rigid, and he let out a strangled cry. Pain flared like a lightning bolt. Darkness crept into his eyes once more, and his vision faded. After what seemed like hours, the surge stopped and he collapsed, spent. He lay there, stars dancing before his eyes, his chest rising and falling as he sucked in air.

The room spun, images and sounds jumbled in his mind. He saw Niall's face and his single uncovered eye flickering open in the hospital bed. He heard gunfire and saw Niall smashing the machete-wielding driver to the ground. Through the mist, a woman's voice began to grow louder. The room gradually righted itself and he could suddenly see Elsa, standing at the counter, her phone clamped to her ear. Her voice sounded distant, like she was talking underwater, but he could just make out a few of her words. 'We have a problem,' she said. 'You need to get back here, now.' She tucked the phone into the pocket of the robe and lowered the taser slightly, fixing him with an intense stare. The ghost of a smile curled across her lips.

'You made a big mistake,' she said, squeezing the trigger again. Twenty thousand volts smashed into the barbs, and his muscles locked. The pain was terrible and all-consuming, like nothing he had ever experienced before. When the darkness finally came, Max felt nothing but relief.

88

MARNIE GRAY'S HEART lurched at what she had just heard. She lowered the phone and stared at it, willing it not to be true. It couldn't last – they knew this – but Elsa had always assured her that they were in control. She felt hot tears well in her eyes, and her breath left her in a gasp.

Max Craigie, in her house, tasered on the floor. This was bad, very bad.

She looked at the Airwave radio by her side. It was chattering away with the usual local policing. Nothing of any assistance required. Nothing unusual at all.

He'd gone there on his own. To do what? Where was his backup, where were the surveillance team?

She had to get a hold of herself, and to act. Elsa would be furious with her if she lost all control now. She jammed a knuckle into her mouth and bit down hard, relishing the pain and the tang of blood in her mouth. She had to control the fear that was threatening to overwhelm her. She breathed deeply, like Elsa had taught her, and a plan popped into her head.

She picked out her phone and made a call.

'Marnie?' Len's voice answered.

'Hi, sweetie. Quick one, are you working?' Her voice was all at once light and breezy.

'Aye, late turn controller, everything okay?' he said.

'Everything's fine, Lenny. Any surveillance teams working out west tonight, hun? There's been some odd activity. I just want to make sure I don't dive in where I'm not required,' she said, and forced what she hoped was a flirty giggle. Len was pathetic, but he was easy to manipulate.

'None that I'm aware of, although I don't always get to hear about it. Anything you need help with?' he said.

'No, it's fine. Thanks,' she said, hanging up.

She looked behind her, but the pitch black, and flashing headlights made it almost impossible to identify any other cars behind.

As they rounded a left-hand bend, she barked at the driver. 'Next left.'

'Jesus, lady. A bit of warning would be nice,' said the driver.

'Just pull over here,' she said, craning her neck to see out of the back of the car as the taxi drew to a stop in the small side street.

Within twenty seconds, she saw it. The same Volvo that she'd seen Billy Bruce – or whoever he really was – get out of in Leith the other day. No doubt about it. She was being followed. She knew what they'd do now. There were procedures and tactics on regaining a subject during a surveillance follow. She'd be unlikely to lose them. She made an instant decision. She wouldn't skulk about and hide; she'd bring the bastards out into the open.

'I'll get out here,' she said, throwing the driver a banknote and jumping out of the car without another word, her stomach churning. A wave of determination began to wash the anxiety away. She had to do this for Elsa.

Tucking her radio into her bag, she walked back out onto the main road and towards a seedy-looking pub in the middle of the parade of shops. Without hesitating she pulled open the door and entered the vestibule that had a grimy window looking out onto the street. As she expected, the Volvo was parking up opposite. There were two in the car, one of whom she recognised. It was the young DC she'd seen with Max Craigie at the PM in Inverness. The passenger seat was occupied by a much older guy, who was staring at something in his lap. A computer of some sort that was illuminating his face.

Her palms felt damp and the silk of her kimono was sticky against her skin. She looked through the double-doors from the entrance room into the decent-sized pub. It was grimy and unloved but buzzing with activity. A big clutch of men in green-and-white football tops were watching the match in front of a widescreen TV. There was a sudden cheer from the group and a great deal of backslapping and general bonhomie as they all looked up at the screen.

She peered out of the window again at the stationary Volvo. The white face of the young cop loomed at the glass on the driver's side, as she peered towards the pub with concern.

Marnie glanced back at the group of men and smiled. She began to calm as she controlled her breathing – just as Elsa had taught her – and a plan began to form. She'd get out of this.

She unbuttoned her coat to reveal the white, silk kimono that she was still wearing underneath. She'd just pulled a coat on over it for the short journey to their favourite curry house to

413

collect the takeaway Elsa had ordered. Elsa was very particular about food, and as they'd consumed a fair bit of wine, it fell to her to go and fetch it. Elsa always seemed to get her way, that was for sure. Elsa had been keen that they relax together, as Marnie had been so stressed-out by events at work, but it was hard to be all romantic with everything that had been going on. Elsa had been her usual charming self, but she hadn't taken it well when Marnie suggested that trying to kill Billy – or whoever he was – was a bad idea. As always, Elsa had talked her round, as she always did.

What was supposed to have been a romantic evening to relax lay in tatters, as did the rest of their lives, most probably. But maybe there was still time. They had, after all, planned for this moment.

She knew what she had to do. Thankful she was alone in the putrid vestibule, she quickly pulled her kimono open revealing her thin and gauzy top and tore at it, ripping the top button off. She dug her long red nails into her chest, grimacing in pain as they carved trails across her pale skin. She did the same on her cheek.

She switched her face from one of determination to one of fear and horror. She burst from the vestibule, through the double-doors and into the main room of the pub, coat flapping open, and approached the mob around the TV. Screwing up her face, as if she'd been crying, she staggered into a chair. She let the coat drop off her shoulders and grabbed someone's arm. He was a huge, shaven-headed man, with an enormous belly. 'Help me, help me. Won't you help me, please?' she wailed.

The big man turned and frowned down at her. His confusion

quickly changed to concern and then to anger as his gaze went to her damaged face and chest.

'Jesus, love. Are you okay?' he said.

'Someone grabbed me and tried to get me into their car. I think they were going to kidnap me,' she said, eyes wide, her breaths short, voice trembling.

'Shit, who?' he said, his jaw tightening. Other members of the group began to turn at the sight of an attractive, partially clad woman in their midst.

'They're outside in a big Volvo. A man and a woman. I think they wanted to rape me,' she said her voice rising to a wail.

The group of fans lost interest in the action on the screen as white-knight syndrome took over in the grotty backstreet Edinburgh pub.

'See if there's a Volvo outside,' said the big man to a much younger man who looked very similar, almost certainly his son.

The smaller man went to the window and looked outside.

'Aye, a big Volvo out there,' he said, his face registering anger.

'Right, let's get the bastards. Bobby, call the cops,' said the big man. At least half of the group surged to the door and disappeared outside, their chests puffed out, bouncing on their toes and ready to fight. They looked just like football thugs, thought Marnie, just about managing to conceal a sneer. Stupid but easy to manipulate.

'You okay, hen?' said an elderly man, wearing a green-and-white scarf. He put an arm on her shoulder. She flinched at the touch, and he quickly withdrew it, his frown deepening.

'I need to go to the ladies',' said Marnie, and disappeared off to the rear of the pub, following the signs for the toilets.

She pushed her way through the door and into the corridor, spotting a fire exit at the rear. Wrapping her coat back around her kimono she stepped outside into the cool evening air, a smile forming on her lips. She entered an alleyway at the back of the pub, followed it for a while, parallel with the road, until she came out further along.

She flagged down a passing taxi.

'Linlithgow,' she said as it pulled over. She took a seat in the back.

'Nae bother, hen,' said the driver, moving off into the night.

As they passed the front of the pub, Gray smiled at the sight of half a dozen Hibernian FC shirted males surrounding the Volvo with angry faces, not allowing it to move.

The radio sparked into life in her bag.

'*Any unit deal with outside the Buchan Arms in Broxburn, allegation of indecent assault and possibly kidnap. Two suspects detained in a vehicle by locals, no further details.*'

The radio exploded with chatter as units offered to attend such a serious call. Gray smiled again. Men were just so bloody stupid.

89

MAX SLUMPED ON the floor next to the door he had only just recently crept through, his back to the wall, his right wrist secured to a heavy pipe. It led from an old and solid radiator into the wall and out of sight. Even his tentative pulls told him it was secure and he wouldn't be ripping it free any time soon. Not without snapping his wrist clean in two, in any case.

Added to that, Elsa Morina was sat on a kitchen chair watching him with interest, like a cat studying an injured bird. Her almost-black eyes seemed to bore into him, and her thick make-up drew his gaze.

'Who knows you're here?'

'Everyone. You think I'd come alone?'

'I think it's unusual that you're in here alone. Marnie's told me enough about police work to know that you don't do things like this on your own. That tells me you don't like sticking to the script,' she said, her voice low. 'I like that.'

Max couldn't think of anything useful to say.

'What were you hoping to do in here?'

Max said nothing.

She peered into his rucksack that was lying on the table in front of her.

'Looks like a load of bugs to me.' Her accent was mild, and barely detectable.

Max just stared at her.

'You don't seem nervous. Despite what you must know is going to happen to you. That interests me,' she said, tossing her hair.

'I'd rather not be here, if that's what you mean,' he said.

She giggled, her mouth twisting into a horrible shape. 'Unfortunate for you that I'm a light sleeper. Marnie only went to buy me some food.'

'She's dedicated.' Max knew he had to play for time.

'She'll do anything for me, Max. She loves me, you see.' She giggled again and the sound made Max's heart lurch.

'Was it the same with John Lorimer?'

'I wouldn't have gone within a mile of the big oaf, but Marnie could wrap him around her little finger. Men are easier to manipulate than women – surely you know this – and Marnie can get them to do anything. She hates them, though, always has done. The poor things never see through her. John had his uses, allowed us to get things done, but he became a liability. It's always fascinating when people buckle under pressure,' she said, her eyes drilling into him.

Max tried to swallow, but his mouth was dry. 'How did you manage to kill John and leave no trace?'

'I'm a bloody pathologist. He was comatose from the GHB in his whisky that miraculously my blood work didn't detect. A simple slice into his femoral and he was gone. You see, Max, I understand the human body. Position the leg properly and then one deep cut at the right angle and the blood will spurt downwards and not all over me. It was easy.'

'How did John kill Shuggie?'

She let out a short cackle, but her eyes remained hard. 'Lorimer was too weak. Far too weak and he developed a fucking conscience. He didn't want to kill Shuggie, so Marnie and I took over. It was easy, but it meant John had outlived his usefulness.'

'Shuggie was a good man,' said Max, spitting on the floor to clear the saliva from his mouth.

'He was disgusting. Practically killed himself, he'd drunk so much.'

There was a buzzing from the table. It was Max's phone. Elsa glanced at it, with scant interest. 'Your little friend Janie is trying to call you. I wonder why? Was she the one you came to Inverness with?'

Max said nothing.

'She was pretty, although she dressed like a boy. Does she prefer the ladies?' She grinned, but none of it was reflected elsewhere on her face. Her eyes remained unfathomable and dark, like a shark's.

Max held her gaze but said nothing.

A sudden brief bolt of pain crashed through Max as she pulled the trigger again, the low amperage twisting and bucking him into indescribable agony once more, but thankfully just for a second or two. Max gritted his teeth, tried to force down the scream. Spit trailed down his chin and he tasted blood on his tongue.

Elsa watched Max until he regained his composure. 'So,' she said. 'Can you hear that?' She waited.

'Complete silence. No armed officers bashing the door down, no sirens, no helicopters, just your little friend phoning you. Are you really so dumb to come here on your own?'

'Fuck you,' he gasped, sucking in another breath.

There was a noise in the hall beyond the kitchen, and Elsa looked up, but there was no panic in her eyes. Instead, she pulled out the cartridge from the taser and slotted a new one into place, levelling it at the kitchen door, all relaxed and composed.

The door opened, and Marnie Gray walked into the room, her face blank but her green eyes glittering, as she looked at Max sitting on the floor. She had a red weal on her face.

'You're back, my sweet, what happened to your face?' said Elsa.

'It's nothing, how did he get in here?'

Elsa returned her gaze to Max, a smile spreading on her face as she levelled the taser at his chest, the two laser dots dancing six inches apart from each other. Max looked down at the red points of light and then looked back at the two women in turn.

'Not like I can do much, is there?' he said, rattling the handcuff against the pipe.

'Were you followed?' Elsa asked.

'I was, by his friend and another in a Volvo. They're a little tied up now, but we don't have long, darling. We're going to have to get out of here, Elsa. They'll come, and soon.' She placed an Airwave police radio down on the kitchen table. Max looked at it, dark and inert apart from a solitary blinking red light on the front.

'Any activity on the radio?'

'Well, all the local cops are occupied by an incident I may have set up. Your buddies will be lucky to get out of it alive.' She giggled in a way that seemed so like Elsa. Max shuddered. Marnie looked at Elsa, hesitantly. Gone was the surety and confidence of the Marnie Max had seen at work. Her hair was awry, her blouse torn. 'Did I do well?' Marnie's voice was unsure.

'You did very well, my baby,' said Elsa, turning and rising to embrace her. The two women stood there in a clinch for a few moments, Gray a head taller than the diminutive pathologist. She buried her face in her thick hair and breathed deeply.

'What now?' said Gray, pulling her face away.

'You know, baby.'

'But we could go. Go now and carry on, somewhere else?'

Elsa stared up at her as if she were a child who had just got an A in her homework.

'We both know what must happen, my darling. We always knew what would happen in the end. We've done so much good work. *You've* done so much. We can be so proud.' She raised her head at the much taller woman, and kissed her on the lips, lingering for a few moments.

'I know, but I'm scared. Can't we just kill him and run, maybe move his body?'

'You know we can't, my love. We wouldn't get far. We knew it could come to this, yes?'

'I'm really scared, Elsa. Will it hurt?'

'No, my baby. We always said this would be how it ended. We'll go together before the police arrive. This is our chance to be remembered forever. Our legacy will live on.'

Marnie said nothing, just stared into Elsa's eyes, tears brimming and spilling. Max watched them run down her bruised cheek. Elsa wiped them away with her thumb. Marnie nodded, just slightly, her lip quivering.

Elsa reached into the pocket of her robe. Max started wrestling with the handcuff again, trying desperately to wrench the pipe from the wall. He watched as her hand came back out clutching what at first he thought was a thick, dark pen. Suddenly, she jammed it against Gray's thigh. There was a muffled click and Gray yelped, softly. There was only fear in her eyes now.

'As we promised?' Marnie said, her eyes on Elsa.

'Yes, sweetheart. You'll just slip away, and then I'll join you. We'll slip away together. Think of all the women we've saved, all the men we've stopped from ruining innocent lives.' Elsa soothed her, stroking her hair.

'What have you done?' said Max, in a hoarse whisper, horror rising in his chest.

'Sit, my angel,' said Elsa, easing Gray down into a chair, ignoring him completely.

'What will happen?' said Gray, her voice slurring.

'You'll just drift off, no pain. No more pain, Marnie, my sweet, sweet girl.' Elsa stroked her hair, almost reverentially.

'We did good work, didn't we? The people we killed, that was justice, wasn't it?'

'It was – true justice. We went where the law couldn't.'

'I feel so tired,' said Gray, beginning to sink in her chair.

'Let's lay you down. Come on, my sweet.'

Gray almost slid from the chair, the last of her strength leaving. Elsa eased her onto the floor.

'Elsa, come with me,' she mumbled, consciousness slipping away.

'Yes, of course, I will,' she said, pulling an identical pen from her pocket. Max could see the word 'Novarapid' was emblazoned on the side in thick letters.

Marnie's eyes fluttered, as she looked at Elsa again. They opened wide, her mouth gaping like a fish.

'Elsa, no,' he shouted. His memory flared from diabetic prisoners in custody. Insulin.

The pathologist kept her eyes locked on Gray's, with what seemed to be tenderness, as she stroked her face.

'My beautiful Marnie,' she whispered as Gray's eyes closed, and she took a breath. She was unconscious. Max knew that within a few minutes DCI Marnie Gray would be dead.

'You bitch,' he spat, his heart thumping as he rattled his cuffs against the radiator, the hard metal biting into the already broken flesh.

Elsa turned slowly from the now-unconscious Gray and stood. Her face changed as if a switch had flicked, from sadness to joy. She smiled, and Max thought it was the ugliest smile he had ever seen, white teeth framed by smudged scarlet lipstick. Her mouth broke into a nasty giggle, that quickly became a throaty laugh. She stood over the almost-dead form of DCI Marnie Gray and howled with laughter, her eyes shining manically.

'Stupid, deluded cow. So easy. She really thought we would float off together.' She giggled again.

Max's eyes went from her to the radio. It sat there blinking silently at him. If only Janie had stayed with him. If only he hadn't asked Niall to deploy on this job. So many regrets and he'd been so bloody selfish. His thoughts turned to Katie, her warm voice, her kind eyes, and her smile. He looked again at the blinking light on the radio.

'Why?' he said.

'Because life is boring, detective, you know that. Death is even more boring. I understand both things, but there's something I don't understand. You saw it there, for the briefest of moments, when Marnie left us here alone. The transition. You know it too, I can tell you've seen it before. Haven't you? You're a smart man, DS Craigie, you must want to know more. Maybe we're more alike than you realise.' Her eyes were locked on his.

Max just stared at her. 'You don't know anything about me. Not one. Fucking. Thing.'

'Let me tell you, then you'll understand. Did you know I was born and raised in Kosovo?'

Max's eyes didn't move. He defiantly continued to hold her stare.

'I was a refugee at fifteen years old. Right during the war, my mother and I fled Kosovo for Albania after my father was murdered by the Serbs. They wanted us all dead.' She paused, staring hard at Max.

Max wanted to say nothing. Not to engage with Elsa, but the blinking light on the radio made him want to play for time. 'That must have been hard,' he said.

'Hard?' Her laugh sounded like the crack of a whip. 'We were captured by the Serbs. The things they did to us, no one should endure. I was young and strong, but my mother was weak. I watched her die, one step at a time. Hour by hour, day after day. The life slipping from her body little by little, whilst our captors watched it happen, laughing and mocking, until she was gone.' Her face remained flat, unmoving, but those dark eyes glittered like two deep pools of hate.

'So, I watched her die, but I didn't understand how. I couldn't understand the journey and I still don't. I thought my career would help me understand, but if anything, it just confused me even more. I thought at one time that I was avenging what happened to my mama by killing very bad men, but now I'm not so sure. I'm still a little confused, if I'm honest, but maybe you can help me understand a little better.' She brandished the insulin pen. 'This time, I'm going to try something different.'

She stood and went to the draining board where she grabbed a pair of pink rubber gloves and snapped them on.

90

ELSA GRABBED A BOTTLE of bleach, which she brought to the table. Max tried again to loosen the cuff, to shift the pipe, but his strength was leaving him. The metal had cut deep grooves into his wrists and they were slick with warm blood.

Elsa methodically tipped a small amount of the bleach onto a cloth and began to wipe down all the surfaces of the taser and the insulin pens. She then took each item and knelt next to the barely breathing Marnie Gray. Pressing them into her right hand, she stood up and placed the items on the table. She sat for a moment, as if composing herself, her eyes flicking around the room, making sure she had left nothing to chance.

'You won't get away with this,' said Max, fear beginning to rise in his chest.

'You clearly didn't know I was in here, so I doubt anyone else does. They'll find both of your bodies and all the evidence they need. DCI Marnie Gray was a serial killer who tasered and killed her pursuer, before committing suicide. And you know what? The learned Dr Elsa Morina, consultant forensic pathologist, will confirm their suspicions.' She smiled, widely, as if discussing her holiday plans.

Max closed his eyes and thought about Katie. He didn't want to die, not here, not now. He'd seen so much death. He wanted to live.

'Now, I could make this easier. I could just jab you, and you'd slip away, but I have a feeling you may make a little fuss, and you're a strong-looking man, so I suspect this is necessary. I also have an idea to try something I haven't done before – it might be fun.'

He began to thrash, the fear now bursting through him in waves, the pain in his wrist overwhelming. She stood, taser in her hand and advanced towards him, until she was just out of range of his flailing legs. Two red dots appeared and began to dance on his chest. Max closed his eyes and turned his head to the side. His body went tense, his jaw clenched.

There was a pause, and the silence that filled the room was almost deafening in its intensity.

Suddenly, the door to Max's immediate right exploded inwards and Janie flew into the room, already shaping a reverse kick which whipped out, catching the pathologist's wrist. The taser flew from her hand and spun across the floor.

Janie followed this up with a lightning-fast front kick that cracked the pathologist in the centre of her chest. She flew backwards and smashed into a chair, which crumpled to the ground in a crash of splinters.

She let out a scream and pulled herself to her feet, a mix of rage and fear which was almost ear-splitting in the kitchen. She grabbed at the bottle of bleach as she stumbled, the contents splashing over the floor. She then threw the bottle at Janie who dived out of its path as it flew towards her. Elsa leaped to her feet, and reached towards the countertop, her hand grabbing at a large kitchen knife. She swung the knife out towards Janie, holding it in her hand like a shield. Janie stood, composed, settling her feet in the puddle of bleach on the floor.

'Give it up, Elsa. It's over,' said Janie, her hands in front of her in a fighting stance.

'Fuck you,' spat Elsa and swung the knife in a sweeping arc at Janie's face. Janie moved her head backwards, the knife whooshing past, missing her cheek by an inch. As it passed, Elsa's ribcage became exposed and Janie let a swift punch go. It crunched into her, just above her kidney. She grunted and a flicker of something crossed her face. But she quickly recovered and rounded, back in her stance, the knife extended again.

'I'll gut you.' Elsa's teeth were bared and her eyes blank. Scarlet lipstick was smeared on her face.

Janie stayed silent and calm, keeping her breathing under control.

'Fuck you,' said Elsa again, the knife flashing out once more, cutting the air between them in two, the blade glittering in the harsh LED light.

Janie waited for Elsa to commit, then shot out her foot. It connected with Elsa's knee and there was an audible crack. Elsa's leg buckled and she fell backwards against the counter, the knife slipping from her grasp. Janie let out a breath and stepped forward, her body relaxing slightly. At that moment, Elsa reached behind her and grabbed a small vase that was by the sink. In a fluid motion she whipped it through the air.

The vase hit Janie's forehead and exploded into a thousand pieces. Janie rocked backwards and dropped to the floor. She lay there, stunned, covered in fragments of vase and blood. Max could see a gash had opened like a zip across the flesh above her eye. She groaned, and her hands went up to the cut. Elsa hobbled forwards, one hand on her leg. Only the table separated them. She lifted the bottle of bleach from the floor and threw the contents into Janie's face. As the corrosive liquid flew into her eyes, Janie screamed, horribly, her hands rubbing it deeper into her eyes, mouth and bloody wound. Janie's legs thrashed, but the slippery surface allowed no purchase. Her foot kicked at something which scuttled along the hard floor towards Max.

'Janie,' bellowed Max, wrestling with the pipe again, his arms now slick with blood. He wriggled forward, and the edges of his fingertip brushed something.

Elsa steadied herself and took the knife from the floor. She rounded the table, her teeth bared and slowly began to limp towards Janie, who was still writhing around on the floor, desperately trying to clear her eyes.

Elsa stood over her, the knife raised, her hair plastered to her face.

Suddenly, there was a pop and she stopped dead, as if a film had been paused, an open-mouthed look of shock on her face. She glanced down at the two red dots on her chest, the two metallic probes buried into the cotton of her robe. There was a crackle of static as the 20,000 volts of low-amperage electricity flowed into her body, and she fell. She hit the ground like a broken ironing board, her head meeting the tiles with a crack, and lay there trembling in the bleach.

Max sat there, breathing hard, gripping the taser in his extended hand, the other still cuffed to the radiator, thankful that Janie's flailing leg had kicked the weapon within reach.

'Janie, do you have a handcuff key?' shouted Max.

'Yeah, shite, this hurts like shite. I can't see a bloody thing.' Blood streamed down Janie's face and covered her T-shirt.

'Okay, walk to my voice, steady now. Don't rub your eyes, understand. Whatever you do, don't rub them.'

She edged towards him sliding her shoes through the acrid bleach. 'Where are you?'

Elsa began to stir, groaning. She stiffened up again, as Max delivered another burst. She let out a tight, strangled cry, her eyes locked, then she was still again.

'Keep coming, Janie,' said Max.

'It's here,' said Janie, her eyes clamped shut, her hand outstretched, a small key in her hand. Max reached up and grabbed it, jamming it into the lock and twisting. He stood quickly and grabbed Elsa's wrist. With a heave, he dragged her towards the radiator and cuffed her to it. The now-recovering Elsa began to groan.

Max grabbed Janie by the wrist and propelled her to the sink. He jammed her face down into it and pulled out the flexible sink tap. Turning the cold tap on, he directed the flow of water into her eyes. The sink began to fill with red liquid as the water washed the still-flowing blood from the gash in her brow. Max grabbed a tea towel from the side and held it against the wound.

'Shit, it hurts. Is she secure?'

'Aye, she's cuffed. It's all good, where's Barney?'

'He had to stay back with the cops outside the pub. Somehow a load of Hibs fans convinced them that he'd attacked a woman who'd disappeared. I only managed to get away by brandishing my warrant card and telling them that it was life or death. Couldn't call it in on the radio or she'd have heard. Barney was on the phone to a pal who was doing something with Gray's radio, not sure what. Was that the pathologist that just tried to blind me? We thought it would just be you and Gray in here.'

'It was. I wasn't expecting her to be there, either. How's the eyes?'

'Clearing, a bit, still sore as buggery. What's happened to Gray?'

'Keep that water flowing. I need to call for help,' said Max.

'I'm gonna bloody stop hanging out with you, bloody teuchter bastard,' said Janie, spluttering as the water went into her mouth.

'Aye, same here, you Sassenach buffoon. I keep having to pull your arse out of the fire.'

Max reached for Gray's radio. 'This is DS Craigie, I need urgent assistance at Lochside Cottage, Whitton Street, Linlithgow. Ambulance required, female with major insulin poisoning, one suspect arrested and tasered with a possible head injury and an officer with irritant burns to the eyes and a cut head.'

Max placed the radio down on the table and went to the prone form of DCI Marnie Gray. He knelt by her side and felt at her neck. Nothing.

He shook his head. Janie was squinting at them, her head tipped to one side, the water trickling into her eyes.

Elsa Morina just lay on the floor motionless and defeated. Her eyes open and flat, projecting nothing at them, a sneer on her face, as she breathed heavily, the two barbs protruding from her chest, small red blooms of blood visible at each site.

'You're all pathetic creatures,' she said. Her face was lifeless. 'They all deserved to die. All of them.'

'Aye, whatever, sweetheart,' said Max as the faint sounds of sirens began to get closer.

91

MAX AND JANIE entered the interview room at Edinburgh Central Police Station and closed the door behind them. Elsa Morina was hunched on her chair, dressed in a baggy white sweatsuit, a blue blanket wrapped around her tiny frame. She looked scared and almost child-like, a far cry from the person she had been when Max had last set eyes on her. Her solicitor, a stocky, middle-aged man in a smart grey suit, sat beside her, displaying a look of indignance.

'Are we ready? My client has been waiting hours for this interview, and she's been through a traumatic event. I've raised my concerns with the duty officer, and you can be sure that she'll be making a formal complaint.'

'Aye, we're ready,' said Max as he and Janie sat down in front of them. Janie had an adhesive dressing on her forehead, and her eyes were brick red.

'Good, well let's get on with it, then,' the lawyer said, puffing out his cheeks.

Max switched the digital recorder on and went through the introduction procedure.

The solicitor cleared his throat. 'My client has a prepared

statement that she would like me to read. After this, she'll make no further answers to any questions.' He looked up at Max and Janie, who sat back in their chairs, an iPad open on the desk in front of them.

'Fine,' said Max with a smile.

The solicitor read from a single sheet of paper. 'I, Dr Elsa Morina, wish to say the following. I'm a friend of the late DCI Marnie Gray. We struck up a friendship several years ago, and this later became a relationship, which we chose to not make public on account of our professions. I went to her home this afternoon where we had agreed to meet for an evening together. She returned from work around 8 p.m. and we had some wine and spent some time in bed. Marnie then decided that she wanted some food, so she took a cab to our favourite restaurant for a takeaway. I then fell asleep. I was later woken by a commotion downstairs. I went to investigate and found DS Craigie secured to the radiator and Marnie unconscious on the floor, an auto-injector of Novarapid in her hand. She was slipping into a coma. I was just about to call for help, when DC Calder burst in and brutally assaulted me. Then DS Craigie tasered me, without any justification. I had no knowledge of the activities of Marnie Gray. I have no knowledge about the murders of Fergus Grigor, Scott Paterson, John Lorimer or Shuggie Gibson. Any post-mortems I undertook were done professionally and I stand by my findings. I do not wish to comment further.' The solicitor removed his spectacles and began to polish them as he eyed the two officers, his eyes flinty.

Max and Janie exchanged a glance and a smile.

'Are you sure about this, Elsa?' said Max, gently.

'My client won't be answering questions and I must say that

I object to both of you conducting this interview, bearing in mind the appalling assault you subjected her to.'

'Okay. Some new evidence has just come into our possession. Did you notice that Marnie Gray had a police radio in her possession when she came back into the house?'

'No comment,' said Morina, in a tiny almost inaudible voice. Her eyes were downcast, and she was shivering.

'Officer, I must protest. If you have new evidence, you should disclose it to me in advance of springing it on my client,' said the solicitor.

'Well, now. We've literally just come into possession of it. Have you heard of a "hot mic" on a radio such as this?' said Max, holding up an Airwave radio handset which was contained in a plastic bag.

'This is completely out of order, DS Craigie. I demand that you disclose this to me now and then I can advise my client appropriately. This is profoundly unfair,' he said.

Max stared straight at the quaking form of Elsa Morina. Tears welled in her dark eyes.

'A hot mic is a rarely known about and even more rarely used feature on these handsets. In certain circumstances the radio mic can be covertly opened and anything nearby will be heard and, of course, recorded. Did you notice Marnie bringing in this handset?'

Morina continued to shiver and didn't meet Max's gaze.

'This is an outrage—'

'I'm going to play a recording that has just been sent to me. It is date- and time-stamped and was recorded covertly on DCI Marnie Gray's Motorola Airwave handset. This is all demonstrable evidentially and I can assure you it will be fully admissible at court and will be presented to the procurator fiscal. Once you've both listened to it, you can have as long as you need to discuss.' Max nodded at Janie, who pressed a finger against the iPad screen.

There was a hissing that erupted from the tablet's speakers. Voices became audible. Clear, if tinny.

'*Any activity on the radio?*'

'*Well, all the local cops are tied up with an incident I may have set up. Your buddies will be lucky to get out of it alive.*'

'*Did I do well?*'

'*You did very well, my baby.*'

'*What now?*'

'*We both know what, my darling. We always knew what would happen in the end. We've done so much good work. You've done so much. We can be so proud.*'

'*I know, but I'm scared.*'

'*No need, my baby. No need. We always said this would be how it ended. We'll go together before the police arrive. This is our chance to be remembered forever. Our legacy will live on.*'

Elsa stopped shivering and her head snapped upwards. Her eyes met Max's. The tears were gone, so was the confused, lost expression. It had been replaced by a blazing defiance, and something else. Amusement. A wide smile stretched across her face and she began to laugh. Just a chuckle at first, soon to be replaced with a throaty cackle that was like nails on a chalkboard.

Her solicitor inched his chair further away from her, his face pale.

'Any comment, Dr Morina?' Max said, his discomfort rising.

The pathologist composed herself, before the paroxysms of

438

mirth overcame her again, and she began to howl with laughter, her shoulders heaving.

When she spoke, her voice was bright, almost excited. 'You're pathetic. All men are pathetic. You're so attached to your corporeal bodies that you live in daily fear of death. But not me. I've been amongst the dead so much that it doesn't scare me. I'm at home with the dead. You're all so terrified of death because you don't understand it. Well, I do. I've been amongst the dead for so long, that I know more about them than I do about the living, but their journey to death eludes me. I wanted to learn its secrets. I have tried so hard, for so long to understand why, Max.' Her eyes blazed, wide and full of madness. 'Why men like those Serbian bastards seemed to enjoy killing my mama. I'd tried to learn more, by killing the men who deserved it, but it didn't help, so when you fell into my lap it suddenly occurred to me where I was maybe going wrong. Maybe killing bad men isn't the answer.'

'Elsa,' said the solicitor, but the tone of his voice was one of defeat and Elsa continued as if he hadn't spoken.

Morina's eyes bored into Max, who had to fight to hold her stare, his stomach tight and knotted. 'You're a good man, Max. Honourable, unlike all the other wretches I've killed. Maybe killing you would have been the final piece of the puzzle, but now I'll never know. A shame, really. Perhaps death's secrets are something that people are too stupid to understand. You should know one thing, though.'

'Elsa, that's enough,' said her solicitor.

'What?' said Max.

'I'd have loved to stare into your eyes as the life drained out of them. It would have been a beautiful thing that we would have shared, almost the ultimate journey.' Her voice became quiet and sympathetic.

'Elsa, stop,' the solicitor said, but there was no conviction in his voice, and his expression was one of extreme discomfort.

'Oh, my love, I'd have held your hand, and stroked your forehead as you drifted away. It would have been the experience of a lifetime.'

Her face softened, her eyes were kind and caring. She believed it. She really did, thought Max. He felt a cold chill descend on him as he looked at the pathologist. Her hand stretched across the table, and her fingers gently brushed against the back of his hand. He pulled his arm away, as if electrocuted.

'Interview suspended,' Max blurted, stabbing at the button on the machine, his heart pounding. He felt a trickle of sweat on his spine. The back of his hand seemed to burn where she had touched him. He had a sudden urge to scrub it until it bled.

'Get her back to her cell, Janie.' Max stood and turned to leave.

'Max?' said Morina.

Max turned.

'Aren't you going to ask me about all the others?' she said, her lips parting, showing white teeth in a broad, almost dazzling smile.

92

MAX, ROSS, JANIE and Norma walked out of the High Court in Edinburgh, a feeling of satisfaction washing over them. It had been Elsa Morina's first appearance since being charged with the murders of Scott Paterson, Fergus Grigor, Shuggie Gibson, John Lorimer and Marnie Gray, and the evidence looked solid. The attempted murder charge on Billy Bruce had been discontinued. It was just too tricky, legally.

After the interview with Morina they'd handed all their evidence to DCI Hughie Johnson who had accepted responsibility for the investigation. Ross's team returned to the shadows, where they belonged, ready to fight another day.

Morina hadn't said another word. Literally not one word. She'd just sat through every further interview, said nothing, and didn't even acknowledge her interviewers or solicitor, who seemed terrified of her.

'I don't like to speak too soon, but it looks fairly tight. All the trophies found at Gray's place, the AFIDs and the taser were a good start,' said Ross.

'Thank Christ for the hot mic on the Airwave,' said Janie.

'It was one of the things in the contract with the company.

They wanted the option to be able to open the handset mic, without the knowledge of the officer, in case they were incapacitated or captured and couldn't press the switch,' said Ross.

'Worth his weight in gold, is Barney. Not bad for an ageing spook who lives in a campervan with a heavy nicotine addiction,' said Ross.

'He lives in a campervan?' said Janie.

'Aye, I found out the other day,' said Ross. 'Who would have thought it?'

'Let's not forget our own Norma. The nationwide ANPR trawl, catching Morina leaving the garage in Perth with her coffee on her journey north. I hear the fiscal's delighted,' said Max.

'Well, defence are already raising mental capacity issues, so we can all see the direction of travel here. Whichever, life in a secure hospital, or in prison, same thing, basically. She's not getting out,' said Janie.

'Aye. Good work, people, and you know how I feel about praise. Shall we go to the pub? Max, I'm sure you're gasping for a cranberry juice,' said Ross.

'How about Niall?'

'Niall's doing okay, I think,' said Ross.

'No, I mean, it's not right that we go to the pub and we don't invite him.'

'Well, he's kinda in traction at RIE. Not much we can do about that.'

'Maybe there is. Come on.'

93

MAX, JANIE, ROSS and Norma burst through the door into Niall's private room, clutching a carry-out bag filled with beer, wine, snacks and a carton of cranberry juice.

'Ah bugger, there goes my peace,' he said, accepting a can of lager from Ross and cracking open the ring-pull.

They all touched drinks. 'Cheers.'

'So, are we good? How did it go?' asked Niall.

'As well as could be expected. You know how it'll go with your case, right?' said Ross.

'Aye. I can see the complications. Am I Billy Bruce or Niall Hastings? Cover blown, either way.'

'She's not getting out, whatever the outcome of the case.'

'What's the latest on your injuries?'

'Legs will be a long road, but orthopaedic surgeon is confident that I'll be back on my feet eventually. It could have been much worse,' he said, slapping his cast.

'How about your heid?' said Ross, exaggerating his accent.

'Bleed stopped easily enough, should be fine and the skull is knitting together well, apparently.'

'Like having a sunroof, eh?'

Everyone paused, looking at Ross, open-mouthed.

'Oops, me and my big geggie,' he said, chuckling with a trace of embarrassment.

'You UCOs are all barking anyway,' said Janie.

'Well, I think that my UC days are behind me, unless they want a Hopalong Cassidy type,' said Niall.

'Aint that the truth,' said Jeri, who had suddenly appeared at the door of the room with Katie, both smiling at the scene in front of them.

'Anyway, sign my bloody casts, you buggers,' said Niall, reaching over to his table, picking up a Sharpie and tossing it to Max.

Max scrawled on the top of the cast and passed the pen to Janie who did likewise. The pen then got passed all around the room until it came to Ross.

He paused over his portion of the plaster, and a slow smile played across his meaty features. A quick squiggle of the pen and he handed it back to Niall.

A charge nurse came into the room and looked around with a disapproving frown. 'Only two visitors per bed, please,' she said, as she scribbled on Niall's chart, a little too assertively.

'Right, we're not all layabouts like you, Niall. We've work to do. Come on, team,' said Ross.

'I'll go home with Katie and Jeri, if that's okay?' said Max.

'Aye, bloody "Half-a-day" Craigie, we'll be calling you. See you tomorrow.'

Ross, Janie and Norma all left the room, chatting and laughing, leaving just Max, Katie and Jeri.

'Niall?' said Max, hesitantly, his stomach tight with nerves.

'Yeah?'

'I'm sorry, pal. I wish I hadn't brought you into this,' he said.

Niall looked at him, his face calm. His eyes went down to the cast. 'Don't worry about it. It's just one of those things.' He continued to look away.

'You sure?'

Suddenly, Niall's face changed from serious and introspective, to a mix of shock and amusement.

'That bastard,' he said, a big smile overtaking the frown as he stared at his plaster.

'What is it?' said Jeri.

'Ross bloody Fraser has drawn a big cock on my bloody cast.'

Acknowledgements

AS ALWAYS THERE are lots of people who have been just so important in helping me get from a collection of half-legible ramblings to something approximating a book.

Thanks, therefore, go to all of you, but I'll just namecheck a few.

Robbie Guillory, my agent. I need your sage advice as much as ever now as we progress with this series of books. Not just your negotiating skills, but your ability to spark the inspiration that keeps me writing. I genuinely don't think the books would be anything like as good as they are without your help.

All the team at HQ. Finn Cotton, for everything, you're a brilliant editor, and you've helped me so much in this journey.

Belinda Toor for all your insight and support with the difficult task of coming into a book at such a late stage. I appreciate it so much.

Jo and Sian for all the marketing jiggery-pokery that makes readers aware that the books exist.

All the others at HQ, who I never hear from, but are beavering away in the background to get these books out into the world. Cover designers, copy-editors, typesetters, proof-readers, sales and analytics types – you guys rock.

Colin Scott. For the inspiration, advice, and shits and giggles.

To Gus Fraser, proprietor of Inverness Crazy Golf, and his mum, Bet. Your casual idea of being in this book morphed into a whole new angle in the book that I'm delighted with. I promise to anyone reading that Gus is innocent of anything questionable, snidey or immoral that his doppelganger did in this book. He just runs a cool crazy golf place by the river and serves ace tea and coffee and the best ice cream in town. He also never, ever fails to make me laugh when I'm buying a tea whilst my son Ollie is racing around the skate park. He's a top man, and if you're passing, buy a cuppa from him.

All my writing pals who are free and easy with advice, who read my books and say such nice things.

As always, my crazy big family for all the fun.

Clare. Love you always.

My boys, Alec, Richard and Ollie.

And of course, all the bloggers, booksellers and people that read and shout about the Max Craigie books.

Last but most importantly, you the reader. Without you, this is just a pile of words bound together with paper and glue. You're the ones who matter.

Neil

Catch up on the series so far …
DEAD MAN'S GRAVE

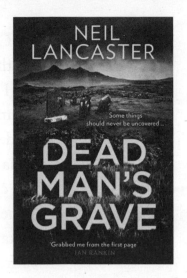

This grave can never be opened.

The head of Scotland's most powerful crime family is brutally murdered, his body dumped inside an ancient grave in a remote cemetery.

This murder can never be forgotten.

Detectives Max Craigie and Janie Calder arrive at the scene, a small town where everyone has secrets to hide. They soon realise this murder is part of a blood feud between two Scottish families that stretches back to the 1800s. One thing's for certain: it might be the latest killing, but it won't be the last …

This killer can never be caught.

As the body count rises, the investigation uncovers large-scale corruption at the heart of the Scottish Police Service. Now Max and Janie must turn against their closest colleagues – to solve a case that could cost them far more than just their lives …

THE BLOOD TIDE

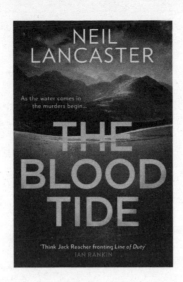

You get away with murder.

In a remote sea loch on the west coast of Scotland, a fisherman vanishes without trace. His remains are never found.

You make people disappear.

A young man jumps from a bridge in Glasgow and falls to his death in the water below. DS Max Craigie uncovers evidence that links both victims. But if he can't find out what cost them their lives, it won't be long before more bodies turn up at the morgue …

You come back for revenge.

Soon cracks start to appear in the investigation, and Max's past hurtles back to haunt him. When his loved ones are threatened, he faces a terrifying choice: let the only man he ever feared walk free, or watch his closest friend die …

Dear Reader,

We hope you enjoyed reading this book. If you did, we'd be so appreciative if you left a review. It really helps us and the author to bring more books like this to you.

Here at HQ Digital we are dedicated to publishing fiction that will keep you turning the pages into the early hours. Don't want to miss a thing? To find out more about our books, promotions, discover exclusive content and enter competitions you can keep in touch in the following ways:

JOIN OUR COMMUNITY:

Sign up to our new email newsletter: http://smarturl.it/SignUpHQ

Read our new blog www.hqstories.co.uk

🐦 https://twitter.com/HQStories

f www.facebook.com/HQStories

BUDDING WRITER?

We're also looking for authors to join the HQ Digital family!

Find out more here:

https://www.hqstories.co.uk/want-to-write-for-us/

Thanks for reading, from the HQ Digital team

If you enjoyed *The Night Watch*, then why not try another gripping crime thriller from HQ Digital?

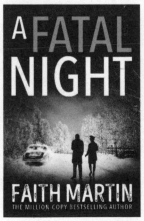

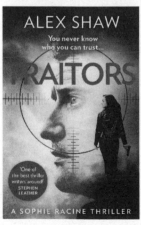